PRAISE FOR THE FICTION OF LEVI S. PETERSON

The Canyons of Grace

"Peterson has raised the Mormon short story to a new level of artistic excellence and sophistication." —The Association for Mormon Letters

"Mormon letters may have found in Levi S. Peterson a sunnier Hawthorne to assist us in interpreting the human condition …" —Richard H. Cracroft

"The quality of Levi Peterson's fiction rises far above that of any other fiction written in the context of Mormon culture which I've encountered." —David Harris

"Peterson's stories are deeply religious, rescuing what is holy in the relationship between lovers and companions, wives and husbands, parents and their children from the jaws of profanation." —William Mulder

"Written so brilliantly … it all rings true." —Joan Sanders

The Backslider

"Mesmerizing! … It deserves a celebration." —Lavina Fielding Anderson

"This is a story of real Mormonism—full of messy, often odd, but mostly good folks. So compelling." —Lisa Patterson Butterworth

"Provocative, entertaining, illuminating, irritating, and, ultimately (at least for the reader who is open to its earthy candor), deeply gratifying." —Richard J. Cummings

"A powerful exploration of grace and suffering and the ways in which we deny ourselves access to the very things that may save us." —Conor Hilton

"It is the humanness of the characters that gives this novel strength … a welcome novel from the hand of an expert story-teller." —Kenneth B. Hunsaker

"Filled with humor, warmth, tolerance, and love." —**Dennis Lythgoe**

"A Mormon cult classic that skillfully but humbly afflicts the self-satisfied and comforts the afflicted." —**Kathryn Lynard Soper**

Night Soil

"Levi Peterson is a lyrical chronicler of rural sensibility. There is a preacher in him that needs to be heard—a caretaker of the underdog, the disregarded, the sinner—and I admire that impulse." —**Phyllis Barber**

"This is the best writing about rural Utah since Wallace Stegner's *Recapitulation*." —**Ron Carlson**

"Suffused with heartbreaking mortal tenderness." —**Eugene England**

"Levi Peterson is widely considered Mormonism's finest writer of fiction, but he is more than that. He is one of America's most skilled and accomplished practitioners of naturalism" —**Harold T. Muir**

"This is a writer completely in command." —**Leslie Norris**

Aspen Marooney

"Levi Peterson is at his tough lyrical best, demonstrating his passion for people and for the physical and cultural landscape where the drama of their living unfolds." —**A. E. Cannon**

"Levi Peterson could give angels lessons in how to love." —**Robert Kirby**

"The leisurely pace is perfect for this tale of love, memory, regret, and guilt." —**Publishers Weekly**

"A realistic portrait of rural Utah life." —**Jane Reilly**

"Piquant, painful, and informed by a harsh lyricism." —**Paul Swenson**

LOSING A BIT OF EDEN

LOSING A BIT OF EDEN

Recent Stories

by

Levi S. Peterson

SIGNATURE BOOKS | 2021 | SALT LAKE CITY

To Althea

The following first appeared in *Dialogue: A Journal of Mormon Thought:* "Badge and Bryant; Or, the Decline and Fall of the Dogfrey Club" (Spring 2010); "Bode and Iris" (Summer 2019); "Jesus Enough" (Winter 2014); "Kid Kirby" (Summer 2016); "Sandrine" (Winter 2012); and "The Shyster" (Spring 2018). "The Return of the Native" first appeared in *Sunstone*, Oct. 2011.

The opinions expressed in this book are not necessarily those of the publisher.

Cover design by Haden Hamblin. Photo courtesy of the author.

FIRST EDITION | 2021

LIBRARY OF CONGRESS CATALOGING-IN-PUBLICATION DATA

Names:	Peterson, Levi S., 1933- author.
Title:	Losing a bit of Eden : recent stories / by Levi S. Peterson.
Other titles:	Losing a bit of Eden (Anthology)
Description:	First edition. | Salt Lake City : Signature Books, 2021. | Summary: "In these ten stories (three of which appear here for the first time), Levi S. Peterson demonstrates his continuing engagement to take seriously the duty of the fiction writer to illuminate and entertain. His subject remains Latter-day Saints caught between the polarities of conscience and passion. Among the stories are sober tellings of rape and misogyny, defiant statements of ascendant feminism and the worship of Heavenly Mother, and-most abundantly-narratives about impermissible love that sometimes lead to heartbreak and other times forges unexpected couplings destined to last a lifetime. Once again, Peterson shows himself as a peerless master of the English language, the tools of his craft, and the artistry of creative fiction"—Provided by publisher.
Identifiers:	LCCN 2021004632 (print) | LCCN 2021004633 (ebook) | ISBN 9781560852926 (paperback) | ISBN 9781560853978 (epub)
Subjects:	LCSH: Mormons—Fiction. | LCGFT: Short stories.
Classification:	LCC PS3566.E7694 L67 2021 (print) | LCC PS3566.E7694 (ebook) | DDC 813/.54—dc23

LC record available at https://lccn.loc.gov/2021004632
LC ebook record available at https://lccn.loc.gov/2021004633

CONTENTS

Losing a Bit of Eden

Nothing happened on the night Ellen spent alone in a Cheyenne motel with the bishop—nothing, that is, of an adulterous sort. Nonetheless, she and he felt compelled to create a doctored version of the incident for their respective spouses. Would they have been better off giving an entirely accurate account? It's hard to say. Either alternative was fraught with nuances of suspicion and guilt for persons of such keenly honed righteousness.

The calamitous incident occurred at the truncated end of a Saturday excursion to the temple in Fort Collins, Colorado. The day started early. At seven sharp, Giles Dolph, bishop of the Banfield Ward in Laramie, and his wife, Nicole, picked up Barry Tolman, first counselor, and his wife, Ellen. Giles was driving his favorite car, an aging Lincoln Continental. Ordinarily, they would have traveled in his wife's van in order to accommodate both counselors and their wives. However, on this weekend, the second counselor and his family happened to be in Utah attending a funeral.

They were dressed for Sunday. It being mid-September—frosty nights and pleasant, sunny days—none of them brought an overcoat. Luckily, as it turned out, Ellen wore a heavy sweater.

Usually, the temple excursion exhilarated Ellen. Under Giles, the bishopric had become a tight-knit group socially as well as spiritually. Their monthly visit at the temple seemed a sort of bonus testimony as to the truthfulness of the gospel, being a harmonious melding of worship and a friendship somehow deeper and more meaningful than ordinary friendship. On the present occasion, a minor worry nagged Ellen. Her youngest daughter, Beth, who lived in Laramie, had a newborn baby. What with having two other children under six, Beth needed Ellen's help. However, given that it was a Saturday and Beth's husband would be at home—and given that the travelers intended to be home by six or seven in the evening—Ellen had decided to stifle her worry and get as much pleasure as possible from the excursion.

Giles drove at a rate a little under the speed limit. He was, Ellen believed, an extraordinarily good man. She admired him for making it a point to obey the law of the land as well as the law of God. He seemed a natural for the job of bishop, being a highly-paid executive of a natural gas hub stationed in Laramie. At sixty-two, he was ruddy-cheeked, well-muscled, and possessed of a full head of graying hair, which he kept neatly trimmed. As for Ellen's husband—well, driving within the speed limit was not a rule he considered important. Barry was, of course, an awfully good man, a one-hundred-percent Latter-day Saint and a kind and considerate companion. He was currently a senior administrator at Laramie's chief hospital. All through graduate school and while working his way up in the profession of hospital administration, he had found time to help Ellen with the children and with the housework, help he continued to give now that she was serving as a volunteer teacher's aide and as an occasional substitute teacher in an elementary school.

The day was proving to be windy and overcast, perhaps a little colder than might be expected in mid-September on the high Wyoming plains. An occasional swirl of dust appeared amid the sage brush. At one moment a small herd of antelope raced beside the freeway, seemingly challenged by the speeding traffic. Shortly, they veered off in an oblique direction—Ellen taking note of their graceful motion with pleasure. She was thinking she ought to procure some pictures of antelope, also some pictures of other forms of Wyoming wildlife for the fourth-grade class in which she served as an aide.

The travelers arrived in Fort Collins in plenty of time to attend the ten o'clock session. When it was over, they attended the noon session as well. As usual, being in the temple gave Ellen an Edenic feeling. She felt childlike, innocent, purified. They emerged from that session a little after two, ready for a late lunch at a French restaurant called the Montmartre, where portions were meager but fancily served. They lingered for nearly an hour discussing their families and mutual friends.

Leaving the restaurant, they got into the Lincoln. Giles steered the sedan onto the street and headed toward a freeway entrance. He slowed upon approaching a red light in an intersection. The light turned green as the Lincoln reached the intersection, and Giles accelerated. At the moment the sedan was completely within the intersection, a speeding pickup entered from the right and—with a resounding roar of deploying airbags and the shriek of fragmenting glass and twisting metal—struck the Lincoln at mid-section. The heavy sedan teetered a moment, then righted itself and left the intersection. Behind it, the pickup spun about and came to rest with a caved-in grill and steaming radiator.

Parking the Lincoln at a curb, Giles looked about. "Who's hurt?"

"I've got a cut," Nicole said. She wiped a hand across her scalp and stared at her bloody palm.

Barry, who had been sitting behind Nicole, gripped his upper right arm with his left hand. "My arm hurts like blazes," he said. "Maybe it's broken."

"How about you, Ellen?"

"I'm okay, I think. Hard to tell, though."

Giles dug out his cell phone and swiped the screen. At that moment, a siren began to wail. "Sounds like somebody has already dialed 911," he said, putting away his phone.

The injured persons ended up in the emergency ward of the Poudre Valley Hospital via two ambulances. The paramedics, suspecting Nicole had a concussion, braced her neck and loaded her into one of the ambulances on a gurney. As for Barry, they placed a temporary splint on his arm and loaded him into the other ambulance on a gurney. The two ambulances pulled away, leaving Giles and Ellen behind for an interview with the police. There was no question that the intoxicated driver of the pickup, apparently unscathed by the accident, was at fault, as a couple of other witnesses verified. Three-quarters of an hour later, the police drove Giles and Ellen to the emergency ward, where they sought the examination rooms of their respective spouses.

Barry was absent from his room, having been taken to the

radiology unit for an X-ray of his broken arm. "It's looking bad," he said when he returned. "It's broken in two places. I won't be going home tonight. Neither will Nicole. They were wheeling her out of radiology as they took me in. She's had a concussion and they want to keep an eye on her overnight."

Ellen had fallen into full-scale worry. She had promised Beth she'd be there by eight that evening. She'd have to phone her and let her know. Things were looking very dismal indeed at this moment. A tough night of sitting up in the hospital waiting area loomed, Ellen being in no mood to call a taxi and find a motel.

Shortly, Giles stuck his head into the examination room. "Nicole says for me to rent a car and head home tonight so somebody will be there to take charge at sacrament meeting tomorrow morning. I've decided to do it. I hate to run out on you, but I'll be back down tomorrow evening."

"Good idea," Barry said. "No use hanging around here."

"Shouldn't I go with him?" Ellen said. "Beth needs me. Sunday's a hard day for her."

"You bet," Barry said. "Just go. There's nothing you can do around here."

Giles nodded his assent and the matter was settled.

An hour later, Giles and Ellen where headed north on the I-25 toward Cheyenne in a rental car. Ellen immediately called Beth on her cell phone, downplaying the seriousness of the accident and promising her daughter to be on hand early the next morning.

The automobile Giles had rented was a hybrid with very few miles on the odometer. He was charmed with the vehicle and marveled at its sensitivity to the conditions of the road. "I've got to get me one of these," he said. Just like Barry, Ellen was thinking—quite fixated on machines. It occurred to Ellen now that there was an implied intimacy to their present situation, which Giles, absorbed by the operation of the automobile, was blessedly indifferent to.

Maybe ten miles out of Fort Collins, flecks of rain hit the windshield. Soon it was raining harder, and Giles turned on the wipers. Ellen found their rhythmical swish comforting. She liked rain if someone else was driving. However, well before they crossed the border into Wyoming, the temperature had dropped drastically and a howling wind was blowing snow in at a slant.

Several miles beyond the border, the travelers turned west toward Laramie on the I-80. By now, it was obvious that a full scale blizzard was in progress. Giles seemed daunted but determined. "Just fifty miles," he said. "We can do it." Seconds later, they encountered a barrier manned by the Wyoming Highway Patrol. "Sorry, folks," said one of the patrolmen. He was dressed, as was his companion, in a fur-collared coat and an arctic trooper cap. "The road's a real mess out there—blown-over semis and a couple of collisions. Best drive back into Cheyenne and get a motel."

Giles sighed. "Guess we'll turn around and head back to Fort Collins."

"Sorry about that, too," the trooper said. "They've just closed the I-25 in both directions. But the county has kept the road between here and Cheyenne plowed. Like I say, best drive back and get a motel. It's just five or six miles."

Giles looked at Ellen. "Well, if we gotta, we gotta," he said. He turned the car onto the median and they crossed over to the eastbound lanes. Exiting at the first Cheyenne exit, they shortly passed a seedy motel with a lit neon vacancy sign. "We can do better than that," Giles said and drove on into the city.

Ellen looked at her watch. It was nearly twelve-thirty. Unfortunately, plowing had stopped in the city center. Only the boulevard leading to the capitol had been plowed recently enough to drive on. Several streets with motels with lit signs appeared impassable. Giles drove back out to the seedy place. He went in and was gone a long time.

"The lady has only got one room," he said on his return. "I took it. It's for you."

"What are you going to do?"

"Sit inside the office," he said. "At least it's warm in there."

He drove Ellen down along a series of closely spaced doors to the end of the motel. Small yellow bulbs burned over the doors. The yellow light gave everything a doubly dilapidated look. Giles and Ellen got out of the car and went into the end room. It had a double bed, a small desk, and a single chair. There was an open gas

5

burner, vented by a small aluminum chimney. Giles tried lighting the burner. Apparently, the gas supply was turned off. "I wouldn't trust it anyway," he said. "A friend of mine died of asphyxiation running a heater like that in a motel room."

The small, crowded bathroom had a washstand, a toilet, and a soiled metal shower booth. There was a single towel and washcloth. The bed had sheets, a single blanket, and a tattered cover. Giles said, "Just take off your shoes and climb in the bed with your clothes on and you'll stay warm." He paused reflectively. "Funny thing is, in the winter I carry a couple of heavy blankets in my Lincoln for just such emergencies as this. But I didn't think even once about throwing them into the rental car."

He used the bathroom and disappeared out the door, heading for the office. Having used the bathroom, Ellen left its door open a crack to serve as a night light and—doing as Giles had suggested— removed her shoes and got under the paltry covers. Shortly there was a knock on the door. She got out of the bed, put on her shoes, and went to the door. Giles came in, closed the door, and turned on the room light.

"The office is locked," he said. "I kept ringing the doorbell and I knocked too, but the lady didn't answer. Darn it. She told me when I rented the room it would be okay to sit there." He pulled the chair away from the desk and sat down. "Do you mind if I stay inside here? I'm wet and I'm cold and I think I've got a touch of hypothermia. I'm leery of running the heater in that hybrid. So if you don't mind, I'll just sit here at the desk."

"Well, of course," Ellen said. She scratched her head, uncertain as to what to do next.

He said, "You better get back under the covers." He switched off the room light. Ellen got into the bed and pulled the covers to her chin. She was reluctant to close her eyes. She wasn't afraid of Giles, just embarrassed, as if going to sleep would exacerbate the adulterous suggestiveness of their situation. She stared at the ceiling for a long time. Gradually, she became warm and, despite her resistance, she began to feel sleepy. Then her peripheral vision caught a motion. She looked and, by the dim light coming from the crack in the bathroom door, she saw Giles rub his palms, then blow on them, and finally shove them into the pockets of his suit coat.

"You are really cold," she said, "and you're not drying off."

"I'm all right."

"Shouldn't you get into this bed?" she said sharply. "You'll get hypothermia for sure just sitting there." She was stunned by her assertiveness.

He stood and began stamping in place.

She said, "All we need is for you to get pneumonia."

"I'm okay," he insisted.

"Actually," she said, "getting under the covers with our clothes on is no different than if we were sitting side by side on a church bench."

He stopped stamping and shuffled to the side of the bed.

"Just do it," she said. "Get in."

He sat and the bed groaned. "This is preposterous," he said.

"Do it anyway," she said.

He untied his shoes and got under the covers.

Ellen was quivering, her veins being charged with adrenalin. No danger now of her going to sleep. Outside, the wind howled madly. Nonetheless, somewhere toward dawn, she went to sleep despite herself. When she awoke, she felt as if something strange was going on. In a moment, she realized the wind had died and daylight showed at the window. She could hear a multitude of little sounds within the room. Giles was breathing with the deep rhythms of sleep. The bedsprings creaked slightly with each of his inhalations. He coughed once, emitted several half-suffocated sighs, then went on with his quiet snoring. Ellen slipped out of bed quietly as possible and ensconced herself in the bathroom for a while. She saw in the cabinet mirror that her dress was wrinkled. The sweater still looked pretty good. She was lucky to have worn it.

When she emerged from the bathroom, Giles had turned on the room light. He was seated on the chair, tying his shoe laces. He looked at Ellen quizzically. "This has been one for the books," he said.

"It has," she agreed.

"I looked out," he went on. "Wouldn't you believe it? The sky is clearing up. Snowplows are on the move."

Giles went into the bathroom and stayed a while. Ellen slipped back into the bed for warmth. A sentence ran through her mind: *I have slept with a man to whom I wasn't married.* It was true, she had. It was odd—in the context of that sentence, the word *slept* was loaded with adultery.

Giles emerged from the bathroom and sat at the table. Apparently, he had been mulling the same problem. "I don't think we can just be straight forward about what has happened here." His fingers were drumming on the table. Ellen remained in the bed, staring at the ceiling.

After a while, still drumming his fingers, he said, "So what kind of a story do we concoct?"

"Two rooms," Ellen said. "The motel had two rooms left when we arrived."

The drumming stopped. "Okay, that's the way it was—two rooms."

Ellen felt a little sick. Maybe she was mourning. Somehow they were losing a bit of Eden just now.

Sandrine

These things happened sixty years ago. It was 1962, the year of the World Fair in Seattle. I was twenty-one and had just finished my junior year at Utah State University in Logan. My forestry advisor there had wrangled me a summer job as an intern with the National Park Service at Mount Rainier. He said I needed to experience the contrast between the dry pine forests of the interior West and the lush fir forests of the Pacific Northwest.

I went home for a few days before leaving—home being a farm in Curlew Valley about fifty miles west of Logan. On the day I headed for the Northwest, my mother said goodbye by taking my hands and making me look directly into her dark, bespectacled eyes. "Remember, Lewis," she said, "if it comes to having to make a choice, I'd rather you be good than happy." Being a conscientious Mormon son, I thought about what she had said for a while after I took to the road. I couldn't imagine a situation where I'd have to make such a choice.

I followed the most direct road between Curlew Valley and Mount Rainier I could find on my Shell Oil road map. I wanted to take in the World's Fair, but I figured I could do that later on in the summer. Nothing had prepared me for the spectacle of Mount Rainier. Although it's considered a part of the Cascade Range, it towers over neighboring peaks. Measuring over 14,000 feet, its perpetually snow-covered summit is visible from a hundred miles away.

I was stationed at the primary visitors' center in the park, appropriately called Paradise, which consisted of a big parking lot, a large lodge for tourists, and several smaller dormitories for park staff and for guides belonging to a professional guiding service. I bunked in one of the dormitories with a pleasant high school teacher who spent summers on the seasonal park staff. I quickly discovered that my duties were far from glorious, consisting mostly of emptying garbage cans, picking up litter, and answering tourist questions. I wasn't unhappy with all that. I was learning a lot about the park, and I loved the mountain, especially at dawn and dusk on clear days, when the towering peak burned with a delicate orange alpenglow. That was a sight I never got tired of.

I was on duty six days a week, including Sunday—with an hour and a half off early Sunday morning to attend a small sacrament service for Mormon tourists in the basement of the lodge. My scheduled day off each week was Tuesday. At first, I didn't drive out much on that day, being caught up by exploring the mountain. I visited viewpoints, followed foot trails through the park, and one Tuesday borrowed boots and parka and climbed in the snow to a climber's base camp. But eventually I began to drive off the mountain to explore logging practices on both public and private forest lands—this on the recommendation of my advisor at Utah State.

One Tuesday I ventured up the Carcelle River, a logged-out valley draining out of the northwest corner of the park. In the evening I stopped at a café in Beaufort, a town of about a hundred inhabitants. It was late and the café was empty except for the proprietor, who served me a hot pork sandwich. His name was Maximilian Stewart, Max for short. He was maybe forty-five years old and bald and soft spoken, and he had a hard time looking me in the eyes when he talked. I asked him what he knew about the logging boom along the river during the early twentieth century. He seemed hesitant at first, as if he didn't know much at all about that topic, but pretty soon he opened up and began to talk, and I realized I had struck gold.

When I left, I asked him if it would be okay for me to come back on the following Tuesday, and he said, sure, he'd be glad to tell me anything he knew about the history of the river. As I got up to leave, his wife came in the front door, and he introduced us and suddenly everything turned topsy-turvy for me. Her name was Sandrine and she was a beauty. There's no other word for it. She was just a beauty—in her early twenties, auburn hair, naturally defined eyebrows, porcelain cheeks.

The problem was I couldn't get her off my mind during the following days, a fact that smacked of a violation of the commandment that says thou shalt not covet thy neighbor's wife. It was so bothersome that I pretty much made up my mind that I wouldn't go back to the café. However, on a routine phone call to my advisor at Utah State, I mentioned Beaufort, and he wanted to know more about the place. I told him it had a post office, a mercantile, a saloon, and of course Max's café. It also had an elementary school to which students were bussed from an even smaller town called Limington, which was located on up the river a few miles. "My gad, Lewis," my advisor said over the phone, "do you realize these little derelict logging towns are prime subjects for a study on the sociology of forest-dependent communities. What an opportunity! Don't miss it."

What he was proposing was graduate-level work, and I was still an undergrad. But I'd be setting myself up for an exceptional master's thesis a couple of years down the road. I resisted the idea for a few minutes on account of Sandrine, but my advisor wouldn't take no for an answer. As I thought things over, my apprehension began to strike me as just plain silly. I was a Mormon, born and bred. I had standards, I recognized boundaries. Admiring Max's wife didn't amount to lusting on her, any more than admiring a beautiful painting amounted to stealing it. So I said okay, and that's how it happened that for the rest of the summer I devoted my day off to a project that I grandiosely entered as "sociological analysis" on my *per diem* requests from the undergraduate research fund at Utah State.

I spent a few Tuesdays creating a population map from county records in Tacoma, which allowed me to document the waxing and waning of Beaufort and Limington. The records also named a couple of sizeable logging camps, Little Quebec and Chambers Landing, that had simply disappeared beneath second growth trees and brush. After that, my research was basically just a matter of talking to people who lived on the river. I won't say I worked hard at it—it was my day off, after all. Some afternoons I just parked my car—a twelve-year-old Chevrolet—on a Forest Service road and took a nap.

In any event, I made a point of ending my day by having a late supper at the café in Beaufort, where I pumped Max for information. My task became easier as Max became interested in my research project and began asking some of his other customers about things I wanted to know. Naturally, I came to know Sandrine and also their daughter, an eight-year-old named Aubrey, who were usually present. Sandrine kept busy, setting tables or preparing menus for the next day, but she listened to my conversation with Max and sometimes added comments of her own. She had a soft voice and was capable of a radiant smile. But much of the time she seemed tense and preoccupied and prone to answer questions tersely. In contrast, Aubrey was relaxed and cheerful. She had auburn hair, a pug nose, and missing top incisors. She and Max were obviously deeply attached, and she quickly took a shine to me. She liked to sit at the counter and lean against me while I ate my supper or chatted with Max.

Sometimes my conversations with Max got onto personal topics. The fact I was an active Mormon pleased Max. He had worked with a Mormon man in Seattle and liked him. He had the idea that Mormons are extra trustworthy. According to him, that's why a lot of Mormon men were recruited into the FBI and Secret Service. I could believe that easily enough, but to keep things honest I had to tell him that the majority of the felons in the Utah State Penitentiary were Mormons. Max asked if I had been a missionary, and when I said no, he wanted to know why. It was because I had qualified for a four-year scholarship at Utah State, which I accepted after promising my mother that when I graduated, I would go on a mission.

At any rate, Max decided that I was to be classified among the trustworthy of the world as I learned toward the end of the summer. It was late one Tuesday night after Sandrine had taken Aubrey to their house across the street to put her to bed. As I prepared to leave, Max came from behind the counter and followed me to the door. He said he wanted to ask a favor of me, but first he needed to tell me something about Sandrine, which he hoped I would keep a secret.

The secret was she was an ex-junkie whom he had rescued from the alleys of Seattle. The first time he ever saw her, he was on duty at a shipping platform under the viaduct on Elliott Bay. He was old enough, of course, to be her father. He was divorced, and his two adult children lived out of state. The shipping platform was a cheerless, noisy place where trucks rumbled in with produce and hardware, and huffing switch engines positioned freight cars for unloading in front of the platform. Around the corner lived a colony of winos and street dwellers—or, at least, they slept there in cardboard boxes and sleeping bags. One summer he noticed a new one, Sandrine, who started sitting in the sun at the far edge of the loading dock. After a couple of days Max began to talk to her, and things went from there. She was a wreck, emaciated, listless, and addicted. The child protection agency had put Aubrey into foster care within weeks of her birth. Sandrine didn't know who Aubrey's father was. She told Max it could have been any of a half dozen fellows who traded her a hit for a session down an alley. But dissipation hadn't erased her beauty. Max took her in, cleaned her up, financed her rehab, and married her when she came out. That's when they bought the café in Beaufort. Max wanted Sandrine a long way from downtown Seattle. After a couple of years, the child protection agency turned Aubrey over to them.

As for the favor, Max introduced it in a roundabout way. Before school ended in May, Aubrey's class had gone on a field trip to the World's Fair in Seattle, and Sandrine had volunteered to go along as one of the adult chaperones. However, as the time approached, she fell apart—that is, she began having bad dreams at night and bouts of weeping during the day. The upshot of the episode was that Max accompanied Aubrey on the field trip and Sandrine stayed home and kept the restaurant going. "She just couldn't take it, Lewis," Max said. "Too many bad things happened to her in Seattle. Her own mother was a junkie, you know, and her father abandoned the two of them while Sandrine was a little girl."

Aubrey returned from the fair in May insisting that Sandrine attend. She wanted her mother to see the giant circular fountain that sprayed jets of water high in the air, and she wanted her to go up the Space Needle and ride the monorail. Sandrine said she'd go, but she kept putting it off until here it was the end of August. Unfortunately, a neighbor lady who had promised to go with her had gone off to California to help out at a niece's confinement. Also, one of the waitresses at the café had quit and moved to Missouri. Being shorthanded at the café, Max felt he couldn't go with

Sandrine. But somebody had to and then, as Max said, it hit him like a bolt of lightning who that would be.

"I don't know why I didn't think of you earlier," he said. "You are the one, Lewis! You're solid, you're religious, you've got ethics. Everybody respects you."

I began shaking my head the instant I understood what he wanted of me.

"Now don't get in a hurry to say no," Max said. "Sandrine has feelings for Seattle. She wants to go. She needs to go. But she shouldn't go alone. Somebody responsible has to go with her. That's just all there is to it."

I shook my head even more emphatically.

"Please, just listen me out," he said. "You are worrying about the appearances of it. Beaufort isn't a place that pays any attention to things like that. After all, this is the twentieth century. We're not a bunch of Victorians. I know it would be a big imposition on you. I'll give you the money for tickets and meals and a tank of gas. And, my gosh, Lewis, you need to go for your own sake. The summer's coming to an end, and you'll be heading back to Utah shortly. You don't want to leave Washington without visiting Seattle."

Eventually I agreed to do it—not that night, but the next Tuesday after I had thought it over for a week. I agreed partly because Max had pressed me so urgently but mostly because it seemed a breach of my faith, a denial of my testimony, to suppose a young man born of goodly Mormon parents might be susceptible to thoughts of adultery even while spending a long, intimate day with the most beautiful woman he had ever met.

The following Tuesday—only a couple of weeks from the scheduled end of my internship—I rolled out of my bunk at a very early hour. My roommate, who was still in his bunk, got up on an elbow and watched me. "Where are you going at this god-awful time of the day?" he said.

"To visit the fair."

He shook his head and lay back. "Well, have a good time."

"I doubt that I will," I said. "It's more or less a duty, just to accommodate a friend."

When I picked up Sandrine, Max came out of the house to see

us off. He wrung my hand with gratitude. As I escorted Sandrine to my old Chevrolet, she paused and looked back. She didn't seem happy. "Go on, honey," Max called. "Have a good time." She waved and we went on. She slid into her seat and I closed the door.

She was wearing a cotton dress and an open sweater. The dress was light blue, with buttons from waist to collar. When she was standing, the hem came slightly below her knees though of course when she was seated in the car, it rested slightly above. A lot of people have bony knees. Not Sandrine. Knees, calves, ankles, whatever—as I've said, she was perfection.

We drove for a while without saying much. The silence made me uncomfortable. Words, even banal ones, cover awkward emotions, and I for one was feeling a lot of awkward emotions. At a station on the outskirts of Puyallup, I stopped for gasoline and used the restroom. As we resumed our drive, Sandrine said, "I'm sorry you have to do this for me. But Max wouldn't give up on it. Neither would Aubrey."

"I'm glad to do it," I lied.

"Max is a good man."

"I know he is," I said.

"It isn't his fault I'm a mess," she said.

What could I say to that?

After awhile we passed some goats in a pasture. "They look peaceful," Sandrine said. Her voice struck me as envious.

"I suppose they are," I said. "Their lives aren't very complicated." It occurred to me then that being beautiful might be a terrible handicap for a girl born into precarious circumstances.

"Do you have goats on your farm in Utah?" she said.

"Yes. A pair of them—Sadie and Eliza."

We glanced at each other, and she gave me a brief flicker of an incandescent smile.

"What's it like on your farm?" she said.

I began to talk, glad for the topic. I told her our farm was in the middle of a long dry valley. There were drab hills on either side, dotted by scrub juniper and sparse yellow range grass—quite a contrast to the green vines, ferns, and flowers flourishing beneath the towering canopy of the Northwest forests. We had a couple

15

of irrigated fields; otherwise, we planted dry land to winter wheat. I attended grade school in a hamlet called Snowville, and I went to high school in Garland, a fifty-mile bus ride each way, which meant I left home long before dawn and got home long after dusk in the middle of the winter. We drove to Tremonton for groceries, and we attended church in Snowville. Sandrine wanted to know who "we" were. I told her it included my father and mother and my sisters, Harriet and Melanie, Harriet being still in grade school and Melanie coming up on her junior year at Bear River High School in Garland. Then, just as an afterthought, I told Sandrine my father was the first Mulenax to become a Mormon, but my mother's line, the Bucyruses, traced their Mormonism back almost to the beginnings in Kirtland, Ohio, which gave her and her family a leg up in the pecking order among their fellow Mormons.

When I glanced at Sandrine, I saw she had relaxed. I supposed she was projecting a lot of wish fulfillment onto my family—likely more than it merited because my father was something of an authoritarian grump and my mother was a world-class worrier.

When we reached Seattle, I parked across the street from the fair, which was taking place on a large spread of land that is now called Seattle Center. While we stood on the street corner waiting for the traffic light to change, I saw that the tense look had returned to Sandrine's face. I felt a bit unnerved myself, being reminded how much I hated the rattle and roar of big city traffic. As far as I was concerned, the traffic in Logan, which had no more than 15,000 residents in 1962, was far too thick.

I couldn't guess how many acres the fair occupied, but it was enough to get lost in. There were exhibits beyond counting, some of them taking up whole buildings. Theoretically, all the exhibits pointed toward the twenty-first century, the title of the fair being Century 21 Exposition. I was pleased to see Sandrine get caught up in some of the exhibits. We both liked the displays about space exploration in the United States Science Pavilion, which consisted of several substantial buildings surrounding a courtyard of Gothic arches perched atop slender spider-like legs. Later on I learned that it was a show of bravado for the United States. Our nation was scrambling to make up for the Soviet Union having put up a satellite ahead of us in 1957.

When we emerged from the United States Science Pavilion, I suggested we go up the Space Needle. At the base, we craned our necks and gaped at the rotating observation deck some 500 feet above us. Ticket holders were queued in a long serpentine line, and a sign at the ticket office predicted a wait of four hours. "It's not worth the wait," Sandrine said.

Just then a man stepped forward and said, "You want to go up? I've got a pair of dinner passes for tonight at 7:00. You get to go to the head of the line. One hundred bucks."

I looked him over. One hundred dollars in 1962 was worth about six hundred today. That's a lot of money for a guy living on a forestry intern's stipend.

"I've got a family emergency," the man said. "I've got to drive to Spokane."

I was about to say nothing doing when I glanced at Sandrine. Her face glowed. So I pulled out my wallet. This was my introduction to scalping. I understood the concept instantly, though it would be several years before I encountered the term for it. It was a good experience for me. The naive have to be trained somehow.

Sandrine and I wandered next into Show Street, a causeway lined with vendor booths. Sandrine paused at a booth selling Alaskan totem figurines. She considered buying one for Aubrey, but decided against it, explaining that Max had bought her a lot of souvenirs when they came in May. A little further along, we came to an arcade featuring peep shows. I stopped and stared, wondering whether a peep show was something like a Punch and Judy show. Smiling slightly, Sandrine said, "I don't think you want to go in there." I realized then that only men were going in and coming out, and my face reddened. I turned and we went back to the entrance of the causeway.

Just outside the entrance, we met an unkempt, sallow-faced fellow who wore a short, patchy beard. Stepping in front of us, he uttered an incredulous, "My God, it's Reen! Babe! Where ya been? Oh, for Christ's sake, imagine running into you here!"

For an instant I assumed it was a case of mistaken identity. But an instant later, I saw it wasn't. Sandrine knew the fellow all too well. Stricken and horrified, she shrank behind me. Something chemical happened inside me. "Get lost," I said to the unkempt fellow, "or I'll put you down." Being a pacifist by nature, I was surprised by the harsh, mean tone in my voice. In any event, the unkempt fellow melted into the crowd and we didn't meet him again.

Sandrine was trembling. No, it was more than that. She was utterly shaken—tears in her eyes, taut shoulders, hands nervously twisting the strap of her purse. Obviously, Max had summarized her past accurately. There was something dire, revolting, truly calamitous about it. The unkempt fellow hadn't seemed *that* ominous to me. In fact, I would have thought him simply nondescript, if indeed I had thought anything about him at all upon some chance encounter. Yet Sandrine's recoil—her terrified eyes, her dive behind my back—implied the presence of a creature who fed on the desolation of others.

Proposing lunch to settle her nerves, I offered her the crook of my arm. She slid her arm through mine and pressed against me as we strolled on. I wondered whether my unthinking offer of the arm was a mistake. I hoped she wouldn't interpret it as something more than a gentlemanly gesture.

We had passed several restaurants in our wandering, but Sandrine chose Greek food from an open-sided van. We sat on a varnished wood bench, eating our gyros and baklava and watching iridescent arcs of water spout from the great circular fountain that had fascinated Aubrey so much. The sun was out, the sky was blue, people flocked around us, hurdy-gurdy music tinkled cheerfully in the background. Sandrine scarcely noticed. She was abstracted and withdrawn, thinking—as I supposed—of those dank alleys from which Max had rescued her. I'll admit that I was abstracted and withdrawn too. I couldn't help pondering the diseases she might have picked up on the streets— herpes, gonorrhea, syphilis, chlamydia, or who knew what else?

Eventually, our silence struck me as a mutual display of poor manners, and I asked Sandrine the name of the unkempt fellow.

She said, "Noose."

"Noose!"

"That's all I ever heard him called."

"It's too bad we ran into him," I said.

She nodded, her eyes averted.

"Though it doesn't really matter," I said. "He's just a reminder of how lucky you are."

I waited for a response that didn't come. "You've got a good home," I explained. "As you say, Max is a good man. You've got Aubrey."

"Yes, I've got Aubrey. If it weren't for her, I'd leave."

"Don't you love Max?"

She raised her eyebrows, surprised.

"I don't love anybody," she said.

"But you do love Aubrey, don't you?"

"Yes, but that's not the kind of love I'm talking about."

It was my turn to look surprised.

"I've never fallen in love with anyone," she said. "I'd like to."

I stood up and moved off a few steps. "Let's go ride the monorail," I suggested. She got up and took my arm without it being offered.

The monorail was a light train that as its name implied ran on a single track. It was next to another single track that bore the return train, the two trains giving the appearance of colliding as they approached each other—one of many illusions of the day, I would later think. The track ran about a mile to a station in the center of the city. We got off and sat on a bench watching people use escalators between the station and the street below.

"We could go to Pike Place and watch the fish mongers," she said. "Or down to Elliott Bay and watch the ferries."

"If you want to," I replied.

We went on watching people as if nothing had been said between us. After a while we got on the monorail and went back to the fair. I suggested we take in the Fine Arts Pavilion, where world-famous works of art had been gathered from dozens of museums. The place was crowded, and we filed along slowly, reading descriptions of the paintings and statues from a printed guide. I was overawed by the artists, El Greco, Caravaggio, Rembrandt, among others, some of whom I had encountered in a humanities class at Utah State. We came to a painting of the dead body of

Jesus being lifted gently from the cross by his desolate followers. Sandrine turned away, shuddering.

"Can we go?" she pleaded.

We returned to the bench near the circular fountain. "I'm sorry to be such a spoil sport," Sandrine said. "I'm a mess, just a mess."

"Do you want to go home?" I asked. "We could give away our dinner tickets. Or maybe somebody will buy them."

She said no, and at seven we went to the entrance to the Space Needle where we found the scalper's promise held good, our tickets admitting us within minutes of being presented. In the restaurant at the top, the maître d' seated us on a terrace somewhat back from the windows but elevated enough to give a view. We dined on steamed mussels and grilled salmon garnished with ginger and orange peel. In the meantime, the pod did a full 360-degree rotation, allowing us to take in the city, the Sound, and two mountain ranges, the Cascades to the east, the Olympics to the west. And, of course, southeastward Rainier loomed in the gathering evening.

Long before the pod had completed its rotation, Sandrine had become radiant, and I was struck again by the intense beauty of her features.

At one point she said, "Can you believe that I love this city?"

"Well, yes, if you say so," I said. "But I wouldn't have thought it. It seems pretty loaded with bad memories for you."

"It is," she agreed, "but I love it anyway."

"I guess I can understand that," I said. I was thinking it was a matter of perspective. Here at the top of the Space Needle, we were above the jostling bodies, the grime, the fetid motivations of predatory human beings. The diminished buildings and streets merged with water, forest, and mountains so that, yes, from this angle it was a beautiful city.

"This has been a very happy day for me," she said. "Thank you for bringing me."

"I've liked it, too," I said. I wasn't lying. From our current vantage point, we could see a couple of ferries, whose wakes plowed a white furrow upon the darkling Sound. It was a surreal scene, a transformation of reality.

Then she said, "May I ask you something personal?" and I intuitively knew trouble lay ahead. "Have you ever been in love?"

"We'd better go," I spluttered. "People are waiting for a table."

"Have you?" she insisted.

"There was a girl I dated during my freshman year at Utah State," I said. "I could have fallen in love with her, if she had let me. The missionary she was waiting for came home at the end of the year and they got married."

We got up and made our way to an elevator. She took my arm while we made our descent. It was full dark by the time we left the elevator and crossed the street to my car. I unlocked the door on the passenger's side and pulled it open. Rather than getting in, she faced me, closely. "Could you fall in love with me, if I let you?" she said.

I froze.

"I'm not waiting for a missionary," she said.

She got into the car. I went around to the other side and got behind the wheel. She slid close to me—the old Chevrolet having a bench seat that allowed for that. "I *do* know what it is to fall in love," she said. "I'm in love with you."

I didn't start the engine immediately. I had to digest, to assimilate, what was happening. Having been invited to fall in love with Sandrine, I had. Or, to put it more accurately, I was able to admit now that I had been in love with her all along. Moreover, as I recognized all too clearly, she had invited me to a moral disaster. If I wanted to make love to her now—on this very night—I had only to ask.

I started the engine and steered the car onto the busy street. My mother's earnest voice sounded in my memory: *If it comes to having to make a choice, I'd rather you be good than happy.* My duty was clear. There was no debate as to what I ought to do. I had had a sound Mormon raising. It was what made Mormon men good candidates for the FBI and Secret Service.

Sandrine turned on the car radio and picked up a disc jockey on a Tacoma station. The first song we heard was Ella Fitzgerald with "My Happiness," an old song that had recently had something of a revival. "Three Coins in the Fountain" followed, also "Vaya Con Dios" and a new one neither of us had ever heard before, "Can't Help Falling in Love with You." When sad love stories are made

21

into movies, they are set to haunting music. It has occurred to me that, if this account were made into a movie, one of the songs we heard on the radio that night might serve for the Sandrine theme, as I suppose it would be called.

Unfortunately, that mellow music undid me. My carefully honed inhibitions receded. They lowered their voices and crept off stage. I kept thinking of a condom machine I had seen in the restroom of the station where I had bought gasoline that morning. My mind was in a dizzy whirl. I couldn't believe Lewis Mulenax would ever purchase a condom.

We passed through Puyallup around midnight. The gas station just beyond the city limits was still open. "I need to use the restroom," I said, pulling over. Inside I used the urinal and washed my hands. I put a couple of quarters in the condom machine and pocketed the tiny packet. I returned to the car and, and as Sandrine slid close to me, drove on. The dash lights illuminated her legs. The hem of her dress lay well above her knees. I took my hand from the wheel and caressed her sculpted knee.

Maybe twenty minutes later I pulled off on a Forest Service road, which I followed until it made a bend and we were out of sight of any cars on the highway. I parked and turned out the headlights. An unbroken wall of trees stood on either side of the road; high overhead stretched a strip of star-lit sky.

"Do you have protection?" she said.

"Yes, but I don't know how to use it," I muttered.

"I'll show you," Sandrine said, opening her door. "Let's get into the back seat."

I opened my door and stepped out of the Mormon universe. Sandrine came around to my side and hugged me. She unbuttoned my shirt and ran her hands across my belly and chest. She unlatched the buttons on her dress and undid her bra and stood expectantly. What could I do but caress her breasts? I was eager, feverish, trembling a bit, fully set on not being deterred, and the words so *this is what it is like, so this is what it is like* cycled impetuously through my mind, not ceasing until we had achieved our full purpose and lay clasped in one another's arms, my energy spent, my self-esteem exhausted.

When we got back into the front seat, she again slid close to me. I gripped the wheel and prepared to start the engine. She lay a hand on my arm and said, "When do you leave for Utah?"

"In a couple of weeks," I replied.

"I want to go with you," she said, snuggling against me.

The idea, the prospect, burned at my elbows and in my finger tips, but I couldn't reply. Sandrine had no idea how visible our liaison would be in Utah, at least, in the part of Utah that I had to return to. I couldn't share an apartment with another man's wife in Logan. Our neighbors would be scandalized. My parents would find out about it, and I wouldn't be able to present her to them. If we met them by accident, they wouldn't refuse to speak to her, but they would be devastated, vastly aggrieved, and their faces would show it.

Sandrine read my thoughts. "You don't want me to go," she said, pulling away.

"I'm not going back to Utah," I said. "At least, not to stay."

I started the engine and turned the car around. I looked at my watch. It was a little after one. Sandrine snuggled against me again.

"I am going to transfer to the forestry program at the University of Washington," I said. "Or maybe I'll take a job in Tacoma. There's a couple of wood product companies that hire people like me. The question I have is when to tell my parents about you. It would be easier for me to tell them in a letter after I have come back. And I will come back. I promise."

"You don't need to promise," she said. "I know you'll come back."

"The toughest thing we face," I said, "is telling Max."

"And Aubrey," she added.

I pulled onto the highway and accelerated.

"How shall we do it?" she said.

"I can't say," I replied. "I'll do whatever you want me to do."

"Immediately then? Both of us?"

"If you say so."

"It will be terrible," she said, "just terrible!"

She was sitting close to me, but no longer snuggling. She stared straight ahead into the tunnel of light projected by our head beams upon the pavement.

"Not tonight," she said at last. "It would ruin a happy day. You go back to the park. I'll tell Max in private tomorrow. I'll ask if we can keep Aubrey part of the time."

"Will he agree?"

"I don't know," she said. "Probably not. There's no way to force him. Legally, he's her sole custodian."

I could see the writing on the wall. It was time for me to articulate the inevitable. "Maybe you should stay with Max and Aubrey. I'll come on weekends."

"And we'd slip around?" she said.

"Slip around?"

"See each other on the sly. No, please, not that. I am going to live wherever you live—Tacoma, Seattle, I don't care where. I want to be there with you, out in the open."

"All right," I said. "That's how it will be."

She snuggled up to me again, affectionate and happy. I felt euphoric too—though also a little lightheaded as if I were coming down with something.

"It's strange, being in love," I said. "It changes everything. Things slide around into new positions."

"Things?"

"Obligations, I mean. You are my obligation now," I said. I meant, of course, that being with her, having her, trumped my Mormon expectations. As I say, I had stepped out of the Mormon universe.

When we arrived, I parked in front of the house and turned off the engine. A porch light burned.

"I won't see you again till next Tuesday?" Sandrine said.

"Yes, as usual."

"I can't do this alone," she said abruptly. "I can't tell them until you come back and are ready to take me with you."

"That makes sense," I said. "Don't tell them. We'll do it together when I come back."

"Yes," she said, "that's what we must do. We'll tell them together."

She kissed me and we both got out of the car. The house door opened and Max stepped onto the porch. She went into the house, murmuring something to Max as she brushed by him. I followed her to the porch. "I'm sorry we're so late," I said to Max. "We kind of did things to the hilt."

"I'm glad you did," Max said. "I can't thank you enough."

"I'll see you next week," I said.

"You better stay here," Max said. "I can fix up the sofa."

"No. I'm on duty at seven. I'd better get on up to the park."

I'll try to abridge my final days at the park. The more I have thought about them over the years, the more I have realized that they qualify hands down as the most painful period of equal duration in my entire life.

The euphoria I felt during our return from the fair didn't survive the night. I arrived at the bunkhouse in time for a couple of hours of sleep. After the alarm went off, I sat on the edge of my bed for a few minutes, still pretty groggy. My roommate came in from the shower room and looked me over. "Man," he said, "you must have painted that town red!"

I shrugged my shoulders and went to my closet and put on my uniform. I left the bunkhouse and started across the main parking lot, which at this early hour was largely empty of automobiles. I found it difficult to focus my thoughts. I wanted to recapture the happy incredulity of the moment I knew Sandrine loved me. But at the back of my mind was one of those half-spoken sentences that govern human behavior even before they have burst into full recognition. When it did come, a couple of days later, it came in connection with my thoughts about Max and Aubrey, who were to lose that which I was to gain. *A decent person doesn't build happiness on another person's devastation*—that was the thought, which, as I realized, was a translation of my mother's wish that, if push came to shove, I should choose to be good rather than happy.

Ironically, as I now saw, I was destined to be neither good nor happy. I was caught between contradictory imperatives. By assuming an obligation toward Sandrine, I had not abrogated an obligation toward Max and Aubrey. For the moment, I chose to honor my newly assumed obligation toward Sandrine. It wasn't an entirely self-serving choice. I had reason to believe her best prospect for happiness lay with me. But I also had reason to believe it would be at best a subdued happiness.

I was eager to see Sandrine on Tuesday—yet profoundly apprehensive. I dithered around the bunkhouse all morning, reviewing my field notes and outlining a report I was required to make to the undergraduate research committee that had funded my summer stipend. In the early afternoon, I drove to Limington, where I interviewed an old woman who had lived her entire life there to see whether she had any memory of Little Quebec and Chambers Landing. Unfortunately, she didn't—which meant those logging camps would appear as no more than names in my report.

Toward evening I backtracked to Beaufort—through which I had driven on my way to Limington. My stomach knotted as I walked into the café. Max beamed with pleasure when he saw me. "Come in, come in!" he said. "Your meal is on the house tonight. You better have a steak with a side of smoked potato salad, which Sandrine made today. It's meet-the-teacher night over at the school, so she's off with Aubrey just now, but they'll be back soon."

I was relieved to find things so normal. I don't know why I should have expected them to be otherwise. I wasn't hungry, not in the slightest, but when Max put the food before me, I ate. Sandrine and Aubrey came in about the time I finished. Aubrey climbed onto the stool next to me and gave me a big gap-toothed smile. Sandrine went behind the counter and stood beside Max. Her face was taut and her fingers fidgety. I told her the potato salad was delicious, and she smiled a little. At that instant I knew, as if by precognition, that I wouldn't be coming back. She and I had had our moment of happiness, and now it was over and we were in for a lot of grieving.

When I left, she followed me out to my car. She put her arms about me and began to sob.

"We can't go through with it, can we?" I said.

"I thought I could," she sobbed. "I really did."

"I know you did. I thought I could, too."

"He's too good a man," she said. "He bet on me when nobody else would. He's kind. He has no end of patience."

"Yes, and he needs you," I said. "And Aubrey needs you, too."

"And I need her," Sandrine said. "I'm split in two."

There wasn't much else to be said—though there was a great deal of pondering to be done, at least, for me. If I had briefly stepped out of the Mormon universe, I was now confronted by the necessity of reentering it. I knew in advance it would take a while.

I came back to Beaufort on the following Friday, which was the day my employment officially ended. I arrived in the early afternoon on that day, having packed my car and said goodbye to a few associates in the morning. Max insisted on serving me the lunch special—remarkably tasty, considering that it was hash. Sandrine stood behind the counter with Max, her face taut and distant. After a few minutes, she pulled a basket with yarn and knitting needles from under the counter and prepared to knit.

"I didn't know you knitted," I said.

"I'm learning," she said. "The woman down the road is showing me how."

When I was through eating, she set the basket under the counter and said, "Drive me over to the school. I promised Aubrey I would come in and bring her out to say goodbye. Her teacher won't mind."

I got out of the car when Aubrey emerged from the school. She wept a little while she hugged me. "You'll come back, won't you?" she said.

"I will."

"And will you write to us while you are gone?"

"You bet I'll write."

"Promise?"

"Yes, I promise," I said.

Sandrine took Aubrey back into the class and when she returned, she slid across the seat to my side of the car and gave me a long, passionate kiss before returning to the passenger's side. We both knew I had lied when I told Aubrey I would come back. But I did send a Christmas card for a few years.

As I started the engine, Sandrine said, "You mustn't stay single. You must find a good woman. I won't be jealous."

"Don't say that!" I protested. The thought of another woman seemed an infidelity, a sacrilege.

When we got back to the café, Max came out onto the steps. Sandrine got out of the car and joined Max on the steps. I waved to them and drove away. I took State Route 410 toward Yakima. Crossing over

Chinook Pass near sunset, I caught spectacular glimpses of Rainier in alpenglow. Passing into shadow on the downward side, I lost sight of the mountain's immense singularity. I tried not to grieve. I wanted to forget the summer of the Seattle Fair. I wanted to forget Max and his café, the fairy child Aubrey, even Sandrine. Yes, especially Sandrine! The sooner forgotten, the better.

But of course forgetting Sandrine was impossible. First of all, as I have said, I had to grapple with the problem of re-entering the Mormon universe. As far as my parents ever knew, I had never left it. But my bishop knew because I told him. I was fortunate in that he gave me a confidential penance, consisting not only of total regularity in performing my duties but also of a quarterly interview with him. Despite his kindliness, I found these interviews harrowing, largely because I judged myself incapable of a complete repentance—I could renounce *being with* Sandrine, but I couldn't renounce *loving* her. So the quarterly interviews stretched on for a second year, at the end of which the bishop got tired of the process and declared me a member in full and unblemished standing.

Three years after that, I met a young Mormon woman whom I wanted to marry. I explained up front what had happened during the summer of the Seattle Fair. When I asked her to marry me, she knew that as far as my private feelings were concerned, it was to be my second marriage. She knew I would come to our wedding as a widower. I am grateful that she accepted me on those terms.

Badge and Bryant; Or, the Decline and Fall of the Dogfrey Club

Badge and Bryant Braunhil were first cousins, but they could have passed for fraternal twins, having—both of them—bright blue eyes, big grins, and unkempt blond hair. They lived in Linroth, a Mormon town in northern Arizona. Their houses sat side by side, and Bryant always came out to accompany Badge to school or church or the Saturday night movie.

Their parents thought they were bound to be a good influence on one another, which they were until their fourteenth year, when they underwent a physiological change. Almost overnight they took up the use of the bad language they had heard their older brothers and the town loafers and wastrels using. With a casual affectation of long-established experience, they talked about doing dirty things with girls and created hilarious parodies of the bishop and their Sunday school teacher. Ambling along in the darkness after a movie or evening church, they were prone to belch, break wind, and write their names in the dust with urine. They vehemently denied being in love with any girl—though secretly both had given their hearts to LillieDale Mortensen, whose family had moved to Linroth at the beginning of their freshman year in high school.

On the last day of their freshman year, Badge and Bryant learned that a junior boy and a senior girl from one of the up-country towns had suddenly had to get married. The sturdy, heavy-set junior boy had already acquired a prominent five-o'clock shadow and a sullen, indolent voice that had settled into the bass range. The senior girl had a thin, sallow face and long brunette hair that brushed her frail shoulders. At dismissal time, Badge and Bryant had seen the girl walking toward her bus with a sober—perhaps even frightened—look on her face. This development provided the dominant topic for their conversation on their lazy stroll toward home on that hot May afternoon.

Bryant, for his part, responded to the sudden wedding with consternation. He was not as ardent as Badge in breaking the commandments, feigning a taste for irreverence and wrongdoing chiefly to maintain his cousin's esteem. Bryant had been an initiate for only a short time into the secret order of those who know that human beings create offspring in the manner of cattle, horses, and hogs. It was one thing to accept that the dignitaries of his town—the bishop, the high school principal, even his own father—begat offspring by connecting to a female. But it was quite another thing to accept that someone near his own age could get a girl pregnant—a fact that began at once to work a curiously cautionary effect upon him. He sensed already that his interest in girls had become more complicated. It wasn't enough that he had elevated LillieDale Mortensen to a station far beyond lust or passion. He also had an obligation, he now recognized, to respect all girls more consistently than he had lately done. In particular, he recognized an obligation to refrain from banter about such things as falsies, the padding with which girls supposedly stuffed their bras, and the bloody rag, the derisive term his schoolmates applied to sanitary napkins. He was to regard all girls as his sisters.

In contrast, the misadventure of the junior boy and senior girl had triggered Badge's vivid imagination. Even as he and Bryant strolled along, he envisioned the couple in their scandalous act, imagining them in the back seat of a car or in a hay loft, where older friends claimed to have done the deed. With a stroke of creative insight, he moved from imagining the junior boy and senior girl in their covert copulation to imagining himself similarly engaged with LillieDale. With that one small step, rich possibilities suddenly burst upon him. Here was new fodder for the daydreams into which he compulsively retreated while milking cows, chopping wood, or suffering through a sermon in church.

At fourteen, Badge had not yet abandoned the habit of fantasy in which children universally engage. From his earliest memory, he had been a scop, a bard, a creator of tales with himself at the center.

Countless times, he had leapt effortlessly over a house or curled his body into a circle and rolled down a hill with the speed of an automobile or dug a hole so deep that it came out on the other side of the earth. He had mastered mustangs, flown biplanes, conducted duels with swords high in the rigging of a sailing vessel. But never before this last day of school in his fourteenth year had the inexhaustible potential of romantic ardor as a subject for his fantasies presented itself to him.

He had been in love precisely seven times before the advent of LillieDale. This phenomenon had first occurred when, at age five, he had said, "I like the looks of you," to a girl with whom he had sat in the back seat of a car while on a stake Relief Society trip with his mother and other members of the stake Relief Society presidency. But compared to the buxom, full-lipped LillieDale, such loves were mere dross and refuse. No wonder then that the misadventure of the junior boy and senior girl who had to get married ignited a mimicking impulse. With a rumble and a jolt, the ecstatic shame of bedding LillieDale in disallowed circumstances locked itself into a preeminent position among Badge's aspirations. With scarcely a moment's reflection, he recognized a consummate theme for the fantasies of an entire summer.

How is it that a person can aspire so eagerly, so ecstatically, to an imagined shame for both himself and his beloved that either of them would have done almost anything to avoid in actuality?

Hardships that prove excruciating in actuality may be borne in fantasy with a good deal of stoic resolve. Boys at play happily imagine themselves in combat conditions that in the real world leave adult soldiers—if they survive—shattered in mind and body. Furthermore, the excoriations of conscience may be borne with much greater fortitude in a daydream than in real life. In fact, in Badge's case, conscience saw no reason whatsoever to be alarmed. The theology preached in the Linroth church house held that God sternly disapproved of fornication—and had the guardians of that theology ever considered the matter, they would undoubtedly have held that God disapproved only a little less sternly of an imagined fornication. However, Badge was so malnourished in theology

31

that it had never occurred to him even to conjecture whether God might pay attention to a person's daydreams.

Also, if Badge had reasoned further on the matter, he would have granted that his neighbors sided with God on the issue of fornication. It is a fact, however, that the human species diverts itself from the tedium of polite behavior by the contemplation of scandal. By simple instinct, Badge understood that, despite their mandate to openly disapprove of an unseemly deed, his neighbors would be subliminally grateful for the distraction its contemplation brought to their otherwise monotonous lives.

When Badge and Bryant had completed their leisurely meander from the high school, they seated themselves on the edge of Badge's porch. Badge needed to expatiate further upon his new-found pleasure, it being his nature to emote, enthuse, and think out loud. He also felt obliged to orient his less imaginative cousin to the satisfactions with which such a wedding swarmed. First of all, Bryant would need an acceptable partner. Obviously, it wouldn't do to direct his attention to LillieDale, given Badge's proprietary interest in her. Badge's duty to his cousin could be satisfied far short of that. Any one of a half dozen other girls in town would do.

"How about we make a pact?" Badge said abruptly. "We'll promise each other to get a girl pregnant. I mean, before we're married to her. And that's how we'll get married."

Bryant grimaced with bewilderment. "Which girl are we going to get pregnant?"

Badge snorted. "We can't get the same girl pregnant. We'll get different girls pregnant. Their fathers and brothers will come after us. They'll rough us up and drag us in front of the bishop and make us marry them. It will be a shotgun wedding, plain and simple." Then, as something of an afterthought, he added, "For example, you could get Panella Wall pregnant."

"Panella Wall! She's a total scag."

"Don't be so dang fussy."

"Well, then, *you* get her pregnant!"

By consensus among the boys in the shower room after PE class, Panella Wall actually fell into a middle rank for dating purposes—the she'll-do-in-a-pinch category. Certainly, she was no queen like

LillieDale Mortensen. However, although she had a large nose, an awkward gait, and a tendency to take the lead while dancing, she was a good-humored, lively conversationalist whom Badge and Bryant had walked home from evening church more than once.

"Besides," Bryant went on, "what's wrong with getting married the regular way?"

"Lots of things are wrong with it."

Bryant shook his head. "A girl won't let us do that to her if we aren't married to her."

"Sure, she will," Badge insisted.

"What do you know about it?"

"If you lick their ear lobe, they let you do it," Badge asserted.

"Who told you that?"

"It doesn't matter who told me. It's true. If you lick on their ear lobe with your tongue, they're helpless. They more or less pass out. So you won't have any excuse for not getting married that way. It's easy to do."

Badge got up from the edge of the porch, opened his pocket knife, and began to carve a tiny image into one of the wooden pillars. "This," he said, "is the sign of the Dogfrey Club, which you and I now belong to."

"What's a Dogfrey Club?" Bryant asked.

"It's just what I'm telling you."

"Where did you get that word? I never heard of any club like that before."

"It's just a word I made up."

Bryant got to his feet and ambled to the pillar. He peered at the minute figure, which looked something like an old-time cannon with a muzzle sitting on top of wheels.

"That's your you-know-what," Badge said. "That's the sign of the Dogfrey Club, the club that guys belong to who have to get married. That's the sign that you and I promise each other faithfully never to get married except by a shotgun wedding."

Bryant took another look. "That doesn't look like my you-know-what," he said.

"Well, that's what it stands for," Badge insisted. "Today is May 17. Every year till we are married we have to come here on May 17 and look at this sign of the Dogfrey Club and promise all over again to have a shotgun wedding."

A Dogfrey Club struck Bryant as taking clubs a little too far. He believed that, in general, clubs were a good thing. He and Badge had formed thirty or forty of them over the years. That is, Badge had thought them up and Bryant had endorsed them. Nothing had ever come of any of them, of course. Badge never bothered to shut them down formally; he just stopped talking about them, at which time Bryant knew they were finished. However, setting up a Dogfrey Club had ominous implications—something like consecrating motor oil instead of olive oil for healing the sick, which their older brothers had been warned not to try because a couple of fellows in Utah had tried it and had been killed by a bolt of lightning.

For one thing, a decent, church-going Mormon girl like Panella Wall was not a likely candidate for getting pregnant before she was married. The only girls in town who might be considered good prospects along that line were the two gentile Fortnight sisters, whose parents lived in a big trailer on the west side of town. Hannah Fortnight might have passed as a she'll-do-in-a-pinch specimen, but Lucinda was a scag by any measure. Nonetheless, they had their followers, the Keefer boys, a clan from two families whose Mormon mothers had married arrant, break-wind-in-your-face gentiles.

This pack of boys had lately been declaring their collective success with getting a hand up under the skirt of one or another of the Fortnight girls at the Saturday night movie. Billy Keefer, a ten-year-old, had gone one better than his older exemplars by claiming that he had been forced to satisfy the sisters' insatiable demands by resorting to a makeshift dildo, an extendable rubber stopper for soda pop bottles, which he flourished before his listeners by way of inarguable evidence.

Such an egregious lie needed no open rebuttal from the likes of Badge and Bryant, who happened by chance to be among Billy's listeners one Sunday afternoon. But as the Braunhil cousins had strolled on from this chance encounter, Badge fulminated with scornful indignation that Billy—a mere gnat, a cockroach, a maggot—should presume upon their credulity, whereas the silent Bryant shrank from the image that the ten-year-old's vaunt called to mind. It had seemed to him then, as it again seemed on the hot May afternoon at the end of their freshman year, that sex was too delicate, too problematic, too fraught with ambiguity, to trifle with by inventing such a superfluity as a Dogfrey Club. Sex being what it had turned out to be, as much of a messy necessity for human beings as for animals, you shouldn't come to it via the backdoor by not even taking the trouble to get married first when getting married was what you had in mind all along.

That summer when the boys were fourteen droned on, failing—like all other summers—to live up to anticipations formed in mucky, frozen corrals during the dismal months of winter. But toward the end of the summer, Badge's father proposed that the boys spend a few days with their Uncle Trevor and Aunt Sybil in Phoenix. Obviously, midsummer wasn't the best time to visit Phoenix, but given that they had never been there and could hitch a free ride down and back on a cucumber truck, it would make a nice, safe, inexpensive break in the summer routine. Badge's father had, in fact, already spoken to one of the truck owners, Diff Greenfleck, who was a good, steady, church-attending man and could be counted on to keep the boys out of trouble in transit.

On a Monday morning Badge's mother delivered the boys to the cucumber-loading shed halfway between Linroth and its somewhat less respectable sister-town of Saller's Cove. Diff's truck was backed up to a dock, and Diff and a couple of Apache helpers were stacking crates of cucumbers on the truck bed. Several pickups and a tractor and wagon waited to be unloaded. Their owners stood nearby, watching while an agent for the pickle factory weighed their cucumbers. Having spoken politely to the men, Badge's mother made sure each boy had his lunch, admonished them both to behave themselves, and left. With her departure, the men resumed interrupted conversations. Paying no attention to Badge and Bryant, they sprinkled their speech with swear words of the sort permissible to men who made some pretension of being good Mormons. Shortly, Diff and his helpers finished loading the truck, and Diff threw a tarp over the load and began to tie it down. However, the end of his rope was frayed and he had trouble feeding it through the first grommet. At that point one of the farmers said something that made all the men laugh. Bryant knew it was a dirty joke though he couldn't figure out precisely why. Badge, who knew more about the anatomy of women than Bryant, saw the point; but he didn't feel authorized to laugh, not being an adult. Sorting out an adult identity was perplexing, to say the least. On the one hand, both boys envied the insouciance, the slouching ease, with which the farmers casually tossed off an obscenity every few minutes. On the other hand—instructed by the secretive lore of their extended family—they esteemed that Braunhils were of a caste sublimely above the ordinary, whose scions were obliged by destiny to shun levity and unclean thoughts.

A half hour later they were on their way in Diff's truck, Bryant in the middle because he found sitting there more tolerable than quarreling with Badge over who got the seat by the window. Diff was a likeable sort of fellow despite having a jutting hawk-beak nose and cheeks that drooped into discernible jowls. He talked slowly, drawling out his words as if he had to pause mid-word to let his thoughts catch up with his language. He seemed glad for the boys' company and confident that they would want to know about his wife's hemorrhoids and his son Kenny's prowess as a football player, also about the strengths and weaknesses of every one of the players on the five teams in the county summer softball league—he being an enthusiastic participant, sometimes playing left field and sometimes third base.

Some of Diff's traits bothered Badge, particularly his drawl and apparent assumption that whatever interested him would interest everybody else. But, generally, both boys felt at ease in his presence. They also liked his wife, a tall, willowy, flat-chested woman, not really pretty but very nice, as Mormon mothers were supposed to be. Besides Kenny, Diff had two other kids, a peaked-looking daughter of twelve and a sniveling boy of eight, but that was nothing to hold against Diff who couldn't help what kind of lackluster kids God gave him—Kenny not being much of a looker, either.

When they got to Show Low, Diff stopped at an auto parts store. "Won't be but a second," he said. "I'm going to overhaul the wife's car. Gotta pick up a couple of gaskets. This place won't be open when I come back through here tonight."

The cigar-smoking proprietor of a curio store was unloading Navajo rugs from a panel truck next to the auto parts store. He paused and stepped closer to the truck. "You boys are Braunhil kids, aren't you?" he said. "I know your daddy." He blew a cloud of cigar smoke through the open window in an absent-minded way, almost as if he hadn't done it on purpose.

"We're not brothers," Badge said. "We're cousins."

"Hitching a ride with Diff Greenfleck I see," the fellow said. "You're riding with a hypocrite, boys. Diff was on the high council that excommunicated me. They ought to excommunicate him, too. More than one night I've seen his truck parked in back of that cathouse in Globe. Though I don't suppose he'll stop there if you're coming home with him tonight." He pulled the cigar from his mouth and stared at the saliva-slickened butt bitterly, as if it was the taste of the tobacco that bothered him rather than the unjust treatment of a church court. Then he turned his back to the truck and went on unloading rugs.

Bryant wasn't sure what a cathouse was. It didn't seem likely that Diff would be picking up cats in Globe. There were more than enough of those around Linroth. Badge, however, knew it was a place where whores lived. That is, given the man's leering intonation, he supposed he meant a whorehouse. "Whore" was a word Badge had looked up in a dictionary in the grade school library, having heard it in the schoolyard at recess. Finding the word hadn't been easy because he assumed that it began with an "h." The librarian asked whether she could help. When he told her the word, she flushed and said, "You shouldn't be interested in words like that." Then she said, just before turning away, "Go ahead and look it up. Find out for yourself. But it begins with a 'w,' like 'where.'"

The cigar-smoking man came back to the truck window and said, "I suppose you're wondering what I was doing driving past the back side of that cathouse in Globe. Well, I'll tell you. Ever since I got unchurched, I've made it my business to do that whenever I come through Globe, which is twice a week in the summer. I want to see whose automobile I might find parked there. It would surprise you who." With that, he blew another cloud of smoke into the truck and went inside his store. A second or two later, Diff came out of the auto parts store and they were on their way.

"Somebody's been smoking a cigar," Diff said, after sniffing two or three times.

"It was that old guy who owns that curio store," Badge said. "He blew it in here on purpose."

"Oh, yeah," Diff said. "That's just like him. He's an old reprobate. Claims the good brethren who go to church try to get downwind from his cigar so they can enjoy it second hand."

Beyond Show Low, they entered a forest of ponderosa pines. About ten miles down the road, they came to a tiny hamlet named Forest Dale, which was nothing more than a small mercantile and a grouping of small, unpainted frame houses. On the porch of the mercantile stood a couple of Apache women wearing billowy ankle-length skirts and long-sleeved over-blouses of brightly colored calico. This was the reservation, Diff explained, and white people couldn't own land or live here—except for one fellow who had married an Indian and could therefore not only live here but also hunt deer and elk and run his bear- and cougar-hounds.

"I wouldn't mind being able to take elk on the reservation," Diff said. "Elk are smart. They know where the reservation boundary is, and they stay inside it. Of course, you would have to feel okay about your wife not bathing very often. These folks don't have bathrooms, and a lot of them cook over outdoor fires."

Badge and Bryant knew about their smell. Every summer Apache families camped in the cottonwoods along the creek and picked cucumbers for the Linroth farmers, and on more than one summer Badge and Bryant had struck up a friendship with Apache boys. When they had time, they haunted the willow patches up and down the creek with these boys, who could talk better English than their parents. The Apaches slept in blankets wrapped in tarps, and as far as Badge and Bryant could tell, they didn't take off their work clothes when they went to bed. There was a spring near their camp that flowed with clear water for drinking and cooking and for hand-washing clothes on a Sunday afternoon. A lot of white people in Linroth looked down on these Indians, but Badge's and

Bryant's parents weren't among them. Their mothers took turns bringing ice-cold sodas out for the pickers in their husbands' fields every afternoon except Sunday. The pickers never said thanks, that not being their custom, but their brown faces beamed with pleasure when they saw the white women approaching.

A couple of miles past Forest Dale, Diff and the boys went by a grassy, treeless flat. At the far end stood the ruin of a sawmill—a caved-in incinerator and a long wood deck-like structure that Diff said had supported a conveyer chain. "Me and an Apache fellow named Horace Clay pulled green chain at that mill one summer before the war," Diff said. "He was a nice guy. Talked good English, except of course all of them use verbs only in the present tense. Horace went on binges a couple times that summer. His wife asked me to drive over to Whiteriver and get him out of jail. Which I did."

By now it was only Bryant who was paying close attention to these details, being the kind of fellow who had to listen to what adults were saying and utter brief exclamations of an affirmative sort that would show his respect for their station, such as "Wow!" and "Gosh!" and "Boy howdy!" For his part, Badge was trying hard to ignore all the interruptions and settle into an important phase of his current episode of having to get married to LillieDale. Ever since school had adjourned in June, Badge had been creating elaborate daydreams about getting her pregnant to occupy his attention while working at vacant, mindless chores such as hoeing corn or tramping hay. He had generously sought to share his pleasant escape with Bryant, even going so far as to remind him of their mutual commitment to the vows of the Dogfrey Club, but Bryant had seemed at best indifferent. Badge's fantasies were essentially a saga, a series of episodes or, as it were, a serial daydream. The problem with a serial daydream such as this, of course, was that over and over Badge had to invent new particulars for what was fundamentally the same story, a task that had become increasingly difficult as the summer progressed.

Nonetheless, on this August day, traveling in Diff's truck through a pine forest on the highway between Show Low and Globe, Badge succeeded at last in screening out all distractions and settled into one of his favorite scenes. In it, a distraught, sobbing LillieDale

informed her parents of her pregnancy. She could bring herself
to do this only when her belly began to swell and concealment
was no longer possible. Her parents were of course thunderstruck,
her mother bursting into tears, her father into a torrent of rage.
That scene quickly melted into another, in which Mr. and Mrs.
Mortensen knocked at Badge's door and, upon being invited in by
his parents, announced the condition of their daughter, who stood
between them with tears of shame gilding her flushed cheeks. On
hearing their accusation against his son, Badge's slack-jawed father strode to the backdoor and called his errant son to come forth
from the barnyard and make his account, only to be informed by
another son that an hour earlier Badge had tied his .22 rifle and
a sack of provisions to his saddle and galloped away down a lane.
In the meantime, Badge's mother sat on the sofa sobbing with
her face buried in her hands. She knew only too well that news of
the disgrace that had fallen upon her family would ricochet about
town within a few hours, and it wouldn't stop at the town limits but
would broadcast itself hither and yon, taking a prominent place in
the repertoire of the county's infamous scandals.

The public nature of his disgrace was an indispensable aspect of
the fantasy with which Badge entertained himself. He was pleased
to imagine furtive conversations held at dinner tables in towns
as far away as Holbrook to the north or McNary to the south.
Women shook their heads indignantly, and men pursed their lips
with incredulity upon hearing that over in Linroth a Mortensen
girl had become pregnant and the Braunhil boy who had done it to
her was hiding out in the mountains. Men were saying things like
"They ought to lynch him" and "Tar and feathering's too good for a
skunk like him." It was a delicious notoriety.

Fifteen or twenty miles beyond Forest Dale, the truck bore the
three travelers past a little valley spread with corn and squash fields
and, alongside a cottonwood-lined creek, a cluster of frame houses.
Just off the highway was a gas station with a sign that said this was
Carrizo. A yellow cat sat on its haunches by one of the gas pumps.
That set Bryant to wondering again what a cathouse might be and
why Diff might be interested in stopping at one of them and, if
he wasn't, then why the owner of the curio store would make up a

preposterous story by claiming that he was. Bryant was almost to the point of wishing he hadn't come on this trip in the first place.

"I'll tell you a story about Carrizo, boys," Diff said. "A couple of years ago, I had a phone call in the middle of the night. I was home in bed. The chief of police over at Whiteriver said his officers were in a standoff with a drunk guy in Carrizo whose wife was being held hostage. These Apache cops were playing it cool and trying to talk the guy into surrendering. The chief of police said on the phone the guy insisted he wouldn't surrender to anyone but his old buddy Diff Greenfleck, so would I drive out to Carrizo and get him to come out peaceful? I said, 'Who the heck is he?' Chief of police said, 'Horace Clay.' So I did it, boys. Took me an hour and a half to get there. It was close to dawn. He came out, handed me the rifle, then broke down and started to sob. He had been through the war since I had seen him last, got shot up on Guadalcanal. All filled out now, a little on the heavy side."

Even Badge had to perk up and pay attention to that story, so much so, in fact, that when Diff stopped talking, he asked, "What happened after that?"

"They kept him in jail in Whiteriver for a while. Talked about a stint in the penitentiary. But it never happened. These folks are pretty lax on carrying out white man's justice. Four or five months later, they let him loose. Him and his wife still live in Carrizo. I stop by once in a while, drop off something out of our garden or maybe a five-pound cheese. That's the kind of gift they like."

"That's awful nice of you to take them some vegetables or a block of cheese," Bryant said thoughtfully.

Diff whistled a little and tapped a finger on a spoke of the steering wheel as if his mind had wandered on to some other topic. A few minutes later, with the truck grinding up a steep dugway, he went on where he had left off. "A sack of potatoes, five pounds of cheese—that ain't much of a gift, is it, boys? I'm just trying to make up for the fact he had to go to war and I didn't. I tried to enlist, I really did. But I had a hernia."

Shortly thereafter, Badge succeeded in slipping away into his fantasy again, being somewhere in these very mountains evading capture by Mr. Mortensen and his elder sons. These earnest individuals, assisted by a shifting variety of townsmen, combed the forested terrain relentlessly, forcing Badge into constant movement. He was, of course, the craftiest of fugitives, having achieved a cunning found only in coyotes or foxes that have survived to old age—grizzled and hatch-marked by scars from traps, bullets, and the slashing fangs of hounds. For example, Badge made sure the thickets and ravines in which he hid had more than one exit. He hid by day and moved by night. He built small, smokeless fires and took small game by snares rather than by rifle. So expert was he in the art of concealment that he sometimes overheard the angry, frustrated speech of his pursuers only yards from where they had dismounted. Such details were enhanced when Badge shifted the scene of his narrative to such places as the Linroth post office where those reporting on the futile search in the mountains were beginning to express a begrudging admiration for the fugitive. "Who would have figured on it?" exclaimed old Wilbur Linroth, current patriarch of the town's founding family, as he fingered through his mail. "That Braunhil boy is one smart cookie!"

Eventually, of course, the plot called for his capture. Overcome by fatigue one morning at daybreak, he fell asleep and failed to muffle the nickering of his horse. By the sheerest accident, his pursuers also heard the sound and raised a mighty clamor. Although he awoke and, with a single leap, mounted his unsaddled steed, they had him surrounded. Pulling him roughly from his horse, LillieDale's eldest brother pummeled him with savage fists while a younger brother lashed him with the knotted end of a lariat.

"Let's hang him, Dad!" exclaimed this zealous punisher.

"No, sir!" said his father. "This boy is going to marry your sister whether he wants to or not. Now listen to me, boy. Are you going to come peaceable, or do we tie you to your saddle?"

The unquenchable spirit of a mountain man of the Olden Days surged in Badge, and he leaped to his feet and sprinted for freedom, only to be knocked to the ground again.

The truck had come to a terrain chopped and broken by arroyos and canyons. Stunted piñons, gnarled junipers, and thickets of rust-brown manzanita dotted the landscape. They passed the junction to Cibecue, an Apache town of some size, as Diff informed the boys, where there had been a battle between the US cavalry and some Apaches in 1881. It had had to do with a medicine man who claimed he had the power to resurrect dead Indians who would drive white people out of Arizona. Six or seven of the troopers and the medicine man were killed in the fight.

"You gotta admire the Apaches," Diff said. "There wasn't all that many of them. But they still tied up most of the US cavalry for five or six years."

About twenty miles past the Cibecue turnoff, they came to Salt River Canyon, a dramatic gorge into which the road dropped nearly two thousand feet via short, steep hairpin curves, only to cross the silvery river by means of an iron truss bridge, and quickly regain its lost altitude by equally steep hairpin curves. On the descent, the odor of burnt brake linings filled the cab, and on the climb out, the truck slowed to a crawl—all of which seemed to trouble Diff not at all. As cool and collected as if he were instructing them in their priesthood class on a Sunday morning, Diff lectured the boys on the vegetation of the canyon, particularly pointing out the bayonet-spiked agave plant, from which long, graceful, white-gray stems reached skyward, culminating in a halo of yellowish blossoms.

At the point where the road emerged from the canyon stood a café with a couple of gas pumps out front and, to the side, a large cottonwood tree whose overarching boughs shaded the café. A sign at the side of the road declared this to be Seneca. Diff steered the truck to a halt beneath the tree and got out. He said he was going to have some lunch and offered to bring the boys a soda to go with the lunches their mothers had prepared. They said no thanks because it seemed on the one hand that, since they had money, they couldn't accept his charity, yet, on the other hand, having hoarded the money for weeks so they could spend it in Phoenix, they didn't feel good about spending it before they even got there.

While they ate their lunch, Bryant noticed a black and white dog sleeping in the shade of an awning. The dog reminded him of the yellow cat at Carrizo, which reminded him to ask Badge what he thought a cathouse might be.

"It's a place where ladies let you screw them for money. It's where whores live," Badge asserted.

Bryant was flabbergasted, having never thought of whores being people who might live in a clean, decent state like Arizona, whose history and constitution he had studied in the eighth grade.

"It's the same as a brothel," Badge said. "That's another word for a whorehouse."

Bryant naturally wanted to ask another question or two, but Diff came out, putting a momentary end to his education in sexual matters. Diff handed them each a grape soda as he climbed into the truck. "Treat's on me," he said.

"You boys are in the teachers' quorum now, aren't you?" he asked as he looked up and down the highway before pulling the truck back onto the road. "We gottta get you assigned to an adult partner for ward teaching. Maybe your dads." After he had the truck on the road, he added, "But you likely would rather go with somebody else, wouldn't you? I went ward teaching with my dad when I was about your age. He wouldn't quit talking. I remember a place or two where our visit lasted more than an hour. Two hours, once in a while. He wouldn't have been rude enough to keep somebody else's boy pinned down so long."

Bryant was feeling doubly grateful to Diff just now, who had not only given him a grape soda but had also reminded him of what a faithful Mormon he was. Even if there was a whore house in Globe, the cigar-smoking owner of the curio store had it all wrong. A man as nice and decent and generous as Diff wouldn't visit a place like that. Not in a thousand years.

Badge was also grateful for the soda. However, unlike Bryant, he wasn't preoccupied just now with Diff and the insinuations of the proprietor of the curio store, being eager to get on with his current episode of having to marry LillieDale. He had left off the narrative at the point where the Mortensen cavalcade entered Linroth following its successful venture in the mountains. Now, with Badge's horse in tow, Mr. Mortensen lifted a hand in triumphant salute to this friend or that along Main Street. Behind him, the slumping Badge—bruised, battered, and securely tied to his saddle—stared indifferently at the ground. As the cavalcade arrived at the Mortensen house, LillieDale shrieked a despairing protest and dashed from the door.

"Back off, girl!" said her father sternly. "You'll have him soon enough."

Ordering one of his sons to fetch the bishop and another to alert the Braunhils to the imminent wedding of their son to his daughter, he ordered yet another son to help him tie Badge to a chair in the living room. "That rascal's a slippery one," he muttered. "Tie him tight. We can't risk his escape. Not after all this trouble."

A considerable crowd of Mortensen and Braunhil relatives assembled in the Mortensen living room for the wedding. Their talk was sober and subdued, nothing like the usual Mormon social gathering. Badge's parents brought his dark blue Sunday suit and a white shirt and tie, which Badge, released from the chair, put on in the bathroom.

LillieDale wore a loose-fitting lavender Sunday dress and held a modest nosegay of white daisies and blue bachelor's buttons gathered from her mother's garden. When asked to say "I do," LillieDale's voice broke and she wiped away tears with the back of a hand, while Badge uttered the same affirmation with a sullen, downcast grunt. When the bishop had declared them man and wife, Badge brushed LillieDale's puckered lips with the merest touch of a kiss.

Badge emerged from his daydream when Diff pointed out, some miles beyond Seneca, a dead coyote on the shoulder of the highway. "That's rare," Diff said. "Coyotes are usually too smart to get hit by a car." They had by now passed beyond the lower-montane forests of juniper and piñon and were upon a wide plain covered by mesquite, chaparral, and patches of dry yellow grass. They saw some cattle sheltering themselves in the shade of a scrubby tamarisk grove near a windmill. "Tough country for animals in the summer," Diff said. "But there are more wild animals here than you'd think. Some mule deer, antelope, bobcats, coyotes, wild pigs—peccaries, that is, a distant cousin to the domestic pig, I understand. Folks around here call them javelinas."

Bryant listened with satisfaction to all these facts. He hoped he'd know about such a wide range of things when he was an adult.

Badge, however, was once again feeling out of sorts with Diff for interrupting his daydream about LillieDale with talk about facts he already knew.

Diff hummed a bit of song, slapping a hand on the steering wheel in keeping with its rhythm. Then, as if there was a connection between peccaries and the song he was humming, he said, "When I was in high school, I drove to Mesa; and a friend and I drove on down to Tucson and went javelina hunting in the desert. Never saw any. My friend decided to relieve himself on a big overhanging rock. So he took down his pants and squatted and did his business. A bobcat jumped out from under the rock. My friend stood up with his pants down around his knees and shot it. Back in Mesa we drove by his girlfriend's house to show off his trophy. She came out in pin curlers. She wasn't interested in the bobcat, but she did seem interested in me. So next time I was in Mesa, I went by her house and asked for a date. Now she's my wife. My buddy was sore for a while. But he got over it."

The truck rumbled on, hot air rushing in both windows. Bryant mulled this latest story, wondering what Sister Greenfleck had looked like in pin curlers when she was high school age. Badge, for his part, had finally managed to shut off the listening machine in his head and turned on his imagination, which had automatically begun to play the finale of his latest episode.

Following the perfunctory wedding ceremony, LillieDale's mother invited the guests to partake of cookies and punch which she and her sister had set out on card tables in the flower garden. The nuptial pair stood at formal attention, glass cups in hand, accepting the solemn salutations of their families, friends, and neighbors. Underneath a veneer of polite cordiality, these good, decent people could scarcely contain their seething indignation against Badge for deflowering such a delicate, defenseless blossom as LillieDale, who wiped tears from her downcast eyes every few moments.

Reveling in the ignominy into which the citizens of Linroth had cast him, Badge lingered on this lachrymose scene at length. Eventually, however, he had to disperse the crowd and imagine himself and LilliDale standing alone in the room where they had been wed.

Glancing piteously up at him, she obviously expected at best a callous indifference on his part. Happily, the narrative now called for Badge to yield to his throbbing love and allow a warm, reassuring smile to replace his hitherto stolid, apathetic countenance— a transmutation which the long-neglected girl at first did not dare accept as sincere. It was not until he took her in his arms and pressed a long, fervent kiss upon her lips that she began to feel the first inklings of a hope that had eluded her for weeks. Suddenly, relief and gratitude swept her wan, fine-featured face and her eyes welled with happy tears. With that, this version of the saga ended.

About a half hour later, the truck pulled into a gas station at the outskirts of Globe. "Better get out and come inside, boys," Diff said. "You can cool off a bit before we hit the desert."

Bryant crawled out of the truck through the driver's door and followed Diff into the station. Badge didn't move. Although he was tired of imagining things just now, he felt compelled to at least outline a new plot before turning his attention elsewhere. He needed something shiny, something innovative, something that made LillieDale's suffering even more poignant and his own reasons for failing to reassure her of his eternal love more tragic. There was, he recognized, an illogic to his weeks-long evasion of capture which could justifiably be interpreted as a lack of pity for the despairing girl. He needed some dark compulsion, a sinister force, which left him no alternative to evasion. But who could call upon his best, most creative, most concentrated energy in such heat? With a surge of disgust, he climbed from the truck and stalked into the station.

Inside, Bryant was extracting a strawberry soda from an insulated container. "Want one?" he asked Badge, who grunted his assent and dug into a pocket for change. Diff stood at a counter feeding a few nickels into a slot machine. Soda in hand, the boys watched while the slot machine's three little wheels, each bearing the image of a lemon, a banana, or an apple, circled frantically, always failing to halt with a winning lineup of a single fruit. "Well, damn!" Diff said at last, turning on his heel and striding from the station. "I won a buck last week," he added as they climbed into the truck. "But it's a fool's game. They adjust those slots to pay off about once every five hundred tries. They're illegal, you know. But, heck, Globe is a mining town. What do you expect?"

Moments later they topped over a hill and a squalid, heat-blistered town stretched before them. It filled a narrow valley, its streets extending up a slope on either hand. Above the houses on the northern slope loomed a crushing mill, conveyer belt, and smelter serving an open pit copper mine. Despite such evidence of a flourishing economy, the residential area presented the decayed, half-ruined aspect of a ghost town, as if none of its present inhabitants expected to remain for long and had no incentive to repair, clean, or paint. There was no hint of trees or lawn around the houses, which floated like small soiled islands in a sea of dust. At the center of town the highway showed some sign of citification—a commercial district six or seven blocks long with curbs and concrete sidewalks. There were stores, a bank, a hotel, a couple of restaurants, and an insurance agency—with an occasional house standing between.

While the truck made its slow progress through town, both Badge and Bryant were entranced by the possibility that one of the tarnished, decayed buildings they were passing served as a brothel.

For Bryant, simply granting the possibility was a disillusionment, an unhappy schooling in the nature of mortality, something like the disillusioning—though also enfranchising—perception that his father and mother had had to couple in the same astonishing fashion as the bucks and does in his rabbit cages to bring him and his siblings into the world. Nonetheless, he remained at peace. He had made up his mind on the key issue, which was whether Diff would frequent such place. He had already decided at Seneca that Diff was too likeable, too regular in attendance at church, too generous and considerate, to have secret associations with evil women. Furthermore, a hitherto tenuous thought had by now coalesced into a firm conviction for Bryant. The cigar-smoking owner of the curio store in Show Low was an arrant mischief maker, a man so given to evil that he could find delight only in tainting genuinely good men with accusations of it. It was such as he who—as the scriptures ordain—are to be cast into outer darkness on the day of judgment, a determination that had released Bryant from further agitation over this matter and allowed his mind to wander on to matters entirely unrelated to evil-doing in Globe, Arizona.

It was otherwise with Badge, who again struggled to lock his thoughts on the task of sketching out a new episode about having to marry LillieDale that would infuse his fantasy with a distinctly new energy. The present obstacle to concentration on this task was the disturbing question whether, late in the night, Diff Greenfleck's truck, loaded with empty cucumber crates, might be found parked behind one of the tarnished, decayed buildings lining this road.

Within moments of Badge's turning his thoughts to that topic, Diff stopped the truck at a traffic light. Waiting for the green signal, he whistled a joyless tune through puckered lips and again tapped a senseless rhythm upon the steering wheel with his fingers. A woman wearing a light blue sundress and white sandals crossed from the opposite side of the street in the crosswalk immediately in front of the truck. The thin straps of her dress made no pretense at covering her bare, tanned shoulders. Below the hem, which came a little under her knees, her legs were similarly tanned. Diff and the boys watched till she reached the curb near the truck. When the light changed, Diff revved the engine and engaged the clutch, and the truck passed through the intersection. For a few seconds, Badge could see the receding figure of the woman in the rearview mirror outside his window. Just before they passed beyond her range, he saw that she had turned and started up the steps of a house.

Badge considered whether she was a prostitute. It wasn't her appearance that put that possibility into his mind. He had no pre-conceptions about what a prostitute might look like—except that she would surely have distinguishing marks of some sort. As far as he could tell, this woman had none. She hadn't a particularly pretty face, nor a nicely contoured body, nor a coiffure of any note. How-ever, even plain and ordinary women were charged with an aura of sexuality that required attention. This one had to be considered, had to be assessed and ranked, if only for a few seconds.

Among the changes Badge had undergone during the past year was the perception that women no longer mingled indistinctly with men in the general population. Within a few short months, they had become, more or less all of them, objects of sexual interest. That this woman—that almost any woman—was sexually attractive to Badge was a discomfiting fact for both practical and moral reasons. Lust was not an emotion that any Mormon male, old or young, could easily admit to, it being generally supposed in the Mormon world that there is no similarity between the sinful emotion of lust and the ardor which drives a husband to beget legitimate babies upon his duly-wed wife. Badge had fed on lust for LillieDale without thinking of it as lust. It was love—tender, grand, unique in the annals of history, light-years beyond mere lust. But a sexual interest in a grown woman had something of the unsavory, even something of the incestuous, about it. It was like lusting after his own mother. Although he had lately fancied himself a man—swaggering and swearing and teaching Bryant to do the same—he refused to imagine what went on in his parents' bedroom or at least, since from time to time he *did* imagine it, he made certain to expel it from his consciousness as quickly as possible.

Even worse, admitting a sexual interest in the woman wearing the light blue dress implied that Diff shared that interest—for among the changes Badge had undergone during the past year was the recognition that his sexual interest in almost any woman was shared by almost any man. This recognition would not have been an issue just now, or in almost any other circumstance, had it not been for the accusation that the cigar-smoking proprietor of the curio shop had made against Diff. Diff had said nothing about the woman at the intersection, nor, to be truthful, could Badge testify that he had watched Diff's eyes follow the woman. But it had to be assumed. The naive, innocent Bryant may have paid her no more attention than he would have paid a man. But if Badge had viewed her with a sexual interest, then so had Diff. The unsettling conviction now grew upon Badge that it was not merely possible, but certain, that Diff would visit a whore house on his way home from Phoenix tonight.

That certitude was something Badge didn't wish to linger on. For a few seconds, he reviewed the exonerating evidence—Diff went to church with his wife and kids every Sunday, he played softball in the county league, and he was generous and thoughtful to a couple of kids who happened to have hitched a ride with him.

For a few seconds more, Badge noted that the evidence against Diff was dubious—the bitter testimony of an angry, rumor-mongering, cigar-smoking reprobate whose very appearance, starkly alien to the model of decency to which Badge adhered, undermined his credibility. Compulsively, Badge resumed his effort to jumpstart a new fantasy about having to marry LillieDale. There was, in fact, a touch of desperation to the gesture.

Try as he might to fix his mind on LillieDale, he could not help envisioning—from the perspective of one who peers through a keyhole or some other tiny aperture—the woman in the light blue dress sitting on the edge of a bed in a room whose perimeter was lost in shadow. He had, he recognized, cast her in the character of a prostitute and from that followed the further recognition that it was not, after all, so much a matter of being certain that Diff would visit a brothel on his way home tonight as of *hoping* that he would. Therein lay the shame. Someday not so far into the future, Badge would have to settle with himself—since no one else could do it for him—whether he himself would or would not stop to visit ladies of the night in Globe, Arizona.

The truck soon carried them through Globe's sister town of Miami. Although it too boasted a smelter and an open-pit mine, it was even smaller and graced by even less of a commercial district. Beyond Miami, the highway began a tortuous descent, passing through a tunnel and giving views of a handsome arched bridge long before passing over it. Emerging from a canyon, the road passed through the town of Superior, set picturesquely amid barren, turreted sandstone mountains. Beyond Superior, at a point where the road began another descent, Diff said, "It's plenty hot, boys. But it's about to get hotter."

Shortly, the road leveled out on the wide, undulating expanse of the Sonoran Desert, which stretched distantly into a horizon hazy with heat and dust. The desert was thick with a gray, dusty, thorny vegetation: saguaro cactus with upthrust arms, giant prickly pear, domed barrel cactus, wicked-looking cholla whose branching joints bristled with sinister spines, and delicately arched ocotillo, which, according to Diff, was often used for fences in Mexico.

Diff wiped his neck with a bandana, muttering as he did so,

"A little heat won't kill you." After a moment he added, "Actually, it *will* kill you if you don't have water. Lots of it. You sweat out a gallon a day in this heat. More if you have to work in it. Roofers in Mesa and Phoenix start work at four and quit at noon in this weather. Some of them take salt tablets."

In time they came to Apache Junction, which was nothing more than a handful of houses and a gas station where a road to Florence and Tucson split off from the highway to Mesa and Phoenix. A couple of miles past Apache Junction, Diff said, "When I get old, I'm going to move to the Northwest and build a house in a rain forest. It will have a corrugated tin roof and a bunk bed just inches from roof, and night and day I'm going to listen to the patter of rain on the tin roof."

The air continued to rush through the open windows of the cab like a blast from an oven, drying off perspiration before it had a chance to form. Bryant bore his misery stoically, his thoughts having pretty much gone into estivation, like a desert salamander or turtle that digs into the soil to escape the baking heat of the surface. For his part, Badge writhed with a poorly suppressed impatience. Almost anything that came to mind irritated him.

First and foremost among the irritants was his inability to find composure enough to generate a new daydream about having to get married to LillieDale. But a list of lesser irritants also presented themselves. He resented Diff anew for drawling when he spoke, a particularly acute irritant, given Diff's propensity for lecturing. He resented Bryant for playing the constant sycophant to any adult and also, as Badge reminded himself, for failing to pay his cousin the same kind of respect, considering that Badge constantly went out his way to think up clever activities, an example of which was the Dogfrey Club, toward which Bryant displayed an almost supercilious indifference. It wasn't easy to think of ways to pass the time of day pleasantly; and if Badge was kind enough to include Bryant in his special projects, then Bryant ought to demonstrate a little more gratitude.

After a while, they passed some pecan and citrus orchards; and shortly after that, houses began to line the highway. Pretty soon they came to the Mesa city limits, and their misery was compounded by the necessity of stopping often at red lights. They passed the Mormon temple, a handsome, flat-roofed, one-story structure with tall recessed windows and date palms and decorative orange trees all around. They toiled on through Tempe and on into the outskirts of Phoenix, where Diff pulled into a service station and made a phone call to the boys' Uncle Trevor, who would come pick them up and save Diff the trouble of crossing the city in heavy traffic with his loaded truck.

Trevor showed up after a while in a fancy new ice-blue Buick with a V-8 engine and air conditioning. He didn't look anything like his brothers, Badge's and Bryant's fathers, who were short, bald, and ruddy-faced and who, like their sons, could have passed for fraternal twins. Endowed with a full head of dark hair, duly oiled, and a carefully clipped pencil-line mustache, Trevor wore office attire—light poplin pants and a white shirt with sleeves rolled up to mid-arm and a tie with a half-loosened knot.

Trevor and Diff made arrangements for Diff to pick up the boys on Friday afternoon for their return to Linroth and then stood chatting in the shade of the store awning for a few minutes. Trevor seemed interested in the cucumber crop this year. Also, he wondered whether the rainy season had started yet up north and if so whether the folks around Linroth and Saller's Cove were getting hit by some good thunderstorms. Eventually, he got around to asking whether Diff had ridden any broncs at the Pioneer Day rodeo in Linroth this year.

"You know better than that!" Diff protested. "It's been years since I was dumb enough to get on a bronc."

"Diff wasn't any older than you fellows when he started riding broncs and bulls," Trevor said to the boys.

"These boys are too smart to get into that game," Diff said, shaking his head ruefully. He turned and walked toward his truck, saying, "Gotta go get this bolt heap unloaded before the cukes wilt in the heat."

"Good old guy, that Diff!" Trevor said.

Trevor drove the boys across town to the brick and cement block yard where he was the superintendent. He bought them ice cream sandwiches from a machine and took them into his air-conditioned office, which wasn't much of a place—a couple of utility desks with swivel chairs, some filing cabinets, and half a dozen metal chairs set against the walls. He said a secretary normally sat at the desk that had a phone on it, but she had left early to make a deposit before the bank closed. After he had phoned his wife to let her know the boys had made it and could be counted on for supper, he said he had to get back out in the yard. He told the boys they could stay in the office where it was cool; or if they wanted to look over the operation, they were welcome to watch from a little roofed balcony where they'd be out of the way of men and machines.

The boys sat for a while cooling off, more or less slumped in a torpor of silence. Bryant was thinking about things at Uncle Trevor's and Aunt Sybil's house. They had five kids, all of them younger than Bryant and Badge. On summer visits to Linroth, the kids had acquired an expectation of wit and mimicry on the part of their cousins, which Bryant hoped he and Badge could live up to during the coming few days. He had in fact sanitized a couple of dirty limericks he had heard at school which he thought his younger cousins would enjoy. He was counting on Badge to lead the way as usual with some farcical ideas to keep the kids in stitches.

Badge sat abstracted, his head cocked a little and his eyes fixed on a plaque on the wall that said Trevor Braunhil had been certified by an institute in Milwaukee as a service master of some kind of a concrete mixing machine. A concrete mixing machine was what Badge felt like just now, his mind being full of inarticulate thoughts and feelings that refused to arrange themselves in an orderly sequence, being just bubbles of awareness that burst almost as quickly as they surfaced.

After a while, Bryant said, "Want to go watch them make blocks?"

"Might just as well," Badge said. However, he didn't move, so Bryant went out and closed the door.

Sitting there, still looking at the plaque on the wall that said Trevor Braunhil had been certified by an institute in Milwaukee, Badge realized he had never felt so depressed in his life. He hadn't known a person could feel so depressed.

He was wishing he hadn't been so certain that Diff would visit a brothel on his way home tonight. He was wishing he hadn't recognized that he *hoped* Diff would. He was especially wishing he hadn't realized, that sometime soon, he would have to decide whether he himself would stop there, too. Then it came to him that he had to make that decision now; and with that recognition, as ordained by a simple line of logic, his depression evaporated. If he could resolve, truly resolve, never to visit a whorehouse, then, very likely, Diff had long ago made a similar resolution.

Then he began to feel depressed again for being irritated with Diff and Bryant out on the highway with the hot wind rushing through the windows of the truck. Also, he recognized it didn't demonstrate much gumption to make up his mind never to visit a cathouse in the future when he wasn't willing to give up his present vices, foremost among which was a non-stop daydream about fornicating with LillieDale. So he decided to abandon his fantasy of having to marry LillieDale, which made him feel depressed in a different sort of way because he could see there wasn't any end to this business of moral reformation, it now being his clear duty to learn how to get through the tedium of the day without fantasies of any sort. With something of an inward groan, he made up his mind to get by with nothing but facts all day long.

But it didn't seem like there was much to live for on a steady diet of only facts all day long. Maybe things would change when he became an adult. But he wasn't sure, having observed good, decent adults for fourteen years. He never saw adults really enjoying themselves. They were mostly dedicated to work and worry and wondering if the price of pinto beans would hold up long enough to allow for a profit on the twenty acres of dryland planted to them. If adults tried to catch a moment of relaxation with a book in the evening, they promptly went to sleep in their chair. If they went to a movie, they went to sleep. At least, Badge's parents did. Also they went to sleep when they went to church—though as far as church was concerned, going to sleep could be considered a mercy. Nonetheless, facts were facts, and sooner or later Badge had to accept them.

Pretty soon, Bryant came back inside the office. "Making concrete blocks with a big machine isn't much different than mixing cement in a trough and pouring it into molds with a shovel," he said.

He sat down in a chair facing Badge and said, "A guy just came into the yard and reported one of the delivery trucks was broken down, and Uncle Trevor just said, 'Dang!'"

"My dad would've said 'Dadgost it!'" Badge observed.

"Where did he get that word?"

"Just made it up, I think."

"Braunhils don't ever swear, I guess," Bryant said.

They sat staring at each other for a while. "I've been thinking," Badge said. "What if we give up on that Dogfrey Club business? I have in mind when we get home I'm going to take my knife and dig that little sign off that pillar on the porch."

Bryant tilted his head and rolled his eyes upward to show he was weighing the matter carefully.

"It was a dumb idea," Badge said.

Bryant nodded. "Yeah," he said, "it kind of was."

The Return of the Native

The Phoenix-bound plane was airborne before I allowed myself to consider the negatives of what I was doing. I told my stepdaughter who lives in Seattle an outright lie about my destination, saying I was flying to Corvallis to visit an old buddy from my Navy days. I knew I would have to expand on that lie when my wife, on a cruise with her sisters, got around to calling me. Even worse, I would have to expand on the lie I had been telling myself for a long time, that there was no resemblance between who I'd become and the fifteen-year-old kid who forced himself on his first cousin in a barn back in 1951.

It was my sister Rosa who phoned me, saying that Uncle Hammond was dead, also that Aunt Sophrina was holding up, but a daughter, who had been taking care of them, had gone to pieces. Not that anybody expected me at the funeral, Rosa said, but it wouldn't be decent not to let me know. To which I replied that she was right, it was something I ought to know even if I hadn't been home for over half a century. I appreciated Rosa greatly. She was the only one left who kept me posted on things in Linroth.

Actually, Rosa's call caught me at a lonesome moment, Patricia having just left on her cruise. I went golfing that first day, and the next day I helped a neighbor put up a cedar fence, but I woke up both nights feeling abandoned, and on the second night the thought hit me like a bullet, Just go! Patricia had been at me for a long time to take her to Linroth. Our friends couldn't believe we had been married for twenty years without a single visit to my hometown. That story had to be a fiction, they said; it just wouldn't happen in real life to a couple as normal as we were. But it wasn't fiction. So I woke up that morning and said to myself, this is it, my one and only chance to scout things out in advance and see if Linroth has turned into a Levi's-and-boots kind of town full of firearm-packing Republicans like the rest of Arizona, because if it has, it isn't a place to take Patricia, who ran out of patience long ago with ultra-right wing folks and can be counted on to stop and quarrel if she runs into any of them. At least that was the reason I gave myself, though later, as I realized once the jetliner was airborne, the real reason was to test myself and see whether I could keep my composure when the old anxiety—the old self-incrimination—came back to me like delirium tremens to a half-cured drunk.

I lived in Phoenix during the last year and a half of high school, so I shouldn't have been surprised at how hot it was when I left the air terminal and climbed on a shuttle bus out to the car rental lot. But I was surprised, and, after navigating onto the freeway heading east toward Mesa and Globe, I was equally surprised at how little I recognized of the city I'd once known so well. But all this wonderment proved a beneficial distraction, so for a while the fantods I had been anticipating on the airplane didn't kick in. When they did kick in, I was eating a hamburger in a fast food place on the east end of Globe. Out a window I could see the junction where the Safford-bound highway split off toward Show Low, and I was struck hard by the fact that the junction looked exactly as it used to fifty years ago, also by the fact that on Thanksgiving Day of the year I turned seventeen, I stood at that very junction trying to thumb a ride home to Linroth because I had heard that Cassia, my cousin, would probably be there. I stood at the junction all day in a cold wind. What little traffic took the Show Low road didn't stop for me. I was broken-hearted, to say the least. A little before dark, I caught a ride back to Phoenix, and when the school year was out, I joined the Navy and never made another attempt to go back to Linroth.

I threshed all this over while sitting in the fast food place, wondering how I ever figured that, even if I had made it home to Linroth and even if Cassia had actually been there—I later learned she wasn't—I would have had the nerve to beg her forgiveness, which made me pause for a moment to wonder how, having more or less ruined her life, I could face her at the present if she happened to turn up at Uncle Hammond's funeral, which—according to my current reasoning—she just might. I sat there after I had finished my hamburger and cola mulling that possibility and, as I say, having the fantods. Then it occurred to me to get Rosa on my cell phone and find out if Cassia was in town, because if she was, I would turn around and go back to Phoenix and catch the first available plane back to Seattle.

Unluckily, Rosa didn't answer her mobile phone, and when I dialed her house phone, a granddaughter—likely a teenager, I thought—answered and said Rosa was out. When I asked the girl whether she had ever heard of her uncle Rulon Braunhil, which is me, she said, "Sure, you're grandma's brother who lives in Seattle." But when I asked if an elderly cousin named Cassia had come home for the funeral, she said nobody had told her anything about that. "I didn't even know I had an elderly cousin Cassia," she said.

*

My trouble with Cassia—which I didn't see as trouble for a long time—came about because we were born within six days of each other and our families regarded us as twins and encouraged us to do things together. As a result, we had feelings for each other from early on that first cousins shouldn't have. Around the time we turned five or six, we got into the habit of getting undressed and checking each other out behind a chicken coop. Luckily, we got past that phase without being caught.

The summer we were ten, we wrestled each other on the back lawn of the seminary building, and she pinned me and kissed me long and hard. "That's the way Betty Grable kisses Victor Mature," she said and kissed me again.

The year we were twelve and in MIA, we rode in the back seat of my parents' car to a stake-wide New Year's Eve party in Holbrook. It was very cold, and Cassia and I huddled under a blanket and we kissed in a way that seemed sinful to me. I put a hand on one of her breasts and she took it off. I felt humiliated. For several months after that I wanted to forego partaking of the sacrament, but doing so would have made me intolerably conspicuous because I was a deacon and had to help pass the bread and water to the Linroth congregation every Sunday. That doubled my worry because I understood people who partook of the sacrament unworthily were eating and drinking damnation unto themselves.

All of that trouble between Cassia and me was nothing compared to the trouble we got into during the summer we were fifteen, and it happened because our fathers owned side-by-side farms on the creek. I had been hoeing corn on a rainy afternoon in June. Near evening, Cassia came down the lane to fetch cows home for evening milking. She wore a dress and scuffed brown and white oxfords with no socks. A squall of rain hit, and she climbed into a barn at the head of the pasture.

"Hey, dummy," she shouted from a window, "come in out of the rain."

I dropped my hoe, crawled through a fence, and climbed into the barn. Damp and shivering, we sat side by side in the hay. Our shoulders touched, and I gazed at her askance. She was beautiful—dark brows, an aquiline nose, slightly hollowed cheeks.

"When we were kids," she said, "you asked me to marry you, here, in this barn."

I couldn't remember that.

"You kissed me," she said. "Don't you remember that?"

"I remember other places, but not here," I said.

She placed a stem of hay on my head. I removed it with an irritable gesture. She replaced it, and I let it stay.

"Did you kiss Lori Ann when you took her home from the junior prom last spring?" she went on.

"That's none of your business."

"You did, didn't you?"

"That just isn't any of your business."

"Would you kiss me now?" she said.

I stared at her.

She puckered her lips and closed her eyes.

Alarmed, I said, "The rain's quitting. We better be going."

She pushed me down and placed a long, lingering kiss on my lips.

To that point I had struggled to maintain an illusion of disinterest. But after that long, lingering kiss, a frantic, furnace-fed flame drove through me and there was no stopping me even though when I tugged up her dress she pleaded for me not to do it, and

60

when the deed was done, she wept. I waited till full dark before I went home, long after she had climbed from the barn and gathered her cows and returned along the lane. Lightening arced madly through a distant cloudburst, a portent and testimony, I felt, of the hell I had suddenly entered.

My nighttime terror was of God, who couldn't overlook a rape, particularly a rape of a first cousin. As weeks passed, I realized God was toying with me, letting me simmer in anxiety, preparing a catastrophic demise for me in the ripeness of his own due time. My daytime terror was that Cassia would tell her parents, who would tell my parents, and who knew what would happen then? Maybe they'd turn me over to the law and I'd end up doing a life sentence down at Florence. In the meantime, Cassia avoided me. One day when I saw her in the store, she turned on her heel and disappeared through the door at the rear that said "Employees Only," even though she wasn't an employee. She didn't come down the lane anymore, either.

When fall approached, the two Braunhil homes were set abuzz by the announcement that Cassia would spend the school year with an aunt on her mother's side in Salt Lake City. The reason given was that her bright mind merited a challenging high school. Weeks after she left, I overheard a mere fragment of conversation between my sisters Carol and Rosa, who were washing dishes at the kitchen sink. A single phrase—*put it up for adoption*—lingered in my mind as I left the house by the kitchen door, heading for a belated duty in the corral, where unmilked cows lowed impatiently. By the time I returned with a pail brimming with foamy milk, I had figured it out. Cassia had been banished to Utah to have a baby.

Years later, I pressed my mother to open up about Cassia. She admitted the real reason that Cassia went to Utah was that Uncle Hammond, informed by Aunt Sophrina of his daughter's pregnancy, had exiled her forever from his house. When the family gathered for prayer before supper on the day he found out, Hammond forbade Cassia to join. "You no longer belong to this family," he said. The next day she left on the afternoon bus. Aunt Sophrina and Dory took her to meet the bus. My mother went, too, and so did Carol and Rosa. I imagine those girls already knew the real reason.

The more I thought about the circumstances under which Cassia left Linroth, the more certain I felt that she wouldn't show up at Uncle Hammond's funeral. I figured that he'd be the next to last man in the whole world—me being the very last—she would want to show some respect for by attending his funeral. In any event, I had got myself as far as Globe, and I wanted to keep on going. So I did, calming my nerves by working out a little plan in case a tactical retreat proved necessary. With the exception of Rosa, nobody presently alive in Linroth had seen me for fifty years, and if I took a little care not to confront persons near my own age face to face, I could easily remain incognito. I would take a motel in Show Low for the night and turn up in Linroth just in time for the funeral and take a seat at the back of the church. If I saw Cassia filing in among the mourners after the closing of the casket, I'd slip away when the funeral adjourned to the cemetery, leaving town as unannounced as I had entered it.

When I got to Show Low, there was still a lot of daylight left, and I kept driving, assuring myself that I would just take a quick look around Linroth and then come back to Show Low for the night. My eyes blurred with tears when I rounded the hill south of Linroth. From that perspective, the little town nestling in a horseshoe-shaped valley looked as familiar as if I had left it the day before. Driving on in, I could see a lot of things had changed. There was a Chevrolet dealership, a bank branch, and, across the street from the church house, a modern post office building and a café. The church house itself, constructed of chiseled yellow stone and topped by a steeple, was unchanged. The doors and window frames must have been painted recently because they looked as fresh and well cared for as when I had last seen the building.

Driving on down the street, I saw a modern small-town version of a supermarket occupying the spot where a mercantile had once stood. Across the street from the supermarket I saw an old red brick home fronted by a white picket fence. Attached to the fence was an ornate sign declaring "Pioneer Bed & Breakfast." I pulled over and with motor idling sat thinking a while. If I registered with a pseudonym—the name of my Corvallis friend came to mind— there was no need to retreat to Show Low for the night. But then it occurred to me that it was pretty craven of a man to rent a room in a bed-and-breakfast place in a town loaded with relatives who would consider it a high privilege to furnish him with a bed. With that, I decided to call Rosa again, and if Cassia was in town, I'd pretend I was calling from Seattle and beat a hasty retreat, and if she wasn't, why, heck, I'd abandon this incognito stuff and go stay at Rosa's house where a brother ought to stay.

However, Rosa didn't answer either her cell phone or her house phone, so, craven or not, I went into the bed-and-breakfast place. The girl behind the counter, maybe seventeen, pulled out a registry and asked my name. "Rulon Braunhil," I blurted, suddenly repulsed by the ploy of a pseudonym.

"Braunhil is a common name here," she said.

"I grew up here," I said. "But I've been gone a long time."

Maybe I struck her as incapacitated because she said, "I'm sorry, we only have an upstairs room available."

"That's okay," I said. "I do a lot of hiking on hilly trails."

As she led me up the stairs, I asked her family name. "Burleson," she said.

"That's not a name I recognize."

"No, my parents are newcomers. We aren't Mormons, but we like it here. I have lots of Mormon friends."

"I'm glad to hear that," I said.

In my room, I heaved my suitcase onto the dresser top and hung my shirts and pants on racks in a closet. I went to a window and looked out. A small, sleek White Mountain Lines bus had stopped at the supermarket across the street. On a Monday evening fifty years ago, Cassia got on another White Mountain Lines bus at that very spot though I wasn't there to see her do it. I went back to the bed, took off my shoes, and lay down, somehow feeling truncated, cut in half, dismembered.

I graduated from high school in Phoenix because after Cassia left for Utah I acted out the complete outlaw at Linroth Union High. I sauntered down corridors slamming locker doors shut, popped bra straps on unwary girls, and knocked a boy over a bench in the shower room after PE, in consequence of which my parents and I met with the principal one morning.

"I just hope you can influence your son to behave," the principal said. "The next step is the state industrial school at Fort Grant. If we expel him, that's where they'll put him."

"What's got into you?" my mother said. "You come home late. You don't do your chores. You sass your dad. This isn't like you at all!"

Fortunately, my father had a plan. "Rulon says he can't take it here anymore," he explained to the principal. "Boys get that way. So I phoned his Uncle Trevor. That's my brother who lives in Phoenix. He says to let Rulon come live with him and Sybil."

Dad looked at me. "Do you want to do that, son? Do you think you could settle down and start getting decent grades again?" I said I would try, and I did, having made up my mind that I really had gone kind of crazy, and Cassia notwithstanding, I had a life to live and needed to get on with it.

My dad was a good man. He wasn't anywhere near as hidebound and punctilious as Uncle Hammond. Neither was Uncle Trevor, for that matter. He was laid back, too.

I went home to Linroth for brief visits, but as I said, after that failed hitchhike on Thanksgiving Day, I never went back. I knew Linroth was like a malaria zone for me. It was as if I had been run through some kind of a magnetizing machine and there was a protective shield around the town that automatically deflected me.

My parents came to my graduation from Camelback High School, and when I told them I wanted to join the Navy, they agreed to sign for me. The Korean War was going full tilt, and like a lot of the other fellows at Camelback, I could see serving in the Navy was ten times smarter than getting drafted into the infantry. I did my basic training at the Great Lakes training station on the shores of Lake Michigan, then was assigned to a logistics unit at the Alameda Naval Air Station across the bay from San Francisco. Although handing out underwear and socks to new arrivals wasn't my idea of excitement, the bustling activity of the base distracted me, and upon returning to my quarters in the evening I often realized that I had gone for hours without thinking of my private hell. But with evening the fantods returned, and I spent long, wakeful nights until I got some sleeping pills from the base medical center and began to knock myself out every night by taking a couple.

After nearly a year at the base, I started to take evening courses in electronic engineering at the University of California at Berkeley. During the first semester, I met and began to date a young woman from Mexico, Emilia, who was finishing a master's degree in philosophy. An atheist, she had a long list of proofs for the absence from the universe of a divine personality, and she was eager to convert me. As things stood, I was eager to be converted. I did some superficial reading in Hume, Nietzsche, Russell, and Sartre, declared myself free from Christianity, and threw away my sleeping pills. As for my social life, I went to movies, museums, and operas around the Bay Area with Emilia, usually at her expense because her father owned a big ranch and sent her plenty of money. Eventually, she made it evident that she would welcome something more than philosophical discussions between us. She wasn't voluptuous, yet with dark braided hair, luminous eyes, and lightly bronzed lips, she was far from unattractive. However, my Mormon scruples hadn't vanished with my Mormon theology. Simply put, I couldn't make love to a woman without marrying her, and I couldn't marry Emilia, not only because I couldn't see spending the rest of my life in Mexico, but even more important, because I judged the rapist of a first cousin to be unworthy of any decent woman. The truth was, I realized, that I couldn't marry at all. And with that realization, I broke off with Emilia and settled into three decades of celibacy. As for Emilia, she graduated in the spring and went home to Mexico to stay.

I understand sublimation well. It's what monks, nuns, and maverick laypersons like me practice in order to lead sexless lives. I developed my skills in sublimation chiefly in and around Seattle, where I eventually migrated, having found employment with the Boeing Company after I resigned from active duty in the Navy. Sometimes I dated women I met at Boeing, and my various male friends occasionally recruited me for blind dates. Not wanting to get to the point of having to explain myself, I rarely dated a woman more than once, even if I was attracted to her.

So how is it that after three decades of celibacy I married Patricia?

I met her on a Sunday afternoon. It was nice weather, and I had driven up from Seattle to see the fields of tulips in the Skagit Valley. I stopped at an ice cream shop on a rural road and had a dish of almond fudge at an outdoor table. Patricia and her teen-aged daughters—Koreen and Alisha—came out of the shop looking for a place to sit. My table was the least occupied, and Patricia asked if they could sit with me.

Things went from there. Patricia had a round, cheerful face and abundant, shoulder-length hair, carefully parted in the middle. She engaged me in conversation with the disarming forwardness of an established friend. She had a home in the Cedar Park district of north Seattle. She was five years past the accidental death of her husband and, as the following months proved, was willing to have a gentleman caller. Luckily for me, she more or less took me as is without asking to see under the hood; that is, she didn't seem perturbed by the blank spaces in my life's story. I was pleased— and a little astonished—that I could at last permit myself to think of marriage owing to the fancy that with age I had been transformed into a different human being, still named Rulon Braunhil, but otherwise an utter stranger to that fifteen-year-old youth who had raped his first cousin in a barn.

*

I dozed off for a while on the bed in the bed-and-breakfast place and woke up wondering how I was going to spend the evening. I went downstairs and asked the Burleson girl whether there was still a movie theater in town.

"Yes, but it just runs on Saturday night."

"What do people do for entertainment during the rest of the week?"

"Friday nights there's usually a dance somewhere—here or in Saller's Cove or up at Show Low. Monday night is family night for the Mormons. Everybody stays home. Other nights, a lot of people play softball. There'll be a game tonight with a team from Holbrook."

"What about that café up the street?" I said. "Do local people seem to like it?"

"A lot of them seem to. We could have fixed you dinner if I had let my dad know early enough that you wanted it."

"That's all right. I'll check out the café."

I drove to the café and went in. I took a seat in a booth, and a girl in a lacy apron came from behind a counter and handed me a menu. "We only offer the full menu on Friday and Saturday night," she said. "Tonight, the entrée is chicken fried steak."

"No lasagna?" I said. "Too bad."

"You could have a hamburger or a sandwich."

"I'll have the chicken fried steak," I said, handing back the menu.

"Chicken fried," she called to the fry cook.

She stood fingering the menu, apparently in no hurry to leave. I looked her over. I wouldn't have called her pretty, yet I was attracted by her dark, curly hair and reassuring smile, which caused me to consider my own less-than-attractive person—a thin fellow, somewhere between tall and short, somewhat stooped, and possessed of a lined, emaciated face and white, close-cropped hair.

"I was wondering ... ," she started to say, then suddenly blurted, "Are you my Uncle Rulon?"

I was totally astonished. "My friend Cindy Burleson phoned me a few minutes ago. I hope you won't be mad at her for telling me you were in town."

"No, I won't be angry."

"You phoned Grandma at noon, didn't you?" she went on.

I nodded.

"I'm the one you talked to. I'm Ashley. I'm Lee Ann's daughter. We live next door to Grandma. Mom asked me to run over and borrow a lemon juicer. But Grandma wasn't there, and I couldn't find it."

A couple of boys of high school age came in and sat at the counter. Ashley served them Cokes and stood behind the counter talking to them. After a while she brought my order. "You wanted to know about Cousin Cassia," she said. "When Mom brought me to work a while ago, she told me Cassia is arriving by Amtrak and Grandma will pick her up in Winslow early tomorrow morning."

"I'm glad to know that," I said—truthfully enough, though I realized Ashley would assume my reason to be quite different than it was.

At this point, a man entered the restaurant and looked around uncertainly. His face was broad and pasty, and a shock of graying hair hung almost to his eyes. His long-sleeved shirt was buttoned at the throat. He shuffled to my booth and slid in opposite to me.

"My name is Clemon Haines," he said, offering me a limp hand.

Ashley set a knife and fork in front of the man and asked, "Is it milk or orange pop tonight?"

"Pop," he said. Then, as she retreated toward the counter, he leaned confidentially toward me. "The church pays for my supper here every night. I've got a bad back. Can't work."

My mind was getting error signals from four or five directions. I was dredging up memories from a series of letters from my mother saying a retarded Haines boy had assaulted a woman and had been castrated and sent home from the state hospital as no longer being a public menace. Also, since there was no way I could face Cassia the next day, I was trying to process how I was going to manage to leave town without her and Rosa knowing I had been there.

Ashley brought the man a chicken-fried steak and glass of orange soda, and he fell to eating with gusto. "Going to the soft-ball game," he said with scarcely a pause in his avid chewing. "That Holbrook feller, he's something else. Can he ever hit!"

I laid a couple of dollar bills on the table and stood up.

"Boy, you're a real tipper!" the man said, eying the bills closely. "Say, stick around a few minutes and you can go to the game with me. You ought to see that Holbrook feller."

"Thanks. I've got things to do," I said.

I went to the counter. I glanced back at the man in the booth. "Do you worry about a fellow like that?" I asked Ashley in a low voice.

"Of course," she said, rolling her eyes with something like vex-ation. "We don't walk places after dark. Girls, I mean. Not alone, that is. When the café closes, Mom will come get me in the car."

"What time does it close?"

"Ten-thirty on week nights. But I won't wait to let Grandma know you're here. I'll phone her right now. I know she'll want you to stay with her."

"That's okay," I said. "There's no need to let her know tonight."

"No, really, she'll want to know you're in town. I'm sorry I didn't phone her sooner."

"Do you mind holding off and letting me surprise her?"

68

"Well, heck no, if that's what you want."

"I mean like tomorrow at the funeral."

She studied me for a long time.

"It's important to me," I said.

"All right."

"Promise?"

"Yes, I promise."

It was getting toward twilight when I went outside. I saw lights in the church and heard an organ, so I crossed the street and went in, taking a seat in the backmost pew. The church was empty except for me and a woman at the organ, who smiled at me and went on playing. Likely she was practicing for the funeral. The dark wood of the pews glistened, and the scent of furniture wax pervaded the atmosphere. The pasty-faced Haines fellow was on my mind. Men who violate women ought to be castrated. That goes for a man who has his way with his first cousin in a barn. That's how I felt. That's how I had been feeling off and on for five decades. Also, sitting in the church, I could see the disadvantages of being a total disbeliever. If I believed in God, I could ask for forgiveness and maybe I could get a feeling that said, "Okay, you've done penance enough. Go your way and sin no more."

However, I knew I had to get my mind off irremediable matters in a hurry. I needed to concentrate on how to leave town without Rosa and Cassia finding out I had been there. Figuratively speaking, I was kicking my own butt over and over for giving the Burleson girl my true name. The key now, of course, was Ashley, who sooner or later would tell her grandmother and Cassia that I had been in town. I had to come up with a reason for her not to tell them—a reason that could at best be only half accurate—and I had to somehow convey it to her before her mother came for her at ten-thirty.

When I went back, the café was empty except for Ashley and the fry cook. Ashley looked surprised when I walked in, of course. "I'd like a cola," I said and went to the back booth.

When she brought the drink, I said, "I need to talk to you for a minute."

"About what?" she said, throwing a quick glance toward the pass-through window into the kitchen.

"I've changed my mind about going to the funeral. I want to leave town first thing in the morning. I don't want Rosa and Cassia to know I've been here. I wish I hadn't come in the first place. I need you to promise not to tell them I've been here. Just that."

Shifting uneasily, she glanced again toward the pass-through window. Time passed. Obviously I had put her between a rock and a hard place.

"There's a reason I have stayed away from Linroth for fifty years," I added.

"And it involves Grandma?"

"No. Cassia."

I was in a pure panic, speechless, maybe shaking a bit and certainly wondering how it was that a pleasant, innocent-looking teenager of whose existence I had had no inkling until a few hours earlier should turn out to be the one soul to whom I had confided even so much as a remote hint of my reason for not returning to Linroth.

"All right," she said at last. "I promise. I won't say a word."

A short, burly man came into the café and took a seat at the counter. Ashley left me and took his order. Then a chattering couple came in and took a seat in a booth, and she took their order.

I got up and walked to the door. As I stepped onto the sidewalk, I saw Ashley had followed me. "Couldn't you settle things with Cassia?" she asked.

"I don't think so," I said. "I ruined her life."

She looked at me for a long time, then shrugged and went inside.

*

I woke up around three a.m. from a nightmare about a swarm of frenzied ants running over my feet and up my legs. I turned on the light and got out of bed and sat in a chair. I felt hollow and heartsick, the way I felt when I first understood that first cousins can marry in Europe and nearly half of the states in the Union. Unanswerable questions came back to me. Did our parents know but choose not to let us marry? Would Cassia have had me? Would

70

I, barely sixteen when her pregnancy showed, have manfully shouldered the duties of a husband and father?

What was certain was that I presently lacked the courage for a face-to-face encounter with Cassia. I couldn't survive looking into her eyes. It might have been otherwise if I could have construed her life as largely a success. I followed her life through my mother, who followed it through Sophrina, who surreptitiously defied her husband by staying in close touch with her banished daughter. After attending college in Utah, Cassia headed east, where she taught school for twenty years. She was married for four or five years during this period. As far as I knew, she and her husband had no children. After she divorced, she got an EdD and served as the principal of an elementary school for fifteen more years. Judging by appearances, she was among those plucky teen girls who pull out of the tailspin of getting pregnant and giving up a baby for adoption and go on to lead adult lives of considerable achievement.

However, she probably suffered a good deal from loneliness and also from the injustice of her exile. I could well imagine how angry she felt whenever she allowed herself to think about either me or her father. Moreover, the longer I lived—and the more keenly I appreciated the fact that having an unknown child somewhere out there in the big world had put me into a tailspin of sorts—the less certain I became that any woman could pull entirely out of the trauma of giving up a baby. Even if Cassia had abhorred the fetus growing within her at first, considering how it got there, wouldn't she have bonded with it when it began to stir and kick inside her womb? And even if the boy child it turned out to be was carried away from her unseen at the instant of his birth, her instinct for mothering couldn't have been disposed of so succinctly. Didn't an unfed hunger, a thwarted desire, leave her perpetually susceptible to bouts of grief—like my mother, who mourned a seven-month stillborn girl to the end of her days?

That's why I couldn't imagine Cassia would want to see me under any circumstance. The least I could do was honor her wish and leave town at dawn as I had originally planned.

I went down to the lobby at daybreak and looked up Seattle-bound flights from Phoenix on the house computer. I decided on a late afternoon departure and secured an online reservation. After a breakfast of sausage gravy and biscuits, I loaded my travel bag into my car and, by way of a final goodbye to Linroth, drove along the back streets. Driving by the cemetery, I saw a man loading a backhoe onto a trailer. I stopped, got out, and—back to playing incognito—said, "There must be a funeral coming up."

"Yeah. Just dug a grave for a feller named Hammond Braunhil. Old as Methuselah. Damn well time for him to go." The backhoe operator had red, scaly cheeks. He looked like a man who didn't worry about washing his face and combing his hair when he got out of bed in the morning.

He scrutinized me closely. "You from around here?"

"I'm just passing through. I've lived in Seattle most of my life. I don't know much about little towns. I get curious sometimes to see what they look like from the back side." I was surprised how slithery and loathsome I felt, though technically nothing I said was a lie.

The backhoe man, who had been digging close to the cemetery gate, got into his truck and left. I decided to take a look at the grave—that serving as a kind of vicarious attendance at the funeral I had chosen to miss. Both the open grave and the excavated soil were covered by a tarp— nothing to see there. Looking around, I realized I was in Braunhil territory. My Braunhil grandparents were here, as were my own parents and the seven-month stillborn girl they insisted on naming. Suddenly, I was beset by the sense of an unfulfilled duty. It seemed a pity a man should pay his respects to the mortal dust of his parents for the first time at my age.

I could vaguely recall the interment of my stillborn sister. But I attended the funeral of neither of my parents. I was spared the guilt of intentionally missing my father's funeral because Boeing had sent me to Mulhouse, France, and without informing anyone, I went to Haute Savoie in the Alps for a weekend of skiing, where I was put even more out-of-touch by a four-day blizzard.

When my mother died, Rosa let me know by telephone. "I hope you'll come for the funeral," she said.

I was silent. "It's time," she said. "I don't know what it is with you, but it's time to get over it. Come home, Rulon." But I couldn't.

Like a felon, I was reluctant to revisit the scene of my crime, the ruin of Cassia.

Nor did I mention the funeral to Patricia, whom I was dating at the time. After that, I always spoke to Patricia of my mother's death—and my father's, too—as vaguely in the past. My mother had faithfully written at least one letter a week from the moment of my departure. Needless to say, my knowledge of matters in Linroth fell off drastically with her death.

When I left the cemetery, I decided to drive along the street I had grown up on, which I quickly decided was a bad mistake because I went to pieces when I passed by the two Braunhil houses, mine and Cassia's, and all of a sudden I wanted to see Cassia—unbeknownst to her, of course, because her gaze would have withered me like an earthworm in the summer sun. So I made up my mind to attend the funeral after all, where I could sit at the back of the church and probably catch a glimpse of Cassia when she filed in with the mourners, and then, as I fervently promised myself, I'd for sure slip away while the first hymn was being sung and get on the road to Phoenix in time to make my plane.

At the church, custodians had opened the sliding doors between the chapel and the recreation hall and filled the latter with folding chairs in anticipation of a crowd as large as a stake conference—a well-founded anticipation, I saw as I took a seat well to the rear of the nearly filled recreation hall. An organist—likely the woman I had seen the evening before, though I couldn't be sure at that distance—played a soft prelude. Shortly, there was a stir, and the organist shifted to a solemn hymn. The family procession, led by pallbearers and the coffin, came from a side hall and turned into the middle aisle of the chapel. Immediately behind the coffin came a tiny, shrunken woman on the arm of a robust, half bald man of approximately my age. I recognized the woman as Aunt Sophrina. The robust man had to be Bryant, her eldest son. As for the others—fifty or sixty of them—I could make out only an occasional face with some cast of the familiar to it. I identified my brother, Badge, and my sisters, Carol and Denise, and also my cousins Jake, Dory, and Brenda.

Among a trailing crowd of teens and children, I recognized

Ashley, who seemed intent on marshaling her younger cousins into pairs. Finally, at a distance from all the others—as if there had been some hesitation on their part about joining the mourners' throng—came two women, whom—with a catch in my throat—I recognized as Rosa and Cassia. The twenty-five years since Rosa had brought Mother to Seattle for my commissioning as a lieutenant commander in the Navy Reserve had been kinder to her than to me. Of sturdy frame, she had a round face, prominent cheeks, and amber-grey hair swept upward to add to her already imposing height. As for Cassia, her slight, slender body was clad in a black dress with a white collar and cuffs. Her hair, once auburn, was silvered—something like light on rippling water. Her forehead was lined, her cheeks seamed, her mouth composed. As she and Rosa passed from my view, I felt apathetic and let down. What had I expected? Perhaps something transcendent, ethereal, other-worldly.

In any event, fragments from the past tumbled through my mind—kaleidoscopic memories of fights, street games, bonfires, and family gatherings. I recalled a day when Bryant intervened in a fight between me and Badge, saving me from a sure beating. I remembered that Rosa tackled me once during a game of football, and I plowed into the gravel with my elbows and knees. I remembered hiding in Uncle Hammond's granary while Dory and Brenda searched for me during hide-and-seek; I held my breath for fear they would hear me. I loved those kids, all of them; siblings and cousins were one and the same to me. Here they were, most of them, at this funeral, the Braunhil family more or less in its entirety, and I longed to claim a place among them. Sitting at the back of the church, a stranger among strangers, I recognized afresh what a fragile and pitiable creature a human being is without a family. I was lucky, of course, to have married Patricia, but considered objectively, my marriage to her was a grafting onto the trunk of a tree planted by her dead husband, whose last name Patricia kept because Koreen and Alisha wanted her to.

I knew it was time for me to leave, but I could no longer muster any sense of urgency. I hadn't seen enough of my kin. I knew

I'd stay as long as there was a reasonable chance of concealing my presence in the crowd.

The funeral began with a hymn, which—though I hadn't so much as thought of it in fifty years—returned to me word for word. A son-in-law of Hammond's, Jasper Cleveland, gave a lengthy invocation, extolling Hammond as a man mighty in the service of the Lord. A daughter, Brenda, read his life story. As a young man, he had served as a missionary in New England. Upon his return, he attended Arizona State University, where he met and married Sophrina. They settled in Linroth, and he became one of the foremost farmers in Navajo County, winning all sorts of prizes for cattle and crops at fairs. He had been on the local school board four or five times. He had been counselor to one bishop and two stake presidents, but had never been a bishop or stake president himself, which, as I conjectured, likely said something about his lack of tact and understanding of human nature.

I wondered what Cassia was making of all this. As for myself, I couldn't quarrel with the facts of his life—the boards and church positions and prizes and all that—but I could quarrel with the lies about what a kind father and devoted husband he had been. I knew from my mother's letters that he put Sophrina through the wringer on a steady basis, and from when I was a kid, I could remember him making Bryant lean over a rabbit pen while he beat him with a belt for forgetting to latch a corral gate. Lies are pretty much the stock in trade of funeral speakers. Somehow it's blasphemous to admit the ugly side of the dead person's life.

Following the closing prayer, I stood with the general congregation while the family filed from the church. I went to my car but made no move to leave until most of the other cars had left the church. Sitting there, I observed my divided emotions with a detached curiosity, being fully aware that further delay meant missing my Seattle flight yet knowing that sooner or later I would start the engine and drive to the cemetery.

When I arrived at the cemetery, I parked at the far end of a line of cars, a position from which I could watch the proceedings at the grave without getting out of my car. Needless to say, I despised myself for being a voyeur, a peeker through a keyhole, as it were, into the doings of a family I no longer belonged to.

A considerable crowd stood around the grave. Observing their bowed heads, I surmised that the dedicatory prayer was in progress. Following that, the formalities of the service were at an end, and the crowd began to disperse, filing through the cemetery gate and getting into cars and driving away. Several persons entering cars near mine glanced my way. I sat tight, confident in my anonymity, a stranger among strangers. My siblings Badge, Carol, and Rosa lingered by the grave, also my cousins Bryant, Dory, and Brenda— to say nothing of Cassia and the girl Ashley, who stood beside a woman I couldn't identify—her mother, Lee Ann, I supposed.

A vague apprehension grew over me when another car parked near the gate and the Burleson girl from the bed-and-breakfast place got out. Before entering the gate, she paused and looked my way. Jolted by a shot of adrenaline, I realized I had missed my chance to escape. Sure enough, an instant later she was conferring with Ashley, and both girls were looking my way.

Ashley left the gravesite, came through the gate, and turned in my direction. She wore half-high heels, a black skirt, and a white blouse, and, despite the frantic thoughts ricocheting off the walls of my mind, I calmly reflected that a girl doesn't have to be pretty to be attractive if she was as decent and good natured as Ashley.

I lowered my window as she approached. "Cindy told me this was your car," she said. "So you haven't left yet."

"No," I said, "but I'm leaving now."

"Don't do that. Not without seeing Grandma."

"I've got to go."

"It'll break Grandma's heart when I tell her it's you I've been talking to over here."

"So you'll tell?"

"They can see I'm talking to somebody. I can't lie about it, can I?"

"You promised not to tell," I said.

"You said you were leaving town first thing this morning," she insisted. "You broke your word, so I can break mine."

I was surprised by her tenacity. She looked altogether too young, too kind and willing to please, to hold to such a hard line. "It's Cassia, isn't it?" she said. "You are absolutely afraid of her."

"Well, yes, I am afraid of her."

"Why?"

"Because I did something very bad to her."

"What was it?"

"The worst thing a man can do to a woman, short of killing her."

Her eyes narrowed with perplexity. How odd, I was thinking, that I should be confessing an offense of these dimensions to this epitome of decency, this unblemished soul whose deepest instincts tended toward propriety and duty.

"In any event," I said, "you can see why I need to leave town unnoticed. I admit it was very foolish of me to come to the cemetery. For that matter, it was very foolish of me to come home to Linroth in the first place."

Ashley looked toward the group around the grave.

"What could I tell them?" she said. "Cindy has probably already told them it's you I'm talking to."

"Just tell them you don't know why I insist on leaving in such a hurry."

Her perplexity increased. "Couldn't you ask Cassia to forgive you?"

"Some things can't be forgiven," I insisted.

"It happened a long time ago, didn't it?"

"Fifty years ago.

"You weren't very old."

"Fifteen."

"Well, then, I think she should forgive you. She's awfully nice. She doesn't seem like somebody who would hold a grudge for fifty years."

I was beginning to wonder what Ashley knew about rape. Hadn't every girl in Linroth, long before she was ten, learned to fear the likes of Clemon Haines, the castrated imbecile who stalked the dark streets of her imagination at all hours of the night? Wasn't it the curse of Eve that her daughters should perpetually fear the rapist who lurked undiscerned among the sons of Adam? Maybe not. Maybe with girls like Ashley, rape is simply a concept. Maybe it is an eventuality that happens to persons so unconnected to them that it has no meaning.

"Are you aware that at the age of sixteen Cassia was exiled to Utah to have a baby?" I asked in exasperation. "Do you realize that this is her first day in Linroth in fifty years? Do you realize that I am the cause of her exile?"

"No, I didn't know that," she said.

"Cassia doesn't want to see me," I repeated. "It would embarrass her profoundly. It would make her angry."

"I could at least ask her if she would like to see you."

"Don't even think about that!"

I hadn't budged her an inch. She looked steadily into my eyes. I began to feel disconcerted and finally looked away. She continued to stand there, her hands on the car door. It dawned on me that she was going to win by default. Just by standing there, just by not giving me permission to leave, she was making my worst nightmare come true. Pretty soon someone else—her mother, for example, or maybe Rosa— would join her. With that thought, I pushed open the door and got out. I felt like a prisoner ready for his execution. "Let's go," I muttered.

She turned and led me through the gate. The group around the grave watched us closely. "It's Rulon!" Rosa cried. Her face beaming, she stepped happily toward me. Cassia, alarmed, sidestepped into the space Rosa vacated. Her brow was more furrowed, her cheeks more seamed, than I had realized from my brief glimpse of her at the church house. Her unadorned, half-pinched lips were ambiguous, perhaps angry, perhaps grieved.

Rosa, having released me from her hug, saw the ambiguity but would have none of it. "Aren't you two going to hug?" she said. It was a command though given as a question. I opened my arms and as Cassia leaned into my embrace, her body shuddered slightly. Rosa saw the shudder and a look of worried enlightenment crossed her face. She suddenly knew, after all these years, who had fathered Cassia's bastard child.

Accordingly, Rosa didn't insist that the occupants of the two side-by-side Braunhil houses intermingle that evening. Ashley and her parents, Rosa's daughter Lee Ann and her husband, Eric, came to supper. A couple of my other siblings, Badge and Carol, dropped in for a while. We talked about high school friends and retired relatives who had moved to Mesa to engage in temple work in their old age. Inevitably, our conversation was subdued and sober. Everyone present was trying to ignore the elephant in the room— the degree to which the condemnation of the fifteen-year-old kid who had raped Cassia in 1951 was to be laid upon the sixty-five-year-old man he had become.

I was up early, needing to check in at the Phoenix airport by noon for my Seattle flight. Rosa, dressed in nightgown and robe, prepared breakfast for me. Unexpectedly, Ashley—fully dressed— came in briefly to say goodbye, or so I assumed, although she didn't actually say goodbye before leaving.

After breakfast, I finished packing my suitcase. Followed by Rosa, I went out to my car. The dawn was just turning into day. Robins sang in the cottonwoods along the ditch bank fronting the two Braunhil houses. Water gurgled beneath the footbridge across the ditch. I placed my suitcase in the trunk of the car. I turned to Rosa. She took both my hands. "You won't be coming back, I guess," she said.

"No, I think not."

At that moment the door on the other Braunhil house opened. Ashley and Cassia emerged, the latter wearing a nightgown and robe. They descended the steps, opened the gate, and crossed the ditch on the footbridge. By then, my cousin Bryant and Aunt So-phrina had come onto the porch.

Ashley and Cassia approached me and Rosa, Ashley leading. "I have told Cousin Cassia," Ashley said, "that if you ask her to forgive you she should do it. Fifty years is long enough."

Cassia and I stared at each other. I was stunned, breathless, unable to think. Then I blurted, "Please forgive me. I am so terribly, terribly sorry for it."

"I will forgive you," she said. "I *do* forgive you, I *do*."

That is how it happened that a Braunhil family reunion was held in Linroth during the following summer, to which I brought Patricia—duly forewarned, of course, to avoid political and religious conversations.

Cedar City

Hoyt McCulley was nineteen that summer. He had come home to Cedar City from his freshman year at BYU in June intending to go on a mission. His sister Winifred met him at the airport. She was sixteen. She brought Effie Butler with her. Effie, also sixteen, had blossomed since Hoyt had last seen her. She had a bust, she had a waist.

Winifred dropped Effie off at her house before driving Hoyt on home. "Dad and Mom don't like me doing things with Effie," Winifred explained. "So I hope you won't tell them I took her along to the airport. I wanted her to see my missionary brother."

Hoyt wanted to know why their parents objected to Effie. Apparently there were a number of reasons. Foremost seemed to be the fact that Effie's aunt—her father's sister—was in the Purgatory prison near St. George for embezzlement.

That fit with what Hoyt knew about his parents. Be polite, but reserved—that was the rule when it came to certain acquaintances. Blake and Patricia McCulley had social standards, and they lived in a posh new development at the southeast end of town. Phil and Beverly Butler lived in an aging section on the north end. Blake McCulley was the wealthy proprietor of a thriving brickyard. Phil Butler was a biology teacher at the high school. He worked as a cashier at the supermarket in the summer. All this didn't add up to much for Hoyt at the moment. He honored Winifred's request and said nothing about Effie to their parents. He more or less forgot the incident.

As for Effie, the shunning ordained by Winifred's parents hurt. However, she didn't hold it against Winifred. If anything, it stiffened her resolve to maintain Winifred's friendship. At the moment, of course, she had no idea of any involvement with Winifred's big brother. That came on the next Saturday evening when, by sheer coincidence, they both showed up at a dance at an open-air pavilion in Parowan.

Parowan was about twenty miles north of Cedar City via the I-15. Effie arrived a half hour earlier than Hoyt. She and the two seminary friends with whom she had driven joined a cluster of girls waiting, according to custom, for boys to ask them to dance. Just as Hoyt paid his way into the pavilion, Effie was listening to a slightly drunk girl from a nearby ranch boast that she had aborted a pregnancy by means of a powder she had bought from an herbalist named Mackie Jane. Effie was horrified. *Mackie Jane*—it was a name she wouldn't forget.

She was relieved as she saw Hoyt approaching her. She smiled happily when he asked her to dance. They chatted for a couple of minutes after they had begun to dance. Then Effie impulsively offered a cheek and Hoyt bent down to it. They stopped talking and danced face-to-face. Hoyt, of course, couldn't help having sexual feelings, what with her body pressed against his. He felt a twinge of guilt. A guy shouldn't have sexual feelings for his little sister's friend.

Effie was wondering why she had tilted her face up with a glance of expectancy—also why she had pulled her body against his without hesitation. It surprised her. She hadn't realized she knew how to do things of that sort. She respected Hoyt enormously. He looked so mature. He was handsome, well-muscled, soft-spoken. She was flattered when he asked if he could drive her home to Cedar City. She asked her seminary friends if they minded if she went home with a guy. They said, heck, no, just do it.

When Hoyt and Effie got to her house, he walked her to the door. The porch light burned. They stood a moment. She looked up at him. She was very pretty—auburn hair, hazel eyes, a perfect complexion. He could have just said goodnight. She could have just thanked him for the ride. But, of course, he hadn't brought her home because she needed a ride. So, porch light notwithstanding, they exchanged a kiss, then another, then a third.

In the immediate aftermath, they both had reservations about the face-to-face dancing, the ride home, the kisses. There was the disparity in age—she was still a juvenile, he was essentially an adult. Of even greater weight was the inevitable disapproval of Hoyt's parents. Independently of each other, they gave up on any further contact.

Confusing circumstances shortly brought them back together. Hoyt went to work at his father's brickyard. Sometimes after work he walked over to watch the greenshow at the Shakespeare festival on the college campus. Cedar City was already famous for hosting the festival. People had to buy tickets to the plays months in advance. But in the late afternoon, six days each week, dancers dressed in Elizabethan costumes performed before all comers on an open-air stage.

Effie also had a part-time job that summer in the stockroom at Vorners drugstore out at the south end of town. Her parents let her drive to work in an old beater of a car that they were keeping for her imprisoned aunt. After work one afternoon, Effie parked near the campus and wandered in to watch the greenshow. Almost immediately she saw Hoyt standing near a maple tree. Her impulse was to turn around and leave. However, their eyes locked for a moment, and they both knew an exchange of a few civil words was mandatory.

She joined him by the maple tree. They stood a while. Both talked about their work. Hoyt said Winifred was spending a week with their grandmother in St. George. He and Effie were warming up, starting to feel like they wanted to be somewhere in private with each other. Both were thinking, this just isn't good. So nothing came of their encounter at that moment. But they went away realizing that, in case their parents asked, the greenshow was a very convenient explanation for unaccounted hours.

Their next encounter was therefore no accident. They both showed up at the greenshow hoping the other would be there. After a brief chat, Hoyt said, "Shall we go somewhere? I have a pickup."

Effie nodded.

Minutes later they were driving eastward toward the mountains. A mile beyond city limits, Hoyt pulled off on a side road. He knew a gentile farmer who didn't care if young Mormons made out in the lane behind his dairy. The pickup had an automatic transmission and a bench seat, allowing them to slide toward each other and embrace. Soon they were kissing passionately. Effie was thinking, this is wrong, just wrong. Hoyt was asking himself, what on earth are we up to? Their hearts were palpitating. They felt like adulterers.

After a while, Effie said, "Shouldn't we go home?" Hoyt started the engine and steered toward town. They both knew one of them needed to say, what we just did can't happen again. Instead, Effie said, "You will be leaving on your mission soon."

"Yes," Hoyt said, "I'll be leaving very soon."

With that, they set themselves up for more secret meetings, being persuaded that the feeling they had for each other—a mixture of lust and budding affection—was like a radio transmission. It could be turned off with the flick of a dial.

Turning off their feeling for each other like a radio transmission was made even more unlikely by the fact that Hoyt didn't leave for his mission in a timely way. He had an interview with the bishop, and the bishop had his clerk send the paperwork on up to the stake president's office. On the very day it arrived, the stake president's father had a massive stroke in San Francisco, and in his rush to get to his father's side, the stake president forgot to instruct the stake clerk to delegate the mission call to one of his counselors.

So Hoyt and Effie pursued a clandestine relationship for more than a month. Usually it was in Hoyt's pickup, but sometimes Effie drove them in her old car. Ordinarily, they parked behind the dairy barn, but on several occasions they drove up the canyon toward Cedar Breaks National Monument, just talking. Of course, even when they were making out, they were engaging in conversation, thus coming to know one another's aspirations and standards.

The net effect of all this was that, by the time Hoyt received a call assigning him to the Seattle mission, it was almost August, and he and Effie confronted the troubling fact that they were deeply in love. They only momentarily entertained the idea of giving each other up. Obviously, they couldn't do that. It isn't the nature of love to self-destruct.

They dismissed the idea of marrying immediately. By the time Hoyt returned from his mission, Effie would have finished both her senior year in high school and her freshman year at the college in Cedar City. They would marry then and move to Provo, where he would pursue a degree at BYU while she worked to help support them, and then, when he had a degree, he would work and she could finish college before they settled down to having children.

It certainly wasn't an implausible plan, but they judged it wise to keep it a secret from Hoyt's parents. As for Effie's parents, she anticipated no objection from them, so an exchange of letters with Hoyt during his mission posed no problem for her.

The approach of Hoyt's departure triggered a number of celebratory preparations among his extended family. A small crowd of relatives accompanied him to the St. George Temple for his initial endowment. The endowment ceremony impressed Hoyt greatly, metaphorically tracking as it did the progress of the human spirit from the pre-existence through mortality and on into the eternal reunion of the spirit and resurrected body. At the end of the ceremony, Hoyt remained awhile in the beautifully decorated celestial room of the temple, where, as he later reported to Effie, he had felt an utter holiness. It was like nothing he had ever experienced before. It was a taste of the Celestial Kingdom, and he hoped he could keep the feeling forever.

Hoyt and Effie had no luck connecting during his final week at home, and he had to tell her about the temple on the telephone. She asked him if she could see him one more time before he left. He said sure, they'd somehow manage it. That was on a Friday evening. He was scheduled to deliver a farewell talk in sacrament meeting on Sunday. On Monday, he'd take a plane to Salt Lake City and enter the mission home for a week of training.

On Saturday morning, things collapsed on them. After breakfast, Hoyt's father called him into his home office and asked him to take a seat. Blake McCulley was tall and broad-shouldered, and he had a deep, resonant voice. When he preached on gospel themes, people believed in what he said.

Speaking to Hoyt across his desk, he said, "I'm informed that you and the Butler girl who is Winifred's age have often been seen together this summer. I take it you have come to some kind of understanding with her. That is too bad. Both last night and this morning, I have consulted the Lord in prayer on this matter, son, and feel instructed to advise you to break off your attachment. It is the will of the Lord that you do it at once. Don't leave this girl with a false hope for the future."

He paused to stare meditatively at his now-clasped hands. "After your mission and a bachelor's degree at BYU," he went on, "we'll send you to Stanford for an MBA. I count on you to make McCulley Bricks competitive in the Las Vegas and Salt Lake City markets—and maybe beyond. Someday you'll be a wealthy man, Hoyt, and you need to set your sights on a wife befitting your station. That can't be a girl whose aunt is serving a prison term for embezzlement."

Hoyt was stunned. For a few moments, his breath failed him. His thoughts also failed, refusing to coalesce into anything con-crete. Then the disaster came through like a flood. When his father spoke, the Lord spoke. It was possible Hoyt could have defied his father, but he couldn't defy the Lord.

He tried to explain all this to Effie that evening by telephone. He was sobbing so hard she failed to grasp his meaning. She won-dered whether someone in his family had been killed in an auto accident. When she finally understood, she began to sob, too. It was as if truly someone had been killed, that someone being Hoyt. She saw she was going to find out what it was like to be a widow without ever having been married.

Then their future took a new unanticipated twist. In her grief, Effie begged Hoyt to live up to his promise to meet with her one more time. In his grief, he agreed. It was about ten in the evening. They met behind the dairy, he having driven in the old pickup, she in her aunt's car. He got out of the pickup and got into the car, and they slid into a sobbing embrace. The moon was out. The car win-dows were rolled down, and they could hear a chorus of frogs from the farmer's pond. In time, their grief wore itself out, and they sat in a stupor, reluctant to release one another to a separate future.

Eventually, Effie dozed, slumping in Hoyt's arms. He held her carefully for a long, benumbing time. When she awoke, they were both in something like a somnambulatory state, being aware of what they were about to do, aware even that it was a devastating, life-changing event, yet helpless to forebear. Driven by the desire to condense into a single desperate act a lifetime of loving sexual union, they persisted until they succeeded in mastering the arcane art of fornicating in the front seat of an automobile. Thereafter, only seconds following the completion of their misbegotten deed, they were struck by an emotion close to horror.

"Effie," Hoyt gasped, "what have we done?"

"It's my fault," she mumbled. "I'm sorry, I'm just so sorry."

They sat on opposite sides of the car now, as if straining to distance themselves from each other. Both were measuring the enormity of their sin and in the process were orienting to a new reality. Hoyt's mission had crumbled. He could see nothing but ruin before himself—confession, excommunication, blank despair, and decades before his self-respect returned. Effie recoiled with a similar guilt, then almost instantly panicked over the possibility of becoming pregnant. What were the odds? Was there something she could do to prevent it? Who could she talk to? Maybe she could go home and take a shower and try to wash herself out. How would she explain taking a midnight shower?

"I can't go on a mission," Hoyt muttered, sending Effie's panic in a new direction. "I'm soiled, I'm unworthy."

"You *have* to go," Effie said.

"They won't let me!" he said angrily.

"Don't tell them what we've done. Just go."

Hoyt shook his head slowly, appalled by her seeming callousness—a reaction she duly registered in the light of the moon.

"Can't we just settle things with the Lord without involving other people?"

"That's not the way it's done with serious sins," Hoyt said. "You have to tell your bishop. That's church policy. I learned that in my religion class last fall."

"Your whole ward expects you to go on a mission. Everybody in town will know what you've done. It'll kill your father and mother."

His throat tightened. He acknowledged her point. Shame loomed, foreboding, dreadful.

"It's not fair to me, is it?" she added. "Your parents will know I'm the one you did it with. Other people will figure it out, too."

He was baffled anew. Did consideration for a partner in sin pre-empt the obligation to confess?

"We really didn't know we weren't meant for each other," Effie went on. "But now we know. So let's tell the Lord we are sorry for what we did, and we'll never do it again, and you go on your mission like everybody expects you to do."

He opened the car door and slid out. He stood for a long time with the door open.

"I don't know what to do," he finally said. He closed the door and got in the pickup. In a moment, Effie was sitting alone with moonlight flooding through the windshield.

At home, Hoyt was a long time going to sleep. Even then, he slept fitfully, feeling feverish, maybe even a little delirious, during his moments of waking. When he got up a little after dawn, he sat on the edge of his bed considering lust. Lust was a dangerous animal. It had to be kept in a locked cage. In their grief, he and Effie had unlocked the cage.

He considered his father's summons to his office. He tried to recall his father's precise words. Apparently, the Lord didn't have a specific girl in mind as his future spouse. He thought in terms of a type, a bride of prominent standing in her community. However that might be, Hoyt had reduced his prospects to ashes. What decent girl would want him now?

His thoughts flicked to Effie. Hope flared inside him. Moments later, the flare subsided. Turning back to Effie would be an affront to the Lord. Heeding her protest against confessing their sin would also be an affront to the Lord. Who was Effie to countermand a rule of the church? With a grim determination, he decided he would see the bishop and tell him what he had done. He wouldn't name his partner. That's all he could do for Effie.

He took a shower and dressed for Sunday. He saw his father leaving the house early to attend the monthly meeting of the stake high council. Hoyt decided to tell his father what he had done. He could tell the bishop later. He went out onto the porch. His father had opened the car door and was about to enter. He paused and looked back at Hoyt. Hoyt's stomach surged with panic. He waved at his father and went back into the house. He went into his bedroom, closing the door behind him, and sat on the edge of his bed. Effie said it right. Confessing would kill his parents. It would kill him too. He'd be shame-wracked, as would they.

He could see he didn't have the nerve, the self-control, to confess at present. He would go on the mission, and when he came home, his parents could glow in the recognition that their eldest son had successfully completed a major rite of passage. After that, at some unspecified time in the distant future, when he was in circumstances that would allow him to conceal his disgrace from his family and friends, he'd do what had to be done.

In the opening exercises of Sunday school, Hoyt sat by his mother and siblings. When the sacrament came along their row, he partook of it. Partaking of the sacrament unworthily was something more to repent of. He could see he'd be doing all kinds of things unworthily during the next two years—and maybe long afterward as well. It was like spending a line of credit. He was building debt. Sooner or later he'd have to pay it back.

As expected, Hoyt gave a farewell talk in sacrament meeting that afternoon. He had in mind he'd talk about the second article of faith because he had written a term paper on it in a religion class at BYU. When he found himself standing before the pulpit, looking out over the congregation, he was speechless. Things seemed unreal. The second hand of the clock at the back of the chapel ticked away. People were beginning to feel embarrassed for him. His eyes lit on his mother. Her face beamed as it had—as he just now remembered—in the celestial room of the St. George Temple. That was before he had sinned. He began to speak.

He went on for fifteen minutes. He said he had been seized by the sheer holiness of the temple. It was nothing like he had ever experienced before. It was a foretaste of the Celestial Kingdom. And spreading the word about that foretaste—wasn't that what a mission was all about?

When he sat down, he could see approval on the faces before him. During his ride home with his family after the meeting, Winifred summed up his family's feelings. "You'll knock 'em dead, big brother!"

His mission beckoned. He was swept along by a deep, swift river, and he lacked the fortitude to climb out. To the sin of fornication he would be adding hypocrisy on a daily basis, accumulating a moral deficit of unfathomable dimensions.

Effie spent an equally distressing day. She had lingered behind the dairy for a half hour after Hoyt left. It was a little after three when she got home. Her mother met her in the hall.

"Thank goodness you're back," her mother said.

Effie needed a plausible lie. Winifred came to mind.

"I met Winifred. We've been doing a lot of things together this summer. She phoned me. She wanted to talk to me. She said she'd rather not do it over the phone. So we met over behind the gym at the college. She said her father and mother don't want her doing things with me anymore. She was crying. So was I."

"Did she say why they don't want her doing things with you?"

"No."

"It's Fran, I suppose," Effie's mother said, referring to Effie's imprisoned aunt. "What she did is pretty well known around here."

Effie went into the bathroom. She considered taking a shower. She knew her mother, still awake, would hear the running water. She decided not to shower. She went into her bedroom, which she shared with her sisters. They slept on a bunk bed, the ten-year-old Ruby on top, the six-year-old Constance on the bottom. They were sound asleep. Effie had a twin bed to herself. She knelt at the side of her bed and asked the Lord to forgive her for breaking the law of chastity with Hoyt. She asked him to forgive her for lying to her mother. She promised him that if he'd keep her from becoming pregnant, she wouldn't feel bad about not having Hoyt as her husband and she wouldn't grumble at her parents or quarrel with her younger siblings or avoid doing her assigned chores quickly and thoroughly.

The next morning, she set and cleared the breakfast table without being asked. She recruited her brother Marvin, who was thirteen, to help her wash the dishes. Afterward, she helped her youngest sibling, Andrew, who was three, dress for church.

Effie partook of the sacrament in both Sunday school in the morning and sacrament meeting in the afternoon. In both instances, she said a silent prayer, again asking the Lord to forgive her sin with Hoyt and to keep her from becoming pregnant.

The following week proved an anxious wait on Effie's part. The Butler household was still operating on a summer schedule. Effie worked afternoons at Vorners. Mornings, she played the role of mother to her siblings while their mother pursued her duties as ward Relief Society president. On Mondays, Effie drove Marvin to soccer practice and Ruby to volleyball practice. Tuesdays and Thursdays, she took all of her siblings to the city swimming pool, where she lingered in the shallow end with Andrew. On Wednesdays, she took them all to the public library, where they each checked out enough books for another week of afternoon and evening reading. She also washed and dried her own clothing and supervised each of her siblings in performing the same task at scheduled intervals during the week.

Ordinarily, Effie enjoyed her summer routine. But during this particular week, she was too on edge, too on alert for the first sign of her period, too anxious about its failure to appear. She tried to remember precisely the day when it had last begun, hoping to reassure herself that it wasn't quite time yet. Adding to her perturbation was an accidental encounter with Winifred at the library. Learning that Hoyt had got off on his mission, just as she had urged, she suffered a fresh jolt of anxiety with the thought that a pregnancy would compromise his mission.

During that week, Hoyt had stayed at the mission home across the street from Temple Square. He and several hundred other new missionaries operated on a strict schedule. They rose at six and retired at ten-thirty. Furnished with a missionary lesson manual, they devoted an hour and a half to memorizing the lessons and related scriptural passages before breakfast and another hour before going to bed. Following breakfast and lunch, they gathered in the Assembly Hall on Temple Square for lectures and sermons by general authorities. Hoyt was in awe of the apostles and other Mormon celebrities who addressed the missionaries, and by moments he forgot the guilt and grief that otherwise confounded his waking hours.

Hoyt flew to Seattle on a Tuesday. The next day he and his senior companion departed in a mission car for the Tri-Cities, Richland, Kennewick, and Pasco, located at the confluence of three major rivers in southern Washington, the Yakima, the Columbia, and the Snake. The pair would be living in Richland, under the supervision of a district president quartered in Kennewick. A pair of sister missionaries was stationed in Pasco.

Hoyt's senior companion was John Scott. He was big, red-haired, and freckled. He liked to talk about himself and his hometown in northern California. He asked how old Hoyt judged him to be. Hoyt figured he had to be thirty. To be tactful, he said twenty-five. Laughing with satisfaction, Elder Scott said he was twenty-two. Hoyt could see he might end up hating the fellow. Mission rules required them to be together, twenty-four hours a day, seven days a week. Missions were a lot tougher than people back home made them out to be.

The missionary quarters in Richland proved to be a studio apartment over a garage in a part of town characterized by older, modestly priced houses. The room was furnished with a shabby sofa that made out into a bed at night. At the end of the room opposite the entrance were two narrow doors, one accessing a small kitchen, the other accessing a bathroom. A telephone hung on the kitchen wall.

The next morning the two missionaries phoned the bishop of Richland Ward and the other missionaries in the Tri-Cities area. The bishop invited them to introduce themselves in sacrament meeting on the following Sunday. Later in the morning, Hoyt and Elder Scott tried their hand at reactivating inactive members—an experience that quickly taught them it would be a discouraging business. The first three on their list no longer lived at the address on their list. The fourth was a woman, Betty Abrams, who, with her non-member husband, operated a vineyard and winery. Betty Abrams had a frank, friendly face. "I appreciate your visit, guys. It's getting close to harvest, and we're going to be real busy. Also, we've got a vintage that's got to be bottled. But come winter, yeah, you bet, I'll get back in the groove and show up at church."

Elder Scott was in a surly mood when they got back into town. Correctly predicting—as time would prove—that Betty Abrams wouldn't show up, he wondered why local officials had approved the owner of a winery for baptism in the first place.

Late in the afternoon, the missionaries went afoot from door to door through a neighborhood of small frame houses inhabited, as they soon discovered, mostly by workers at the nearby Hanford nuclear site. On that first afternoon, they had no success whatsoever. Hoyt could see the Mormon message was a hard sell. Men tended to shut the door with a scowl of impatience. Women tended to consider the missionaries' request for a few moments before shaking their heads and saying something like, "That isn't something we'd be interested in."

On Sunday they spoke in sacrament meeting. Elder Scott gave an inspiring sermon and bore a fervent testimony. Hoyt read his talk, having written it out the evening before. When he was through, he bore a quick, perfunctory testimony, being unable to get past the feeling that an unforgiven fornicator had no right to bear a testimony even if he had one.

The fall term at the high school in Cedar City began during the first week of September. On the first day, registration went on at tables crowded into the central hallway of the main building. There was a loud, happy hubbub among the students. Effie didn't share the excitement. Nearly four weeks had passed since her disastrous night with Hoyt. She knew she was pregnant. She was more than depressed. She felt as if she was wearing dark glasses. It was as if her shaded emotions projected into the spaces around her.

Having talked to a counselor, she registered for algebra, physical education, and choir in the morning and American history and English in the afternoon. She wouldn't be working at Vorners during the fall term. Nonetheless, her schedule presupposed an unimpeded energy. It presupposed a girl who wasn't pregnant. So again she asked herself whether there was a convenient way not to be pregnant—a pill to take, a syrup to drink. Where would she find it? Who could she ask?

Then she remembered. At the Saturday night open-air dance at Parowan, an inebriated girl had boasted of an abortion induced by an herb sold by an herbalist named Mackie Jane. *Mackie Jane!* Effie was certain that was the name the girl had mentioned.

Leaving campus, Effie drove north to Parowan. Sure enough, there was a tiny shop across the street from the post office with a sign reading *Mackie Jane's Herbal Remedies*. Effie sat awhile without getting out of the car. Abortion was a doubly serious sin. The church accepted it in cases of rape and incest, also in cases of a deformed fetus. But in the case of a girl like Effie—she just had to tough out a pregnancy and give the baby up for adoption so she could go back to being a regular teenager.

She got out of the car and went into the shop. It smelled of lavender. An obese woman, clad in a black dress overlain by a white lace stole, sat on a stool behind a cash-register.

"What can I do for you, honey?"

Effie froze.

"Are you pregnant?"

Effie nodded.

"How far along, dear?"

"A month."

"Just a month? That's good, that's just fine."

She went to a shelf and pulled off a packet of finely chopped herbs.

"Boil this in enough water to make two quarts when you are finished. Strain it and let it cool and then drink it, one quart during the first twenty-four hours, then the other during the second twenty-four. Pretty soon, clotted blood will come out. You'll need to stay close to a toilet for a day or two. Two or three weeks later, your period will start again, and you'll be back to normal."

Effie shook her head. "I wouldn't dare make it at home. There are too many people around. Could you make me some?"

The obese woman led Effie through a dark hallway into a cluttered kitchen. She filled a kettle with water and set it on a burner.

"You watch this kettle, honey, and when it starts to boil, pour the packet in and let it simmer for forty-five minutes. Then come get me and I'll find something to put it in so you can take it home."

An hour-and-a-half later, Mackie Jane charged Effie fifteen dollars for the herbal packet and a dollar apiece for the quart jars into which she poured the resulting tea. She refused to take money for the use of her kitchen.

"I'm just happy to help, sweetie," she said as she followed Effie out to her car.

Effie secreted the jars in the basement of her home. She waited till Friday to drink the potion. She drank two cups that evening and two more before breakfast the next morning. The tea was bitter and made her feel nauseous. Nonetheless, she went on with the tea regimen, begging off on attending church on Sunday by telling her parents she had a touch of diarrhea. They agreed she should stay home from meetings. However, no clotted blood appeared—just urine as usual. On Monday morning, Effie gave up hope and went to school as expected. She tried not to think about the church's policy on abortion. She knew she was guilty of attempted murder.

As the autumn advanced, Effie was depressed, angry, and frightened. She had totally given up on having an abortion. She knew she had a tough time ahead, recalling all too vividly her mother's pregnancies with her sister Constance and her brother Andrew. She had been old enough by then to take full account of her mother's swollen ankles, her bloated belly, the terrifying travail of the at-home delivery, the nursing of the infants with her elongated, bulbous breasts.

Curious, maybe morbidly so, Effie browsed in books about pregnancy in the open stacks of the city library. She was repulsed by the images of fetuses and wished she hadn't seen them. She tried to find information on when a pregnancy would begin to show but couldn't. When hers showed, she'd have to tell her parents and quit going to school. Maybe they'd want to send her away somewhere until the baby was born. Anyhow, she wasn't going to tell them until she had to, that was for sure.

At about seven weeks into the pregnancy, nausea began. Effie went back to the city library and read up on morning sickness. She kept little snacks in her school bag so she could eat between classes. Luckily, she had to ask to go to the restroom only a couple of times. When it hit her at home, she tried to vomit quietly and without splashing outside the toilet bowl. Small wonder then that at midterm she did poorly on her examinations—doubly humiliating because during her sophomore and junior years she had qualified for the school's chapter of the National Honor Society.

In the meantime, Hoyt had met the kind of prospective wife the Lord had in mind for him, as had been made manifest to his father. Soon after their introductory talks in Richland ward, he and his companion were invited to dinner at the home of Murray Cameron and his wife. Murray was one of the chief engineers at the Hanford nuclear site, a position that gave his family a particularly high standing in Tri-Cities society, as the missionaries had already been informed by other members of the ward. The Camerons lived in a magnificent house overlooking the Columbia River. As twilight came on, sliding glass doors gave those seated at the dining table a perspective upon the twinkling lights of Pasco, directly across the wide expanse of water. The Cameron children, a daughter of eighteen and three younger sons, joined their parents in questioning the missionaries closely as to their families and homes. They were a delightful, good-natured group, and the two missionaries were happy to receive other invitations to dinner as the fall progressed.

As Halloween approached, the daughter, Heather, phoned the missionaries on a Wednesday evening, soliciting their aid the next day in decorating the church recreation hall for a Halloween dance because the other girls in the ward's Young Women program had for one reason or another reneged on their duty to help. Heather assured the missionaries her mother would be present as a chaperone. Her mother arrived with her daughter as promised, but quickly disappeared in the building, leaving Heather and the two missionaries at work in the recreation hall. Circumstances soon proved that Heather could use only one of the missionaries, and she made it plain that Hoyt was her choice.

Elder Scott seemed happy with this arrangement. He sat on a folding chair near an entrance to the hall and read a book by an apostle. Accordingly, Hoyt spent four hours clambering up and down a tall tripod ladder, taping festoons of orange and black crepe paper high on the walls. Standing at the base of the ladder with rolls of crepe paper in a basket, Heather gave orders with a loud good humor. She also made statements and asked questions that, in retrospect, Hoyt would interpret as demonstrative of more than a casual interest in him. He of course had found her attractive from the start. She was tall and lithe and had prominent cheeks and lips that seemed ready to laugh at any moment. Moreover, she was a freshman at Columbia Basin College in Pasco with a major in English.

Up to this point, Hoyt had no thoughts of her as a prospective mate. It was his companion's comment, as they drove back to their quarters for a late lunch, that opened his eyes. "She's in love with you, Elder," his companion said. "Be careful or you'll be transferred to another city."

Hoyt was startled. His first impulse was disbelief. Love? Not possible. Then he remembered her hand on his arm, steadying him as he stepped off the ladder in the recreation hall. He mulled the matter all afternoon and on into the evening.

The dangerous thing was how he was feeling. What does it do to a guy when a very attractive girl somehow reveals she would like to know him more intimately? What does it do to him when he realizes she is precisely the sort of wife his father could approve of for his son, being a devout Latter-day Saint and derived from a well-to-do, prestigious family?

He awoke before the alarm clock sounded the next morning. He was feeling forgiven. He hadn't asked for forgiveness. The Lord had just given it to him. How else could he account for the Lord putting a girl like Heather in his way? It was as if she was *the* one the Lord had in mind all along.

So maybe Effie was correct after all, saying she and he should just tell the Lord that they understood they weren't to be married to one another and they were very, very sorry for what they had done and they wouldn't ever do it again. In that case, Hoyt had done exactly the right thing by going on his mission as everybody expected him to do. It was a sweet thought, and as time went on, it made the hours of tracting from door to door slip along faster.

However, from time to time Hoyt reflected uncomfortably on the fact that his secret prayers, said at his bedside morning and night, were hurried and perfunctory. At moments of honesty, he acknowledged that the church expected a person guilty of fornication to confess it to his ecclesiastical shepherd, in Hoyt's present case that person being his mission president. Moreover, he acknowledged that he still grieved for Effie. He truly had reduced his prospects to ashes.

Such dismal moments were rare. Generally, his dread of shame was in command, and while he believed that in the undefined future he would confess, he acknowledged that it might not be until the end of a long, successful Latter-day Saint life. Be it said to his credit that, despite whiling away the tedium of tracting by thinking about

Heather, Hoyt's actual conversations with her demonstrated nothing other than the friendliness that one Latter-day Saint owed another.

Far away in Cedar City, Effie experienced an improvement of mood of a different sort. Although she still dreaded the exposure of her pregnancy, her attitude toward her unborn child underwent an abrupt change for the better.

One evening at dinner, her father announced to his children that their aunt, Fran Butler Thomas, was to be released from the Purgatory prison on the following afternoon. She would be on parole, which meant she had to live at a particular residence of record and report in at regular intervals to a probation and parole office. As the children already knew, he and their mother had agreed they would make their home Fran's particular residence of record. Unfortunately, the bedroom and bath he had been constructing in the basement for their aunt weren't quite finished. He would push forward to complete that project. In the meantime, he hoped the children would adapt to their crowded house with good will and laughter.

"Now to a sensitive matter," their father went on. "I am sorry to predict that certain people will disapprove of your aunt's presence in our city, to say nothing of her presence in our home. To them, she is a criminal, pure and simple. I think it is time for you to understand why she embezzled a large sum of money from the company where she served as office manager."

With that introduction, he went on to explain, in a simplified version, a sad story that Effie, being the oldest child, already knew in greater detail.

Ralph Thomas, Fran's husband, divorced her in order to marry another woman on whom he had spent so lavishly before the divorce that he depleted the savings he and Fran had in common. By the terms of the divorce, they had split custody of their three sons, Eric, Gordon, and Danny. Nearly a year following the divorce, tragedy struck Danny, who was in the first grade. He underwent a loss of appetite and energy and the ability to concentrate on tasks. Doctors at the University of Utah medical center in Salt Lake City diagnosed him with a rare debilitating disease with no known cure. True to their prediction, he was soon confined to the pediatric ward of a nursing home in St. George.

As Danny continued to decline, Fran learned of a clinic in Nogales, Mexico—just across the border from its sister city, Nogales,
Arizona—that claimed a cure for this and other debilitating diseases. The remedy—daily hour-long baths in a solution made from
the bark of a tree native to Yucatan—had been expressly classified
as useless by the FDA. Nonetheless, assured by friends that they
knew of persons who had been cured by the baths, Fran undertook
a desperate scheme.

On a Friday evening at the machining shop where she worked,
she kept the week's cash intake of nearly $10,000 instead of depos-
iting it in the bank. The next day she took Danny from the nursing
home in a wheelchair, which she placed in the trunk after she had
seated Danny in her car. Their failure to return was not noticed
by the staff until late that night, by which time they were well on
their way toward Nogales—this during a period when Fran's other
sons were with their father. The next morning Fran checked herself
and Danny into a motel on the American side of the border. Each
morning thereafter, she rolled Danny in the wheelchair across the
border to take baths at the Mexican clinic, returning late in the
afternoon. This was at a time when people could cross the border
without a passport.

She and Danny otherwise spent most of their time in the
motel, watching television and rented movies on a cassette player.
Ten days later, her money exhausted, she drove her son back to St.
George and returned him to the nursing home. Moments later, as
she walked out of the nursing home, she was arrested. Only days
later, he died.

The point Effie's father wanted his children to grasp was that
their aunt wasn't a criminal by nature. She was simply desperate
and willing to grasp at straws. She knew she would go to prison,
but she hoped the baths would heal her son—which of course they
failed to do.

It fell to Effie to bring her aunt from the prison, her parents
wishing to devote the afternoon to putting the basement rooms into
a serviceable condition. Leaving school early, Effie arrived at the
prison by mid-afternoon. It was the Tuesday before Thanksgiving.

It was about forty-five miles to the prison. Effie sat in the parking lot for a while. Twin high woven-wire fences topped by fierce rolls of concertina wire surrounded the place. People took confinement very seriously here.

Effie finally got up her nerve and went inside the administration building. Fran sat on a bench near the reception desk. She was small, thin, and gaunt-cheeked. She was dressed in grey slacks, a blue chambray shirt, and a denim jacket. A small suitcase sat at her feet.

"Remember me?" Effie said.

Fran nodded. Her lips twitched into the start of a smile, then went sober again.

Effie turned to the uniformed woman at the desk. "Anything for me to sign?"

"No. Mrs. Thomas is good to go."

Effie moved toward the entrance. Fran picked up the suitcase and followed. Before starting the car, Effie asked Fran whether she wanted something to eat. She said no.

"What I want," she went on, "is to go to St. George right now and get it over with."

"Get what over with?"

Fran pulled a folded envelope from her shirt pocket. She said it was from Phyllis, her ex's new wife. It contained directions to Danny's grave in the St. George cemetery. Fran explained that she hadn't attended Danny's funeral, being in jail waiting to be sentenced. She knew that someday she would have to visit his grave but, fearing it would be a traumatic experience, she had planned to put it off for a long time. About three months before her release, Phyllis sent the letter. Although Phyllis had broken up her marriage, Fran took the letter as a kindness.

She doubted her ex knew that Phyllis had sent the letter. He was vindictive. He persuaded a caretaker at the nursing home to testify that the time in Nogales was torture for Danny and shortened his life. After Fran's conviction, he petitioned to abrogate her custody and visitation rights forever. In consequence, she was now forbidden to see her sons Eric and Gordon.

Fran didn't know whether their time in Nogales shortened Danny's life, but it wasn't torture. He hated the nursing home and rejoiced in his escape from it. He tolerated the baths, which occupied about three hours a day. Otherwise, he and Fran stayed in their motel room on the American side of the border, eating their meals and doing things Danny liked to do. It was a sweet, beautiful, sacred time, and she was glad they had it. What was torture was coming back to the nursing home when their money had run out.

All of that came out of Fran in hesitant, stumbling phrases as she and Effie sat in the parking lot before the prison.

"So do we go to the cemetery?" Effie said.

"Yes. Let's get it over with."

The cemetery was in the middle of St. George. Effie parked and they got out of the car. The air was clear and cool and the autumn sun hung low in the west. Fran unfolded the letter. Following its directions, the two of them made their way among the grass-covered graves, coming at last to a small stone that read:

Daniel Butler Thomas
Sept 4, 1966 – Apr 16, 1971

A withered bouquet of flowers lay on the stone. Fran knelt and took them in her hand. A few leaves from the bouquet remained on the stone. Fran brushed them off. She stood and sniffed the wilted flowers.

"He didn't quite know what it meant to be dead. But he was afraid of it." She frowned. "You never recover when your child dies. You never get over it." She bit her lip. Tears tracked her cheeks. She began to wail. It was an eerie, gasping, lost-in-a-forest sound.

Effie absorbed her aunt's grief. Then an electric charge arced inside her. With an overwhelming rush of guilt and relief, Effie rejoiced that *her* child was alive.

They were soon on the freeway, heading toward Cedar City. Fran was silent. Effie's mind churned with the implications of her sudden determination to keep her child following its birth. Could she toughen herself to the shame? Wouldn't she have to continue to rely on her parents for board and room? How could she pay for the additional expense of another infant in the Butler household? How would her parents react to their daughters Ruby and Constance sleeping in the same bedroom and sharing the same bathroom with an unwed sister whose pregnancy would become increasingly visible? At some point, wouldn't she have to drop out of school? That would be too bad, given that she now had an even stronger motive to finish. And what about Hoyt? Should he be forced to acknowledge paternity? He came from a family that could easily afford child support payments. But it would ruin his mission. He'd be sent home in disgrace.

It was well after dark when they arrived. Effie led Fran into the house. Effie's mother approached them.

"I hate to crowd in," Fran said.

Effie's mother hugged her. "This is your home, Fran. Don't think of going anywhere else."

The enlarged family sat to a late supper, then remained at the table while Effie's father updated his sister on their extended family. The three-year-old Andrew slipped off his stool and climbed onto Fran's lap. She brushed his hair with a hand and pressed a cheek against his ear. Effie could see she had relaxed. She looked almost happy. A deep reassurance came over Effie. Her own problem, tough as it was, would find a solution in this family. Things would work out. The Butler family would somehow heal both a paroled felon and an unwed pregnant daughter.

Effie went to school the next day—the day before Thanksgiving—determined to work hard on her neglected homework with an eye to returning to the top rank of students. Assigned to write a report on Hawthorne's *The Scarlet Letter*, Effie spent the day after Thanksgiving reading the book. She immediately identified herself with the adulteress Hester Prynne, who emerged from the Puritan prison with a newborn baby in her arms and stood on the pillory scaffold in the public square surrounded by jeering town folk. She similarly identified Hoyt with Hester's pastor, Arthur Dimmesdale, who at the insistence of the chief minister pled with her to reveal the name of her fellow sinner. This she sturdily refused to do, eliciting from the shame-silenced Dimmesdale an utterance of admiration: *"Wondrous strength and generosity of a woman's heart! She will not speak!"*

Ignoring the fact that at the novel's end, Dimmesdale did mount the pillory scaffold with Hester and their child, Effie focused upon

Hester's reluctance to betray her lover. Effie realized at this moment
that one of the chief obstacles to confessing her condition to her
parents was the pressure they were certain to bring to bear upon her
to reveal the father of her child. Effie took from Hester the strength
to conceal his name. She saw herself as rising to a truer sort of righteousness by leaving Hoyt free to finish his mission and marry the
sort of woman the Lord had intended for him from the start.

Effie finished reading the book near midnight. She quietly entered her parents' bedroom and, after closing the door, woke them.

"Dad, Mom, I need to tell you something."

Her mother turned on a bedside lamp.

"I'm pregnant."

"What's that?" her mother said.

"I'm pregnant."

"You can't be," her father said abruptly. "You're just a child."

"I haven't had a period for over three months."

From her mother: "That can't be true."

"It *is* true."

Her parents got out of bed and put on their bathrobes, then
seated themselves on the side of the bed.

"You're truly not joking?" her father said.

"No, I'm not joking."

"So who is this fellow?"

"He's a guy I met at the greenshow one day last summer."

"What do you mean, a guy? Is he somebody we know?"

"He's just a guy. He doesn't live in Utah."

"Effie, how could you!" her mother said.

"I know. It was dumb, very dumb."

They were all silent for a long moment. Then her father: "Has it
truly been three months since you had a period?"

"Yes."

"We can settle the question by taking her to the doctor tomorrow," her mother said. "But I'm afraid it'll be as she says."

"So what do we do?" her father said.

"We could send her to Mabel's. She'd take her in." Mabel was an
aunt who lived in Idaho.

"Good idea."

"I'll go if you want me to," Effie said, "but if it means I'm supposed to give up the baby for adoption, I won't do that. I want to keep the baby, no matter what."

"You're just a child, Effie," her father said.

"I won't do it. I can't give it up. I just can't." She began to sob.

There was a long silence. Her father broke it, saying, "Well, then, this fellow you met at the greenshow—we need to tap him for child support."

"I don't know where he lives. I don't want to have anything to do with him. I don't want my baby to have anything to do with him."

Again silence. Then her mother said, "We have to build another bedroom in the basement, don't we?"

"We do. But it will take a while. And we'll have to scrimp a bit harder to finance the materials. We'll have to be careful how we present this situation to Fran. We can't have her feeling like she's an inconvenient intruder. In the meantime, Effie will just have to go on sleeping in the same room as her sisters. They'll have to adapt to her condition."

"We'll need to talk to the bishop, won't we?" her mother said. "I think he'll want me to resign as Relief Society president."

"I suppose Effie ought to stop going to meetings immediately. And after a while, when she begins to show, she'll have to stop going to class at the high school. But she can go on with her studies at home. She can submit and pick up assignments once or twice a week at the counselor's house. It's something like taking correspondence courses."

Effie saw that she had succeeded. Somehow they would manage things. Her parents were the best of people. Her baby would grow up in the Butler household. It would have the Butler name. But inevitably, Effie felt bedraggled, wrung out, contemptible. She was a poor example for her sisters—and for her brothers too, for that matter. She wasn't the only one on the pillory scaffold. She had put her whole family there.

Nonetheless, as the winter wore on, Effie excelled in her studies, which soon shifted over to being conducted at home, with a weekly visit at the home of a school counselor to receive and submit assignments.

In Richland, very little snow fell that winter. Temperatures were low, and Hoyt and Elder Scott wore heavy underwear, overcoats, and scarves. While they tracted, people often took pity on them and invited them in. As a result, two families were receiving a weekly lesson and seemed likely to convert. In addition, the two elders reactivated an elderly widow who had refused to attend meetings for nearly twenty years on account of a grievance with a bishop.

In early March, almost exactly seven months into Effie's pregnancy and Hoyt's mission, their drastically separate trajectories suddenly merged, resulting in a major reorientation of their lives.

The merging began on a Sunday evening. On Sunday evenings, Hoyt's family had the custom of talking with him via the conference phone in his father's home office. On this particular evening, the family chat had gone on for three-quarters of an hour. About twenty minutes after the conference call ended, the missionaries' phone rang again. Hoyt answered. It was Winifred.

"There's something maybe you ought to know," she said. "I haven't seen Effie at school for a long time. Last Thursday I saw her coming out of Mrs. Channing's house with some books in her arms. You remember Mrs. Channing, don't you? She's one of the counselors at the high school. It was almost dark. But I could see Effie is pregnant."

There was a long silence. Then Hoyt said, "You say it was almost dark?" There was doubt in his voice.

"Yes. But not that dark. She's pregnant. She's *very* pregnant. You couldn't miss it."

There was another long silence. He was already sorting implications and had shut down on Winifred's presence on the phone. I can go home, he was thinking, I can have Effie.

"Are you still there?" Winifred said.

"Yes."

"Okay. I'll hang up now. I just thought maybe you'd want to know."

He heard a click and a dial tone came on his phone. He knew he couldn't just go home. Things were way more complicated than that. He had some tall thinking to do.

As he left the kitchen, his companion, who sat on the pullout bed, looked at him expectantly. "It was my sister," Hoyt said, "telling me some things she forgot to talk about before."

He lay awake most of the night. Sharp edges whirred relentlessly in his mind, slashing thoughts and emotions into tiny, incoherent bits. He would be several days sorting and assembling facts and probabilities from those bits and pieces. He would be several days beyond that before deciding what to do about them.

These were the facts and probabilities. Effie was about seven months along. Her parents—and likely her bishop as well—had to be fully aware that she was pregnant. For both moral and financial reasons, they would have pressured her to reveal her child's father. Obviously, she had refused. That meant she wanted Hoyt to serve a mission. And then—this thought came to him reluctantly, yet the more he considered it, the more likely it seemed—she intended that he would return from his mission and sooner or later fulfill the Lord's intention, as revealed to his father, that he marry a woman supposedly more befitting his station.

If that was her intention—his first response to that possibility was a sort of craven gratitude. He had sheltered himself from shame by serving a mission as expected these seven months. He was loath to give up that shelter although he was troubled by the possibility of a protest on Winifred's part. He surmised Winifred had informed him of the pregnancy in the expectation that he would own up to being Effie's partner, even though that eventuality ran counter to Winifred's self-interest, given that she and the rest of the McCulley family would share in the indelible humiliation of Hoyt's early return and subsequent excommunication.

What would Winifred do if he simply continued his mission? Probably nothing. It would just be a matter of the two of them knowing throughout the rest of their lives that Hoyt had accepted Effie's gift of silence. So it wasn't Winifred who finally brought Hoyt to confession. It was the unborn child.

In the wee hours of another sleepless night, Hoyt found himself wondering whether Effie's delivery would be at the Butler home with the assistance of a midwife, that being the manner in which Effie and her siblings had been born, according to what she had told him during their clandestine meetings of the previous summer.

Would Effie scream in agony as, according to what he understood, women always did while giving birth? What would the child look like after it had emerged, wet and still connected by an umbilical cord to Effie's womb?

All at once, Hoyt was struck by the staggering, miraculous enigma of copulation, pregnancy, and birth and felt impelled to acknowledge his paternity. He knew instantly he couldn't remain a missionary. He had to go home. That determination came of course with a fresh jolt of panic—but along with the panic was the comfort of knowing he had resisted the temptation of showing more than a conventional friendliness to Heather Cameron.

Hoyt phoned Effie early one evening. The phone rang in the living room where her mother was helping Fran sew a dress. Effie sat on the nearby sofa, studying. Her mother handed her the phone.

"This is Hoyt," he said. "I need to talk to you."

"Wait a sec," she said.

She put a hand over the speaker. "It's him," she said to her mother.

"Him?"

"Yes, him."

"Oh, *him!*" With that, her mother rose and signaled Fran, and they left the room.

"Why do you want to talk to me?" Effie said into the speaker.

"Winifred says you are pregnant."

Effie considered his statement for a long moment. "I don't want you to come home, Hoyt. I want you to finish your mission."

"I can't. I'm unworthy, and I'm tired of it gnawing on me day and night. I have to own up to the child. I'm its father. I have obligations. The law says so. I have rights, too. But the best thing would be if you and me got married, wouldn't it?"

"Your father said the Lord doesn't want us to be married."

"That doesn't count now. The baby counts. The Lord wants it that way."

"Do you really believe that?"

"That's how I feel, Effie. The Lord didn't let me know soon enough if he had somebody else in mind for me because he let me fall in love with you, and you're the one I want to be with."

"I feel terrible," Effie said. "I've ruined your mission."

107

"My father ruined it," Hoyt said abruptly. It had just now struck him.

"Your father?"

"You and I, we had a plan, didn't we? You were going to go to school while I went on my mission, and when I came home we were going to get married. Then my father said that wasn't in the books. So we did what we did. And now the baby is coming. So let's just go forward from there. I'm coming home."

The next morning Hoyt set about preparing for his departure. Searching the yellow pages of the phone book, he learned there was a Greyhound station across the river in Pasco. There was also a telegraph office in Pasco.

On the evening before he left, he calmly packed his two suitcases in the presence of his astonished companion, telling him why he was abandoning his mission and asking him to wait until after he had departed before phoning the mission president. Hoyt phoned for a taxi, and when it arrived, his companion followed him down to the street. Hoyt shook his hand and thanked him for all the good things he had done.

"I hate to see you go home," his companion said morosely. Hoyt could see they had become attached to each other, despite their differences.

Hoyt sent two telegrams before the telegraph office closed. One was addressed to his father and mother. It read: *I am leaving mission because of unworthiness. Home tomorrow night. Hoyt.* The other was addressed to Effie. It read: *Please meet me at Greyhound station 11:45 tomorrow night. Hope you will marry me. Hoyt.*

When Effie's telegram arrived, her mother brought it to her. Effie read it while her mother watched. She handed the telegram to her mother.

"Hoyt McCulley! He's the one?"

"I didn't want him to come home. I wanted him to finish his mission."

"Child," her mother said, "the Lord has answered our prayers."

The east-bound bus arrived at the Greyhound station in Pasco at 1:15 in the morning. Hoyt boarded, and as the bus pulled away, his courage tumbled. Maybe his parents would say, "Don't bother unpacking your suitcases. You don't belong with us anymore." At the very least, there'd be an inevitable interrogation in his father's office. "I needn't tell you how disappointed I am with you," his father would say while they gazed at each other across the desk. And then later, his father—being a member of the stake high council—might well participate in the church disciplinary hearing that excommunicated his son. Thinking about all that was a waking nightmare.

By the time the bus made Pendleton, Oregon—just short of 3:30—Hoyt was worrying about the possibility of Effie bowing up and refusing to marry him. She hadn't actually said she would go through with a wedding during their phone conversation. If she wouldn't—well, there would have to be some detailed negotiations on custody and child support.

Two hours later—not quite dawn—the bus stopped in Baker, Oregon, and the driver took a half hour break. Hoyt was wondering who Effie and her parents would ask to officiate at the marriage—their bishop, or maybe the county clerk. As for his own parents—they wouldn't attend and he certainly wouldn't want them to. He and his pregnant bride, side by side—it would be a perfection of shame, wouldn't it?

The bus reached Boise, Idaho, at mid-morning and the driver took a forty-five-minute break. While Hoyt had a pancake and sausage breakfast, he tried to decide what he'd say when he ran into people that didn't know he'd come home from his mission—which was bound to happen, because he would have to get a job and go to work.

The bus made brief stops at Twin Falls, Idaho, and Tremonton, Utah. It pulled into Salt Lake City about an hour before sundown. Hoyt had to make a transfer to a bus that wouldn't leave for an hour and a half. He had a hamburger for supper, and then, as if pulled by a magnet, he walked seven or eight blocks in the gathering darkness up to Temple Square and took a look at the temple, which glowed with floodlight. Who knew? Maybe after a couple of years he and Effie would go to a temple somewhere—most likely St. George—and be married for time and eternity and have their baby sealed to them. It was a comforting thought. Sooner or later they could be just an ordinary, run-of-the-mill Latter-day Saint couple.

Hoyt's bus stopped briefly in Provo and for a half hour in Parowan. Slightly less than an hour later, it pulled into Cedar City. It stopped on the street next to a closed service station and Hoyt got off. The driver set his suitcases on the curb. Shortly the bus rumbled on down the street, its red and amber taillights casting swirling patterns in the exhaust. A car was parked across the street from the service station. A door opened and Effie got out. Suitcases in hand, Hoyt crossed the street. He dropped the suitcases. They stood a moment, eyeing each other in the semi-darkness, then, impeded by her belly, they closed in an awkward embrace.

"Did you really have to come home?" she said.

"I had enough," he said. "I want to get straight with the world."

Feeling the clasp of his arms, she felt like crying. She hated to give in, hated to admit her loneliness.

"You will marry me, won't you," he said anxiously.

"I will."

"I hope it can be soon."

"Yes. Let it be soon."

They talked awhile after getting into the car. They agreed they needed to find an inexpensive apartment. He said he'd start looking for work the very next day. They decided to secure the backing of Effie's parents as to the time and place of the wedding before Effie dropped him off at his house. At the door of the Butler home, Hoyt braced himself. Phil and Beverly Butler had plenty of reason to assign him the larger share of blame for their daughter's condition.

He was surprised by the warmth with which he was greeted. He could tell Effie's parents were simply relieved that he had at last appeared on the scene. They approved of a quick wedding though they wondered whether it ought to be postponed at least until Hoyt had a job and he and Effie could rent an apartment. Effie and Hoyt, seated on a sofa, gave each other a searching look. Both were afraid of waiting. The fact they were in each other's presence at this moment seemed too tenuous, too fragile, too likely to declare itself a dream.

Accordingly, they made plans to apply for a wedding license the next day and to be married at the Butler home on the day after that. They would recruit the bishop of the Butlers' ward to officiate or, if he proved unavailable, the county clerk or the justice of the peace. Fran would sew Effie a cute new maternity outfit to be married in, and Effie would have a bouquet to hold and Hoyt would wear a boutonnière. They would have an extra nice dinner by way of celebration. And then Hoyt and Effie could spend a honeymoon night at the new motel out south of town. After that? They weren't certain where the bride and groom would lodge until Hoyt had a job and a paycheck in hand.

It was Effie's mother who spoke of a honeymoon night at a motel. That word *honeymoon*—it was scented with carnality. It embarrassed both Effie and Hoyt, though neither mentioned it.

Before leaving the Butler home, Hoyt phoned his house. Winifred answered. Hoyt told her he was with Effie and her parents and Effie would be driving him home now.

"Will there be a wedding?" Winifred asked.

"Yes. Day after tomorrow, if we can arrange it."

Ten minutes later Effie and Hoyt pulled into the McCulley driveway. The house lights were on. Hoyt's mother, wearing a robe, came out. She walked to Effie's side of the car and waited until Effie had lowered the window.

"We understand there's to be a wedding. May we be present?"

It came to Effie then that she would be marrying a family—a family that didn't want her, a family the Lord didn't want her to have. Her mind stuttered blankly, refusing to flex. Her kinetic energy expended itself in the fierce grip of her two hands upon the steering wheel of the car.

Time passed. Turning toward the house, Hoyt's mother said, "I understand. It's all very overwhelming, isn't it?" Her voice was soft, kind, resigned.

"If you truly want to, then do come," Effie burst out.

Hoyt's mother turned back toward the car. "Thank you. We do want to come. Just let us know when."

Obviously, the wedding couldn't be held in the small, incommodious Butler home. Moreover, as Effie now realized, this wedding suddenly seemed destined to emphasize, rather than efface, the sin of the bridal couple.

In the meantime, the listening Hoyt revised his hope that he

and Effie would soon transform into just another run-of-the-mill
Latter-day Saint couple. He could see that they were destined
to make innumerable adjustments to one another's customs and
expectations. However, he found an immediate relief in the fact
there would be no stern interview in his father's office. His parents
had obviously accepted the inevitability of his marriage to Effie—
thanks, in all probability, to Winifred's effort.

The next morning, Hoyt joined his family at an early breakfast. It
was a school day and Winifred and their two younger siblings soon
left with their father, who would drop them off at school on his way
to work. Hoyt and his mother remained at the breakfast table for a
while. His mother said she and his father planned to fund a deposit
and two months' rent on an apartment for him and Effie, also to
lend them one of the family cars. She said his father would give
him a job at the brickyard, but she advised against taking it. Maybe
Hoyt's little brother Jordan, now eight, would grow up to fulfill their
father's ambition to establish his brickyard as a family dynasty.

They sat a while longer at the table, both of them silent. Finally,
Hoyt said, "I guess I'll be cut off the church."

"Yes, likely," his mother said.

"What do you think I ought to do—go visit the stake president
up front or wait for a summons?"

"I guess I'd go visit him up front." She had tears in her eyes.

"Sorry, Mom," he said. He felt muddled and angry as if there was
some sort of injustice to the humiliation that confronted his family.

At mid-morning he went to the city employment office. A
low-paying janitor's job was the only one he was qualified to take.
Next he drove out to big truck-repair shop on the freeway at the
north end of town and looked up Theo Rasmussen, a backsliding
friend from high school days who had never gone to college.

"Long time no see," Theo said. "Thought you was on a mission."

Hoyt knew he had to hit that statement head-on. "I came home
early. Effie Butler and I are getting married."

Theo figured out the situation in a hurry. "Shotgun wedding,
huh! Well, dadgum, who'd a thought it! She's a good-lookin' babe."
There was admiration in his voice.

Theo also had good news regarding employment. The open-pit

iron mine twenty miles west of Cedar City had re-opened and was paying big bucks for truck drivers. If Hoyt passed the written part of the test for a commercial driver's license, the company would hire him to drive at the mine site, enabling him to master the techniques of handling eighteen wheelers and double-bed dump trucks well enough to later pass the driving test for a commercial drivers license. Hoyt therefore routed himself by the Iron County Justice's Court building and picked up the required training booklet.

Hoyt knocked at the Butler door after lunch. Effie opened the door. They stood a moment in the open doorway. They both felt uncertain. A hug, a kiss, or maybe just a pat on the shoulder seemed right, but neither of them knew which it ought to be. She turned and led him through the living room and on into the kitchen. An opened schoolbook and a writing pad lay on the table. Sitting down, she invited Hoyt to sit.

She was alone. Her mother had taken little Andrew shopping. Her father and her other siblings were at school and Fran was at Vorners drugstore where she had an eight-hour-a-day job.

Effie said, "Do you still want to get married?"

"Well, heck, yes. Don't you?"

"Yes, but it likely can't happen till next week sometime."

She went on to explain that her mother had phoned the courthouse about a marriage license and was informed that a person under the age of eighteen had to have permission from the juvenile court to marry.

"You and me and Mom and Dad have an appointment day after tomorrow. I hope that's okay."

"Sure."

"Also, our bishop says he would be glad to officiate at our wedding. I hope that's okay."

"You bet."

"Something else—he would like to talk to you and me. He said he could meet us at five o'clock in his office in the church. Is that okay with you?"

Hoyt nodded.

Effie had been doodling on the writing pad. She turned the writing pad sideways as if to examine her mindless figures from a new angle. "When I first knew I was pregnant for sure, Hoyt, I tried to have an abortion. I tried to kill our baby."

Tears streaked her cheeks. "So maybe I need to be excommunicated, too."

Hoyt's mouth rounded into a horrified O. "Don't say that!" He reached for her hand.

"Shouldn't I bring it up with the bishop?"

"I don't know. Maybe you shouldn't."

The two spent a restless afternoon, Effie trying to concentrate on her schoolbooks, Hoyt trying to digest the commercial truck driving booklet.

Effie's mother and Andrew returned around four. "Well, that's just pretty," Effie's mother said, upon finding them at the kitchen table.

A little after five the young couple met with the bishop as appointed. He shook hands with both of them and had them take seats. He pulled his desk chair around so that they formed an intimate discussion circle.

"I was quite startled," the bishop said, "when Effie phoned me that you had decided to come home early from your mission."

"Yes, sir," Hoyt said, "I shouldn't have gone on a mission. I have a lot to answer for."

"You do understand that the stake presidency will be holding a disciplinary hearing."

"Yes, sir, I understand that."

The bishop turned to Effie. "You understand that he will be excommunicated?"

Effie nodded.

"I have told you to refrain from partaking of the sacrament until your baby has been born and then blessed by a worthy priesthood holder. I believe you need to understand that Hoyt will likely be a much longer time becoming worthy to partake of the sacrament again."

Effie was trembling. Hoyt could see trouble coming. She began to sob. "When I first knew I was pregnant, I tried to have an abortion."

The bishop flinched.

"I need to be excommunicated, too," she said.

Hoyt and Effie left the church about forty-five minutes later.

The sun hung low in the western sky. Hoyt steered the car eastward out of town toward the mountains. Things had been settled, far better than either had expected. Still, the ambient atmosphere seemed volatile, somehow likely to change for the worse. They were both thinking of the bishop's perplexity as he dealt with the details of the attempted abortion. In the end he had just shaken his head and said to Effie, "Let's just leave things where they are. When your baby is blessed by a worthy holder of the priesthood, you can start partaking of the sacrament again."

When they reached the side road to the dairy farm, they took it, parking by the pond.

"This is where it started," Hoyt said.

He remembered thinking, in the aftermath of their sin, that lust was wild and had to be kept under lock and key. On that feverish night he and Effie, with their Christian will weakened by the grief of renouncing one another, had unlocked the cage and let lust have its way. On the present sunny March afternoon, Hoyt realized he felt no remorse for their sin.

"I'm glad we did it," he said. "I'm glad we made love that night. Otherwise, we wouldn't be together now."

His calm, baritone voice roused uncanny feelings in Effie. She remembered Hester Prynne in the forest with Arthur Dimmesdale. *"What we did had a consecration of its own. We felt it so! We said so to each other."* It was a paradox, a thing both right and wrong.

Worry hovered in the background of her feelings. The next few days would be grating—the appearance in the juvenile court, the application for a marriage license, and the wedding, now scheduled for the Relief Society room at the church with both the Butler and McCulley families present.

And then a worry that Hoyt shared with her, the approach of their nuptial night, their honeymoon night, as Effie's mother had termed it. The center of their worry was the unborn child, manifest now as Effie's swollen belly. For Hoyt, the worry had to do with a possible injury to the child. For Effie, the worry had to do with the grossness, the ugliness, of her body.

It was Effie who broached the anxiety. Impulsively, she told Hoyt that upon returning to her home on the previous evening, she had asked Fran whether intercourse was okay for a pregnant woman. Fran said it was. Lots of couples did it. Just figure it out, Fran said.

Problem solved. Hoyt, set ablaze, bent across the console and kissed Effie passionately. Come their wedding night, they'd figure it out.

Jesus Enough

1886

When Darby turned fifteen, his mother, Cora, said if he didn't make up his mind to accept Jesus pretty soon, it would be too late. She said he had to make the choice either to make public his profession of faith or to write himself off as a bad debt and go to Hell. So during the spring, instead of going out to the ranch to be with Jack on Saturday as usual, he stayed in town and tried to memorize the 115 items of the catechism presented to him by the pastor of the Baptist church out on Mullen Road. He never came anywhere near to retaining all of them. What he did retain boiled down to the following:

By praying to God in the name of Jesus, you send mail to God through Jesus. In effect, Jesus and God are one and the same. You don't really die when you die. Your soul is still alive. This is good if you manage to live righteously because your soul will go to Heaven to dwell with Jesus in bliss forever. Also, Jesus will bless you with a long, prosperous sojourn in mortality. But you are in big trouble if you can't live righteously because Jesus will make sure you die young from accident or disease, and your soul will go down into the fire that shall never be quenched where its worm dieth not.

When the pastor asked Darby if he felt he had received an effectual calling to shake off sin and ignorance and be enlightened by faith in the Lord Jesus, Darby said yes, and on a bright Saturday in early May he was baptized in Clark's Fork River just below the bridge at the far end of Missoula. Before the ceremony, he counted on Jesus giving him the same sweet assurance of faith that his mother had, but Jesus didn't live up to his end of the bargain. While his mother was very pleased by his baptism, Darby still didn't believe, and now he had twice as much to worry about, having added deceit to disbelief.

When school was out, Darby went to the ranch to help Jack—his stepfather—tend livestock and harvest hay. At fifteen, he could work alongside any man. Of medium stature, he had broad shoulders and well-muscled arms. He had short, blond hair, parted in the middle, and blue eyes, sensitive to the sun, hence in a perpetual squint, even indoors. He was quiet and polite by temperament. He was handy with a rope and had already developed a knack for breaking horses.

Sometimes his mother came out to the ranch, but mostly she stayed at the house in Missoula so she could help out with the church's charitable projects. Darby and Jack came in to town on Sunday for the 11:00 service at the church. They came in a buggy pulled by two prancers—"Just to prove we ain't barbarians," Jack said. "Ain't everybody in town got a rig this fancy." Jack was around fifty years old. He wasn't handsome, having a scarred face from a mine explosion. He never tried to discipline Darby. Generally, Darby didn't require it, and when he did, Jack reported him to his mother and left the matter to her.

One day Darby and Jack were mending some fence on the northern boundary of the ranch, and Darby brought up a fact likely to shock Jack but requiring some advice.

"Jack," he said, "I've got something bad to tell you."

Jack stopped driving a staple and looked up.

"I don't believe in Jesus," Darby said.

Jack went back to pounding the staple.

"You got any advice?"

"No, sir," Jack said. "I don't believe in him either."

So it was Darby who ended up being shocked.

After a while Jack said, "Maybe I do have some advice. Not believing don't give you no license to live on the wild side of life. Leave the whores alone and don't get no girl pregnant you don't intend to marry."

It was advice that Darby had the good sense to follow, which meant that he went on relieving his lust by practicing the solitary vice, as the Baptist minister called it during a sermon denouncing the abominations of the modern-day Sodoms and Gomorrahs of Montana.

1890

The year he turned nineteen, Darby got a job in one of the underground silver mines in Butte. Once a month he took a weekend off and went up to Missoula to visit his mother and Jack. At noon on Saturday, Jack met him at the train station with the buggy and drove him to the house, and come Sunday evening he drove him back to the station. One Sunday evening, Darby said, "An old guy at the mine says my father wasn't killed in a railroad accident. He says my mother worked in a whorehouse, and that's where I came from."

"Well, if that ain't the wildest damn story I ever heard," Jack said. "Who is this old horse turd that told you that?"

"He's a tally keeper at the mine. He used to run a saloon up in the redlight district."

"Your mother wasn't no whore, and I'll kill the son-of-a-bitch who says she was," Jack said.

"So where was I born?"

"In a boarding house."

"And my dad really was killed in a railroad accident?"

Jack pulled at his mustache with nervous fingers.

"Well, was he or wasn't he?" Darby insisted.

"No, he wasn't," Jack said. "And his name wasn't Henry Shaw, either. Your ma just made that name up. I never asked her what his real name was, and she never offered to tell me. She was just seventeen and she was slinging hash in a boarding house, and a man took advantage of her, and when she told him she was pregnant, he lit out, and that's where I come in, because when I moved into the boarding house, your poor little ma was as puffed out as a toad and feeling pretty bleak about things, so when I offered to marry her, she took me up on it even if I had this smashed-up face. I gotta say, Darby, your ma really is one hell of a good woman, and I hope you ain't ashamed of her."

"No, sir, I'm not ashamed of her."

Jack slapped the reins down hard on the butts of the prancers. "I hope you ain't ashamed of me, neither," he said. "I've tried to be a good dad."

"You *have* been a good dad," Darby said.

1891

Darby's best friend in Butte was Harley McAlister, a young fellow from a ranch near Bozeman. Although he was only twenty, same as Darby, he had done some hard living, having signed on for a couple of trail drives into Canada, during which he did what cowboys are famous for, which is boozing and visiting soiled doves and shooting up little towns. But when one of his buddies was killed in a barroom fight, Harley did an instant turn-around. He quit the cowboy life and got a job at the mine in Butte and started saving his money because there was serious talk of a new college in Bozeman, and he had in mind getting an education so he could become a Methodist minister.

Darby met Harley on the night shift at the mine, and they hit it off right away. Harley took a bunk at the boarding house where Darby rented, and they spent Sundays together on the weekends when Darby didn't go up to Missoula to visit his mother and Jack. On Saturday nights Darby and Harley had a bath and a shave and then went to the Butte Miners' Union reading room and caught up on the newspapers. On Sunday, they'd attend a service at the Methodist chapel. Afterward, if the weather was good, they'd hike in the hills beyond town; if it was bad, they'd go back to the Union reading room to finish the day. Either way Harley talked a lot about religion. It was a marvel and a glorious wonder, Harley said, how the Carpenter of Nazareth had framed us a doorway into a better life on the Other Side. Darby was fascinated by Harley's fervor for religion even if he didn't share it. It was a strength to be around somebody who wasn't worried about dying.

1893

Things changed between Darby and Harley when Colin Morrell hired on at the mine and rented a bed in the boarding house where Darby and Harley stayed. They became a threesome—except that Darby found himself left out of the conversation a good deal of the time. Furthermore, Harley did another turn-around, this time going back to what he must have been while he was still a cowboy. Darby was confounded by the change in Harley. It was as if he had never had a religious feeling in his entire life. What surprised him most was that when Colin started talking about getting out of the rut of hard labor in the mine by robbing a bank, Harley took to the idea. Darby was therefore not surprised when he came in from a night shift in the pit to find that Harley and Colin had left town. Midsummer, Darby received a letter from Harley's mother, Rhetta McAlister, which said:

> *My boy has played the fool they will hang him on August 16. Would you be so kind as to fetch him home his corpse I mean. His father has disowned him.*

Colin and Harley had robbed a bank in Cody, Wyoming. The teller was slow in forking over the cash, and Colin killed him. A posse formed and kept on their trail. By nightfall, when an utterly dark, rainy sky forced them to bivouac, Harley's horse developed a limp. Soon after dawn, the posse caught up with Harley, while Colin made good his escape with the booty. Harley was sentenced to hang at the penitentiary in Rawlins as an accomplice to the murder.

On the night before the execution, Darby spent a half hour with Harley in the prison. There was a man of the cloth there, too, an Episcopal minister. Harley had the shakes, his cheeks were grey, his lips were blue. "I don't want to die, I don't want to die," he said over and over.

"Pray with me, son," the minister said. "Trust in the blood of your Savior."

It was as if the minister wasn't there. Harley stared past him, as if he could see something beside the brick walls and iron door of the cell. When he looked at Darby, Darby could see deep pools of eternal nothingness in his eyes.

The next day, riding with the coffin in the baggage car, Darby mulled the words of the minister at the prison gate. The priest had gripped Darby's arm with iron fingers and in a voice choked with grief said, "Let us trust in the blood of our Savior," and Darby wondered if the minister was exhorting himself. Remembering the strange, bottomless pools of nothingness in Harley's eyes, Darby wept, silently he hoped, stifling a sob from time to time, consumed by the inexhaustible pity of being a creature destined to meditate upon the certainty of its own demise. The only good of it all was that, when the baggage car attendant helped him load the coffin onto a waiting wagon at the Bozeman station, he was drained of his weeping. He could now put on a manly impassivity.

Rhetta McAlister rode on the wagon seat beside Darby, her face as stolid and emotionless as Darby's. By and by they passed a ranch house. A man stood on the porch, his arms folded, his forehead creased by a frown.

"It's my husband," Rhetta said. "We can't stop here. We'll take Harley to my brother's ranch."

Her brother's ranch was on Bozeman Creek—a pretty spread, Darby could see. It was what he wanted, what he intended someday to have: a mountain valley, grassy with a creek running through it. It was late in the day, and the brother said to bring the coffin into the house. "Better not," Darby said. "It stinks." So they unhitched the horses and left the wagon sitting outside the pole fence, about a rod from the porch. After supper, the brother brought chairs out onto the porch, saying, "We'll sit up with him tonight and dig his grave in the morning."

His wife said they ought to talk about his virtues and strengths.

"Harley was a good hand at roping," the brother said. "Never missed."

"He was a thoughtful boy, real considerate of others," Rhetta said.

"He was my best friend," Darby said.

"What I don't understand," Rhetta said, "is how he got together with that Morrell fellow."

"We roomed in the same boarding house up at Butte. First thing I knew, he and Harley were working the same shift, and after that things weren't the same for me. Harley kind of forgot me. Colin Morrell is a strange guy. He's like a fast river when you fall in it. Once you're in, you can't get out. It sweeps you downstream."

Late in the night they dozed in their chairs. Darby roused from time to time, feeling guilty for not watching the night through.

The family cemetery was on a ridge south of the ranch house. It was a pretty place to be buried—yellow bunch grass, some scarlet

Indian paintbrush, a few ponderosa pines. They dug the grave at dawn and after breakfast brought the coffin up. The brother's wife brought a Bible. "What shall we read?" she said. They decided on the Beatitudes, also Psalm 23. Before they filled the grave, Rhetta said, "He really was a good boy. I hope the Lord will forgive him."

Darby seized a shovel and went to work filling the grave. At least he didn't believe Harley had gone to Hell. As Jack said, when you're dead, you're dead.

1899

When the bottom dropped out from under the world price for silver, Darby went down to Park City, Utah, where he heard the silver mines were still hiring. A foreman at the Silver King mine told Darby, "What I need is a man on the timbering crew. Can you handle an axe and your end of a crosscut saw?" He could, and that's how he ended up working in a timbering camp on the north slope of the Uinta Mountains, felling and sectioning lodge pole pines for shoring up shafts in the Silver King and Ontario mines.

There were three other men on Darby's crew: Curly, Dean, and Albert. Albert, whose last name was Mason, was a Mormon, and he had some family in a little town called Oakley. Once in a while, Curly and Dean made fun of Albert for being a Mormon, but Albert didn't get riled or flustered. He just laughed with them. Darby could see he believed in Mormonism lock, stock, and barrel—Joseph Smith, the gold plates, the Book of Mormon. It was curious, bunking with someone who knelt at the side of his cot at bedtime saying a silent prayer for ten or fifteen minutes. What did he pray about?

After a couple of weeks, Albert invited Darby to spend Sunday in Oakley with him. When they got off the train at Wanship, they found a waiting buggy, driven by Albert's sister Tilly—a girl of nineteen or twenty, who had dark, shoulder-length hair and blue eyes set in a long, slightly freckled face. Relegating her to the back of the buggy, Albert took the reins and invited Darby onto the seat beside him.

Albert's mother struck Darby as something like a duchess or countess. Her chief function was the supervision of her daughters, who were busy setting the table and preparing supper. These

123

included—besides Tilly—Belle, Madge, Ona, and Myreel, descending in age from Tilly, the eldest, by increments of three or four years till it came to Myreel, who was only three.

When it came time for the meal, Albert sat at the head of the table and asked Belle to say a blessing on the food. "We honor the priesthood in this home," Mrs. Mason explained to Darby as she passed a bowl of creamed green beans.

Darby slept that night with Albert in an upstairs bedroom. "I should have explained earlier," Albert said, "that my father has two families."

"He's a polygamist, I guess," Darby said.

"Yes. I hope it won't offend you. In the eyes of the law, he is not married to my mother. He spent six months in the penitentiary in Sugar House, and he can't live in this house anymore. He has to stay in Kamas with Aunt Sheila. Sometimes he visits."

"At least you know who your father is," Darby said. "I can't say the same for myself."

The next morning, Albert took Darby to priesthood meeting at 9:30 and then Sunday School at 10:30. At noon they went home for a big dinner that Tilly and her sisters had prepared, and then at 2:00 they all went to sacrament meeting, which went on till nearly 4:30. He had to hand it to the Mormons: they could preach. After meeting, they went home for a light supper of bread and milk and bottled fruit. After that, while the younger girls did the dishes, Tilly took Darby to the henhouse to gather eggs. Tilly wore a dress of light blue cotton with collar and cuffs of white. She asked him to hold the basket while she picked eggs from the nesting boxes. At the last nesting box, they faced each other wordlessly. It seemed to Darby that something needed to be said. At least, it was obvious that they both wanted to say something. What was it? He didn't know.

Albert and Darby got up at 3:00 the next morning, and after a quick breakfast Tilly drove them to the Wanship station, where they caught the train headed for the timbering camp. They sat on crates in the swaying caboose. After a while Albert said, "Tilly is gone on you."

Darby showed his surprise.

"I know you wouldn't lead her on," Albert added.

"No, sir, I wouldn't."

"Because whoever she marries has to be a Mormon."

Darby thought about Tilly for several days in the timbering camp. At breakfast one morning he said to Albert, "What does it take to be a Mormon?"

1900

To Mr. & Mrs. Jack Wilson, Missoula Mont Dear Mother and Jack It's best I tell you I have been courting a Mormon girl. Her name is Tilly Mason. She has freckles but is very pretty. She has dark hair and blue eyes. I have never seen that in a girl before. She comes from a good family. Mormons are people just like everybody else. I wish you could meet Tilly. Your loving son, Darby.

To Darby Wilson, Park City, Utah Dere Darby; Yore mother says to tell you you are trifling with damnation to tye in with the Mormons. She says to tell you you are welcum here any old time but your gal is not. That aint my idea Darby For me, you are grown up and know yore own mind Best of luck, Jack.

Darby tried hard to convince himself he wasn't becoming a Mormon just so he could court Tilly with a free hand. He wanted to take on Mormonism lock, stock, and barrel, just like Albert. He had a lot to overcome. He wasn't sure he could master the long list of do's and don'ts. Giving up tea, whiskey, and an occasional cigar was no problem, but coffee was another matter. Also, the Mormons spent a lot of time in meetings. Furthermore, Darby had his doubts about mastering the ins and outs of Mormon theology, which was strange stuff.

Albert said Mormons don't believe in hell, just in heaven—a different sort of heaven, a multiple one. There were three kingdoms in the Hereafter. The highest was called the Celestial Kingdom. Nobody but good Mormons went there. The middle one was called the Terrestrial Kingdom. That one was for all the good folk on earth who hadn't managed to hear about Mormonism or who had been tricked into disbelief by the craftiness of men. That would include his mother, for sure, who had been misled by Baptist ministers. As for Jack, Darby wasn't sure, Jack being a disbeliever. Jack might end up in the bottom tier, which was called the Telestial

Kingdom. This kingdom was reserved for the truly wicked—adulterers and thieves and sorcerers, etc., etc.—which, if Albert was to be believed, would include about nine-tenths of the people ever born. Darby could see that he himself would end up there if he couldn't manage to get past his disbelief.

Ironically, it'd be the place where Harley McAlister and Colin Morrell would be. That would be okay for Harley, who had paid for his participation in a crime with his life. But it would be far too nice a place for Colin Morrell. Maybe there ought to be a place of eternal torment for people like him.

1901

To Mr. and Mrs. Jack Wilson, Missoula Mont Dear Folks It is my honor to tell you Miss Tilly Mason has consented to become my bride on Oct 17th in the Mormon temple in Salt Lake City. There will be a wedding supper after in the Redman Hotel. Please come. Someone will meet you at the train station and make sure you get there. The Masons have many relatives in Salt Lake who can put you up just fine. Your loving son, Darby.
To Darby Wilson, Park City, Utah Deare Darby Yore mother says don't bother her with no more newes about yore doings amungst the Mormons That aint my idea If you luv this gurl I luv her too A ten doller bill is enclosed Yore affecshunite father Jack Wilson.

Unfortunately, once again the Holy Ghost didn't measure up to Darby's expectation and turn him into a believer. Darby was somewhat ashamed of himself for accepting this fact so easily. However, he knew he had to bear testimony as to the truthfulness of the Latter-day Saint view of the gospel in testimony meeting once in a while. He chose to do this in the testimony meeting closest to the quarterly stake conference. This kept him on the good side not only of Tilly but also his father-in-law, Harold Mason, who happened to be the second counselor in the stake presidency.

Tougher duty than that was presiding over his own household—that is, over himself and Tilly in the apartment they rented at the back of a farmhouse a couple of miles out of Park City. As a holder of the priesthood, he called on Tilly to say family prayer before supper on one day and on himself to say it on the next. It couldn't be a brief prayer. He had to call on the Lord to bless the president

of the church and the Quorum of the Twelve, also to bless by name
each member of the stake presidency and the Oakley Ward bishopric as well as each member of the immediate Mason family and
a lengthy retinue of uncles, aunts, and cousins, also to bless Darby's
mother and Jack, since Tilly expected it. Luckily, this didn't snuff
out his love for Tilly. In fact, he sometimes felt he ought to be paying an even stiffer toll for the privilege of being her husband.

1902

Tilly went into labor at dawn on the day before Christmas, and
her screams went on throughout the day. It didn't matter where
Darby went, in the house or outside, he could hear her screams.
About 9:00 on Christmas Eve, the screams stopped and an infant
wailed. Darby was in an adjacent room. Tilly's mother opened
the door briefly and said, "You have a daughter." They had already
decided on a name—Millicent. After a while his mother-in-law
called him into the bedroom and laid the infant, wrapped in
flannel, in his arms. Darby sat beside the sleeping Tilly, carefully
cradling the tiny bundle in his arms. About 4:00 on Christmas
morning, Tilly awoke and nursed their child. Darby floated weight-
lessly above the earth, lost in an ecstasy not far below the moon. He
loved Tilly beyond bounds, he loved their child beyond bounds. He
regretted giving up on those long prayers at bedtime. He really was
going to try harder to believe.

1905

*Western Union May 5 1905 Darby Wilson, Oakley Utah. Your ma Cora
Wilson has died of typhoid -stop- your pa is besot with grief -stop- best
come. Hanna Simmons.*
*Western Union May 6 1905 Hanna Simmons, Missoula Montana. Will
arrive tomorrow night -stop- please hold on funeral. Darby Wilson.*

The minister of the Mullen Road Baptist church preached the
funeral sermon, assuring his listeners that Sister Cora Wilson had
died in a state of grace. He also made sure everybody understood
there were certain ones among the congregation that day who perhaps would not die in a state of grace were they so misfortunate as
to be unexpectedly cut off from this mortal coil. "There are those,

even among us at this instant, who have not opened their hearts to Jesus." He looked hard at Jack and Darby while he spoke.

Jack and Darby lingered at the grave for a while after everyone else had left.

"She was a beautiful woman," Jack said.

"She was," Darby agreed.

"I hate to leave her here," Jack said. "Somehow it seems wrong just to put her in the ground like that and walk away. Funny damn thing, ain't it? Dying, I mean. Just suddenly not existing anymore."

Darby nodded.

"It could make you wish Jesus was real."

"Yes, sir, it could. It does."

"Folks you live with believe he's real, I expect."

"They do."

Jack loosened his tie. "Just having *her* was Jesus enough for me."

Hannah and Wilmer Simmons had Jack and Darby in for supper that night. "What's your plans?" Wilmer said to Jack.

Jack shook his head dismally. He pulled out a bandana and wiped his cheeks—something Darby had seen him do every few minutes since he had got out of bed that morning.

"I think he ought to come down to Utah with me," Darby said. "It's time he met his granddaughters."

"So how many have you got?" Hannah said. "I'll bet they're real pretty."

"They are so," Darby said. "Millicent is two-and-a-half—no question who is boss when she's around. Katie isn't three months old yet. Big, bright blue eyes, like her mother."

"Well, there you go," Hannah said. "You just do that now, Jack. Go down to Utah and get acquainted with those pretty little girls."

Jack shook his head and dabbed again at his cheeks. The next day, as he accompanied Darby to the train station, he agreed to get someone to look out for things out at the ranch and come down to Utah for a visit. About an hour after Darby got aboard, his train passed through Butte. He couldn't help thinking of Harley McAlister and Colin Morrell. Wasn't it time for him to find Colin Morrell and kill him? Didn't he owe that to Harley? Then he reproached himself for such thoughts. They weren't proper for a man married to a woman as kind and decent as Tilly.

1906

Jack moved to Utah to stay in the spring. He sold the house and lot in Missoula and traded his ranch for a ranch in the Heber Valley, about sixteen miles from where Darby and Tilly lived on the outskirts of Park City. Darby spent some Sundays helping Jack put up barbed wire fences and a corral. They also did some repairs on the dilapidated old ranch house. This troubled Tilly, of course. She liked Jack, but she was down on Sabbath breaking.

1908

In the middle of October, Darby and Jack rounded up some cows on the flank of Mount Timpanogos. Tilly had been in Oakley with her mother for a month, giving birth to daughter number three, Deborah. After they had the cattle gathered and moving nicely toward the ranch, Jack said, "I've got something to tell you. I have met a sweet little Jew lady from Salt Lake City, up visiting a friend in Heber. Her name is Aliza, Aliza Sharner. She don't practice the Jew religion. She has converted to no religion at all, which is my sort of religion. Me and her want to get married and start up a boarding house in Salt Lake." Darby's mind churned. He was bowled over, knocked down. It wasn't right for Jack to betray Cora by marrying somebody else. "That ain't all," Jack said. "You been itching for a ranch of your own for years. Let's get my ranch appraised. We'll figure half of it is already yours, an inheritance from your mother. The other half, you buy out, and that's what Aliza and me will use to set up a boarding house. I'm tired of ranching, Darby. I just want a little time to enjoy life before they cart me to the cemetery."

Darby was still speechless.

"I've been hell for lonesome," Jack went on. "It's eating me up. Your ma told me the day she died, 'Get yourself another wife, Jack.' I said, 'I can't do that! I can't never forget you,' and she said, 'You don't have to forget me, but you ain't cut out to be alone.' And you know, Darby, I truly ain't."

Darby sighed and shook his head. "Do whatever you've got to do," he said. "It isn't for me to stop you."

"I'm still your dad," Jack said. "That ain't going to change."

1909

Western Union June 9, 1909. Mr & Mrs Jack Wilson, Salt Lake City. Wife's brother Albert killed -stop- funeral Oakley Fri -stop- please come. Darby.

A horse Albert was riding shied, and he fell among some rocks, splitting the back of his skull. At the viewing, he lay in a satin-covered coffin with his skull bandaged. He was dressed for Sunday in a black suit and white shirt and tie.

Darby had Jack with him when he took a final look at Albert before the closing of the coffin.

"He sure looks dead, doesn't he?" Darby said.

"They always do," Jack replied.

"My mother-in-law has gone to pieces. Melted like butter in a frying pan."

"It's pretty tough, I imagine, losing your only son."

"Tilly is taking it pretty good," Darby said. "'He's just gone on a trip,' she says. 'He's gone to visit grandpa and grandma. He's gone to Jesus.'"

Jack nodded.

"It's best if you can see it that way."

"I wish I could."

In bed that night, Tilly asked Darby to hold her tight, and while he did, she sobbed. He knew then that her talk about Albert just being gone on a visit was whistling in the dark. He pitied her but that didn't keep him from taking advantage of her vulnerability and doing what a married man has a right to do. Moreover, he didn't withdraw in time and went off inside her. He went on holding her after he had finished, and eventually she went to sleep. The next morning, feeling depressed and guilty for exploiting her grief, he sat on the edge of the bed before dressing for the day. Though he and she had figured they weren't ready for another baby, he had very likely got them one. Just as he made a motion toward standing, she put her arms around his waist and held him tight. "I do love you so," she said, and his emotions changed. "I love you, too," he murmured, powerless to express the strength of his feelings. Love was a prairie alive with wind-whipped grass. That was how he felt about Tilly.

Tilly stayed on at Oakley, mothering her little sisters and taking care of her mother, who didn't get out of bed except to use the chamber pot. Darby thought maybe his father-in-law's other wife would pitch in and help out, but she didn't. Darby lived by himself at the ranch all week and came into Oakley on Saturday night, leaving the ranch in the hands of a hired hand, a Ute Indian named Chester.

1910

April 14, 1910 To Mr. Jack Wilson, Salt Lake City, Utah Dear Jack, It is 2:00 am and I can't sleep. I am in Oakley right now. I hope to hell things are okay out on the ranch. Chester is a pretty good hand so I likely don't need to worry. I used to come in from the ranch Saturday nights and spend Sunday. Now it's rare I spend more than a day at the ranch each week. It's been nearly a year since Albert was killed. You'd think we'd start to recover by now. My mother in law is pretty much an invalid. Ditto for Tilly just now. The new baby is fine. Another girl as you might guess. We named her Cora for my mother.

We've hired a neighbor lady to come in and help out around the house during the daytime, also to stay with Tilly on the nights I go back out to the ranch. Tilly takes a good deal of propping up. Surprises me. The way she used to rely on the Lord, etc., I thought she was tougher than me. Not so, it turns out.

Well, here I go giving in to my feelings again. I am going to quit feeling sorry for myself though to be truthful Albert's going has hit me in the belly very hard too. Sorry to say, it has brought up my feelings over Harley McAlister. I haven't ever said this to anybody before but it's true. It has been a rare day ever since I watched them hang poor Harley that I haven't had dismal thoughts about him. What's worse, I can't put down thoughts of finding that son of a bitch Colin Morrell and killing him. That isn't right, is it, Jack, thinking every day of wanting to find a guy and kill him?

As it turned out, Darby tore up this letter. He couldn't admit to wanting to kill somebody. Also he didn't want Jack thinking he was feeling sorry for himself.

1911

*Sept 14, 1911 Mr & Mrs Jack Wilson, Salt Lake City Dear Jack & Aliza,
I have got where I don't know how I should be feeling over the way things
are turning out. I spend two, sometimes three nights every week out at the
ranch but it's still mostly in Chester's care and doing okay. We ought to make
some money on our steer shipment this fall.*

*But the damnedest thing has happened. My dad in law has finagled me
onto the board of the Utah Horse and Cattle Growers Association. I hope
you can put me up a night or two toward the middle of October when I
come down to Salt Lake to attend my first board meeting. I don't feel up to
it, Jack. But I know what you'd say. You'd say, hell, yes, you are up to it. If I
know anything at all about ranching it's because of you, Jack. Thanks for all
the things you taught me.*

On the day before the board meeting convened in Salt Lake, the
neighbor lady, Mrs. Morris, came over to spend the night so Darby
could leave Oakley at a very early hour. She said she would tend the
kids so Darby and Tilly could go to bed early. As usual at bedtime,
Darby and Tilly knelt beside their bed to say their secret prayers,
Darby feeling bad because he was merely pretending to pray.

Tilly didn't rise immediately after her prayer. "Why has Jesus
abandoned us?" she said.

"Abandoned us?"

"Why has he sent us so many tribulations? Why did he desert
Albert? Why won't he heal Mother?"

He edged close to her and placed a hand on her shoulder. "Trib-
ulation is what this world is for," he said.

"At least, I have you," she murmured. "You are such a good man."

They rose, turned out the light, and got into bed.

Darby had hoped to make love to her, but the moment seemed
too troubled, too fraught with concern, for such a carnal deed. Re-
signing himself, he rummaged about his mind a bit, seeking some
thoughts that would help him fall asleep. Then she spoke in a tone
with just an edge of surprise. "Don't you want to do it?"

"Do you mind?"

"It feels good to have you hold me," she said. She tugged her
night gown to her waist and lay waiting.

*

Darby arrived in Salt Lake in time to take lunch with the other board members in a small conference room in the just-completed Hotel Utah. Counting himself, there were seven members of the board, some of them hailing from faraway ranches. The chairman of the board owned a giant ranch in the northwest corner of Utah. "This is Harold Mason's son-in-law," the chairman said while introducing Darby. "He comes highly recommended, being not only a gentleman of the first water but a practitioner of the latest methods of livestock and range improvement." Darby could see that an ability to slather on the compliments was one of the requirements for a chairman.

After lunch, the board settled down to business, which was principally concerned with sending a delegation from the Utah Horse and Cattle Growers Association to the annual convention of the Western States Livestock Association, assembling in February in Phoenix, Arizona. The board's immediate duty was to prepare a revision of the bylaws of the larger association for consideration at the convention. A lesser duty was to designate a speaker for the opening session of the convention.

"It's an honor for the Utah delegation," the chairman said, "to be asked to provide the keynote speaker for the opening plenary session of the convention. It shows that Utah has got beyond the stigma of polygamy in the minds of our associates from other states."

Hobart pulled two photographs from his briefcase, saying, "I propose that we choose one of these two ranchers as our speaker. They are prominent men, both of them, one from Uintah County in the northeastern part of the state, another from Iron County in the southwestern part."

He pushed the photographs toward the board member who sat on his left, "Take a look and pass them along."

He paused as if debating what he should say next. "I am modern, gentlemen," he said at last in a voice in which pride and embarrassment mingled. "I took along a photographer and had photographs taken of both—including myself in both, of course, to overcome their natural reluctance to be thought desirous of prominence. They are truly solid, down-to-earth men. Take your choice. I am convinced either will give us a stellar performance."

Another photograph had slipped from Hobart's briefcase, which

lay on its side on the table. He took up the photograph and con-
templated it for a moment before replacing it. "Here's one that got
away," he said. "William Prothman is his name. He has a ranch out
east of Kanab on the border with Arizona. In fact, his spread laps
over into the House Rock Valley east of the Kaibab Plateau. That
would have been something, wouldn't it, a speaker with holdings in
both Utah and Arizona? But he said no, very emphatically. Didn't
want to be photographed, but I already had this one from the
county clerk in Kanab."

Sitting at Hobart's right, Darby saw the photograph clearly before Hobart placed in his briefcase. He saw it and froze, for staring
at him in black and white was a man who looked very much like
Colin Morrell.

Darby had supper that night at Jack and Aliza's boarding house.
The boarders, all of them men, were university students and a couple of professors. Their conversation was lively, but Darby scarcely
listened. His mind cycled furiously around the question of traveling to Kanab to see for himself whether this William Prothman
were truly Colin Morrell. If he were, he was no one for a novice
like Darby to stalk. What capacity for self-defense did a man have
who found it distasteful to cut off the head of a chicken for Sunday dinner? And say Darby somehow bested Colin in a shoot-out,
wouldn't the law hold him liable for having taken on a duty proper
to an officer? Yet it still galled him to leave Harley unavenged.
Harley hadn't died easy. When he dropped through the trap door
of the gallows in the Wyoming penitentiary, he was supposed to die
instantly of a broken neck, but instead he had suffered a long, slow
strangulation—another particular for which Colin needed to pay.

At bedtime, Jack took Darby up a back stairway to a room
in the attic. Though it was tiny, it was clean and had a dormer
window, which let him look out on the lights of the city. Darby
undressed, turned out the light, and got into bed. He was still in
a state of panic. His stomach was tight, his muscles tense. Then,
suddenly, it came to him what he could do—what he *should* do.
He would attend the convention in Phoenix, but he would leave
early and, unknown to anyone else, he would visit Kanab to ascertain whether this prosperous rancher William Prothman was truly

Colin Morrell. Moreover, he would go incognito in case chance brought him face-to-face with Colin. And if Prothman proved to be Colin, Darby could alert authorities in Wyoming and Utah as to his whereabouts, and, if asked, he could serve as a witness. He could exert every legal effort, make whatever expenditure it required, to see Colin bereft of the spoils of his crime. And with that determination, Darby fell into a deep, tranquil sleep.

1912

Darby disliked deceiving anyone. He especially disliked deceiving Tilly, which he did by failing to tell her that his itinerary for Phoenix included an arduous detour by way of Kanab—a detour, moreover, that might be of such length that it would altogether preclude his attendance at the convention. As a disguise, he had grown a beard and mustache. Though his whiskers were modestly trimmed, Tilly had protested. "It's not you," she wailed in mock despair, welcome words in Darby's ears, that being exactly the effect he hoped for. To complete his disguise, he carried literature and samples from a saddle and harness shop in Salt Lake City, and, after boarding the train, he put on a derby common to traveling salesmen. In his pocket nestled a snub-nosed, double-action, hammerless revolver. He had bought it in Salt Lake before returning home from the board meeting, and he had fired it enough to believe it reliable.

> A note in Darby's handwriting: *Feb. 8, 1912. I shall keep this log in case I am called upon to testify in court. I departed Salt Lake City this morning at 9:17, bound for Marysvale, a very small mining town, as I understand, where a spur of the Utah Central ends. From there I must take the mail stage tomorrow morning, which will stop tomorrow night in Panguitch. I expect to arrive in Kanab on Saturday evening. I am in for a bad shaking I am told, the roads being in poor condition due to the hard winter. I had no idea making my way to Kanab would prove so onerous. It's almost enough to turn me back.*

Truly Kanab was a hard place to get to. For miles the road from Panguitch was no more than two tracks over the crusted snow. Moreover, it was a dark, broody day, and gusts of wind rocked the stagecoach from time to time. Kanab itself counted scarcely forty houses. But it had a hotel, a bank, a courthouse, and a livery barn where Darby arranged to hire a buggy and a team of horses for a few days.

"We don't see a lot of fellows like you around here in the winter," the owner of the livery barn said. "There ain't but maybe thirty ranches between here and the canyon."

"Maybe I've made a mistake," Darby granted, "but as long as I'm here, I just well see what I can sell. We've got a superior line."

He started to walk away, then turned back. "You ought to get in this line yourself," he said to the owner. "This country is going to grow. You can get in on the ground floor. You can do more than just make a living. You can leave your kids an inheritance." Darby stopped, ashamed of himself for talking like a real drummer.

He took a room at the hotel, which was a two-story house with rooms off a central corridor upstairs and down and two outdoor privies in the back, one for women, another with a three-hole seat for men. It was while using the latter that Darby was advised to consult the postmistress for the whereabouts of local ranches.

"She knows everybody," his advisor said, who happened to be a judge of the circuit court, in town for hearing grievances and property disputes. Darby took account of the judge's presence with a double satisfaction, knowing that such a magistrate was precisely the sort to whom the presence of a fugitive from the law like Colin Morrell should be reported.

A note in Darby's handwriting: *Feb. 10, 1912. Arrived this evening. Cold wind rising. Not much difference between this hotel and a run of the mill boarding house. Three Forest Service men at table for supper. They are on their way to measure snow depth on the Kaibab plateau thirty or forty miles south of here which I am told butts onto the Grand Canyon. We gathered in the parlor after supper with a nice rumbling fire in a glazed German stove. That must have cost a pretty penny to tote way out here.*

By the time Darby turned off the kerosene lantern and got into bed, a blizzard was in progress outside. At dawn, the wind abated and the sky began to clear, but wild, irregular dunes of fresh snow obliterated the roads that led from town. That was ominous.

Making his way to the ranch of William Prothman was a dubious proposition given the best of weather. Once again, the precariousness—no, the utter foolishness—of his plan bore in on him, and he was of half a mind to take the northbound stage when it left, though that wouldn't be until the next morning. Like it or not, he had a Sunday to spend in Kanab.

His prospects improved while he and the Forest Service men still sat at the breakfast table. While the girl who had waited on the table was clearing dishes, the hotel's manager—a portly woman—came into the dining room. "Would one of you men be so kind as to help Mrs. Prothman who rents the back rooms get in some wood?" the manager said. "Her husband didn't show up in that storm yesterday, and she's trying to split wood in this snow. She's been sickish, and her baby's got the croup too."

"I guess I could do that," one of the Forest Service men said.

"Let me," said Darby, quickly standing up. "The exercise would do me good."

Out the back door and around the corner of the house, Darby found a small woman wearing a long coat buttoned at the collar and a scarf tied over her head. In her bare hands she held an axe with which she tried to scrape snow from a mound of wood.

"Let me do that for you, ma'am," he said, reaching for the axe. She seemed reluctant to give it up. He tugged and she released her grip.

"Go in," he said, and she did.

He split an armload of wood and took it in. The woman stoked the stove, which fortunately had embers enough to ignite the snow-dampened juniper. A boy of maybe six years sat at a small dining table writing on a slate. An infant of less than a year lay on a sofa, breathing noisily. An empty crib stood in a corner. "She's got the croup," the woman said.

Darby split wood steadily for a couple of hours, filling the wood-box next to the kitchen range. Each time he brought in an armload, he looked about the room. A shelf was hung on the wall next to the door. On it were silver salt and pepper shakers, a few knickknacks, and several photographs in frames. There was none of a person who resembled Colin Morrell.

Without her coat, the woman appeared close to being

emaciated. Her cheeks were sunken, her long blond hair tied back. She seemed eager to talk, responding readily to Darby's questions. She said she was ill. It wasn't the croup. Something in her lungs. She said it was lonely in town. She didn't feel lonely out at the ranch, though it was just her and Bill and the kids out there, plus a Paiute family that worked for them. This was her first year in town. Their boy, Bobby, was six now and needed to go to school. But Kanab wasn't an easy town to live in if you weren't a Mormon.

She didn't tell Darby that until after she had asked him in a timid, roundabout way whether he was Mormon and he had decided he would learn more from her if he told her he wasn't, which in a sense was true. As for this woman—Agnes was her name—she said she and Bill didn't belong to any church. They just believed in Jesus. They read the Bible on Sunday nights when they were together, especially the parts about Jesus.

She was a native of Barstow, California. She was working as a waitress in a restaurant when she met Bill. He was in town selling cattle. He swept her off her feet. She had never met anybody like him. They were both orphans, more or less. That is, her daddy died when she was a little girl and her mother died the year Agnes turned fifteen, and Bill's parents were killed by Indians in Kansas. A kind couple from Wichita raised him, but they were dead now, and so neither Agnes nor Bill had anywhere to go back home to. But she didn't mind. Bill was so kind, so gentle. It was something to watch him with the kids. She didn't know what she would do without him. She just hoped and prayed he didn't have an accident or a renegade Indian didn't come along and shoot him. She prayed hard Jesus would protect him. "Jesus! He's our hope, he's our sustainer," she said.

All this Darby gathered intermittently as he brought in the split wood. It was interesting but unrevealing. He felt let down, frustrated, even angry, being no closer to knowing whether William Prothman—her Bill—was Colin Morrell than before he had launched himself upon this fool's errand.

And then things changed with a cataclysmic suddenness: the sun stood still, the waters of the Red Sea parted, Vesuvius erupted. As he entered the kitchen with a final armload of wood, Darby heard an exclamation of delighted surprise from Agnes, a happy shout from Bobby, and the murmuring intonation of a deep masculine voice, and he knew with no doubt whatsoever that Colin Morrell had just come home to his wife and children.

Darby panicked. He thought of dropping his armload of wood on the floor and running, but finally froze and stood where he was. Agnes entered the kitchen, closely followed by Colin and Bobby. "This nice man has filled our wood-box to overflowing," Agnes said.

"I'm in your debt," Colin said.

"It's nothing to speak of," Darby mumbled, bending to conceal his face while he carefully deposited each stick upon the overfull wood-box.

"I meant to be here last night," Colin said, "but the storm forced me to hole up along the way."

Darby backed from the kitchen into the snowy outdoors, waving a hand as he closed the door. Though he had been working in his shirtsleeves, he was sweating. He retrieved his jacket and his bowler from a fence post where he had hung them and trudged to the front entrance of the hotel and went to his room. For the moment, he was feeling superior, triumphant, on top of the world. William Prothman and Colin Morrell were one and the same person. "We've got him!" Darby said silently to Harley McAlister. "We've nailed him!"

The room was cold so he put on the jacket and also his overcoat. He took off his shoes and lay on the bed. He could feel the revolver in the pocket of his jacket. It comforted him. Also it sobered him, brought him down off the top of the world. Colin wasn't in custody yet, and taking him could prove a dangerous business. So what was Darby's next move? Inform the circuit judge of the presence of a felon wanted for robbery and murder in Cody, Wyoming? Or first look up the county sheriff, assuming there would be such an officer in Kanab, the seat of Kane County? Or might there be a federal marshal in town?

He could hear the tolling of a bell, probably the signal for the Mormons of Kanab to gather for sacrament meeting. He wondered how many of them truly believed in a living Jesus. A strange question, that, just now. Or maybe not so strange. Those who believed were the lucky ones. They had an antidote, a cure, for fear. They felt watched over and protected. *Felt* watched over, *felt* protected. Sooner or later, Jesus would let them down just as he would very, very shortly let Agnes Prothman down. She relied on him to protect her husband from accidents and renegade Indians. At this moment she basked in her husband's presence, blissfully unaware of the looming presence, not of a protective Jesus, but of the blind goddess who in one hand held the scales of impartial judgment and in the other the double-edged sword of Justice.

What was there about Agnes that reminded him of Tilly? Agnes was blond and had grayish eyes and a sweet, plaintive smile, quite unlike his blue-eyed, dark-haired, befreckled Tilly. Wasn't the common bond between them their wifeliness, their motherliness? He regretted having thought of Tilly just now. For years he had imagined her grief and devastation should calamity befall him. For years he had tried to be cautious, to foresee and thereby forestall danger, to keep himself hale, hearty, and whole for the benefit of those who depended on him. And now, far too easily, he could imagine the approaching devastation of Agnes Prothman.

He could see where his sympathy for her led, and he tried to steel himself against it. "I won't abandon you," he said to Harley. He imagined himself rising from the bed and finding the judge this instant, but he didn't. Later, reading a days-old newspaper in the dining room, which served as the hotel foyer between meals, he continued to assure himself that he would shortly seek out the judge, but he didn't. Nor did he say a word to the judge after sitting with him at supper. In bed, he lay rigidly awake much of the night, determined to see the thing through at first opportunity in the morning.

At breakfast the stage driver announced that a cowboy from Long Valley had informed him the road to Panguitch was passable, and he therefore intended to start north as scheduled. After the others had left the breakfast table, Darby remained sitting there for a few moments, but no longer in a state of paralysis. He *had* abandoned Harley, he saw. He *couldn't* ruin Agnes Prothman, *couldn't* plunge her into widowhood. This gross miscarriage of justice had to be, whereby Colin Morrell went on enjoying the fruits of robbery and murder. Darby rose and went out to tell the stage driver he intended to be in the coach when it rolled northward.

As much as possible Darby kept his thoughts centered upon Harley throughout the long day in the pitching, jolting coach. It was a memorial session of sorts, a way of paying respect and affirming their friendship, also a way of begging forgiveness for conceding to Agnes Prothman's greater need. By way of compensation, Darby tried to recall scenes from those happy two and a half years in Butte when they had spent sabbaths together, rambling over the hills in good weather and frequenting the union reading room in bad weather.

On the second day of the journey northward, the coach driver halted the stage briefly and pointed out the log cabin in which the famous bank and train robber Butch Cassidy had grown up. His present whereabouts were, of course, a matter of debate. Some said he was living out at Robber's Roost or in New York City under a new alias. Others said he and the Sundance Kid had migrated to South America and had been killed in a shootout with Bolivian soldiers. Darby couldn't help wondering whether such stories had grown up in the vicinity of Colin Morrell's boyhood, wherever that might be—certainly not in Kansas, as Agnes Prothman had been led to believe.

This reflection brought Darby back to the ambiguity, the moral uncertainty, of his decision to spare Colin for the sake of his wife. His wife prayed to Jesus to keep her husband safe from accidents and renegade Indians. Ironically, it was a mortal Jesus acting in proxy who had saved him most recently. But wasn't that the way with the real Jesus? The real Jesus was the Jesus in good men and good women who did the right thing when it was needed. A make-do Jesus? Yes, but under the present circumstances, wasn't that Jesus enough?

Bachelor Stallions

Irvin had a disrespectful ex-wife who kept him pinned to the wall for alimony and child support. He sold cars, but times were tough, and his father wouldn't advance him any more money. The last three times he ran short, his friend Mort made up the difference. He gave it to him. Wouldn't hear of Irvin paying it back. "Hell, no, Little Buddy," Mort insisted. "I got it. You need it. What are friends for?"

Mort rode a stallion. Sooner or later, Irvin hoped to keep a stallion. His mount was a gelding, which he quartered at a stable at the edge of Salt Lake City. He kept his boots and hat at the stable because if he wore them at home his father would break into a sarcastic laugh and say, "Who are you, Billy the Kid or maybe Jesse James?" Irvin wasn't a big guy. He liked the fact his boots and hat made him four or five inches taller. Unlike Irvin, Mort was a giant. He had hands big as frying pans.

The following happened on a Sunday when Irvin should have been in town attending church. He and Mort were in the Cedar Mountains chasing wild horses. It should be pointed out in Irvin's defense that he always felt something godly about a band of wild horses in full flight: angels of the desert, pure essences of freedom and bliss.

Mort and Irvin weren't supposed to be there because the entire range was closed to pleasure riders. Some scientists at the university were conducting a long-term study of wild horse behavior and they didn't want the wild horses disturbed by the presence of domesticated horses. All morning the two riders avoided their favorite canyon because there was an observation post there and somebody would be in it. Mort figured it would probably be that woman who had run them off once before. After lunch, which they ate just over the crest from the canyon, Mort said, "Let's leave our horses here and slip over the top and see if it isn't that professor lady in the observation post."

When they got close to where they could see into the head of the canyon, they crawled through the sagebrush on their hands and knees. Lying on his belly, Mort took a long look through his binoculars at the observation point, which was on a lower ridge. He said, "It's her, Little Buddy. Big as life. Lord, I hate a woman who thinks she's somebody."

Then they were diverted by a spectacle near the spring that made this canyon a gathering place for wild horses. The canyon head was a wide amphitheater of sagebrush, dry grass, and mountain mahoganies. Near the spring grazed three bachelor stallions. Nearby, head drooping, stood a small grey mare. One of the bachelors, a bay, threw up his head, whinnied, circled about, and, with his great erect penis swaying, approached the mare from the rear. The mare laid back her ears and kicked back with both hind hooves. With perfect timing the bachelor avoided her kick and mounted her, riding her staggering form perhaps thirty yards across the steep slope. Soon the mare stood again with drooping head. After about ten minutes, another of the stallions circled around and mounted her. Then the third stallion did it.

A stallion with a harem mounts his mares only when they are in heat. Free roaming bachelor stallions will rape any unprotected mare, and they will do it over and over. A harem stallion will do the same with an unfamiliar mare. It's a way of killing another stallion's fetus.

"That's exactly what we are going to do with that woman down there," Mort said.

"What do you mean?" Irvin asked.

"We are going to rape her," Mort said.

"I couldn't do that," Irvin said.

"All right," Mort said. "Nobody says you have to."

They returned to their horses and rode along the circling crest, then angled down the ridge on which the observation point was stationed. The point was out of sight behind a brushy knob. Their mounts, interested in going home, trotted eagerly. Mort, wearing an undented, round-topped Stetson, bobbed nonchalantly atop his stallion. Irvin followed.

At one point Irvin called, "She will have a gun."

"Very likely," Mort called back.

"How will you get it away from her?"

"Leave it to me, Little Buddy. Just don't get between me and her at any time."

"I don't think we ought to do this," Irvin called.

"Rape is just a word," Mort said. "When it's over, women accept it. It's natural for them to do so."

"We'll get a life sentence," Irvin said.

Mort swung his stallion about. "Little Buddy," he said with wearied patience, "don't cross bridges till we get to them." He started on, then swung around again. "I worry a good deal about you. I lie awake at nights trying to think of things I could do to help you develop a little spine. Now just keep this in mind. We are not playing cowboy anymore. This is the real thing."

There was also this other, more subtle matter, that when they were out on a ride Irvin fused with Mort. There was no provision for anything else. One was not without the other. They were two fetuses in a womb or, as Irvin now judged, two prisoners in a cell, two corpses in a body bag. He was feeling very bad. A shadow seemed to circle his irises. Whatever direction he turned his eyes, every object seemed outlined by a smoky aura.

They found the woman squatting by her tent brushing her long grey-streaked hair. The tent was at the edge of a clearing in the junipers about fifty yards from the observation point. The woman stood and twisted her hair into a bun. She wore khaki mid-thigh shorts, hiking boots, and a navy-blue T-shirt. A pistol hung on her belt. Her face was long, her nose beaked, her cheeks furrowed. She might have been forty-five or fifty.

"You are not supposed to be here," she said.

"Yes, ma'am," Mort said, dismounting and unstrapping a saddle bag.

"Your horses are a major disturbance to our study," the woman said. "Especially that stallion. Would you please ride out of here without delay?"

Mort took a flask of whiskey from the bulky saddle bag, a paper cup, and a small insulated pack. "Ice," he said, rattling a couple of cubes into the cup. "Would you have a drink, ma'am?" he inquired.

"If you don't leave immediately, I'll have to get on my radio and report you," she said.

"Calm down," Mort said. "We're on our way. Soon as I finish my drink."

Into the other end of the clearing, maybe thirty yards away, ambled a strange though not unfamiliar apparition—in single file, a grey jack burro, a small dun mare, and a red mule foal.

"I'll be goddamned," Mort said. "That donkey has got himself another mule colt."

The jack burro had grazed in the Cedar Mountains for maybe five years. No one knew where he came from. Other riders confirmed what Mort and Irvin knew, that the burro bore an uncanny exemption with the fifteen or twenty harem stallions of the range. Without exception, they allowed him and his mare to wander at will.

The little family disappeared into the junipers on the other side of the clearing. "Nothing turns my belly worse than a donkey," Mort said to the woman. "Jesus was a donkey rider, now wasn't he? Little Buddy here feels guilty for not going to church on Sunday. He thinks Jesus is watching him. So what about you, ma'am? Do you think Jesus is watching us on this fine bright day?"

"My religious sentiments are none of your business," the woman said. She removed the pistol from its holster and let it dangle in her hand.

"Jesus was a hybrid," Mort said. "Isn't that true? Something like a mule, which is half donkey, half horse, Jesus being, as people say, half God, half man. Jesus couldn't have had children. Jack mules screw, but when they do, they are firing blanks."

"Why don't you get him out of here?" the woman said to Irvin.

"He doesn't mean any harm," Irvin said. "He's just joking."

There was no question Mort was bad company for a man with scruples. But he was Irvin's best friend. His only friend. It wasn't just the loans he gave Irvin that he didn't have to pay back. Mort had nearly killed a fellow in a bar one night for picking on Irvin. Pounded him to a pulp.

Mort finished his drink and threw down the cup. He was a weekend drinker. He left the stuff alone from Monday morning till Friday night. He was an engineer at the Kennecott concentrator where he made big money.

The woman said, "Put that cup in your saddle bag."

"Anything else you want?" he said, picking up the cup. "Can I sweep the clearing for you?"

He mounted the stallion and swung around. The stallion pawed the earth and reared, then backed in a circle with nervous, crow-hopping steps. "You pie-biting son of a bitch, mind up, will you?" Mort muttered, kicking the animal savagely.

Suddenly the stallion lunged toward the woman. As the animal dodged past, Mort threw himself from the saddle onto the woman and thudded into the ground with her. The pistol spun from her hand and landed in the dust. Mort got up and dragged her into the shade of a tree, where she lay moaning.

"You didn't figure on any rodeo stunts, did you?" he said. "I'm an old steer wrestler."

He brushed dust off his pants and examined a gash on his forearm from which blood was welling. He picked up the pistol and checked its clip. "Full load," he said, "with a live one in the chamber." He stuck the pistol in his belt.

Irvin galloped after the stallion and brought him back. He offered the reins to Mort, who waved them off. "I'm hurt, Little Buddy," he said. "I'm afraid I've broken some ribs. There's something bubbling in my lungs."

He lay down under a juniper maybe twenty yards from the woman. "Keep an eye on her," he said.

Irvin dismounted and tied both horses to a tree. He offered the woman some water from a canteen, which she drank in big gulps. She rolled onto her side into a curled position. Irvin returned to Mort, who had placed his hat over his face. The sun was hot in the clearing. The horses stamped their hooves and swished their long tails. Black flies buzzed around piles of green stinking dung.

"I ain't up to screwing her just yet," Mort said from beneath his hat. "I hurt too bad. If you want to do it to her, go ahead."

Irvin offered Mort a couple of aspirin tablets from his saddle bags. He took a couple to the woman. He supported her while she drank them down, then let her curl on her side again in the dust.

"What are you going to do with me?" she said.

"When my friend feels better, we are pulling out of here."

"He wants to rape me," she said. "Don't let him do it."

Irvin stood over her trying to decide what to do next. He despised himself for being disappointed, despised himself for wanting to watch Mort do it. One of his cousins had been raped. Her assailant had accosted her at midnight at the far side of a parking lot of a ski lodge where she worked. He dragged her into the trees, raped her, and then, for good measure, dragged her back to the parking lot and slammed her down on the ice.

"Why would he do that to her?" Irvin's mother said. "Didn't he know she is a person? Didn't he know she has feelings?"

The woman got up. She steadied herself by hanging to a juniper bough. "Give me a break," she said. "Give me a chance."

"I'll ask him," Irvin said.

He crossed the clearing and knelt beside Mort. "Shouldn't we be getting out of here?" he said.

Mort brushed the hat from his face and got onto an elbow. He looked for the woman, squinted, looked again. "Where is she?" he said.

"She was there," Irvin said. "Just now. I just barely turned my back on her."

"Goddamned woman!" Mort said. "We'll get a twenty-year sentence if she gets away." He pulled himself up, untethered his stallion, and climbed into the saddle. He took the lariat from his pommel and shook out a loop. He was groaning from the pain in his lungs.

"If she'd stayed out of these mountains, this wouldn't have happened," he said. "Why do they have to study wild horses? What makes them so different?"

Irvin climbed onto his gelding. Mort handed him the pistol. "If you want to be merciful, you find her first and shoot her," he said. "Because if I find her first, I'll drag her to death with this rope."

Mort had Irvin ride on his uphill side, and they trotted into the junipers. The woman's footprints angled gradually toward the bottom of the canyon. "Easy to see," Mort said. "She doesn't have any sense at all about concealing her tracks."

Irvin could see it was true, somebody was going to die. Mort often said, "I have never killed a person. Sooner or later, that is an experience I intend to have."

They lost the tracks for a minute. They spread out, looking hard. Then Mort shouted. "She's flanked us. Headed uphill, still running. There's a radio in camp. I'm going back and pick it up before she beats us to it. You come on down here and stay on her trail. Ride in semi-circles and keep your eyes open." He reined around and lashed the stallion into a fierce uphill run.

Irvin found a couple of boot prints in the soil. He followed their direction, which was uphill but not precisely toward camp. Grass and sagebrush grew among the junipers here, obscuring the track. He circled wide till he found the tracks again, now leading away from camp into the canyon. He followed till he emerged from the junipers a few yards above the sage-filled bottom.

The jack burro, the dun mare, and the red mule foal were in the bottom. They stood staring at Irvin and his gelding. Irvin remembered Joseph and Mary took Jesus down to Egypt on a donkey. Jesus rode a donkey into Jerusalem on the day of the palms. Irvin was wishing Mort hadn't said those things about Jesus being a kind of spiritual mule, half human, half deity.

The woman's tracks returned to the junipers. The pattern of her movement so far suggested hysteria. That wasn't surprising. Even the junipers made for poor hiding. Scarcely twenty yards into the junipers, Irvin caught a glimpse of the running woman. His gelding broke into a gallop and he caught up with her. She flung herself into a small bushy juniper. Her breath came and went in gasps. Her eyes rolled, she muttered incoherent things. Irvin couldn't help thinking of how people must have felt, naked and standing in line waiting to be gassed in Nazi death camps. He was scalded with pity. He stopped trying to think and gave in to a wild impulse.

He urged his horse closer to the woman. Holding the pistol by the muzzle, he extended it toward her. "Take it," he said.

She tried to push herself deeper into the juniper boughs. He could see she was paralyzed. He dismounted. Still holding the pistol by its muzzle, he approached her.

"Just take this pistol," he pleaded. "You'll have to help yourself,"

149

he said. "I could never shoot him. Not in a hundred years." He placed the handle of the pistol in her hand. She was on her knees, string at the pistol blankly as if she failed to recognize what it was.

Irvin returned to his horse. A shadow again seemed to circle his irises. Again, objects around him seemed outlined by a smoky aura. He put a boot into the stirrup and mounted. At that moment Mort rode into the opposite side of the clearing. He reined the stallion to a halt. "My God," he said, "how did she get that gun?"

The woman rose and stepped away from the juniper. Her clothes were dusty, her bare legs and arms bloody from multiple scratches. Gripping the pistol with both hands, she stood with her feet well apart, as if bracing herself. She fired repeatedly until the action clicked shut on an empty chamber. One of the shots hit home. A red spout of blood burst from Mort's chest. His eyes, wide with astonishment, flicked back and forth between Irvin and the woman.

"Little Buddy…," he muttered in a failing voice. He toppled from the saddle. With a loud bleat of fear, the stallion bolted from the clearing.

The woman lowered the pistol. She seemed puzzled, as if she couldn't believe she had fired. Slowly, comprehension appeared on her face. Shaking her head, she holstered the pistol. She felt the back of her neck and winced—an injury, maybe, from Mort's tackle in the camp.

Irvin was weeping. His gelding was restless. It wanted to follow the stallion and Irvin had to rein it in over and over.

The woman said, "I take it you've got a truck and trailer down at the mouth of the canyon."

"It's Mort's outfit," Irvin said.

"The keys are probably in his pocket. Get them, will you?"

"I couldn't. I just couldn't."

She crossed the clearing, muttering. She squatted by the bleeding body and extracted a ring of keys from a pocket of his jeans. She studied his face for a long moment. She stood and said, "I'm going to up to the camp. Please go get that stallion. We can't have it loose on this range."

When Irvin arrived with the stallion, he saw the camp was a

strewn mess. The woman stood arms akimbo, thinking out loud. "The radio's a wreck. Can't call for a copter. So I walk out of here."

"This horse will ride double," Irvin said.

"I prefer to walk," she said.

She rummaged about among the scattered artifacts of the camp. She reloaded her pistol and belted on a waist pack into which she had placed packets of trail mix.

"Well, let's get going," she said. "While we're at it, we'll work out a story about all this that will keep you out of prison."

She set off at a surprising pace for a battered person. Leading the stallion by a rope, the weeping Irvin reined his gelding into the trail behind her.

Kid Kirby

His name was Reeves Kirby and he was eighteen that summer. He was small of stature and unlikely to grow bigger. Moreover, he had a mild temperament, blond hair, bland blue eyes, and a downy upper lip—truly an unlikely candidate for the fast-draw artist the public later made him out to be.

He came up to the ranch at Almy to help his dad, Tull Kirby. Reeves meant to go back to Tooele in the fall and marry his high school sweetheart, Mary Beth McAllister. She was the pharmacist's daughter. Reeves planned to go to pharmacy school over in Pocatello. He for sure wasn't going to be a rancher.

His dad's ranch at Almy was down the Bear River five miles from Evanston, Wyoming. Tooele was in Utah. The distance between the two towns was about eighty-five miles. Culturally, it could have been a thousand. Reeves didn't figure on stumbling into a gunfight that summer with the notorious killer, gambler, and bawdy-house proprietor, Thomas Galt. Reeves didn't own a revolver; he didn't know how to load one. All he knew was you had to pull the trigger.

The ranch at Almy was called the Elkhorn. Long ago somebody had nailed an elk antler to the barn. There were cattle to tend at the Elkhorn, also fields of alfalfa to harvest and irrigate. For maybe a week after he arrived, Reeves found the work tolerable. But when a rancher from upriver showed up wanting to hire him to break some horses, he was ready to listen.

This fellow's name was Homer Blanchard, and he had a contract to provide twenty-five well-broken horses to the US Cavalry stationed at Fort Duchesne by the middle of September. He had some prime mustangs, and he need someone who was extra good at breaking horses to take them. "I need them mustangs broke pronto," he said, "and I need'em broke right, and your granddad says you can do it."

He had just been out to visit Reeves's grandfather, Riel Kirby, who raised horses at the Narrows of the Bear River. "A horse has pitched your granddad onto a fence and he's too stove up to take on my project," Homer said, looking Reeves over as if he were inspecting him for blemishes. "He says his Ute helper ain't up to the task, but he says you can handle it. Says you are extra good at breaking horses. Says you are a genius at it."

Reeves scuffed the toe of his shoe in the dirt. It had been a while since he'd tried his hand at sweet-talking a bronco into letting him on its back without a lot of fire and fustian—ever since his grandfather had sold his ranch at Tooele. "I could give it a try, I guess, if my folks will let me," he said.

"Let me fix it up with your dad and mom," Homer said. "You come stay in the bunkhouse for a week, and I'll pay you triple. You gentle a couple of broncs, and I'll have my buckeroos finish them off. And no hard feelings if it don't work."

Tull was okay with this proposition, having found out that a neighboring rancher had some big sons willing to work for a lot less than Reeves would be making with Homer. Predictably, Eula said an emphatic no, and it took several days for Reeves to over-come her objections by persuading her that, rather than allowing Homer's cowboys to corrupt his morals, he would impress them by his resolute adherence to Mormon standards, thereby opening their hearts to becoming members of the church. Moreover, he solemnly promised to ride home on Saturday evening in plenty of time to get a good night's sleep and prepare for driving to sacrament meet-ing with his folks.

Reeves did as he had promised at the end of the first week, telling his mother with considerable pride that Homer was satisfied with his work and wanted to hire him for gentling the entire herd of twenty-five horses. Reeves hoped she'd let him accept. It seemed like breaking horses was a gift Heavenly Father had given him, and he ought to exercise it, especially since the pay was so gener-ous and he'd have enough money to go forward with his plans to ask Mary Beth to marry him and to apply for pharmacy school at Idaho State University in Pocatello. Eula prayed about it that night, and it came to her that, yes, Reeves should take advantage of Mr. Blanchard's offer and acquire the means to escape not only from the polluting influences of Wyoming but also from a rancher's hardscrabble way of life. As for Mary Beth, Eula would welcome her as a daughter, if the Lord saw fit to make her Reeves's wife.

What Reeves didn't tell his mother at the end of his first week—largely because he hadn't taken it fully into account just yet—was that while his bunkmates, Homer's three buckeroos, Andy, Jack, and Morley, were respectful of his Mormon scruples, they had already influenced him more than he had influenced them. He was curious about their indifference to sin. They didn't seem to recognize there was such a thing. Profanity and bawdy stories, punctuated by raucous laughter, were as innocent with them as breathing.

For his part, Reeves was keenly aware of sin. From his own perspective, he was a soul who paid close attention to the costs of sin without being able to check his spendthrift ways in accruing those costs. His bad side got the upper hand all too often, and he'd stroke his stack in the privy or some other private place. The solitary vice, as people called it, was a nasty business, and he knew if he didn't stop doing it, he'd be called to account for it. In the meantime, if he were to suddenly die by accident or disease, his soul would certainly not ascend to the Celestial Kingdom. The best a fellow of such a flawed character as his could expect on the ladder of glory would be a middling position in the Terrestrial Kingdom. But at least—so he reasoned—sins of his sort wouldn't consign him to the Telestial Kingdom, the dreary abode of murderers, thieves, and whoremongers, which was where the three buckeroos were likely to spend eternity.

For a couple of weeks more, Reeves got home around sundown as expected on Saturday evening. A week later, however, he didn't. It happened to be the last Saturday of the month—the day when Homer paid his hands their wages and they customarily rode into Evanston to blow a portion of them. Gathered with Andy, Jack, and Morley in Homer's office, Reeves asked if he could accompany them into Evanston. The road he followed toward home was the same the three buckeroos would follow on their night in town, branching off at the outskirts of Evanston.

Homer looked at Reeves with astonishment. "So, you're going to take up with booze and wild women!"

"I'm already part way home when I'm in Evanston," Reeves said. "I was thinking I'd just look around a little and then get on home."

"Well, I ain't in charge of nobody's morals," Homer said, "but I don't want your folks to pull you off my bronc-breaking project. So, by damn, you other fellers make sure he gets on his way home at a good early hour."

"You bet," Morley said. "We'll do that."

As the small cavalcade jogged toward town, Reeves learned that the buckeroos planned on visiting a dance hall called the Buckingham, which featured a bar, a vaudeville theater, and a brothel, owned by a couple called Flossie Kabane and Tom Galt.

"Thing you need to know," Andy said to Reeves, "is when Tom Galt knocks on your door, you've got to leave your lady pronto. Also, if the police raid the place, the drill is you skedaddle quick out the window and drop down into the alley in the back, which runs right back up to the livery barn where our horses are tied up."

"I don't believe Reeves will want to go upstairs to the ladies," Morley intervened. "Mormons don't do that kind of thing."

"Is that so, Reeves?" Jack said. "Not even before you get married?"

Reeves, flustered, started to say something, but his voice died in a squeak.

"That's just the way Mormons are," Morley said.

"Eighteen and he ain't ever shugged nobody!" Andy marveled.

When the road split, one branch heading into Evanston, the other branch heading toward Almy and the Elkhorn ranch, Reeves's good side told him to just head on home, but his bad side wouldn't let him disappoint his sturdy comrades, who were pleased with the prospect of showing him the vices of a western railroad town. They each quaffed a shot of whiskey at the bar while Reeves waited; then they went into the restaurant and had salmon and oysters that had been shipped in ice from San Francisco. Their waitress was a pretty blue-eyed girl of maybe fifteen. A white apron was tied around her waist. Her blond hair was coiled into a tight bun, atop which a tiny tiara of starched white cloth perched. Her glances did strange things to Reeves, making him straighten his posture and assume what he hoped was a nonchalant look.

Following their meal, Reeves's comrades took him into the vaudeville show. There was a dog that jumped through hoops with incredible speed and another that could pedal a tricycle. There was a magician from Albany, New York, who locked a lady in a cabinet and sawed her in two and then waved his wand and opened the cabinet and, lo and behold, he had put her back together without any harm. There was a minstrel with black paint on his face who sang "Old Black Joe" very soulfully, which set the audience to weeping.

The grand finale was dancing ladies who came onto the stage with flouncing skirts and high-kicking legs—each upward flounce revealing above their black, be-gartered stockings an expanse of white, sensuous flesh. It was those glimpses of white, sensuous flesh that caused Reeves to envy his comrades when they disappeared up the stairway that led to the brothel. Moments later, his moral compass swung back to true north, and he was ashamed of himself.

He stationed himself on a bench in the passageway between the theater and the restaurant to await his comrades. By and by, the cute little waitress who had served them at dinner came from the restaurant and chalked the following day's menu onto a blackboard. That task accomplished, she stood a moment, arms akimbo, gazing at Reeves. A strand of blond hair, loosened from the bun on top of her head, hung over an ear. He confirmed his earlier judgment as to her age—fifteen, at most, maybe younger. Once again he felt compelled to appear manly. He straightened his slumping back and nonchalantly crossed one leg over the other.

Stepping close to the bench, the girl said, "Where are your friends?"

Reeves nodded toward the entrance to the brothel stairway.

"You're too young to go with them, I guess."

"I'm eighteen," he said.

"You don't look eighteen."

"I know it," he said. "I'm eighteen even if I don't look it. Reason I didn't go with them is I'm a Mormon. I'm not supposed to do that kind of thing."

"I know some Mormons who do," she said.

He flushed.

"But I'm glad you don't," she quickly added. "Me, I'm an Episcopalian. We aren't supposed to do that kind of thing either."

Eyes averted, Reeves picked at a thread on a cuff.

"I don't go to church, of course," she said. "Anybody who works for the Buckingham can't go to communion."

That wasn't a big loss as far as Reeves could see. The Episcopal communion didn't count for anything, anyway.

"What's your name?" she said.

"Reeves Kirby."

"Reeves Kirby," she repeated, appearing to savor the sound.

The flicker of intimacy in her voice disturbed Reeves. He planted both feet on the floor.

"I'm Jennie O'Brien," she said. "I'm sixteen. I'm like you. People don't believe I'm that old. But I am."

Reeves gave a doubtful glance.

"I *am!*" she insisted.

He nodded acquiescently.

She tilted her head toward the brothel stairway. "Flossie wants me to work up there."

"Why don't you quit?" Reeves said. "Why don't you go home to your folks?"

"I can't. They're in Fresno. We had a farm in Nebraska. Uncle Dean told Daddy to come on out to Fresno. But we ran out of money by the time we got to Evanston. Daddy had to borrow from Flossie and Tom to go on. They made him put me up for collateral. My folks said they'd come back for me. But they won't. There are too many mouths to feed."

Reeves's eyes widened.

"I've got to go," she said. "Flossie will scold me if she catches me loafing out here."

She put a hand on the door handle. Suddenly she blurted, "You probably think I'm tarnished."

"Tarnished?"

"I'm *not.*" She glanced back toward the brothel stairway. "If I worked up there, I'd have a room to myself. I could buy nice clothes. But I can't. I *won't.*"

Reeves stared at his feet. A stitched pattern decorated the toe of his boots.

"I guess somebody like you wouldn't ever come calling on a girl like me even if I'm not tarnished," she said.

Just then the three buckeroos burst from the brothel stairway. "Reeves, little buddy," Morley hooted, "it's time to get you started on your way home."

Reaching the Elkhorn ranch a little after dawn, Reeves told his worried parents a lie about his horse throwing a shoe, requiring him to turn back to get the animal reshod, and when that task was accomplished, Homer's wife had asked him to help her finish pressing whey from a tub of cheese curds that threatened to spoil before morning.

As expected, Reeves drove into Almy with his parents for sacrament meeting. He considered not partaking of the sacrament, but, unwilling to rouse his mother's suspicions, he took the morsel of bread and sipped from the tiny cup when they were offered.

Thoughts, worries, stray emotions of all sorts swam frantically round and round inside him like minnows trapped in a tub. He had stepped down a few rungs on the ladder to glory—no question of that. He hoped he would still qualify for the Terrestrial Kingdom in case one of the broncos stumbled and fell on him.

Moreover, he couldn't stop thinking about Jennie O'Brien. She said her parents had sold her. It seemed incredible, yet he believed her. She claimed she wasn't tarnished. He believed that, too. In a sense, that just made matters worse. She was too forward, too bold. She supposed a fellow like him would never keep company with a girl like her, even if she wasn't tarnished. Well, that was a fact, and he resented her for making him feel guilty about it just now. For one thing, a Mormon boy couldn't keep company with a Episcopalian girl. For another, it wasn't a girl's place to invite a boy to pay court to her. And on top of all that, he had a sweetheart back in Tooele.

By the time sacrament meeting ended, Reeves had got back around to feeling sorry for Jennie O'Brien. He granted she was a virtuous girl who had reason to feel desperate. She needed a rescue, but he wasn't the fellow to provide it.

Things went along as expected for a couple of weeks, and then on a Monday morning Tull asked Reeves to take a day off from working for Homer in order to convey supplies to his grandfather at the Narrows ranch. He'd have to transport the supplies by pack-horse because of a washed-out bank in the ford across the river. Tull normally would have taken them, but he was pressed to clear several fields of newly mown hay before an extended irrigation turn came round. Accordingly, Reeves saddled his gelding, cinched a pack frame on a mare, and with Tull's help loaded the frame with beans, flour, dried apples, and coffee.

Reeves had no difficulty following the trail although the horses had a tough scramble up the bank at the washed-out ford. Approaching the ranch house, Reeves shouted, "Grandpa, it's me! Reeves!" Hearing no reply, he repeated the shout.

He dismounted and tethered the horses to the hitching rail. As he climbed the porch steps, he shouted again. He knocked, then pushed open the door and peered inside. There were unwashed dishes on the table and a frying pan with a burned pancake on the stove. He shouted again. He closed the front door and walked around the corner of the house. He paused at the barn and looked in. The loft on either side of the bay was full of grass hay.

"Grandpa!" Reeves shouted into the bay.

He heard a faint voice calling from behind the barn. About twenty yards past the barn, he saw his grandfather, sitting on the ground with his back to a wagon wheel. His shirt was drenched with blood and he held a crumpled felt hat, equally bloody, against his chest. A pool of gleaming blood gathered on the ground beside him. There was another pool of blood—considerably darker—maybe four yards away.

"I am dying, boy," his grandfather said. "I have been shot from the back."

Reeves knelt beside him, his breath sucked down to nothing. His head swung with the unreality of what was going on. It wasn't possible someone he knew would get shot in the back. It wasn't possible someone he knew would bleed to death in his own barnyard.

"I fell on my face," his grandfather rasped. "I played dead, tried not to breathe, blood draining out of me. Son-of-a-bitch who shot me gave me a kick. He said, 'You've had this coming for a long time, Riel Kirby.' I knew the voice—Tom Galt, no mistake about it."

Reeves remained in stunned silence, mouth agape.

"I let Lester go to a powwow on the reservation," his grandfather said. "Lucky thing he wasn't here. Galt would've shot him too. I had a chance to kill that son-of-a-bitch years ago. I should have done it. He was running with a bunch of rustlers over in Grouse Creek. We lynched four of his compadres and let him go. Tell your daddy who it was, Reeves. Tell him it was Tom Galt who shot me."

Reeves was trying hard not to sob, trying hard to suppress his surging panic, trying hard to comprehend each word and phrase as precisely as possible.

"I have been a wicked man, Reeves. I have visited whores. I have killed men that didn't need killing. I have defied the promptings of the Holy Ghost many a time. I'm going to hell, Reeves. I'm headed for Outer Darkness."

Soon his hands fell limp and the crumpled hat dropped into his lap, revealing a bloody crater of shredded flesh and bone where the bullet had emerged from his chest. Reeves looked into his face and saw what a dead man looked like. There was something emptied about a dead body. It seemed suddenly smaller.

Reeves stood and backed away. Giving in to panic, he turned and began to trot. He came to the tethered horses. He untied the gelding's reins and prepared to mount. Then he realized it would be a desecration, a dishonor, to leave his grandfather's body behind. Whatever was required, whatever postponement of panic and grief and self-recrimination might be necessary, he had to take the body with him.

He attached the gelding's reins to the hitching rail, then untied the load from the pack frame and carried it into the house. He led the mare to the barn and exchanged the pack frame for a saddle. Dragging his grandfather into the barn on a tarp, he tied a loop of rope beneath his grandfather's arms and hoisted him by means of a block and tackle dangling from a rafter. Having positioned the mare, he lowered his grandfather into the saddle, securing it by tying his hands to the saddle horn and his ankles to the fenders just above the stirrups.

Reeves led the mare from the barn, climbed onto his gelding, and urged the horses forward. At the ford, the mare stumbled and fell to her knees. With a strenuous lunge, she recovered and followed the gelding from the ford. Looking back, Reeves saw that his grandfather's body dangled bizarrely out of kilter. There was nothing to do but proceed.

Reeves got to the Elkhorn ranch after nightfall. Tull came from the house with a lantern and stared at the grisly burden strapped to the packhorse. Over and over he muttered, "Merciful heavens! Merciful heavens!" Eula stood on the porch watching.

"He talked to me some before he died," Reeves said.

"You watched him die!"

"Yes, sir."

"Tough duty. Very tough duty."

"He was in the barnyard. He got shot from the back. He fell on his face and played dead. The man said, 'You've had this coming for a long time.' Grandpa said he knew the voice. He said it was Tom Galt."

"Tom Galt!"

"Yes, sir."

Eula left the porch, calling, "I'm coming down."

"Don't," Tull called back. "He isn't pretty."

"I intend to see him," she said.

The mare shifted nervously. Riel's body listed grotesquely to one side of the saddle, face downward. Eula took the lantern from Tull and raised it, illuminating Riel's drawn, grimacing face. The glazed eyes were open, and tiny stalactites of dried blood hung from his nostrils.

She stepped back, shuddering.

Tull saddled a fresh horse, took the lead rope in hand, and left for Evanston. Inside the house, Reeves tasted little of his supper. At his mother's insistence, he recounted the event at the Narrows ranch, asking when he had finished, "Will he be cast into Outer Darkness?"

"He lived a hellish life for as long as I knew him," Eula said, "but I doubt he ever knew enough about the Holy Ghost to be cast into Outer Darkness."

Reeves lay awake for a long time, rigid with anxiety. An hour or so after he fell asleep, he woke in a cold sweat and sat upright in bed, shouting. He had dreamed of diving into a deep pool of blood. He had the shakes, no question of that. He couldn't help wondering whether he had denied the Holy Ghost without knowing he was doing it.

The next day Tull returned with the county sheriff, Orville Roberts, who asked Reeves to accompany them to the scene of the murder. Tull rode in lead, the sheriff just behind, and Reeves at the rear. Listening to the sheriff talk about local politics helped Reeves keep a grip on his emotions.

At the site of the murder, the sheriff paced off the distance between the pools of dried blood and the corral fence, recording it in a notebook he pulled from his shirt pocket. "That's where he fell when he was shot," the sheriff said, pointing to the first pool of blood. "Then he crawled over to the wagon to prop himself up. Lots of stamina, old Riel. Hard to kill."

Next they traced Galt's tracks to a trampled campsite in a grove of junipers about a half mile from the ranch. "Looks like he staked Riel out for a couple of days," the sheriff said. "He wanted to kill him pretty bad." Reeves felt a rush of anger. Anger felt good. He saw he wasn't free just yet to quail and cower. He had to keep himself pulled together, had to do whatever was required to see Galt get his just deserts.

Early the next morning, Tull left on an overnight trip to Randolph, Utah, where his mother had made her domicile despite its considerable distance from the Kirby ranches. Tull hoped to persuade Hortense to return with him to the Elkhorn ranch, where she would occupy Reeves's bedroom. Reeves, for his part, agreed to sleep in a bunk in the tack room of the barn.

Soon after Tull left for Randolph, Reeves decided to ride upriver to the Blanchard ranch to let Homer know why he was taking a week off from bronco breaking. As he saddled his horse, his mother asked him to pass through Evanston on his return to buy maple sugar and baking powder at Rinsler's mercantile. "I have in mind some special desserts for your grandmother Kirby," she explained.

That's how it happened that on his return Reeves tethered his horse at the livery barn in Evanston and crossed the street to the mercantile. He couldn't find the baking section right away. He entered an aisle featuring dry goods—denim jeans, jackets, bolts of brightly colored cloth. A girl stood at the end of this aisle, fingering some material. Approaching her, he saw it was Jennie O'Brien. She wore a drab skirt, and her hair was wound into an untidy bun upon her head.

Reeves halted, and they stood immobile and wordless before each other, as if their sudden encounter required a carefully considered response.

"You never came back," she said at last.

He took her statement as an accusation. "My grandfather has been killed," he blurted, as if his recent devastation justified the dereliction of a hitherto unrecognized duty toward her.

"What happened?"

"It wasn't an accident," Reeves said. "Someone shot him. I watched him die. Then I tied him on a horse and ..." His voice broke. He was wishing he hadn't told her.

"I'm sorry," she said, "really sorry." There were tears in her eyes.

She laid a hand on his arm. He looked at it. She had no right to touch him. He had no right to let her.

"I've had a bad turn, too," she said. "I've caved in. I've said yes to Flossie. I'm going to start working upstairs." Her hand gripped his arm more tightly, and her eyes peered into his. "You probably think I shouldn't. But what else can I do? She'll turn me out onto the town. I've got nowhere else to go."

Her face remained impassive, but her grip on his arm became fierce—it was if she were clinging to a branch to keep from falling into a river.

"It's too bad you are a Mormon," she said. "I would let you be the first one. For free."

Anxiety rippled through him, followed by confusion. Grief was giving way to something else. She lusted on him and he knew it. Furthermore, he lusted on her. An animal inside him had come awake, had gone on the prowl, alert to a clandestine opportunity. His bad side had taken charge just now—a fact she must have sensed through some slight motion or inclination of his body that Reeves took no account of.

"We could cross the street," she said, "and go around behind the livery barn. There's a back door to a hayloft. Some of the ladies use it when they want to work on their own—when they don't want Flossie taking her cut."

She turned and walked from the store, Reeves close behind her. In a split second, he had made an irrevocable, cataclysmic, life-changing decision. A quarter of an hour later, he emerged from behind the livery barn alone. He returned to the mercantile and bought the maple sugar and baking powder. Retracing his steps, he tucked the goods into his saddle bags. Mounting, he urged his horse into a trot. Passing the corner of the barn, he saw Jennie, looking forlorn. He noted a wisp of hay clinging to her tousled hair.

For a while, he felt numb and un-centered. Once again, things didn't seem real. The world had taken on a different color. The mid-day sun blazed, yet its light seemed filtered as if by smoke from a prairie fire. After a while, his ideas coalesced, bringing him around to his desperate situation. He couldn't understand what had come over him, couldn't believe he had succumbed so easily. He recognized he had hitherto known next to nothing of sin, neither of its enticements nor of its consequences. Stroking his stack in the barn was penny ante sin. In contrast, to pay for the dubious privilege of deflowering Jennie O'Brien, he had written an IOU pledging his salvation as a forfeit. How did a fellow repent of a sin like that? What currency would satisfy the debt?

Tull didn't arrive back with Hortense until near noon of the next day. She descended from the buggy with her head held high. Her abundant grey hair was bunched about her head and her cheeks were deeply seamed. "Was it you, then," she said to Reeves, "who found my poor, beloved Riel shot in the back and dying?" She pulled Reeves to her bosom and wept.

After supper that evening, Tull and Hortense prepared a brief obituary of Riel for the Evanston newspaper. When Tull proposed one for the Tooele newspaper, she objected. "Riel was not dealt with justly in Tooele," she said. "I wash my hands of the people there. Knowing of Riel's service as a Union officer, stake authorities called him on a mission to halt rustling in the Grouse Creek country. But these self-same beneficiaries turned on him for hanging the thieves—as if there were some other way of stopping cattle theft in a lawless region. And the disfavor of the authorities allowed the spirit of persecution against him to flourish in Tooele. Those we took to be our best friends turned against him, and we were forced to sell our ranch and our beautiful house and come to this godforsaken country."

The next day, Tull accompanied Reeves to the inquest in the Uinta County courthouse, which was overflowing with participants and curious onlookers. The inquest board, composed of the coroner and two upright citizens, occupied the elevated judge's bench. At another table, somewhat to the side, sat Reeves and Sheriff Roberts as witnesses. At a table immediately in front of the judge's bench sat Thomas Galt and an attorney, Galt having been subpoenaed on basis of the sheriff's report. Tall and broad-shouldered, Galt was dressed in a handsome western suit. His expressionless face was accented by a thin, pencil-line mustache.

Pounding a gavel, the coroner called the meeting to order. "We are assembled here to inquire into the death of Riel Kirby, rancher, found within the precincts of this county by his grandson Reeves Kirby alive but dying from a gunshot wound on Monday, September 4, in the year of our Lord 1899."

The coroner first asked Reeves to testify. For a few moments, Reeves was paralyzed by stage-fright. Then, in a subdued voice he recounted the sequence of events from his arrival at the Narrows ranch to his departure scarcely an hour later. He ended by repeating the words his grandfather had attributed to Tom Galt. "The man who shot him said, 'You've had this coming for a long time, Riel Kirby.' Grandpa said he knew the voice." Reeves paused for a moment. Eyes downcast, he continued, dropping his voice to little above a whisper. "He said it was Tom Galt."

The coroner next called on the sheriff, who ended his report by saying circumstantial evidence pointed toward Tom Galt as the perpetrator. Following that, the coroner called Tom Galt into the witness box. "We have subpoenaed you, Mr. Galt, to appear before this inquest because of the testimony of young Mr. Kirby. Are you able to provide evidence exonerating yourself in this matter?"

"Yes, sir."

Galt's attorney stepped forward at this point, asking permission to speak. The coroner nodded approval. "My client," the attorney said, "is employed as the chief security officer at the Buckingham, a resort offering the citizens of Evanston entertainment of the highest order. On the day of Riel Kirby's demise, Mr. Galt was on duty at this establishment and likewise during the preceding night, as his employer, Miss Flossie Kabane, and a number of other employees stand ready to testify. Miss Kabane, I will add, is among the spectators in this room and stands ready to so testify if the inquest board desires."

He turned and pointed to a woman sitting on the first row of spectator seats, only a few feet from Reeves. She wore a dress made of velveteen, having a high collar and long sleeves. Her lips and cheeks were rouged, her lashes were long and dark, and beneath those lashes, her eyes were restless and wary.

"Miss Kabane, you've heard what Mr. Geary has said regarding Mr. Galt's whereabouts on the day of Riel Kirby's assassination," the coroner said. "Are you able to verify that he was on duty at your establishment not only throughout that day but during the previous night as well?"

"Certainly," she said.

"Well, then, I don't see any need to prolong this hearing," the coroner said, turning to his two associates on the bench. These two nodded their agreement. "Sorry to go against your opinion, Orville," the coroner said to the sheriff, "but this board of inquiry finds that Riel Kirby died from gunshot wounds inflicted by an unknown assailant. Thomas H. Galt, hitherto suspected as the assassin, is hereby declared cleared and exonerated. The board extends its condolences to the family of Riel Kirby." And with that, the coroner struck the desk before him with a gavel and declared the inquest adjourned.

Outside the courthouse was a busy scene—clusters of people talking, riders mounting, buggies pulling out of the hitching area onto the street. Reeves reached the Kirby buggy ahead of Tull. While he watched, Galt and Kabane got into a buggy, which Galt, who handled the reins, guided onto the street. Galt turned the buggy about and brought it to a halt within a few feet of Reeves.

"You have run up a bill for entertainment provided by one of Miss Kabane's employees, Jennie O'Brien. You owe Miss Kabane $200 for that session. That's the going price on virgins. Miss Kabane is willing to extend your credit till next Friday. On that day she expects you to deposit $200 in gold coin with the cashier's office in the Buckingham. If you don't make it, what happened to Riel Kirby is going to happen to you." He looked at Flossie Kabane, and when she nodded, he added, "It appears Jennie has got balky on the idea of working upstairs with the ladies. If she don't change her mind, we may be asking you to make up the deficit on that score, too."

The next day, Saturday, a funeral was held for Riel in the Almy Ward chapel—with burial in the Almy cemetery. At the viewing preceding the funeral, the Kirby family stood beside the coffin while members from the Almy Ward filed by to pay their respects, most of them unknown to Reeves. Riel's face struck Reeves as unnatural. It was peaceful enough, but shrunk and eerily pale.

To his surprise, Homer Blanchard and his wife filed by. "I had dealings with him," Homer said. "If he agreed to sell me horses, I didn't need a contract. I knew he'd deliver." As he passed on by, he said, "I'm counting on you showing up Monday, Reeves. I'm needing you to get on with them broncs."

"Yes, sir, I'll be there," Reeves said.

But he wasn't sure he would be. He'd have $100 coming when he finished breaking the broncs. That was good money for a ranch hand for half a summer's work—about a quarter of his father's former nine-month salary as a schoolteacher. But he wouldn't finish the job for a couple of weeks. Then there was the problem of borrowing another $100, and, along with that, the problem of talking Jennie O'Brien into going to work as a whore. All of which gave him reason to consider skipping the country, disappearing down in Arizona or maybe up in Idaho.

The funeral wasn't long. Tull read a sketch of Riel's life, composed the evening before by Hortense. The sketch made him out to be a man without flaws. Following that, the bishop of Almy Ward preached a sermon on the resurrection, in which he assured his listeners that at the dawn of that glorious event, the kin of the deceased, here assembled, would be reunited with him. Reeves could see the bishop didn't know much about Riel Kirby, who, by his own account, had been a wicked man, at best, destined to pass eternity in the Telestial Kingdom—unlikely, therefore, to be greeting any of his righteous relatives at the moment of the resurrection.

This thought reminded Reeves that at present he himself was unforgiven of a sin meriting consignment to that lower realm. Wouldn't it be the damnedest thing if he got shot by Tom Galt and ended up in the Telestial Kingdom shortly after his grandfather? Could they talk to each other from time to time? Or would it be solitary confinement, worlds without end?

Come Monday, Reeves went back to work, being unable to make up his mind about leaving the country. He skirted Evanston widely on his ride home on the next Saturday night, hoping Tom Galt wouldn't anticipate his ruse. He accompanied his parents to church, knowing Galt's deadline had passed and therefore half expecting to be shot.

He finished working with the broncs on Thursday of the following week. That evening, Homer gave him a draft for $120 drawn on the Stockmen's Bank in Evanston—$20 more than Reeves expected. "For good, timely work," Homer explained. He went on then to advise Reeves to cash the draft at the bank it was drawn upon. An out-of-town bank, he explained, would likely discount it 10 or 15 percent.

Homer's draft put Reeves in a quandary. On the one hand, he didn't like taking a 10 or 15 percent discount on his summer wages. On the other hand, he was afraid—no, terrified—of running into Tom Galt in Evanston. Good sense dictated that he take the draft, ride home to the Elkhorn by an entirely different route, say goodbye to his parents, and continue riding on to some distant place before cashing his draft. Eventually, beset by greed, he failed to listen to good sense and stayed another night in the bunkhouse with the three buckeroos. By morning, he had worked out a plan for cashing the draft at the Stockmen's Bank before he rode on down to the Elkhorn ranch. It wasn't an unlikely plan—except that, as Reeves learned later, Tom Galt had persuaded, through friendship and threat, a number of persons to inform him if Reeves Kirby should show up in town. These persons included an employee at the livery barn where Reeves tethered his horse a little before noon that fateful day.

Scarcely a half-hour later, in a stunning reversal of the usual dynamics of a confrontation between an armed and an unarmed opponent, Tom Galt lay dead in a growing pool of his own blood with an utterly dumbfounded Reeves Kirby standing nearby with a smoking revolver in his hand.

The action culminating in this, one of the most storied gunfights in Evanston's bloody history, devolved in a two block area just west of the railway station, which stood at the head of Tenth Street. The Buckingham sat on this street as did—a couple of blocks down— the Stockmen's Bank. The livery barn, where Reeves tethered his horse, stood on the next street to the south. Reeves walked a roundabout way, returning to Tenth Street well below the bank. After exchanging Homer's draft for greenbacks, he left the bank and retraced his steps. Approaching the livery barn, his limbs froze. Crossing the intersection ahead of him was Tom Galt, preoccupied with loading cartridges from his gun belt into the open cylinder of a revolver. Reeves wheeled about and retreated, hoping Galt would not look down the street and spot him, yet expecting at every moment to be shot in the back. Frantic, he returned to Tenth Street and headed toward the train station, supposing he might hide in some nook or corner there. However, as he crossed another inter-section, he saw that Tom Galt had turned about and was scarcely thirty yards away.

Reeves broke into a run toward the station. As he approached the arcade sheltering the main entrance to the Buckingham, he remembered the advice from Andy on the night of his visit to the Buckingham. In case of a police raid, Andy had said, they were instructed to climb out a window into an alley leading to the livery barn—where, as Reeves now assumed, his horse, his means of escape, stood ready. Impulsively, Reeves swung into the arcade and shoved through the swinging doors. He ran down the hall and tried to open the door to the stairs leading to the brothel. It was locked. Looking back, he saw Galt coming through the entrance door. Reeves crossed the hall and pushed through the restaurant door. Waitresses were setting out napkins and silverware. One of them was Jennie O'Brien.

"Tom Galt is going to kill me," Reeves said hoarsely. "How do I get to the alley?"

"This way!" Jennie said, dumping silverware upon the floor with a clatter. She led him through a side door, down a dim, narrow hall, and into a dimly-lit room with a narrow bed on either side of the window. She shut the door and locked it, then went to the window, pulled a curtain aside, and raised the sash. "Climb out," she said, "and go left."

At that instant Galt began to pound on the door and shout, "Open up, by God, open up!" Jennie turned back to one of the beds and pulled a hammerless revolver from beneath the mattress. She thrust it into Reeves's hand just as Galt kicked open the door and burst into the room. Two shots rang out, and, as Galt tumbled to the floor, Reeves realized he had fired one of them. Galt emitted a sighing sound, twitched several times, and was still.

Reeves stared a moment at the hole in the wall where Galt's shot had struck. Then he stared at the hammerless revolver in his hand. He had never seen a revolver without an external hammer before. He threw it on a bed. He looked again at Galt on the floor. Blood flowed from a small round hole in his chest, drenching his handsome coat. Reeves was suddenly aghast. He had killed a man. The commandment said *Thou shalt not kill*. It didn't say *Thou shalt not kill except in self-defense*. He was at fault for not leaving town without trying to cash the draft. He was at fault for having gone into the hayloft with Jennie. He was at fault for signing on with Homer Blanchard in the first place.

Reeves sat on the bed beside the revolver. Jennie seated herself on the opposite bed, her face blank. What was she thinking, this girl whose father and mother and seven siblings had sold her, the Joseph of her family, into Egypt?

Reeves heard people in the hall. He heard a woman's voice. "Oh, my God, Tom's been shot!" Then a man shouted, "Clear out! He's just killed Tom!"

From outside the building came the clanging bells and the galloping hooves of horses drawing a police wagon. Shortly, someone entered the hall, and a man said, "That's Tom, there in the doorway. I think the kid who shot him is still in the room."

"I'll handle this," another man said. Reeves heard more steps in the hall. "Come out with your hands up!" the most recent voice said.

"All right," Reeves said, "I'm coming out."

He stepped into the hall, his hands high. "He came after me with a gun," he said. "I was trying to get away."

The cop locked handcuffs onto Reeves's wrists. A door opened and Flossie Kabane pushed into the hall.

"Where is he?" she cried hysterically. She threw herself onto the body. "Is he dead, is he dead? Say something, Tom, say something!"

She looked up. "Who did it?"

"Him," the cop said.

"Reeves Kirby!" she exclaimed.

"He came after me with a gun in his hand," Reeves repeated.

"Save that for the judge," the cop said and led him away. Flossie threw herself back on the body and resumed her wailing. No sound came from the room where Jennie still sat.

The driver of the police wagon whipped the horses into a near gallop and, with warning bell clanging, transported Reeves to the county building where city as well as county prisoners were jailed.

After Reeves's personal effects—a pocket knife, a handkerchief, his sheaf of greenbacks, a small medallion given him by Mary Beth—were inventoried, he was conducted into a cell already containing three men, all of them vagabonds, judging from the tattered quality of their clothing.

"He just killed a man," the incarcerating officer—a desk sergeant—told these three, who murmured uneasily.

For a while, Reeves sat on a long bench beside his fellow inmates, wanting to believe the shooting hadn't actually happened. But it had happened, and he was presently in a very bad way. He was bound to be tried for murdering Tom Galt, and how was that going to shake out in front of a jury? What could he expect by way of help from Jennie O'Brien? It was all very confusing, all very ominous.

About eight that evening, the prisoners were offered a bowl of cabbage soup and a slice of bread for supper. Having no appetite, Reeves gave his serving to one of the vagabonds. A little later a door opened, and Sheriff Roberts sauntered into the cell block. Gazing through the bars, he said, "Well, Reeves, I never figured on this. I'm told you have killed Tom Galt."

"He came after me with a gun in his hand," Reeves said.

"I didn't know you had took up packing a gun," the sheriff said.

"It was Jennie O'Brien's gun. She's a waitress. I was in her room."

"She gave you the gun?"

"Yes, sir."

"What were you doing in her room?"

Reeves was silent.

"Are you sure she's just a waitress?"

Reeves could see he was cornered. He looked at his fellow prisoners, who listened intently. "I'll tell you the whole story," he said to the sheriff. "But not here."

"All right," the sheriff said. "I'll get the desk sergeant to let me take you into my office."

Shortly the sergeant led Reeves into the sheriff's office. "I wouldn't trust this boy," he said. "He's a desperado. Meaner than he looks."

"Leave the worrying to me," the sheriff said. "I'll bring him back in a half hour."

"He broke into a waitress's bedroom," the sergeant insisted. "Tom Galt caught him in the act."

"I expect there's more to this story than meets the eye," the sheriff said. "I want to hear what the boy has to say."

After the sergeant had left, the sheriff said, "Now, then, set me straight on what happened. How come you were in that room? How come Jennie O'Brien handed you a gun?"

Reeves flushed. He'd almost rather cut off a hand than tell what he and Jennie had done in the hayloft of the livery barn. But it had to be told. Nothing else would make sense if it weren't. So he started by telling about riding into Evanston with Homer's buckeroos and meeting Jennie in the hall of the Buckingham opposite to the stairs leading to the brothel. Then he progressed to the hard part of the story, their meeting in Rinsler's mercantile and their subsequent visit to the hayloft.

He didn't try to soften the sordid story any. He told how Jennie had given in to Flossie Kabane and decided to start working as a

whore, and when she met him in the store, she said if he wanted
to, he could be the first to have her and he could have her for free.
With that he gave in to his lust, plain and simple, which being a
Mormon boy, he had no right to do. What was worse, it had got
him on the bad side of Flossie and Tom Galt, who told him he had
five days to deposit $200 at the payroll office of the Buckingham
for ruining Jennie for some railroad nabob who'd pay that much for
the privilege of being the first to have her, and if he didn't deposit
it, Tom Galt would do to Reeves what he'd done to his grandfather.
Reeves wouldn't have that much money on hand even after Homer
had paid him off. So he figured he would disappear somewhere. But
he had foolishly decided to slip into Evanston to cash Homer's draft
at the Stockmen's Bank, because out-of-town banks would have dis-
counted it 10 or 15 percent. As bad luck would have it, he had run
into Tom Galt, and being in a total, senseless panic and not being
able to think of anything smarter, he dashed inside the Buckingham
because he knew its back windows opened on the alley that ran to
the livery barn where his horse was tied. Jennie took him to her
room but before he could crawl out a window, Tom kicked the door
down, and when he came through, he had a gun in his hand.

At the conclusion of their interview, the sheriff said, "What
counts now is can we get this gal to verify your story. If she will,
you will likely be let out on bail till the matter is cleared up. You
ain't the first boy to pull a girl's skirt up when he had no business
doing it, and she ain't the first girl to let him." That cheered Reeves
up momentarily. But once he was back in his cell, engulfed in darkness and shivering under a thin blanket on a top bunk, he couldn't
keep his mind off the possibility that she would make him out to
be the unwanted intruder in her room that the other employees of
the Buckingham claimed he was. This, of course, led his thoughts
around to the rapidly growing list of sins set down against him
in the Book of Judgment. It seemed as if sinning was the only
thing he was really good at, which led him to wonder if there were
descending degrees of ingloriousness a fellow could sink to in the
Telestial Kingdom. Likely there were, and he had just achieved a
new level of degradation and ignominy by getting himself stashed
away in jail. As for repentance, it seemed likely he had long since

passed the point of no return. There was truly nothing he could do to come clean of the burden of sin he had accumulated. It just kept getting bigger and bigger.

Toward noon the next day, the desk sergeant brought Reeves out of the cell and returned his personal effects. It turned out that Jennie had backed Reeves's story and, there being no other eye witness to contradict it, Reeves was free to go—with the understanding, the desk sergeant emphasized, that Reeves would show up at an inquest, which was scheduled for the following day. He also said the sheriff would like to see him in his office.

The sheriff, leaning back in his creaking desk chair, said, "I've been up all night. I went back to the Buckingham and had a little chat with Jennie O'Brien. Lucky for you, she tells the same story you're telling. That ain't all. She asked me to fetch her away, so I took her home to my wife. Now, what I want to emphasize is Flossie and her bunch may still try to make out you are in the wrong at the inquest. So, like it or not, you're going to have to tell the whole story you told me. Don't try to leave any of it out, or you'll get tripped up."

Reeves sighed and rubbed a hand across his forehead.

"My advice is you ought to just go home and come clean with your folks right now. Then you can relax in the witness box and tell the story like it happened."

Thanking the sheriff, Reeves headed for the livery barn. When the desk-sergeant had first told Reeves he was free to leave, he couldn't believe it. It seemed too good to be true. Well, now he saw it actually was too good to be true. He was out of jail but he wasn't out of trouble, not by a long sight.

How would he go about confessing to his folks? There wasn't a soft way to do it. "Dad, Mom, Grandma," he could hear himself saying, "I have to show up at an inquest tomorrow at eleven because I have had carnal knowledge of a girl in the hayloft of a livery barn up at Evanston and I have killed a man on account of it."

This was pretty much how he blurted it out upon his arrival at the Elkhorn, except that he named the man he had killed. His folks, all three of them, stared for a moment, obviously unable to digest what they had just been told.

"You shouldn't joke about things like that," his father said.

Eyes downcast, Reeves said, "It isn't a joke. I wish it was."

His father scratched the back of his head. His grandmother sat bolt upright in her chair, her face becoming even more pale and drawn than before. "You have killed a man!" his mother burst out.

"Yes, ma'am. He was coming after me with a gun."

"And fornicated with a gentile!"

"Yes, ma'am," Reeves said.

"How could you? How could you?" Eula cried. "What did I ever do to deserve this?"

"You never did anything. I just got weak, I just got tempted."

With that, his mother stalked into her bedroom and shut the door.

On Monday morning, Tull accompanied Reeves to Evanston in the buggy. Once again, the inquest board was composed of the coroner and the same two upright citizens. At the witness table sat Reeves, Jennie, the city policeman who had arrested Reeves, and Sheriff Roberts. At the attorneys' table sat both the county and the city attorneys and Mr. Geary, the attorney for the Buckingham. In the audience, unknown to Reeves, sat a journalist from the East who happened to be passing through Evanston on a western tour. It was he who would create the myth of the fast-draw artist, Kid Kirby.

Pounding a gavel, the coroner called the meeting to order and declared that the board had been assembled to inquire into the death of Thomas H. Galt, security guard at the Buckingham pleasure resort. Mr. Galt had been shot through the heart at the entrance to the bedroom shared by two waitresses, one of whom was at the inquest in the capacity of witness to the shooting. Having examined the body of the deceased, the coroner went on to say, he had found Galt had expired from a bullet from a .38 special revolver, which penetrated his chest and perforated the left ventricle of his heart, resulting in near instant death. The Evanston police arrested Mr. Reeves Kirby on suspicion of illegally entering the bedroom of a waitress and shooting Mr. Galt, who in pursuit of his duty, had accosted Mr. Kirby. Some hours later, the police released Mr. Kirby from custody on basis of testimony of the waitress, Miss Jennie O'Brien, the only eyewitness to the actual shooting, Miss O'Brien's testimony having corroborated Mr. Kirby's claim that he shot Mr. Galt in self-defense. The stated purpose of the present inquest was to not only ascertain whether Miss O'Brien's testimony was accurate, but also, if her testimony was deemed accurate, to re-examine the alibi offered by Thomas Galt and Flossie Kabane at the inquest into the assassination of Riel Kirby.

"Shortly before I called this inquest to order," the coroner declared, "Mr. Geary, counsel and trustee for the Buckingham pleasure resort, informed me that Miss Kabane has withdrawn the assets of the resort from the Stockmen's Bank and, in the company of four of her female employees, has decamped from the city of Evanston for an unstated destination in Nevada, where she will presumably re-establish her entertainment enterprise. Mr. Geary informs me that Miss Kabane has left in his hands the sale of the Buckingham's remaining assets. It would therefore seem a useless endeavor to go further with this inquest, the testimony of both Reeves Kirby and Jennie O'Brien going uncontested. For reasons unknown, Mr. Galt assassinated Riel Kirby and attempted to assassinate his grandson, who defended himself by means of a weapon handed him by Miss O'Brien. This homicide is therefore judged to be justifiable. This inquest is adjourned."

The sheriff and city cop stood and stepped away from the witness table. The sheriff had sat between Reeves and Jennie, who only now could turn and regard each other. Her eyes searched his.

She appeared ready to say something, but she didn't. Maybe she wanted him to thank her. He owed her a lot. He'd be dead if she hadn't handed him the pistol. He'd be in big legal trouble if she hadn't testified in his behalf before the authorities. However, she was the cause of his trouble in the first place, having offered to let him be the first to have her. He was a public shame now, his parents, too. The bishop of Almy Ward would be calling him to account soon, and he'd likely be excommunicated. Moreover, he couldn't pretend to any future with Mary Beth McAllister, no matter what.

"Thank you for everything," he mumbled.

She seemed not to hear. "My blood hasn't come," she said, her cheeks flushing. There were tears in her eyes.

The sheriff's wife approached, a large, portly woman with a kind, motherly face. On the vertical, she outdid the sheriff by six inches—though sidewise the sheriff held his own, being plenty portly, too. "It's settled, dear," the sheriff's wife said to Jennie. "You're to stay with us till your parents can be located."

Grasping Mrs. Roberts's outstretched hand, Jennie rose. She looked back as she walked away. Reeves saw disappointment on her face. What did she mean by "My blood hasn't come"? Then it came to him with a rush of despair. She was pregnant.

On the ride back to the Elkhorn ranch, he told his father he was ruined. "Everybody knows what I've been up to," he said. "I'm thinking I ought to light out of this country. Maybe I ought to go find a job on a ranch in Idaho or Arizona."

"I hope you won't do that."

"I'm not respectable anymore," Reeves said. "Anybody that is halfway decent will look down on me. They'll cross the street so they won't have to meet me if they see me coming down the sidewalk."

"Why don't you take over the Narrows ranch?" Tull said. "It's out of the way. Nobody goes there unless they want to buy a horse. It would relieve me of a lot of worry if you were down there managing things. Lester will be back shortly, and he can show you the ropes."

"I might do it," Reeves said.

That evening the ward clerk showed up at the Elkhorn to let Reeves know the bishop would like to have a chat with him before church on the following Sunday. Reeves said he'd be there. During the night he considered leaving the country again, but by morning he'd made up his mind to do one better on the bishop and ride over to his house in Almy and get the process of excommunication going immediately.

He found the bishop, a heavily bearded man, in his corral milking a cow.

The bishop said, "You have done some terrible things, Reeves—downright wicked things."

"Yes, sir, that's true."

"I hope you've learned your lesson."

"Yes, sir, I have."

"Are you sure?"

"Yes, sir, I'm sure."

"I have favored cutting you off the church, but President Murdock has counseled otherwise." He was referring to his superior, the president of the Evanston Stake. "President Murdoch wants you to groom yourself up for becoming an elder shortly. He sets a priority on strengthening the Elders Quorum in Almy Ward."

Needless to say, Eula was vastly cheered up by Reeves's report. "An elder!" she said. "Well, that does give me satisfaction."

Reeves didn't feel forgiven. In fact, he *knew* he wasn't forgiven. On top of all his other sins, he had managed to get a girl he didn't love pregnant, and his intention was to disappear, vamoose, shuck out of the country. Sin *did* have a way of compounding itself.

However, in his bunk that night out in the tack room of the barn, he dreamed he saw his grandfather listing in the saddle during that long, grisly ride from the Narrows ranch on the day of his murder. Though he was dead, he could still talk. "What are you going to do to make it up to that girl?" he said to Reeves. He meant Jennie O'Brien. Reeves awoke in a fit of the shakes. He got out of bed and lit a candle. He sat on the side of the bed in his underwear, thinking about being married to Jennie.

He had no idea whether she would wake up mornings cheerful or foul, whether she'd have anything to talk about at the table, whether she'd want to keep house or make a garden or help out in the barnyard. Also, being an Episcopalian, she would likely to take umbrage at a husband who, even if he couldn't get squared up with God, figured God favored Mormons over all other kinds of believers. Also, his mother would object to his marrying an outsider for any reason whatsoever.

After a while, he blew out the candle and crawled into bed. He remembered then the night he had first talked with Jennie while he waited for the buckeroos to finish with their ladies. She had supposed aloud that somebody like him would never come calling on a girl like her, which implied a wish that he *would* come calling. What Jennie wanted, he could see, was for some decent-looking fellow to marry her, and as things had fallen out, Reeves happened to be the handiest candidate. He admitted he still lusted on Jennie, but lust wasn't love, and it seemed like being married to her would just be one more sin piled on top of all the others he was guilty of. Nonetheless, there was nothing to do but ride into Evanston and call on her at the sheriff's house.

Arriving in town, he asked the way to the sheriff's house. He tied his horse to the picket fence surrounding the house, went through the gate, and knocked on the door. The sheriff's wife answered.

"Mrs. Roberts," Reeves said, "I'd like to come calling on Jennie O'Brien, if I may."

She stared speechlessly for a long moment.

"I mean, if it's all right with her," Reeves added.

Just then, Jennie crowded into the doorway beside the sheriff's wife. "It's you," she said.

"Yes, it's me."

"I don't feel at liberty to say yes or no in this matter," the sheriff's wife said. "You'll have to ask Mr. Roberts' permission. He's at his office just now."

An hour later, a lengthy deliberation was in progress in the Roberts's parlor, the sheriff and his wife seated in easy chairs facing Reeves and Jennie and these two seated on opposite ends of a sofa. The sheriff and his wife both had round, cherubic faces, the sheriff's face sporting a bushy mustache. Their bulk loomed in the small parlor.

The sheriff seemed embarrassed. "Do I understand you have courtship in mind, Reeves?"

"Yes, sir."

"And Jennie, is this acceptable to you."

"Oh, yes."

The sheriff looked at his wife. "It might be a good idea—considering everything that has gone on, that is."

"I'm not so sure," Mrs. Roberts said. "To call a spade a spade, I'll just say it: Jennie will regret tying in with the Mormons. They are a strange bunch."

The sheriff coughed. "Well, yes—and another matter is are you ready to start making a living, Reeves?"

Reeves could see he needed to invent a livelihood in a hurry. He said he was going to take over the operation of the Narrows ranch. Drawing on things he'd heard his father say about it, he said he meant to expand the horse herd there by recovering a bunch of his grandfather's branded horses running wild, and also by helping himself to some unbranded stock out on the public domain. He figured on shipping a carload down to the Ogden auction every spring and fall.

"The house down at that ranch ain't no palace," the sheriff said, turning to Jennie. "It's more or less a shack—an outer room with a stove and table in it and a bedroom with a tiny closet. Water comes out of the river. Better count on cooking and washing the dishes, not just for you and Reeves, but for that Ute fellow too."

"That's all right," Jennie said. "That's what a woman is supposed to do. That's what I want to do."

Nothing was said about Jennie's pregnancy during this discussion. Moreover, as he rode back toward the Elkhorn, Reeves had no intention of saying anything about it to his folks. They'd find out about it soon enough. For the moment, all they needed to know was that he planned to marry Jennie. On that score, he knew he had to be assertive, knew he had to not sound like he was asking permission to marry her. But by the time he got to the Elkhorn, he had lost his valor and made no mention of Jennie. Furthermore, he was wishing he had acted on his notion of disappearing in Arizona or Idaho.

Nonetheless, he rode back to Evanston the next day, as promised, leaving his folks puzzled as to his destination. Mrs. Roberts greeted him at the door and left the two of them, Reeves and Jennie, alone in the parlor, seated on opposite ends of the sofa. Jennie was silent and downcast, quite the opposite of her demeanor on the previous day. "I was mistaken," she finally said. "You don't have to marry me."

He chewed on that for a while, uncertain of her meaning. Then it came to him. Her bleeding had started overnight. He was free. For a moment, his feelings surged. Then—as he viewed the tears rolling down her cheeks—his feelings dropped. He couldn't walk out on her. He had to consider himself engaged. He told her so, and when Mrs. Roberts returned to the parlor, she found them seated closely together in the middle of the sofa. Just like that, by a transaction that had lasted no more than thirty seconds, Reeves Kirby and Jennie O'Brien were bound into a union destined to last for half a century.

Reeves announced his intention at the Elkhorn that night. "This girl I did wrong with, Jennie O'Brien," he said, "her and me, we're going to get married. I want to bring her over tomorrow and have you meet her."

"You can't be serious!" his mother said.

"I am serious," he asserted.

"A gentile girl! My son marrying a gentile girl!" Eula said, bursting into tears.

"Is this definitely the direction the wind is blowing?" Tull said. "Is your mind truly made up?"

"Yes, sir, it is."

"Do you think she'll want to accompany you to the Narrows?"

"Yes, sir, she says she will."

Eula was weeping into a handkerchief.

"It's better he marry her, Eula," Tull said. "Just much better."

"I'd rather he was dead," she said.

"Well, he isn't, so we've just got to make the best of it."

"Please, dear," Hortense said, placing a hand on Eula's arm, "shouldn't we make her welcome?"

Eula stared morosely off into a corner of the room. "All right," she said in a weak, despondent voice, "bring her home to meet us."

A final obstacle to be overcome had to do with the construction of Jennie's wedding dress. When Reeves asked his mother to undertake the task—Mrs. Roberts having no skill in that business—she objected to the white, satiny material Jennie had chosen.

"It just won't do," Eula declared. "White stands for the purity of the bride."

What she said was true. Jennie had no claim on virginity. But after he had left the house and had a few minutes to think things over, Reeves decided to be firm. He went back into the house and said, "I'd like you to make it anyway. Jennie has her heart set on it."

Eula was startled. She looked at Hortense, who sat in an easy chair darning socks. "Should I do it?" Eula asked. Hortense put the darning into her lap and glanced back and forth between Reeves and his mother. "What would it hurt?" she said.

"All right," Eula said to Reeves, "bring her back so I can take her measurements."

At Eula's behest, Reeves asked the bishop of Almy Ward to perform the ceremony, which was conducted in the home of Sheriff and Mrs. Roberts. The bishop made no issue of the irregularity of this wedding. In attendance were not only the Kirbys and the sheriff and his wife but also Homer Blanchard, his wife, and the three buckeroos. The latter three were slicked up in their fanciest shirts and newest jeans. "Got to hand it to you, Reeves," Andy said admiringly at a private moment. "You had us plumb fooled. Never had no idea you was getting into Jennie O'Brien's britches."

Watching Jennie, luminous with joy, Reeves felt puzzled. He granted he might be mistaken, but it seemed he had come up a rung or two on the ladder toward glory.

Within days of their wedding, Reeves and Jennie made the Narrows ranch their domicile. Eventually, they became the parents of two daughters and three sons. When their first child reached the age of eight, her grandmother, Eula, persuaded her to be baptized a Mormon. As it happened, Jennie surprised her husband and in-laws by asking to be baptized. By that time, Reeves was known as the provider of superior roping and cutting horses. With Tull's help, he enlarged and modernized the house at the Narrows ranch. It is to be noted that Tull's cattle enterprise at the Elkhorn prospered enough for Tull to build Eula a substantial two-story house—which included a bedroom and small parlor for Hortense.

Little remains to be narrated here other than Reeves's acquisition of the sobriquet of Kid Kirby. Although Reeves and Jennie at first lived in some isolation, they soon discovered that a small book written by the eastern newspaper correspondent in attendance at the second inquest had placed Reeves at the center of a heroic legend. Titled *The Saga of Kid Kirby; or, The Wild West Lives among the Mormons!*, this book characterized Reeves as a fast-draw artist who had heroically avenged the assassination of his grandfather. With a surprising frequency throughout the remainder of their lives, Reeves and Jennie were annoyed by tourists and novelty seekers who made their way to the Narrows ranch to take a look at a Mormon Billy the Kid.

The Shyster

Arne met Leanne Holburn at church during his final year in an MBA program at the University of Washington. He found her very attractive. Of medium height, she had sculpted cheeks, an aquiline nose, and bright, intelligent eyes. Arne was tall and had a thatch of sandy hair and placid blue eyes, and by moments he supposed they might make a pair. He altered that supposition abruptly one evening when they were assigned cleanup duty following a Sunday School party. During the conversation that accompanied their work, Leanne let him know that she intended to go by her maiden name after marriage. "It's a lot of work to change your name on all the public records," she said. "Even worse, it's demeaning to take on a man's surname. It messes with a woman's identity. It demotes her. It makes her a junior partner."

She paused to place a serving tray into a cupboard. "If I am asked to pray in public," she went on, "I address my prayer to Heavenly Father. But I don't understand why I have to. I think it's wrong to leave Heavenly Mother out of our prayers. I address my private prayers to her, and if I ever have any daughters, I will teach them to do the same."

She was a feminist and proud of it. He might have guessed that from the fact that she was in her final year in law school. He respected feminists at a distance, but their battle wasn't his, and he certainly couldn't see marrying one. Having been raised in a proper Latter-day Saint home and having served a mission, he had firmly in mind a wife like his mother, maybe more culturally aware and more attuned to urban life than his mother but, like her, fully in accord with the authorities of ward, stake, and church.

A couple of weeks later, Arne saw Leanne at a study table in the main university library. Impulsively, he took a seat beside her. She looked up and broke into a broad smile, and they exchanged a few words. Law students typically studied in the law library. Maybe she had switched to the main library on the chance of running into him. The thought pleased him—but seconds later, as he left the library, he became worried. He recognized that his attraction to her was stronger than he had believed. It required conscious restraint on his part—deliberate choices aimed at avoiding her at church and on campus.

This proved hard to do. Following sacrament meeting the next Sunday afternoon, Arne saw Leanne as he prepared to leave the church parking lot. She gave him a cheerful wave, and he rolled down a window and offered her a ride. It seemed barbaric not to. As she got out of the car at her apartment building, she said, "Do you want to do pizza and a cheap movie Saturday night? Dutch, of course." What could he say but yes? He couldn't fault her for asking. Being forthright, taking the lead, went with feminism. But he assured himself this Saturday night date would be absolutely the first and the last. If he had to, he'd stop attending church for a while.

Things didn't turn out as planned. After the movie he parked the car in front of her apartment building, and they walked to the entrance to the building, where he figured on saying good-night. However, she invited him in for cookies and milk. It would have been rude to refuse. The cookies tasted good. She said her roommate had baked them. Being a law student, Leanne didn't cook much. After they had finished the snack, he said he guessed he'd better get going. She followed him out of the apartment to the front door of the building. As he turned to say goodbye, she stepped close and kissed him. The unexpected kiss anchored to something inside him.

At the car, he looked back. She was still in the doorway. "It was nice," she called. She was thanking him, although it was he who should be thanking her. It was she who had suggested the Dutch evening out and who had just provided the nightcap of cookies and milk. She radiated signs that she liked being with him. With that thought, his reserves crumbled and he accepted that he was in love with her. What did being in love consist of? It consisted of being addicted to the presence of the loved one. Arne wanted to live with Leanne. He wanted to kiss her goodbye in the morning and come home to her at night. He wanted this despite her fixed views on going by her maiden name and addressing her prayers to Mother in Heaven. He could regard those as foibles, and love demanded tolerance for one another's foibles.

From then on, they dated steadily, usually taking in an inexpensive event on the university campus on Saturday night and, like a married couple, always sitting together in sacrament meeting and gospel doctrine class on Sunday. A couple of months before their graduation, Arne asked her to marry him, and she accepted with a simple yes, not requiring, as Arne noted, express confirmation that he accepted her prerequisites. That went without saying.

After Arne got to his apartment on the evening he proposed to Leanne, he steeled himself and phoned his parents back home on a wheat farm in eastern Washington. His mother murmured a sad disapproval when he told them Leanne intended to go by her maiden name. His father said, "Well, it's easy to see who'll have the upper hand in your house." It hadn't occurred to Arne that he needed to worry about having the upper hand. Leanne didn't strike him as wanting to boss anybody. She just didn't want to be bossed.

"I'm going to remind you of something, Arne," his father went on. "You hold the priesthood. A priesthood holder is supposed to be in charge in his household. There isn't any ands, ifs, and buts about it. It's the way the Lord set things up."

Arne proceeded then to let them know she intended to be a lawyer. After a long silence, his father said, "Are you sure you want to marry this woman?"

"Yes, sir, I am." He hoped he sounded confident.

"You know what I think about lawyers."

"Yes, sir, I do."

"I don't say all lawyers are shysters, but most of them are. They're deceitful and on the take."

"She won't be that kind," Arne said. Nonetheless, for a moment he regretted having become engaged.

Arne graduated from the MBA program and Leanne from law school at the June commencement. A week later they were married in the Seattle Temple, located in the nearby suburb of Bellevue. With them were both sets of parents, one of Leanne's sisters, who served as her bridesmaid, and a friend of Arne's from their Seattle ward, who served as his best man. Following the ceremony, there was a photo shoot in front of the temple. They were standing in the flower garden in front of the imposing white structure, whose single steeple featured a golden Moroni blowing his trumpet toward the late afternoon sun. While the photographer was taking a picture of Leanne and her bridesmaid sister, Arne felt a touch on his elbow and, turning, saw his mother-in-law.

"I hope she's given up on that notion of going by her maiden name," she said, with a nod toward Leanne.

"No, ma'am, she hasn't."

His mother-in-law shook her head dismally. "I don't know where it came from. It struck her about the time she started attending Mutual. I want you to know she didn't get it from me."

"It's okay," Arne said. "It's just the way she is."

"I'm just grateful a good, upright Mormon man would have her," she finished, giving his elbow a squeeze as she turned away.

Arne was left with the enigma. How could Leanne have derived from a mother like that? Her feminism defied her genetic line, it defied the culture she was born into.

As the wedding group melted toward the parking lot after the photo session, Arne found himself walking beside his father. Arne's father was a short, solid man with sun-tanned cheeks and a pale upper forehead where his hat shaded him from the Palouse sun.

"Well, you've tied the knot," he said to Arne. "I hope you make each other happy."

Arne knew his father meant to be kind to Leanne, and he was grateful for it. Nonetheless, he knew his father hadn't changed his view on who ought to have the upper hand in their household. Ironically, he and Leanne had to deal with the issue of someone having the upper hand within several hours of the foregoing conversation. As they sat on the edge of their nuptial bed, still dressed in the clothes they had worn to the wedding supper, Leanne mentioned some wording in the temple ceremony that instructed a wife to obey her husband's counsel as he obeyed the counsel of the Lord.

"I guess that means you are in charge," she said. There was an edge in her voice.

"I don't know what it means," he said, "but I'm not in charge."

Neither of them said more about it, but Arne couldn't stop worrying. A married woman had to approach the Lord through her husband—is that what came of a woman being married in the temple? That didn't seem just. But undoubtedly it was acceptable to Leanne's mother and his mother, too—to say nothing of their fathers. One thing was for sure: it wasn't going to work in his marriage.

Arne and Leanne went on a three-day honeymoon in Victoria, Canada. Predictably, the aforementioned issue festered in Arne's mind, and by the time they returned to take up residence in a small apartment in the Fremont district of Seattle, he had devised a helpful procedure. As they sat to their first meal in the apartment, Arne laid a quarter on the table. "You flip and if it's heads, I say the blessing. If it's tails, you say it. And after that we take turns."

Leanne said, "Okay," and when it came up tails, she said the blessing.

Before their evening meal that evening, Arne proposed they determine who would offer family prayer by again flipping a coin. "Don't bother," Leanne said. "You do it tonight. I'll do it tomorrow."

Arne was relieved and a little proud of himself for so deftly disproving his father's predictions of discord—though, of course, Arne had to accept his wife's addressing her blessings and prayers to Heavenly Mother. Given that he did accept it, they settled down to a busy but happy first summer as a married couple, Arne taking a bus downtown to work at an exporting firm and Leanne catching another bus to the university to cram for the Washington state bar exam.

As things turned out, Arne did a lot of the cooking and cleaning, though Leanne pitched in and helped on weekends. When it came to making decisions, either of them was as likely as the other to take the initiative. Arne could see that they were operating their marriage like a New England town meeting without a mayor to convene it and establish its agenda. One of them would say, "What do you think? Should we do such and so?" or "Hadn't we better do this or that?" making it easy for the other one either to agree or else to object in a polite way. Leanne behaved in this way without apparent forethought. Arne, for his part, granted it was a happy, stress-free way to live, yet from time to time he wondered whether his father was right in believing the truly righteous Mormon household had to operate like a subsidiary of the church, with a priesthood holder distinctly in charge.

*

Leanne passed the bar exam in late July but had no luck in finding a position in Seattle. There was an opening for a researcher in a large legal firm, but she wanted a position that would give her trial experience. When a position for public defender in Hampton, a town down in Pierce County, came open in mid-September, Leanne asked Arne how he would feel if she applied for it. He said he was okay with the idea. Having two salaries, they could buy another car and she could drive back to Seattle on one weekend and he could drive down to Hampton on the next.

On the day of Leanne's interview with the mayor and town council, Arne wrangled a day off from work and drove her to Hampton. Although he didn't say so, Arne had growing doubts about a commuter marriage. They would be apart five days out of seven. Maybe being physically apart would foster being emotionally apart. Given his reservations about Leanne's maverick ways, maybe he'd succumb to getting along without her.

While Leanne was in her interview, Arne went into a convenience store at a truck stop to pay for gasoline and saw a sign that said a general manager was wanted for the truck stop. It was a big place—separate stations for gasoline and diesel fuel, ample parking for semis, a truck repair shop, and a large convenience store with an attached restaurant. Arne saw its implication instantly and applied for the job. It didn't pay much, and neither did Leanne's, for that matter. Together they wouldn't be making much more than he had been bringing home in Seattle. But, at least, they could live together year-around. Also, an old van went with the truck-stop job, which meant they wouldn't have to buy a second car.

Both of them being successful in their applications, they rented a small house in Hampton and, after they had finished the moving process, settled into a routine close to the one they had followed in Seattle. They got up at five and went for a jog, had breakfast, and went to work by seven. Leanne thrived on her heavy load of cases. Arne found managing the truck stop challenging, though in a different way from his former job. He especially got a kick out of relating to the personnel of the truck stop. He learned a lot from the mechanics in the repair shop and early on found the guts to fire one of them, who had been missing a lot of work on account of a drug problem. In the evening, Arne usually got home first and prepared dinner. After their meal, they worked together in the kitchen, Leanne reviewing legal documents at the cleared table while Arne washed the day's accumulation of dishes. He didn't mind cleaning up, and he liked to listen to her elaborate on the documents she was perusing.

On Sunday, of course, they went to church. The Hampton Ward was large, and Leanne and Arne had their membership records transferred there immediately after their move. The members of the ward gave them a warm welcome but, unlike the members of their more liberal Seattle ward, they were obviously troubled that they couldn't say the customary, "Good morning, Brother and Sister Jarvis." Since it didn't seem natural to say, "Good morning, Brother Jarvis and Sister Holburn," they mumbled something like, "Good to see you," or "Hope you're doing well." Arne envied Leanne's indifference to their discomfort. As for himself, he felt to some degree like an oddity in the ward.

*

A couple of months after they had moved to Hampton, Arne became aware that a house just across the road from the truck stop was more than the massage parlor it claimed to be. According to his head cashier in the convenience store, all its employees were young women, and it drew an all-male clientele from nearby cities like Tacoma, Auburn, and Puyallup. The place was inordinately busy around noon on weekdays. A quick massage at lunchtime, it seemed, was just the thing to soothe the nerves of a harried businessman.

Once Arne became aware of this interesting situation, he began to keep a tally of condom sales in the convenience store, which proved more than a person might expect in an ordinary convenience store. Having become sensitized to this fact, Arne began to feel uneasy about selling condoms. There was something unsavory about the promotion of prostitution, which his retail trade in condoms facilitated. It made him an accomplice, as it were, in an evil held by Mormon doctrine to be second only to murder.

He talked this over with Leanne, who failed to take his view of it. She could understand his scruples, but she didn't think he ought to quit selling condoms. That wouldn't stop illicit sex. It would just make more people take a chance on having it without the protection of a condom. If out-of-town businessmen fueled the local economy by buying their condoms in his convenience store, that was all to the better. This struck Arne as a little callous on Leanne's part. However, one evening, a day or two after they had talked the matter over, she admitted that the proximity of a brothel made her uneasy.

She said, "Does it ever cross your mind to have sex with somebody other than me?"

"No," he said. Then he said, "Well, it crosses my mind, but that doesn't mean I'm going to do it."

He was placing dishes in the dishwasher while this conversation went on. She was at the table studying court documents.

"When you need sex," she said to Arne, "please get it from me." It was true her job as public defender had taken its toll on their sex life. They had developed a routine of making love only on Saturday and sometimes on Sunday. He hadn't complained about it. He figured sooner or later her work would become less strenuous and things would go back to the way they had been in Seattle. He was therefore unprepared to hear her say, a little later that night, after they had got into bed and turned out the light, "If you want to tonight, it's okay."

From then on, thanks to the presence of the massage parlor, Arne's side of their sex life improved considerably. Once in a while mid-week, Leanne would be in the mood for being emotionally engaged, but usually it was otherwise, in which case Arne got the business over with in a hurry. No drawn-out foreplay, no romantic utterances, just plain, quick sex so she could relax and go to sleep.

*

After dinner one rainy Friday evening, Arne drove back over to the truck stop to tidy up a quarterly business income tax report. On his way home—it was around ten-thirty—he saw police cars parked with flashing red and blue lights in front of the massage parlor.

"I guess there's been a bust over at the massage parlor," he told Leanne when he got home.

The bust was mentioned in priesthood meeting on the following Sunday. The president of the elders quorum, Jerome Milson, was a member of the Hampton police force. He had been in on the bust and was eager to talk about it. People called him Spud. Arne wasn't sure why. Arne could tell the bust had been a lark for him. He was chewing gum rapidly, and his eyes sparkled with pleasure. There were seven prostitutes, plus the madam—a big haul. "Been working on it for months," Spud said. "A real sting. Better than the ones you see in the TV shows. Worked like a charm."

The next day, the documents that had come in by fax to Leanne's office over the weekend included, as usual, the docket for the present day's court sessions. The docket listed two cases carried over from trials begun during the prior week. It listed a transient charged with both public drunkenness and public lewdness because the arresting officer had seen him pee on a sidewalk. A man from a trailer court was charged with assaulting his wife. As for the ladies from the massage parlor, the madam who ran it had hired a lawyer and posted bail on the night of her arrest. The seven young women who worked for her were still jailed and awaiting arraignment, indicating that they lacked the means to hire a defense attorney. That meant Leanne was obliged to take on their defense.

Arne found out all this at mid-morning when Leanne phoned him at his office at the convenience store and asked him to lend her a hand. Leaving his head cashier in charge, Arne drove to the town hall. When he arrived, Leanne handed him a clipboard and asked him to take notes while she talked to the seven prostitutes, who, by now, were sitting in a row just outside the courtroom. Guarded by a single policeman, they wore orange jail coveralls but weren't handcuffed or chained.

They were an odd assortment. With the exception of a tall, willowy, somewhat older blond named Elsa Holst, they were short and young—girls rather than women. Two of them, Le Hahn and Nguyen Cam, were from Vietnam and spoke broken English. The willowy Elsa appeared to have taken them under her wing. According to her, their given names were Hahn and Cam, it being Vietnamese custom for the family name to come first. Elsa wanted it known their given names had meanings. Hahn meant "good conduct" and Cam meant "orange blossom." Elsa also wanted it known that Hahn and Cam had green cards, the permits that allow aliens to reside and work in the United States.

Another of the girls, Adell Miller, was African-American. There were two Latinas, Flora Gonzales and Luz Trujillo, who spoke fluent but accented English. The seventh, an Anglo girl named Vivian Parker, was obviously embarrassed by her upper incisors, which had grown in crooked, with the result that her lips became wet from saliva when she spoke.

Leanne spoke briefly with each of the prostitutes, glancing at the police report on each as she spoke and relying on Elsa to help her understand Hahn's and Cam's fractured English. Then, addressing them as a group, she said that, although they might already be familiar with the process of arraignment, she was going to go over it with them. She intended to take them before the judge one at a time, and she wanted them to plead not guilty so that she could have some time to study the charges and see if there were mitigating circumstances. She hoped each of them could muster $90 for bail, that being the sum the local bail bonding company was likely to require by way of a fee. In conclusion, she said it was possible she would turn some of them over to other lawyers. "Trying to represent all of you might pose a conflict of interest for a single attorney," she said.

Mid-afternoon, after each had been before the judge and bail had been arranged, Leanne warned them to show up promptly at the pretrial hearing, set for the following Friday, being sure to dress in sober, modest attire such as they might wear to church. Finally, she told them she hadn't had time to decide whether she would represent all of them. She would be letting them know about that on Friday.

Elsa responded to this statement by shaking her head. "We don't want any other lawyers," she said. "We all like you." The others murmured their agreement.

Later Arne asked Leanne how she felt about their faith in her abilities. It was after dinner and they sat on opposite sides of the dining table, she working on a thick sheaf of documents, he tabulating receipts from sales at the truck stop.

"Their confidence in me won't last," she replied. "They were caught red-handed in a misdemeanor. The penalties for a misdemeanor are ninety days in the county jail or a one thousand dollar fine or both. The best any lawyer can do for them will be a plea bargain of some sort." With that, they settled down to a period of silent work, broken a quarter-hour later when she snorted and said, "I can't believe this!" She pulled her cell phone from her briefcase and made a call.

"Is this Spud?" she said into the receiver. Then: "I'm reading the police reports on those women from the massage parlor, and I'd like you to verify something. In two of the rooms you found men in bed with the ladies, but you didn't arrest the men. You let them go. You just arrested the women!"

There was a pause, and then Arne could hear Spud's deep voice resonating from the receiver. Spud went on and on, obviously trying to head Leanne off at the pass somehow. Eventually, she turned off her phone and replaced it in the briefcase.

"I'm plenty steamed," she said to Arne. "They staked that place out for six weeks and saw nobody but men going in and coming out, and when they did their bust, in a couple of rooms they found a man in bed with the girl and they told the man to get dressed and clear out so they could arrest the girl. That does steam me!"

Leanne came to bed that night somewhere in the wee hours, around three o'clock, Arne figured. She tugged at his shoulder till he woke up, then said, "You can't guess what I've discovered. I'm going to get them off, all seven of them." He was too groggy to ask for details, but later he could recall her repeating, "Who would have thought it?" three or four times before he went back to sleep.

When Arne got up, she was already at the table with her laptop, typing furiously. When he took a shower, he saw no sign she had had one. Moreover, when he came out, she didn't offer to help make breakfast, being still busy at her laptop. A little later she paid no attention to the eggs, toast, and milk he set beside her computer before placing his own on the opposite side of the table. "Come take a look at this," she said. "Come and sit by me so you can see this screen."

When he had positioned himself beside her, she read from the screen. "'A person is guilty of prostitution if such person engages or agrees or offers to engage in sexual conduct with another person in return for a fee.'"

"That's the way the state law reads," she said. "But a municipality has the right to pass its own law prohibiting prostitution, which supersedes the state law."

She scrolled down a notch on the screen. "This is how Hampton's law reads. 'A person is guilty of prostitution if such person engages in or agrees to engage in sexual conduct with another person in return for a fee.' Can you see what's missing?"

"Just a couple of words, *or offers.*"

"What that means is it's not against the law to offer to engage in sexual conduct for a fee in Hampton. But that's what the police have charged them with. It's *all* they have charged them with! The town doesn't have a case. The judge will have to dismiss the charges."

Arne was doing some soul searching, and his face showed it. It was wrong, just plain wrong, for her clients to get off with no penalty whatsoever.

He could feel Leanne bristle. "The thing is," she said, in a tone of exaggerated patience, "the police have staked them out for six weeks and watched all kinds of men walk in and out of the place, and even caught two of them in bed with girls on the night of the bust, and they let them go scot-free. As far as I'm concerned, if the men go scot-free, the ladies go scot-free too. Fair's fair, I say."

Arne knew it was time for him to demonstrate family solidarity if he had an interest in preserving his domestic tranquility. "I can see your point," he said. "What's sauce for the goose is sauce for the gander."

Legally, she was in the right. Due process—the strict adherence to the protocol established by law—was one of the most sacrosanct principles of American jurisprudence. As Leanne herself had passionately declared to Arne while she prepared for the bar exam, it was better that a few guilty persons go unpunished than that the public at large be susceptible to false accusations and coerced confessions. But, at best, as Arne could now see, due process dealt in approximate justice, justice for the largest number of persons in a world where, realistically speaking, absolute justice was an impossibility. That didn't keep a person from regretting that impossibility. Leanne seemed all too pleased, all too vindictive, about discovering the gap in Hampton's law forbidding prostitution. Arne knew he still had things to learn about his wife. He hoped they would be good things.

*

On the day of the pre-trial hearing, Leanne again asked Arne to help her by supervising the girls in the hall while she took them one by one before the judge to confirm their acceptance of her procedure. When Arne arrived, the girls were seated in the hall, dressed in blouses of subdued colors and in skirts with hems below the knee. Leanne was explaining that she had gone over the police reports carefully and found no conflict of interest in representing all of them. Going on, she outlined her procedure.

She had decided to expedite matters by filing for a single group trial of all seven of the girls. Also, even though she could present her case for dismissal of the charges at the pre-trial, she would instead ask that the case go forward for trial and enter a plea for judgment with prejudice—"judgment with prejudice" being a legal term indicating that if the charges were dismissed, amended charges could not be re-filed, as they might be if she were to re-quest dismissal at the pre-trial hearing. Finally, she would ask for a bench trial, that is, a trial by a judge without the involvement of a jury, because a zealous prosecutor could play upon the prejudices of the members of a jury, whereas a judge in a bench trial would be likely to stick to the facts of the case. Although the girls were bewildered by the details, they obviously trusted Leanne.

Near the end of her explanation, a couple arrived. "That's her," Leanne said to Arne. "Havana Hild, proprietor of the massage parlor. I don't think that's her real name. That lawyer with her is Douglas Reid from Seattle. He isn't cheap." The woman paused a moment as she came abreast of the girls. The girls shifted uneasily under her gaze. It was as if she held them accountable for the bust. The lawyer touched her elbow and they moved on.

While Leanne accompanied each girl into the courtroom, Arne had time for more soul searching. He wasn't sure what the girls thought of him. He wore a sports shirt and a billed cap featuring the logo of the truck stop. Assuming he and Leanne shared the same surname, they called him Mr. Holburn. He saw no advantage in correcting them.

He glanced down the hall toward Havana Hild from time to time. He wondered how much of the girls' nightly take she had allowed them to keep. He could see no hint of generosity in her frowning face. He wondered whether the girls found any entice-ment in their work beyond the money they were paid. He found it hard to believe their métier satisfied their own sensuous needs. They certainly didn't exude the saucy impudence of prostitutes in certain famous movies. With the exception perhaps of Elsa, they struck him as depressed. He wondered whether they found a vicar-ious gratification in their clients' gratification—a matter of giving good measure for value tendered. Likely not, he decided.

He felt a twinge of guilt for pondering such a topic. However, he returned to it shortly. He wondered how the girls had got into the profession in the first place. Were they shanghaied, like sailors in the era of sailing vessels? Why did they stick with it? Was it because they assumed their moral taint was visible to the naked eye and no decent employer would hire them? Or was it simply a matter of get-ting a job in an economy that offered few opportunities to young, uneducated women? In any event, Arne found himself feeling sorry for them—a sentiment that, upon reflection, disturbed him a little.

At the end of the day, Leanne reminded the girls to show up promptly and again to be respectably dressed for their trial on the following Friday. She also inquired where they had been staying. She was particularly interested in whether they had nearby rela-tives. As it turned out, none did. Having decided to stick together, they had rented two rooms in a motel in Enumclaw, about seven miles up the road from Hampton. Their rooms had no kitchen fa-cilities, and they were buying prepared foods in a supermarket and eating in their rooms. Leanne asked about their finances.

"It's all okay," Elsa said. "Our finances are fine."

Adell shifted uneasily. Vivian frowned. Hahn and Cam looked distressed.

"It looks like your finances aren't okay," Leanne said.

Cam broke into tears, and Vivian's frown turned into a scowl. "Hahn and Cam are free-loading," she said. "They're living off the rest of us."

"It's all okay," Elsa insisted. "We don't mind."

"Is there a reason why they're broke?" Leanne said.

Their distress mounting, the seven fell into a tight-lipped silence.

"Okay, don't tell me," Leanne said. "Have you got any other problems that need to be dealt with?"

"The library won't give us a card," Elsa said. "They won't let us check out books and magazines to take to the motel. They won't let us use the computers."

"Did you try talking to the director?"

"He's the one who said we couldn't have a card. He doesn't like us. His desk is close to the entrance. He frowns when we come in."

Leanne called Arne aside. "Would you take them back to Enumclaw in your van?" she asked. "And maybe go into the library and lean on that director to treat them like human beings."

Arne hesitated. Squiring these young women about struck him as an impropriety. He was, in fact, surprised that Leanne would ask him to.

"Please," she said.

He said nothing, and she laid a hand on his arm. "Pretty please," she said.

He couldn't resist that. He would just have to depend on his propriety outweighing their impropriety in the judgment of anyone they might encounter.

"Thank you," Leanne said.

She left her hand on his arm, restraining him, while they watched the girls file toward the entrance. After a moment, she murmured, "I do love you. You may not think so when I'm all strung up, but I do." It was an odd place to be told that his wife loved him, but he was grateful for it.

Releasing him, Leanne closed her briefcase. "It occurs to me," she said, "that Hahn and Cam haven't any money on hand because Havana Hild has been keeping their entire take to pay off somebody for smuggling them into the country. If that's the case, I don't want to know about it."

Arne pondered this statement as he drove the girls toward Enumclaw. Was Leanne acting the part of a shyster? He felt guilty for entertaining the thought. As he understood the law, defense attorneys had an obligation to report evidence of hitherto unrevealed felonies on the part of their clients—murders, assaults, or other serious threats to persons or property. But a forged green card likely wasn't an offense of that sort. Maybe it was just a matter of Leanne not wanting unnecessary complications.

The girls were pleased with the ride. They had obviously got around to feeling comfortable with Arne. They seemed to regard him as a father figure, a role which upon reflection he decided had both its pros and its cons. As requested, he stopped at the library before he took the girls to their motel. He asked them to wait in the van while he went in.

The director was sitting at his desk. He was a small, balding man who parted his thin hair precisely in the middle. He began to shake his head before Arne had completed his request. "I know who those creatures are," he said. "I know what they do for a living. We don't tolerate that kind of thing in Enumclaw."

"Justly so," Arne agreed. "But they aren't pursuing that line of work anymore. They've been busted. My wife is the public defender in Hampton municipal court. These young women are her clients. She wants to help them reform. She wants to help them figure out a better way to make a living."

The director pursed his lips tightly. The scornful disbelief in his eyes angered Arne. Arne was standing immediately before the desk. Gripping the edges of the desk, he leaned forward and thrust his face close to that of the director. Alarmed, the director rolled his chair back.

Speaking slowly and distinctly, Arne said, "My wife has asked me to drive the girls from the court back to their rooms here in Enumclaw. I'm a businessman—a respectable businessman. I operate the truck stop in Hampton. I regard it as my duty to help these young women straighten up, and I regard it as your duty, too. I want you to extend full library privileges to these young women, all seven of them, and I'm not going to leave until you say you'll do it."

The two men stared into each other's eyes for a long minute. The director flinched first. "All right," he said, "tell them to come in. I'll give them cards."

Returning to the van, Arne was astonished by his tough talk—also disturbed that he really was behaving like a father to the errant girls. There was no guarantee that, with the case dismissed, they wouldn't go right back to prostitution. His suspicion was reinforced when, on the drive between the library and the motel, he discovered that a scheme was afoot. Elsa was proposing that, following their dismissal at the trial, the seven of them start a massage parlor in Prosser, a town in southern Washington where Elsa had a friend who would rent them a small house at a reasonable price. Forming a co-op, they would slip out from under Havana Hild's net and keep their proceeds entirely for themselves.

She didn't say whether she meant for them to stick strictly to massaging. Prosser was a town of maybe 5,000 people. It was on an interstate, about fifty miles southeast of Yakima and thirty-five miles west of the Tri-Cities. Obviously, travelers on the interstate wouldn't be stopping for massages. What frequent travelers like truck drivers might stop for, as word of mouth made its availability known, was the service extraneous to massaging for which the girls currently stood indicted.

Only Luz appeared to favor Elsa's proposal. The other Latina, Flora, said she wanted to go home to the barrio in Pasco and get married. Adell wanted to go back to Seattle because there would be more customers there. Apparently, she had the massage business in mind. Vivian made no comment on Elsa's proposal other than to doubt Havana would let Hahn and Cam go. "They haven't worked off half what they owe her," she said. With that, someone in the back emitted a slight hiss, and a sudden silence fell on the others, as if Vivian had inadvertently mentioned the unmentionable in Arne's hearing.

Arne began to whistle "Rock of Ages," hoping to appear totally blanked out on the conversation he had just overheard. He knew

Leanne would want to know about Elsa's proposal for establishing a co-op massage parlor in Prosser. As for Vivian's confirmation of Hahn's and Cam's illegal status, Leanne had already said she didn't want to know about that.

That evening, Arne was surprised when Leanne shrugged her shoulders over the possibility of the girls returning to their illicit trade. "I hope they don't," she said. "But I can't stop them."

Later, after they had gone to bed and Leanne had gone to sleep, Arne found himself troubled by the degree to which his wife was forced into ethical neutrality by her role as a defense attorney. With a rising distress, he realized that he himself was being forced to set aside his scruples. He liked to think of himself as a representative citizen, the sort of ordinary, everyday, run-of-the-mill person who makes a democracy function. But now he had Hahn and Cam on his hands, and he had strong reason to believe they were illegal immigrants and had forged green cards. If acquitted, they would likely go back to prostitution, and even if they chose to pursue the respectable occupation of masseuse, they would compete directly with poor citizens or the bearers of authentic green cards.

Obviously, the easiest way to forestall either of those eventualities—also, the just way—would be to inform the US Immigration Services of the girls' illegal status. But after threshing restlessly about for a while, Arne realized he wasn't the person to rat out Hahn and Cam. It was the father-figure thing. The girls looked for assistance and protection from him as well as from Leanne. So he'd just have to put up with feeling guilty about aiding and abetting a couple of illegal aliens. Having decided that, he went to sleep.

*

Trial lawyers have a protocol called discovery. Discovery means that by a given deadline—a certain number of days before a trial is scheduled—the prosecution and the defense have the obligation to furnish each other with the complete details of their argument at the trial. In the case of the seven prostitutes, with the trial set for the following Friday, discovery was required by Wednesday. Having worked on her brief over the weekend, Leanne filed her discovery on Tuesday, a day early. That evening, Spud Milson rang the doorbell and asked Arne to step out for a private conversation. Spud was in uniform, complete with badge, pistol, and handcuffs.

"I took a look at that brief on those whores your wife is defending," he said. "She is fixing to turn them loose. Did you know that?"

"Well, yeah, I know she has it in mind."

"And you are okay with that?" he said belligerently. "She's a shyster, that's what she is."

Arne winced at the word shyster. "She's just doing what all defense attorneys do," he said lamely. "They are supposed to do the best they can for their clients."

"We charged them with solicitation," Spud went on in an agitated voice. "We went into the place one at a time in plain clothes and asked for a massage. We went to a lot of trouble to look different from each other. I looked like a Fed Ex driver. As soon as the so-called masseuse asked the one who had gone in if he wanted the premium service for fifty bucks more, he arrested her and then just stayed in the room with her while another one of us came into the place and went into a room with another girl. By the time the fourth one of us had done that, the madam was getting edgy so this fourth guy radioed our uniformed guys to come in and bust the rest of them. Like I say, we charged them with solicitation. Now your wife says Hampton's law doesn't say anything about soliciting sex for a fee, and she means to let all seven of them go. That just won't do, Arne. We caught two of them in bed with clients. We caught them red-handed. And she's going to let them all go. And you tell me you're okay with that!"

Arne sighed and rubbed an eye with the palm of his hand. "I didn't say I was okay with that. I just said defense attorneys are supposed to do the best they can for their clients. That's what they are trained to do."

"If you're not okay with it, then I'll tell you what I think you ought to do. You ought to lean on your wife and tell her to back off."

Arne swung his head back and forth. He was between a rock and a hard place.

"You know the reputation of the church is at stake, don't you?" Spud said loudly. "People in this town know Leanne is a Mormon. They know I'm a Mormon. Come on, Arne. Man up!"

"It wouldn't work," Arne said. "I don't have that kind of influence over Leanne. I'd just mess up my marriage if I tried. She'd accuse me of trying to exercise unrighteous dominion."

"Unrighteous dominion! Boy, has she got you brainwashed."

Arne's stomach was in a roil when he went back into the house. He went to the sink and went on rinsing dishes and placing them in the dishwasher. Leanne was at the table working on the case of the fellow from the trailer court who had given his wife a black eye. The wife had decided not to press charges, which didn't please Leanne. She figured he needed a penalty that would make him hesitate to hit her again.

Arne could feel her eyes on his back. He knew she wanted to know what Spud was after. He couldn't think of a way to let her know that wouldn't make her angry.

"So does he want you to do something in the elders' quorum?" she said.

"He's peeved," Arne said at last. "He went over to the prosecutor's office and took a look at your brief for the massage parlor bunch."

"Peeved?"

Arne rummaged in the dishwasher, repositioning a couple of plates so that he could crowd a third one in.

"Why didn't he come inside and talk to me?" Leanne said in an insistent voice.

"I guess he's afraid of you," Arne said. That idea had just now occurred to him. There was something about Leanne that challenged the average male's instinctive sense of superiority.

"What does he expect you to do for him?"

"He thinks it's wrong to turn the girls loose without any punishment."

"But what does he expect you to do about it?"

Arne said, "Well, I told him I couldn't." With that, Leanne dropped the matter, much to his relief.

When Leanne got home the next evening, she heaved her briefcase onto a chair and disappeared into the bathroom. When she came out, she said, "I'm wondering now just exactly what you told Spud last night," she said. Her voice didn't sound angry, just curious.

Flustered, Arne didn't respond immediately. He had brought

lentil soup from a deli. He was presently chopping a salad. When they sat down to eat, he spoke. "Spud said the whole town knows he's a Mormon and you're a Mormon. He said you getting the girls off without any penalty will do the church damage. He said I should lean on you to change your mind, and I said it wouldn't work, it would just mess up my marriage. I said you'd accuse me of trying to exercise unrighteous dominion."

She eyed him askance. "That's exactly what I'd do. Damn old Spud! He knows very well I can't change the brief. The judge wouldn't allow it at this point. Spud is just trying to punish me for ruining their bust."

For a while she concentrated on her soup. Eventually she said, "Chantal came to see me today."

Arne could smell trouble, Chantal being Spud's wife.

"She also wanted me to change my brief," Leanne said. "I explained why I couldn't. I told her it's out of my hands. Then she said I dishonor womankind. I said I didn't agree. I said the men who pay money for those girls' services are the ones who dishonor womankind. She left in a huff, but just before she did, she said, 'I pity your husband.'"

Leanne ladled more soup into her bowl. "Am I hard to live with?" she asked.

He was flustered again.

"You don't have to answer that question."

He rallied and said, "I knew how living with you would be. I'm okay with it."

She reached across the table and squeezed his hand. "I'm grateful," she said.

As Leanne prepared to leave the house on Friday, the day of the trial, she told Arne that from things she had heard on the previous day, she expected the entire police force would be present at the trial and maybe some townspeople, too, by way of putting pressure on the judge—and on her, too, of course. Arne asked her if she wanted him to come to the trial, which was scheduled for 1 p.m. He said he'd dress up in a suit and tie. She thought a moment and said, yes, she'd appreciate the moral support. Accordingly, he showed up in front of the town hall about a quarter to one. A uniformed woman stood at the courtroom door. Several people sat on the nearby bench. "She won't let you in," one of these said, nodding toward the guard. "The place is packed."

Arne returned to his van and phoned Leanne on her cell phone. "Looks like I can't get in," he said.

"Yeah," she said. "It's a can of sardines in here. Most of the front row is occupied by cops in uniform. A couple of deputy sheriffs are with them. The bailiff let them in, guns and all. The back row is packed with townspeople, also the standing space behind the back row. Somebody has gone all out to let the judge know he might not get re-elected if he doesn't support the police in this matter. I'll let you know how it goes tonight. But I'm not worried. Also, for your information, this morning Havana Hild was acquitted of all charges except keeping the back door locked during business hours—which isn't going to lighten up the mood of the cops any."

Arne went back to the van and put the key into the ignition, thinking he'd go back to the truck stop. He sat a while without turning the key. It was cloudy and raindrops spattered the windshield. He was depressed and wishing Leanne was a nurse or a schoolteacher or, since she was ambitious, a university professor—anything but a lawyer. In any event, he was glad he wasn't inside watching the drama unfold.

That made him even more depressed. He owed Leanne his support. She was his wife, he was her husband.

Glancing at the litter of discarded mail in the footwell of his van, he saw an opened manila clasp envelope from the manufacturer of a line of diesel additives. This sort of envelope, he abruptly realized, might be passed off as containing documents relevant to the current trial. Carrying it, he could likely get inside, where he might be able to worm his way into the standing space behind the rear spectator benches. He wished he hadn't thought of that. Nonetheless, flourishing the large envelope, he returned along the hallway. When he came to the uniformed woman at the courtroom door, he said, "For Ms. Holburn," and the woman opened the door and he went in.

He found himself standing beside an armed policeman. As Leanne had said, the place was packed. He'd have to stand right where he was, alongside the guard.

A railing separated the spectator section from the court proper. The spectator section contained two rows of benches divided by an aisle. Uniformed officers and several respectably dressed citizens occupied the front row. Other respectably dressed citizens occupied the second row. A similar number stood in the space between the benches and the wall. It was clear how the citizenry of Hampton felt about letting the prostitutes go unpunished.

Although no one appeared to be looking at him, Arne felt conspicuous and was within a few seconds of retreat. Then Leanne saw him. She was standing at her desk with a sheaf of papers in her hand. Immediately behind her were the seven defendants, seated in chairs placed along the railing. Leanne pushed through the gate and approached Arne. "Is that for me?" she said, nodding toward the envelope.

He stepped close to her and said in scarcely more than a whisper, "It's a fake—just something to get me past the bailiff. I shouldn't have done it."

"That's okay," she said, taking the envelope.

"I'll clear out of here," he said. "There's absolutely no space anywhere."

"Oh, don't go. Just stay right where you are. It's good to know somebody's got my back." She returned to her desk and, after seating herself, completed Arne's charade by pulling a couple of sheets from the envelope and laying them among her other papers. In the meantime, heads turned among the spectators to regard Arne. Among those spectators was Spud, who, having caught Arne's eye, gave a frowning shake of his head.

Shortly, the judge entered, and the clerk called for all to rise. There was a scraping of chairs and a shuffling of feet, then sudden silence. The judge, duly robed in black, had pouches beneath his eyes and a downward dip at the corner of his lips. He struck Arne as a man who found his present duty to be particularly distasteful.

Having allowed those in attendance to sit, the judge shuffled a few papers and announced that at the request of the defense attorney and her clients, this was to be a bench trial. He paused, then, directing his words to the spectators, said the accused had the right to a bench trial, and as they had requested it, he had no alternative but to grant it. Arne took it that there had been requests from persons among the spectators for a jury trial.

The judge shuffled a few more papers, then looked at the prosecutor and said, "Please proceed, Mr. Hill."

"Thank you, Your Honor," the prosecutor said. Holding a clipboard in his hand, he stepped from behind his table and stood before the judge. A handsome, well-dressed man, he was an associate in an Auburn law firm, contracted to serve as Hampton's municipal attorney and prosecutor.

The prosecutor began, stating that by a clerical error or some other oversight, the recorded ordinance forbidding prostitution within Hampton town limits failed to specify that solicitation was unlawful. Accordingly, the defense would insist that the charge against the accused be dismissed. However, any person of an untrammeled and objective mind could only consider this an egregious miscarriage of justice.

Arne was impressed. This Hill fellow was articulate, and he had a baritone voice somehow suggestive of wisdom and insight.

Sweeping a hand from front to rear of the courtroom, the prosecutor went on to declare that at the court today was the complete embodiment of the rule of law in Hampton. Present were members of the town council, law officers, court officials, and a large delegation of prominent citizens representing a cross section of professions, churches, and service clubs. Other citizens awaited in the entrance hall for the outcome of this trial. The presence of all these officials and citizens constituted a silent plea for justice. Their collective sense of morality held that prostitution was an evil, and their collective sense of equity demanded that this evil be punished. It was their earnest desire that the magistrate of this court make amends for the oversight of the municipal ordinance and find the accused guilty as charged. With a final burst of eloquence, the prosecutor urged the judge to be daring and to break with the expected and find not according to the timorous stance of due process but according to the grand principle of justice.

With the flourish of a hand, the prosecutor sat down, as if exhausted by his short but emotional appeal. As far as Arne was concerned, the prosecutor had hit the nail squarely on the head. It simply wasn't right for the accused—young, unwitting creatures though they might be—to go without some sort of punishment.

The judge sighed and shuffled through several documents absentmindedly. Rousing himself, he said, "Have you anything to add, counsel?"

"No, Your Honor," Mr. Hill said.

Turning his regard toward Leanne, the judge said, "Ms. Holburn, your presentation, please."

Leanne rose and stepped in front of her desk. Though she often wore a dress to court, today she wore a black pantsuit with a white blouse. Arne judged a pantsuit to be more active, more assertive of strength, than a dress.

After consulting a clipboard in her hand, she began by naming each of her clients. "These young women have been charged with solicitation, that is, with offering to engage in sexual conduct for a fee. However, at present it is not a misdemeanor to offer to engage in sexual conduct for a fee in the town of Hampton. The town council, which created the existing law forbidding prostitution, had the option of relying on the law as written by the state of Washington. The law as written by the state of Washington reads: 'A person is guilty of prostitution if such person engages or agrees or offers to engage in sexual conduct with another person in return for a fee.' However, as it had the right to do, the town council chose to create its own law prohibiting prostitution, which supersedes the state law. The law approved by the town council reads: 'A person is guilty of prostitution if such person engages or agrees to engage in sexual conduct with another person in return for a fee.' Notably absent from the law as written by the town council is the word 'offers.' I therefore request that Your Honor dismiss this charge and to do so with prejudice so that an amended charge cannot be filed."

She turned, stepped back to her desk, and exchanged the clipboard for a yellow pad. "The prosecutor," she went on, "has just urged Your Honor to ignore the actual wording of the municipal ordinance against prostitution and to interpret it as if it explicitly forbids solicitation. He has just urged Your Honor to violate due process on the presumption of a collective sense of justice that supersedes written law. I am wondering what difference there might be between such a presumption and vigilante law. I can see none. Hasn't due process come into being precisely because of the cruel inequities of vigilante law?"

Leanne paused to glance at her pad. "I find the prosecutor's plea an affront to Your Honor," she said and promptly sat down.

The judge buried his face in his hands for a moment. When he looked up, Arne saw Leanne had won her case. A man who looked as doleful, as anguished, as downright haunted, as this judge wasn't about to render a judgment favorable to the prosecutor.

"I am cognizant of the many persons who have shown special interest in the present case," the judge said. "Their presence testifies as to the high level of morality in our community. I am cognizant of the integrity and zeal of our municipal police force. I am cognizant of Mr. Hill's stellar service as municipal attorney and prosecutor. All the more reason, then, that I regret to say that Ms. Holburn is correct. According to the law of the town of Hampton, solicitation is not an infraction, and solicitation is what the defendants have been charged with. I have no alternative but to dismiss this case with prejudice. If I failed to do so, my verdict to the contrary would be overturned in the appellate court and I would be sanctioned for rendering a frivolous verdict. Moreover, the defendants' court costs would be charged against the town of Hampton."

The judge directed his gaze toward the defendants. "Young ladies, you are free to go. I recommend that you take advantage of this opportunity to amend your ways."

He redirected his gaze toward the spectator section. "I advise the town council to call an emergency meeting and remedy this faulty law at once."

With that he pounded his gavel, gathered his papers, and left. A buzz of angry conversation now filled the room. Arne glanced at Spud. Grimacing, Spud shook his head—a gesture Arne took to be an accusation of rank betrayal. Spud mouthed, "Damned shyster," silent but unmistakable. Startled, Arne realized Spud was including him in that pejorative term. And with that, he also realized he had made a serious tactical error by attending the trial. As if fleeing, he stepped forward, pushed through the gate, and joined the girls, who stood in a smiling knot around Leanne.

"Wait till the courtroom clears," Leanne said to the girls, "and Arne will drive you back to your rooms." Eventually, the spectator section cleared of all persons except, as Arne now recognized, Douglas Reid, Havana Hild's high-power Seattle lawyer. He waited as the seven girls filed through the gate. As Leanne came through, he said, "Well done, counsel." "Thank you," she said. "Our firm is looking for an associate," he said. "Consider applying." "I will," she said and walked on. Before she allowed the girls to enter the van, Leanne asked about their plans for the future. Five of them hoped to find work as masseuses, Elsa and Luz in Prosser, Flora in Pasco, and Adell and Vivian in Seattle. Hahn and Cam stood apart, on the verge of tears. "Dig out your green cards," Leanne said to the Vietnamese girls, "and maybe Arne will hire you at the truck stop till you can find something better." Leaving Arne speechless, she hugged each of the girls and headed off across the street to her office.

*

Arne ended the afternoon at the truck stop. Arriving home around six, he went on a short jog, hoping it would calm him. It didn't. It seemed, in fact, to merely stir agitating thoughts. Spud said Leanne was a shyster. He said Arne was a shyster, too. Arne had to agree. Being a shyster was built into Leanne's job. She had to adhere to due process. It was her duty to get the girls off. But she seemed to have no regret whatsoever for securing the dismissal of their case. She seemed to sympathize with them as if they were total victims of a sexual crime rather than co-perpetrators of it. Arne admitted that it was wrong for the men who visited the girls to go without punishment, but that didn't justify the exoneration of the girls, nor did it justify Leanne's taking a vindictive pleasure in taunting the police for their botched arrest. The police, after all, had been merely carrying out their sworn duty in making the arrest. Moreover, the respectable citizens of Hampton were in the right to protest their exculpation. As for Arne, he was a shyster by complicity, first, for continuing to shelter Hahn and Cam and, second, for simply having been at the trial. Everyone took his presence at the trial as an open declaration of support for his wife. Nobody knew about his reservations, not even Leanne.

After the jog, Arne prepared a supper of lasagna and salad. Lasagna wasn't the easiest dish in the world to prepare, and he ordinarily took some pride in the seasonings he had learned to add. But on this occasion it merely added to his agitation. Generally he liked to cook, and he didn't mind doing other kitchen work in the evening when Leanne was present to discuss her current cases. However, there was a dubious word for a fellow like Arne—househusband. It was obviously a takeoff on housewife, and it likely hadn't been coined to carry a pejorative connotation—which brought Arne back around to Spud. There was no question Spud scorned Arne. His contempt—and undoubtedly Chantal's contempt as well—would double if they knew the extent to which Arne played the role of househusband so his wife could practice law. Spud was a man's man. Arne wasn't—that's all there was to it. Arne's father was a man's man, too. His contempt would equal that of Spud and Chantal if he knew the extent to which Arne's domestic life failed to fit the model of a proper priesthood-led household.

By the time Leanne came home, the supper was ready. As soon as she had freshened up a bit, they sat down.

"Whose turn is it to say the blessing?" she asked.

"Gosh, I've forgotten," Arne replied. "It's been a while."

"Shall I do it?"

"Yes, please," he said.

As usual, she addressed her request for a blessing on their food to Heavenly Mother. She ate the lasagna with relish. "Nobody makes it like you do," she said warmly. "Not even my mother."

After they had finished the meal, she helped Arne clear the table and wash the dishes. She reviewed the trial with obvious satisfaction. She announced that she planned on attending the city council meeting at which the faulty law against prostitution would be amended. "I am going to gloat in their presence—pure and simple, just gloat!" she said.

She also mentioned Douglas Reid, the high-power lawyer from Seattle, who had invited her to apply for a position in his firm. "What do you think?" she said. "Should I do it? Or should we just stay here and I could go off the pill and we could start a family?"

Arne was speechless. He couldn't respond to eventualities of such moment without time to ponder. At bedtime she was in the mood for languorous, romantic love making, during which Arne set aside his perturbations. Afterward, she fell asleep quickly. Arne, however, lay wide awake, his perturbations very much revivified. Her talk of starting a family—wasn't that the straw that broke the camel's back? Arne had all along assumed he and Leanne would have children. But only now did it bear in upon him that they would be inevitably conditioned to a heretical manner of worship. Sons and daughters alike—all of them would grow up believing it acceptable to address prayers to Heavenly Mother. Maybe they'd grow up believing it was not just acceptable but preferable to worship Heavenly Mother. And with that, a bolt of shock went through him and an eventuality he had been evading all evening broke to the surface. Didn't all this perturbation add up to divorce?

At three-thirty, he could no longer tolerate lying abed with an adrenalin-fed anxiety pumping through him. He got up and went to the truck stop, where he tried to distract himself by ordering parts for refurbishing a hydraulic lift in the repair shop. He quickly realized that he was grieving, as if he took separation from Leanne as inevitable. For all his disapproval of her practice of the law and her manner of prayer, there was no doubt whatsoever that he was still in love with her. Divorce would amount to a death, a burial.

As the first hint of dawn began to show at his office windows, he realized images from his wedding day had been recurring to him during the last hour or two. He had paid them no heed, as if they were simply a part of the random mixture of memories his distraught mind was churning up. But now he wondered whether they had a premonitory significance. The temple wedding ceremony had ordained that a wife should approach Deity through her husband. As they prepared to enter their nuptial bed, Leanne had protested and Arne had concurred. It was wrong, just plain wrong, to consider a priesthood holder as superior to his wife in any respect. Wasn't it also possible, Arne suddenly allowed himself to think, that it was similarly wrong to restrict worship only to Heavenly Father? And with that thought, he saw the way to erase the abrasions of living with Leanne. It was to convert, to go over completely, to her way of viewing matters.

A little after dawn, he went into the restaurant and ordered breakfast. After eating, he sat a while, working out the articles of his new faith. He wanted them broad and inclusive. He could stop thinking of Leanne (and himself by association) as a shyster. Accepting her stance on due process, he could admit that the deliberateness of established law should calm the anarchic outrage of a morally offended community. Moreover, he could acknowledge that the premises of Leanne's feminism were sound. She was right to be angry. Women were suppressed and there was no civilized justification for it. Hampton's policemen had committed a serious injustice when they arrested only the girls and let two men go uncharged.

Going further, Arne could stop feeling ashamed of not being a man's man like Spud. He could accept himself as a househusband who also held down the job of a man's man by managing a large truck stop. Going further yet, he could adopt the worship of both Heavenly Parents. For him as well as for Leanne, prayers addressed to Heavenly Father or to Heavenly Mother or to both at the same time would be equally acceptable. Granted it would be a private mode of worship, done in the confines of their own household. It would be for now and in the future when they might have children, whom they'd help master the nuances of worshiping only the divine male parent at church and both divine parents at home.

*

Arne got home around ten-thirty. Leanne was up, reading the newspaper while she finished her breakfast. It was the latest she had slept in on a Saturday morning for months. Having taken note of the clear, sunny sky, she proposed an outing. "Let's drive up to the Paradise visitor center on Mount Rainier and see how deep the snow is, and on the way home have dinner somewhere."

An hour later, they left in their aging compact sedan with Arne at the wheel. It was the car Leanne ordinarily drove but when they went somewhere together, Arne took the wheel. It was an arrangement that had persisted from before their marriage, the auto being the one Arne had courted her in. While they drove, Leanne hummed snatches of songs and repeated, "What a day!" over and over. The sun was bright, and puffy white clouds floated

in the azure sky. For a while their road went through farmland
and pastures spotted by grazing cattle and horses. The snowpack
circling Mount Rainier glistened in the noonday sun. Eventually,
the highway entered a towering fir forest, offering only momentary
glimpses of the mammoth peak. At the Longmire entrance to the
national park, wildflowers lined the highway, but soon the ascend-
ing road became banked with snow. At the Paradise parking lot,
snowplows had heaped a high bank of snow around its perimeter.
Accoutered with jackets and sun glasses, Arne and Leanne trekked
up an icy trail to the snowfield where heavily burdened climbers
were departing for Camp Muir, from which, after a few restless
hours in their sleeping bags, the climbers would launch their bid
for a pre-dawn summit on the towering peak.

On their return, Arne and Leanne had dinner in a rustic café
just outside the park boundary. Dusk was falling outside, and
electric lanterns cast an intimate light upon the log walls and plank
floor. Soft, melodic music hummed from a speaker above them.
Arne glanced at a menu and made a quick decision. He watched
Leann study the card. She was relaxed, at ease, happy. He perceived
anew how tense, how on guard, she generally was during the work-
week. By all appearances, she thrived on adrenalin. But the tension
had been gone all day—since the night before, actually. She was on
furlough just now.

She looked up suddenly and, seeing his eyes upon her, smiled
and again reached for his hand and gave it a squeeze. The lantern
light shadowed her sculpted cheeks and aquiline nose. The day had
been a furlough for Arne, too. It had confirmed the decision he had
reached early that morning at the truck stop. Harmony would reign
in the household of Leanne Holburn and Arne Jarvis, not only
now but later when it might be filled with children.

A few days later, Hahn and Cam showed up at the truck stop
with their green cards, and Arne hired them as clean-up girls in the
restaurant and convenience store. He found them a small studio
apartment over a garage and paid their rent as a part of their pay
package. With Leanne's help, he got them enrolled in an English-
as-a-Second-Language course that met two evenings a week at the
community college in Enumclaw. Arne calculated that he suffered

a considerable net loss of income by doing all this for them, but, following a suggestion from Leanne, he made up for the loss by shifting funds from their tithing account. At their next tithing settlement, they told the bishop they'd have to pass on getting a temple recommend for the coming year.

As for Spud and Chantal, they never again spoke a word to either Arne or Leanne. However, Spud wrinkled his brow in a dark, dour way when he met them at church, which told them what he thought of them. That was just fine with Arne. He didn't suppose Leanne was losing any sleep over it, either.

Bode and Iris

It may seem odd that an experienced fornicator like Bode Carpenter would get the girl pregnant in the first place—particularly because he carried a condom in the watch pocket of his jeans on that fateful evening. Be it said here, Bode had knock-out good looks—five eleven, neatly trimmed blond hair, a just-right nose, a square jaw, muscular arms, and a taut belly. He lived in Richfield, a town in central Utah. He was a Mormon, and he had an eight-hour-a-day job at the AgriCo-op, a feed and farm supply store, with a half day's work on Saturdays at overtime rate. As for room and board, his parents let him live at home for free because they hoped to nudge him back into the paths of righteousness.

The girl was Iris Denning. She worked in a café in Salina, a town about twenty miles north of Richfield. Another waitress at the café, Sibyl Holinshed, dated a backsliding buddy of Bode's, Abe Larkin. On a Saturday evening in June, Abe brought Bode along, and, after the two girls had come out of the café at quitting time, he introduced Bode to Iris.

She wasn't pretty. She had a hawk nose and a prominent overbite—a true Plain Jane, according to Bode's judgment. That didn't matter, of course, Bode being chiefly interested in her nether parts. Abe drove his old Cadillac up to a reservoir, and while he and Sibyl got busy doing unwholesome things in the front seat, Bode and Iris got out of the back seat and walked up a nearby hill.

For an eighteen-year-old just out of high school, Iris had a lot of savvy about religion. Also, she was aggressive about putting down Mormonism. Maybe it was just the natural result of belonging to a religious minority in a predominantly Mormon town. She was a Baptist, as she let Bode know immediately, and she wanted to know why Mormons believed in three heavens.

"We don't believe in three heavens," he said. "We just think heaven is divided into three degrees of glory."

"That sounds like three heavens to me," she said. "But this is a free country. If you like believing in three heavens, nobody is going to stop you."

Bode was thinking this Plain Jane was somehow running circles around him. Time to fight back.

"So what do Baptists believe?"

"They believe in salvation by faith, not by works. They believe in the Bible. It's all you need to find out how to be saved. They believe in baptism by immersion—after you are old enough to make decisions for yourself. They believe in just one heaven. They don't think you need three of them."

She said this crisply—no sign of hesitation. Nonetheless, Bode decided to take another swing.

"Baptists believe in fire and brimstone," he said. "They believe the devil tortures people in hell."

"Fire and brimstone! That's just silly. The torment of hell comes just from knowing you'll never be with God or Jesus forever and ever."

Bode could see he wasn't going to be running any circles around this chick. Time to back off and leave well enough alone.

They stopped walking and faced each other. Moonlight didn't help her features much. She edged toward Bode, and on an impulse, he kissed her. It was kind of a duty, he was thinking. Homely girls needed to make out once in a while just like anybody else. The important question was, would she be interested in something a little more substantial than mere making out? She put her arms around him, and they went on kissing. "You're so good looking," she murmured. Shortly, the sensuous flexing of her lips got to him, and he tried to slide his hand down through the open collar of her blouse. She grasped his hand and placed it on her waist. They continued to kiss, but the spirit had gone out of it for Bode.

Later, after Abe and Bode had dropped off the girls at their homes and were heading back to Richfield, Abe said, "Well, how was it, ol' buddy?"

"Not so good," Bode said. "She isn't exactly a Marilyn Monroe, and she doesn't want anybody messing around below the neckline."

"That's tough," Abe said apologetically. "You run into girls like that once in a while."

For various reasons, Bode kept dating Iris. For one thing, a couple of his former steadies—girls he could count on for a quick session in the back seat of his car after a movie or a dance—became unavailable, one of them getting married and the other moving to Oregon. For another thing, he had become obsessed by the abruptness with which Iris had pulled his hand from her blouse and placed it on her waist. He couldn't quit thinking about her. On a Saturday night when he had nothing else to do, he drove up to Salina and went into the café at quitting time.

There were no customers present. Iris tidied up behind the counter. Through a serving window Bode could see Sibyl and Larry Forbes, the fellow who owned the café, working in the kitchen.

Iris didn't seem surprised to see Bode. When he said he had come up just to take her home, she said okay, but he needed to understand some things.

"First of all, just remember, I'm a Baptist and you're a Mormon."

He understood they weren't to form an attachment. There was no danger of that, of course, at least, not on his part. He was actually feeling pretty good—somewhat generous and benevolent. Plain Janes have feelings just like anybody else, and it didn't hurt a fellow to accommodate those feelings once in a while.

"Also, I don't drink," she added, "and I don't like to go with guys who do."

"No problem," Bode said. "I'm not into booze. Also I don't use tobacco or pot." He meant, of course, that he wasn't into them as a matter of habit. No need for her to know he wouldn't turn liquor or pot down if they were offered at a party.

They left the café a half-hour later. Bode asked whether they should drive back up to the reservoir. She said she knew a place closer to town. She had him pull onto a dead-end road scarcely a quarter mile from the café. It led to an abandoned prisoner of war camp from World War II—more than sixty years in the past. It was an eerie, unhallowed place, and people rarely went there, especially at night. One night shortly after the war, a guard, an angry American soldier, had sprayed the tents of the sleeping German prisoners with a machine gun, killing ten and wounding twice that many.

"If you want to be undisturbed, this is the place to come," Iris said.

After they had kissed a couple of times across the console that separated their seats, she said, "I like to snuggle. Shall we get in the back seat?"

For a few moments, Bode got his hopes up. Back seats were meant for more serious business than just making out. However, making out was all Iris intended by snuggling. They sat hugging each other while they alternately kissed and fell into snatches of conversation. Eventually their conversation died and their kissing became intense and prolonged, Iris putting a surprising energy into the process. Quite abruptly, about forty-five minutes after they had arrived, she said, "Please take me home."

That's the way weekend nights went for a couple of months. It was an unsatisfactory arrangement for Bode. About five minutes of kissing—with Iris's lips working on his with an uncanny sensuousness—roused him to the point of wanting to finish the job in the way Nature intended, leaving him in a state of frustration. Of course, he'd lope his mule when he got home, but that was tame stuff compared to having carnal knowledge of a girl when he and she were both heated up and wanting it.

Moreover, Iris teased him about Mormonism enough to keep him on the defensive. She had read parts of the Book of Mormon when her family first moved to Salina—her pastor having said they had just as well deal with it up front since the vast majority of their neighbors were Mormon. She said there were good things in the Book of Mormon, but according to her pastor, it was like the Apocrypha in the Catholic Bible. It was a book-length sermon. It explained scripture, but it wasn't scripture. The Protestant Bible—that's all the scripture anybody needed, she said.

Bode didn't know how to respond to that, so he phoned his brother, Avery, who had been on a mission and was currently a senior at BYU. Bode doctored the truth a little, telling Avery he had met a nice Baptist girl who looked like she might be open to the truths of Mormonism if he could correct some false notions

somebody had fed her. Avery latched onto the project in a flash.
As a first step, he advised Bode to emphasize the fact that whereas
Mormons had the bona-fide, genuine trade-mark church of God,
Baptists were a generic brand of Christianity. Like most other
Christian denominations, the Baptists had bought into the Nicene
Creed, which held that God is one in substance but three in person. Only the Mormons, Avery explained, had the straight dope on
the doctrine of the Trinity. God the Father had a resurrected body
of flesh and bone, as did God the Son, whereas the Holy Ghost
had a spirit body, which was why the Holy Ghost could inspire
righteous people at any time and place.

However, the long and the short of it was that Iris was unim-
pressed. She just scoffed at the mention of God the Father having a
resurrected body of flesh and bone. She finally did agree to back off
on talking about religion altogether, since it obviously tainted their
moments together with acrimony. Naturally, Bode brooded on his
dissatisfactions, and he made up his mind multiple times to stop
seeing Iris. But he kept going back. He was hooked, he was an ad-
dict. As far as his sex life was concerned, he knew he would have to
write the summer off as a loss. He just hoped when it was over and
Iris had gone off to the University of Utah, he could build himself
up a fresh inventory of local girls willing to go all the way.

Then one night near the first of August, disaster struck. Bode
carried a condom in his watch pocket, but by the time he realized
he needed it, he and Iris had already got beyond being influenced
by a sense of the consequences. He, of course, had relied on her.
It was she, after all, who had set the boundaries on their intimate
behavior that summer. He could at least console himself on that
fateful evening with the fact that she took the first step by whisper-
ing, "Shall we do it?" Taking that as permission, Bode proceeded as
an experienced practitioner of backseat intercourse.

Within seconds of their having completed the act, Iris whispered
hoarsely, "Bode, what have we done?" During the brief duration of
the act, Bode had congratulated himself on his good fortune. Now
he realized how stupid he had been to proceed without a condom.
Moreover, he realized he shouldn't have gone all the way for a
reason beyond the danger of getting her pregnant. Even though she

had given him permission, he shouldn't have taken advantage of her in a moment of weakness. She was too good a girl for that.

Neither of them spoke after that until they arrived at her house. As she opened the car door, she said, "We're not good for each other, Bode, so don't come back."

"I'll behave," Bode said. "I'll keep my hands to myself. I promise."

"Don't come back, Bode. Just don't come back—ever."

For a while on his drive home, Bode grieved. That was the only word for it. Iris had dug into him deeper than he had realized. But pretty soon he began to fret over the chances of her becoming pregnant. He wasn't ready to be a daddy, especially not with a girl as homely as Iris. So she was absolutely right to put her foot down. They weren't good for each other.

Arriving home, he immediately got onto the internet and re-searched the likelihood of a single instance of unprotected intercourse resulting in pregnancy—a 2.5 percent chance, one site claimed. That meant a 97.5 percent chance that he had got away free.

With that reassurance, he decided to forget his little episode with Iris Denning and get back to his former habits. He could start taking in dances in little towns like Venice or Glenwood or Monroe and scout out some willing girls. Then there was a bar in Marysvale, where he had had luck with an older woman. Maybe she was a regular there. And he sure as hell wouldn't get carried away and have sex without putting on a condom.

The next day was a Sunday. As usual, Bode slept in. He was having a belated bowl of cereal and milk when his parents and his younger siblings, Alan and Janet, returned from church in the early afternoon. Listening to their chatter, he realized he was anxious. For a long time he had believed it unnecessary to be in a hurry to repent. He had figured on changing his ways at the age of twen-ty-five at the earliest and maybe as late as thirty. But now he was feeling strangely vulnerable, as if something drastic would happen to him soon. By evening, Bode had it figured out. His increased anxiety was a result of hanging out with Iris. By poking fun at Mormonism, she had put him on the defensive. Forced to assert his Mormonism, he had begun to realize the commandments were for real and they were for right now. A guy couldn't choose to validate them just any old time.

Bode's life changed drastically. He stopped going out at night, even on weekends. He went on with his back-breaking work at the AgriCo-op, ate meals with his family, and otherwise hung out in his basement room reading the Book of Mormon for the first time in his life. The more he read, the worse he felt about himself. He was in a special stew on Sundays. He started going to church with his family, which pleased his parents greatly. The bishop welcomed him back, as did family friends. Naturally, Bode didn't have the guts to forego partaking of the sacrament because everybody would know he had serious sins on his conscience. So he went along partaking of the sacred bread and water unworthily even though he knew he was digging himself deeper and deeper into the pit of damnation. Any way he looked at it, his life had become downright hellish. It was the life of a spiritual galley slave.

Bode was grateful when Avery and their sister Anna came home from their summer term at BYU. Their good cheer diverted his parents' attention from his silent, moody presence. They were there for three weeks, filling the house with banter and chatter. By the time they went back to Provo for fall semester, Bode had started to cheer up a little. His improved mood lasted through September, when the weather turned cool, and the storage sheds where he worked weren't nearly as hot as in the summer. Sometimes he felt like maybe the Lord had decided to forgive him for fornicating with Iris and all the others and it was time for him to figure out how to make something of himself. However, he was shortly disabused of the notion things were starting to go well for him. On a sunny Saturday morning in early October, Abe Larkin showed up at the loading dock where Bode was taking in a new shipment of chicken mash.

"Got something to impart to you, ol' buddy," Abe said. "Iris is pregnant. Last night I was at the café up in Salina, and Sibyl and Larry told me I've got to let you know."

Bode chewed on his words for a long moment before their meaning sank in. Then it hit him hard. He could feel a blush coming up his neck onto his cheeks. "Well, damn," he said, seating himself on the edge of the dock.

"You know, you could just up and marry her."

"Marry her!"

"That's Sibyl's idea, not mine."

"I don't see her and me getting married," Bode said. "She's a Baptist and I'm a Mormon even if I haven't been a very good one up till now." Also, he hadn't planned on marrying a homely girl. That counted against her more than being a Baptist, although he didn't mention that to Abe.

"Maybe I better tell you something else," Abe said. "According to Larry, you'll have to pay child support till the baby turns eighteen even if you don't marry her. The law makes you do it."

Bode was stunned. Ten seconds of ecstasy in the back seat of a car cost eighteen years of child support!

"Larry says you and Iris will have to fill out a legal document that spells out what you're going to do with the kid."

Bode pulled off his gloves and scratched his neck.

"He and Sibyl think you ought to come on up to the café and start thrashing things out with Iris."

"Does she want to see me?"

"I can't say she's real enthusiastic about the idea. But Sibyl says for you just to show up at quitting time tomorrow night. She will make sure Iris doesn't take off early."

"All right, I'll be there," Bode said grimly.

"Don't take it too hard, ol' buddy," Abe said as he prepared to leave. "You ain't the only feller in the county that has got a kid he didn't plan on."

When Bode walked into the café the next evening, the dining area was empty except for Iris, who sat on a stool at the counter. Larry and Sibyl were in the kitchen, as Bode could see through the serving window. A document composed of maybe two dozen sheets of paper lay on the counter before Iris.

Bode slid onto the stool next to hers. He could see his face and hers, side by side, in a round mirror that hung above the coffee urn.

"You've heard the bad news," Iris said.

"Yes. Abe brought me word yesterday."

They watched each other in the mirror. Funny thing—in Bode's judgment, she was pretty in the mirror

"I'm not blaming you any more than I'm blaming myself," she said. "We weren't smart, Bode, neither one of us."

"That's true."

"My mother told me, don't be dumb, Iris. Don't get pregnant. Then I went and did it."

"I'm sorry," Bode said. "I really am."

Her gaze dropped from the mirror to the document on the counter. She patted it with a hand. "Larry gave me this. It comes from the website of the Utah court system. It tells us how to make a parenting plan. We've got to work out custody and visitation rights—other things, too. It isn't going to be easy. You'll want our baby to grow up a Mormon. I'll want it to grow up a Baptist."

She uttered a short, bitter laugh. "So what do we do—flip a coin?"

He picked up the document and scanned through it. He could see she was right. They were in for some long talks.

Shortly, she asked him to drive her home. As they passed the road into the abandoned prisoner of war camp, she asked him to stop for a moment. "There's something else I just as well tell you. When I first knew for sure I was pregnant, I decided to have an abortion. It's legal in Utah if you do it early. But the doctor has to explain the procedure and show you a movie about it, and then you have to wait three days to have the abortion. All the clinics are in Salt Lake City. Sibyl said she'd drive up with me both times if that's what I really wanted. But I couldn't make up my mind—neither one way nor the other. I knew if I was going to have an abortion, I should do it soon. One night I drove out here. It's a murderous place, and I hoped it would help me harden my heart. It didn't, Bode. It did just the opposite. I gave up on getting an abortion."

Disappointment rippled through Bode. Too bad she hadn't gone through with it. An abortion would have saved them both a lot of trouble. Then guilt took over. He knew he shouldn't feel so disappointed about her not having the abortion. He had an inclination toward wickedness. That's all there was to it.

When they arrived at her house, she asked him to come inside while she confronted her parents with the fact she was pregnant.

He was too startled to say no. A lamp was lit in the Denning living room when they went in. "Wait here," she said to Bode, then disappeared down a hall.

He heard a door opening, then a woman's voice. "Is that you, Iris?"

"Yes, Mom."

"I'm glad you are home. Have a good sleep, dear."

"Mama, Daddy, I need to talk to you," Iris said. "I'm pregnant."

"What's that?" a deep masculine voice said.

"I let a Mormon guy make love to me and I'm pregnant."

"For God's sake," the deep masculine voice bellowed, "don't make jokes about something like that!"

"It's not a joke," Iris said. "He's out in the living room. His name is Bode Carpenter. We've got to work out a parenting plan for our baby."

"I'll kill the son of a bitch!" the deep voice said.

"Woodrow!" Iris's mother cried.

"Well, let's go out and take a look at him."

Iris's parents were Woodrow and Merle Denning. As Bode already knew, Woodrow was a petroleum engineer, transferred from an oil field near Greeley, Colorado, to a drilling site in Salina Canyon.

Hearing the tread of his slippers in the hall, the quaking Bode prepared for the worst.

Woodrow paused in the doorway from the hall. A muscular, heavyset man, he wore a belted robe over his pajamas. A moment later, Merle pushed past him. She wore a robe over her nightgown, which hung nearly to her ankles.

"Let's take a little time to talk things over," she said. "Iris, you and your young man sit on the sofa. Woodrow, let's take the easy chairs."

When they were all seated, she turned to Iris. "First of all, are you sure you are pregnant?"

"I missed my period. It should have happened over a month ago. So I bought a kit and I tested positive."

"Well, then, you probably are pregnant."

Sighing, she turned to Bode. "Tell us about yourself. And, please, I didn't catch your name."

"I'm Bode Carpenter," he said. "I'm from Richfield. My folks are Martin and Esther Carpenter."

"Presumably, you have a job."

"Yes, ma'am. I work for the AgriCo-op feed and farm supply store out on the south side of Richfield."

"What's your pay there?" Iris's father asked.

"Ten dollars an hour, eight hours every week day, and time-and-a-half for another four hours on Saturday."

"Let's see—that's going to be a little over twenty thousand a year. How much do you spend on car payments?"

"Nothing. My dad gave me an old car. I have to maintain it, of course."

"How much do you spend on room and board?"

"Nothing. I live at home with my parents."

"How long are you going to go on living with them?" Woodrow's voice had turned sarcastic.

"I'm not sure. Not forever, of course." Bode could see he didn't count heavier than a piss-ant with Iris's father.

At this point, Merle intervened. "I hope you two aren't planning on getting married."

"No way," Iris said. "We are going to work out a parenting plan on how we are going to raise the baby. Larry Forbes says the law requires us to do that."

"Have you considered putting it up for adoption? You could stay with Aunt Dorothy in Denver till it's born."

"I'm keeping the baby," Iris said stubbornly.

"At our cost," Woodrow grumbled.

"We can handle it," Merle said. "By all means, you two, go ahead with your parenting plan. If you want a place to hang out while you work up the agreement, you can use our den. Nights are too cold for sitting in your car."

"Is that all right, then?" Iris said to Bode.

Bode nodded. He wasn't the negotiator here and his mind was a scramble.

"Hold on just a minute," Woodrow said. "Let me take a look at that document."

He strode to Iris and took it, glancing through its pages as he returned to his seat. "Mr. Carpenter," he said, "what if Mrs. Denning and I make you a deal? We'll get my lawyer to make up a contract that relieves you of all financial obligations toward this child in return for just clearing out of the picture altogether. Merle and I will guarantee the finances of the situation."

Bode's jaw dropped with astonishment. He glanced at Iris. She shrugged her shoulders.

"Is it a deal?" Woodrow said insistently.

"Okay," Bode replied.

"Is this okay with you?" Merle asked her daughter.

"It makes things less complicated," Iris said.

"We'll try hard to keep things uncomplicated," Merle went on. "With me as a backup nanny, maybe you can get on with your education."

Bode could see it was time to leave. He stood and looked around. Abruptly walking out like this left a raw edge. He sighed, scratched behind an ear, and headed for the door.

Woodrow followed him onto the porch. Having closed the door, he said, "I'll make sure that contract is ready as soon as possible. I'll have my lawyer bring it by where you work. Now, there's a little something else I want to mention. If you stick with this deal and sign that contract, there'll be ten thousand dollars cash for you under the table. That's close to half a year's income for you. That'll be yours free and clear."

Bode was thunderstruck. Ten thousand dollars cash! What a guy couldn't do with that kind of money!

"No need to mention this little cash deal to anybody," Woodrow added. "That's strictly between you and me, just a little something to sweeten the pot."

Bode drove home on cloud nine. When it looked certain that the entire population of Sevier County would know what he and Iris had done, the nightmare had suddenly evaporated—with a promise of eighteen years of salvaged income and some instant big bucks on the side! He hoped he could smarten up now. He should get on with making something of himself. He would put the ten thousand toward college. He'd pursue a degree in wildlife resource management. That's what he really wanted, a life in the outdoors—and marriage to a beautiful Latter-day Saint woman with whom he'd raise a righteous family.

Bode had a troubled sleep that night. Somewhere toward morning, he awoke from a strange dream. In the dream, he saw a kangaroo grazing on the strip of grass next to the parking lot at the AgriCo-op store. The kangaroo paused, balanced on its tail, and chewed a while. Then a beautiful human child, maybe six months old, pushed its head and upper torso out of the kangaroo's pouch. Bode knew it was his baby though he didn't know how it had got into the pouch.

He mulled the dream for a few minutes before getting out of his bunk. The baby in the kangaroo pouch reminded him of his sister, Janet, whom his mother had briefly placed in his arms on the day of her birth. He realized suddenly he had come down off cloud nine. He was grieving. He had agreed to walk out on his child before it was born.

He swung out of his bunk and sat with his feet on the cold concrete floor. A stark idea came to him. He wouldn't sign a contract. He wouldn't walk out on the kid. Anxiety stirred in his belly. He knew he was in for eighteen years of child support payments, to say nothing of losing an under-the-table instant bonus of ten thousand dollars. Likely he would bring shame to himself and his family. Maybe he would be excommunicated from the church. Well, that was the way it had to be.

Just before breakfast, he took his cell phone outside to call Woodrow so that his parents wouldn't overhear the conversation. "I'm sorry, sir," he said, "to put you and Mrs. Denning to a lot of trouble, but I've changed my mind. I'm not going to sign any contract. I respect you and Mrs. Denning a whole lot and I hope we can get along okay."

Woodrow began to splutter something about giving Bode twenty thousand dollars under the table. Shutting off his phone, Bode went back into the house to have breakfast. What with his anxiety ratcheted up, he didn't have a good day at work. That night around bedtime, the house phone rang and Bode's mother told him that a girl wanted to talk to him. It was Iris. "Daddy threw a fit this morning. He says you backed out on signing a contract."

Bode didn't know what to say. His anxiety went up another notch.

"From what I could gather, he offered you some money on the side."

Bode remained silent.

"Are you still there?" she said.

"I'm sorry to upset your daddy," Bode blurted, "but I'm like you. You can't go through with an abortion. Well, I can't go through with signing away my right to spend some time with our kid."

"I can respect that—although," Iris added wearily, "it does make things more complicated for both of us."

"I'm ready to tackle the parenting plan. How do you want to work it out?"

Iris suggested they accept her mother's offer to let them meet in the den of the Denning house. She told him she had arranged to work a midday shift at the café Monday through Friday. Accordingly, she proposed now that he and she meet in the den on Saturday and Sunday evenings. The den had both an inside and outside door. Bode was to use the outside door, which would allow him to avoid meeting her father.

Bode felt hollow after he had hung up. It was time now to come clean with his parents. He knew a rancher who had chopped off a gangrenous finger with a hatchet. He was wishing he could trade places with the rancher. Chopping off a finger would be nothing compared to telling his parents he was a fornicator.

Bode's parents, Martin and Esther, were preparing for bed as he entered their room. A single lamp burned on the nightstand beside his mother. She was already in bed, wearing glasses and sitting up propped against a pillow with the Book of Mormon in her hands. His father sat on the opposite side of the bed, bare footed but still clad in his suit pants and his unbuttoned white shirt.

"I've got some bad news," Bode said. "A while back when I was still helling around, I broke the law of chastity with a Baptist girl and now she's pregnant."

"Oh, my word!" Esther gasped.

A long silence followed. Then, from Martin: "We knew you were dating a Baptist girl. Avery gave us to understand she was interested in the church."

"As it turns out, she isn't interested. She has read parts of the Book of Mormon and doesn't believe it. She's a dyed-in-the-wool Baptist. She just believes in the Bible."

"And you say she's pregnant?"

"Yes, sir."

"Oh, Bodie," Esther wailed, using his childhood nickname, "where did we go wrong? How did we fail you?"

"You never did anything wrong. I just turned rebellious on my own."

"What's the girl's name?" Martin said.

"Her name is Iris Denning and she lives in Salina."

"Are you thinking of getting married?"

"No, sir, we aren't. Do you think we ought to?"

"If she's not interested in the church, you are likely just as well off not getting married."

"This is just terrible," Esther said. "An illegitimate child in our family! Who would have thought it?"

"We might have expected it, given how things are nowadays," Martin said. "But what counts now, I guess, is making the best of it. For starters, you've got some tall repenting to do, Bode. You'd better go talk this over with the bishop."

"Yes, sir, I guess I'd better."

A little later, lying in his bunk, Bode pondered the fact that he hadn't told his parents about the six other girls and the middle-aged woman at the bar in Marysvale with whom he had also fornicated. Shortly he decided it was okay not to have told them. But the bishop—that was another matter. He'd rather chop off two fingers than tell him. But it couldn't be avoided. Bode would have to come completely clean with him.

On his way home from work the next day, Bode called by the bishop's house. The bishop was having supper when Bode rang the doorbell. The bishop stood in the doorway chewing food while Bode came straight to his point. "Bishop," he said, "I am in a real pickle. I did what I shouldn't have done with a Baptist girl and now she's pregnant."

"You better come inside," the bishop said, peering out into the street as if there might be eavesdroppers. He had Bode sit in an easy chair while he closed the door between the living room and the dining room where his wife was still at supper. He listened gravely, shaking his head from time to time, while Bode explained his situation in further detail.

"I'm sorry to hear all that," the bishop said when Bode had finished. "Lately, it has looked like you had cleaned up your act, and I've been thinking about suggesting to the stake president that it was time to advance you to the Melchizedek priesthood. But now you tell me all your hell-raising has got you in big trouble with an outside girl."

The bishop's fingers drummed on the wooden arm of his chair. He was a large, bald man—a farmer whose kids had grown up and moved away from home.

"Do you think I ought to marry her?" Bode said.

"Do you want to marry her?"

"No, sir."

"Does she want you to marry her?"

"No, sir. But I guess I could try to talk her into it if you think I ought to."

"Has she shown any interest in the church?"

"No, sir. She makes fun of it."

"Well, I will say I've known some very righteous Latter-day Saints who were married to outsiders. The important thing is to keep the commandments. But if she makes fun of Mormonism, I wouldn't waste time trying to talk her into getting married if I were you."

"There's something else I'd better tell you. Before I met this girl, I broke the law of chastity with some other girls, plus a lady down in Piute County. None of them got pregnant. I made sure of that."

"How many girls?"

"Six."

The bishop shook his head. "Anything else I ought to know?"

"I did some drinking. I tampered with tobacco. I smoked a little pot. But not lately. I quit all that."

The bishop scrutinized one of his knuckles. "You are a tough case. I'm not sure what ought to be done here. I maybe ought to cut you off the church. Might serve you right."

He paused to rub the knuckle. "On the other hand, you've done the right thing to come talk to me. I respect you for that."

He began to drum his fingers again on the arm of his chair. "Guess I won't cut you off. You'd never come back. So where do we go from here? I want you to keep on going to church but hold off on partaking of the sacrament. Do that for a year. In case people ask questions, just tell them you'd rather not talk about it. No need to advertise your predicament any more than we have to. Hold steady and come next summer, you can start partaking of the sacrament again and I'll recommend your advancement to the Melchizedek priesthood."

The sun was setting over the western mountains when Bode emerged from the bishop's house. He could see that getting on the right side of the Lord was going to be tough. The fact he couldn't participate in the sacrament would hit his family hard. Other people would know he'd somehow got in trouble with a girl. Likely as not, word of who the girl happened to be would leak out.

On his drive to Salina to see Iris on the following Saturday evening, Bode considered the dubious prospects of taking care of their child if he had custody of it. He obviously couldn't turn the child over to his mother during his working hours—at least not until she had got over being horrified by the scandal. To put it bluntly, Bode was in no position during his negotiation with Iris to insist on anything close to equal custodial time for the foreseeable future. Maybe he would never want equal custodial time—just regular weekends and some holidays and, every other year, the kid's birthday. Maybe that would be contact enough.

He arrived in Salina a little after seven. Iris welcomed him into the den and disappeared for a plate of cookies. At that point, her little brother and sister entered the den. The brother was maybe eight, the sister maybe four.

"We're Rodney and Ellen," the boy said.

"Glad to meet you," Bode said.

Rodney stationed himself near an arm of the sofa on which Bode was seated. "Are you Iris's boyfriend?"

"In a way you could say I am."

"Dad says you are poor white trash," Rodney went on.

"I expect he's right. I don't have a whole lot going for me."

"You don't look like trash to me," Ellen said.

"Thank you," Bode said.

Shortly, Iris returned. "You've had a chat with the kids, I take it."

"Yes. They have more or less welcomed me into the family."

After the children left, Iris sat beside Bode on the sofa and handed him a copy of the parenting plan, keeping another for herself.

The template for the plan was over twenty pages long. She and Bode were each required to complete a plan, being named respectively petitioner in one and respondent in the other. There were boxes to tick off and blanks to fill in by the dozens, presenting them at this juncture, long before the birth of their child, with issues loaded with imponderables. They were to provide the name, sex, date of birth, and social security number of the child. They could opt for joint custody, in which case they would have to agree on important decisions about the child's education, health and dental care, and religious training, or they could opt for one of them having custody—with sole responsibility for making important decisions—and the other having the right to periods of visitation.

"Custody is the big question, isn't it?" Iris said. "When does our child stay with me, when does it stay with you?"

"For sure it has to stay with you till it's weaned," Bode responded. "Later on—well, I don't know. I likely won't have anybody to take care of the kid on long term. So maybe the arrangement ought to be all along that you have custody and I have visitation rights."

Iris looked relieved. In a moment, a worried look returned to her face. "You'll likely want to take our child to church with you."

"Well, yes, I suppose I will want to do that."

"I don't fault you for it. But it does pose a problem, doesn't it—a Mormon service one Sunday, a Baptist service the next? What's more, according to these instructions, we can't badmouth each other's religion. No matter what, our child is going to grow up in a two-church environment."

She turned to look him in the eyes. "Who knows? Maybe someday I'll have Mormon grandkids. So I wish you'd explain Mormonism to me. I promise not to say anything sarcastic."

That began a series of respectful discussions about the doctrines and practices of their two faiths—discussions that went on for more than a month. For the time being, they put the parenting plan on hold and concentrated on their religious differences. However, without truly taking it into account, they often managed to squander a good portion of an evening together by chatting about personal matters or even, on several occasions, by watching a movie from the ample Denning collection of DVDs.

On an impulse one evening, Bode confessed to having had carnal relations with seven women before meeting Iris. At first, he wasn't sure why he told her. He could see his confession shocked and disappointed her, just as if he had owed her the fidelity of being, like herself, a virgin on the occasion of their passionate misdeed at the prisoner of war camp. Eventually, Bode realized he had, in fact, told her because he did owe her that sort of fidelity. Their relationship was turning strange and unpredictable.

"I'm through with that sort of thing," Bode explained. "I've told my bishop. He more or less disfellowshipped me. It's a sort of probation. He told me if I live righteously for a year, he'll put me back in good standing. In the meantime, I have to go to church on Sunday, but I can't partake of the sacrament."

"The sacrament?"

"The bread and the water for the Lord's Last Supper."

"We call that communion," Iris said. "We don't use water. We use grape juice."

"Did you talk to your pastor about what we did?"

"No, but he knows. Mother told him I'm pregnant."

"Do you partake of the communion?"

"Yes, I accept it. I accept it to show I accept Jesus."

"Do you feel forgiven?"

"Jesus knows what I've done. He knows I'm not going to do it again. My pastor isn't like your bishop. He doesn't get between me and the Lord."

"I hope I feel forgiven when my year is up. But even if I do, I've pretty well messed up my life. I can't hide what I've done. What decent Mormon girl is going to want me now?"

Iris stared at him. "You're dumb to think that way. You're good looking, Bode. There'll be a lot of Mormon girls eager to catch you. I just hope you get one who'll treat our child right when it's at your house."

That's when once again things went south, so to speak. Bode grasped that her words implicitly acknowledged her own attraction to him—and forced him to acknowledge the strength of his attraction to her. He warmed to the idea of coming home to her every evening for a lifetime, then, worried, struggled to put it out of his mind.

A couple of weeks later Iris made her attraction to him even more explicit. It was a Sunday evening in early November. They were on the sofa in the den. "I keep wishing we could get married," she said. "It would be so much better for our baby. Besides, I've got used to you, Bode. I like to be with you. You are very kind, very gentle."

Immediately afterward, she frowned, obviously annoyed with herself. She stood and moved toward the outside door, her customary signal that it was time for Bode to go home. He followed her to the door. She opened it and stood with her hand on the knob. "I've said more than I should have said. Don't attach any importance to it. Let's just get the parenting plan finished and be done with it. We've been neglecting it for weeks."

Driving home, Bode's mind was a swirl. Iris had intentionally put marriage on the table as a topic of discussion, then pulled it off. Did he want to put it back on?

He granted he looked forward to their evenings in the den. He granted that he lusted on her. But marriage? His bishop had said it was okay to marry an outsider. But if he married Iris, there would probably be other children, who like the child who was presently on its way would be intimately exposed to Iris's erroneous faith. Then there was the Plain Jane factor. Wouldn't the first question to come to mind among his friends and relatives be something like this—*Couldn't you do better than that? How did you get tangled up with a girl that homely in the first place? Don't you have any pride?*

Finally, there was the question of finances—a question that made the following week a period of uncomfortable self-interrogation while Bode heaved sacks in the storage sheds or, inside the store, inventoried new shipments. At twenty-one, he was still living the life of a sixteen-year-old, engaged in brute grunt labor for a subsistence wage and mooching off his parents for room and board. If he and Iris married—he could see the handwriting on the wall. They'd be dirt poor and dependent on hand-outs from relatives and the Richfield food bank.

While returning to Salina on the following Saturday evening,

Bode decided to leave the topic of marriage off the table. He planned to agree that they get on with the parenting plan without further delay. However, his resolve evaporated when Iris met him at the door of the den. She looked so good to him—so desirable. He was wondering if he hadn't been half in love with her all along. He didn't really care, did he, if she was a Plain Jane? Who had invented that demeaning term in the first place?

"Shall we sit?" she said, leading him to the sofa. Stapled copies of the parenting plan template lay on the side table. Next to them was a pitcher of lemonade. She poured him a glass.

Handing him a document, she said, "Are you are still okay with letting me have custody with visitation rights for you?"

Ignoring the question, he set down his glass. "When you thought about us getting married, how did you think it could work?"

She seemed surprised, then thoughtful—then maybe even eager. "I had in mind taking turns at doing things your way for a while and then doing things my way for a while. We could go to the Mormon service one Sunday and to the Baptist service the next. Or maybe we could go to both services every Sunday. We would *have* to be a real two-church family. That would be a way of show-ing our respect for each other's faith."

He lifted his glass and took sip. He was dubious. Her idea seemed too simple.

"There are a lot of different ways we could work it out," she went on. "But however we arrange it, it will only work if we really want it to."

His resistance softened. Say their family, he and Iris and three or four kids, did things full tilt the Mormon way for a couple of weeks and then did things full tilt the Baptist way for couple of weeks—the idea was appealing. Maybe they'd end up with a bunch of screwed-up kids, but maybe they wouldn't.

"For starters," Iris said, "we could attend each other's church. Maybe you could come with me to my Baptist service tomorrow."

He pondered a moment. "I'm afraid of your dad."

"Then take me to your sacrament meeting. I'll drive down and meet you there."

"Not in my ward," he said hastily.

"Well, then, somewhere else."

A tremor went up his backbone. They were behaving as if a two-church family was a cut-and-dried matter. "Okay," he said, "but it's just an experiment."

"Yes," she agreed, "it's just an experiment. So where shall we go?"

"Get your laptop and let's see what we can find over in San Pete County."

Returning with the laptop, she said, "Maybe we can squeeze in a Baptist service somewhere, too."

The most promising venues were churches in a couple of small towns in upper Sanpete County—an LDS ward in the village of Bristol and, scarcely five miles from Bristol, a Baptist congregation in the even smaller village of St. Albans. As it turned out, the schedules and proximity of the churches were such that Bode and Iris could take in both meetings on a single day.

He picked Iris up at 8:30 the next morning. They were both in their Sunday best, he in a dark blue suit with a white shirt and tie, she in a tan skirt suit with half-high pumps.

The November sun was bright, and the fields along the highway glistened with frost. Passing through Manti, they saw the Mormon temple, capped at either end by a cupola-fitted tower. Its walls, built of a cream-colored limestone from a local quarry, gleamed in the sun.

"I hear Mormons don't use a temple on Sunday," Iris said.

"That's right. They go to a church for Sunday services."

"So what's a temple for?"

"So people can get married for time and eternity," Bode said. "Also, so they can get baptized for their dead ancestors who died without the gospel."

"I guess I can't enter a temple."

"That's right," Bode said. "I can't either. Not right now. Maybe next year after the bishop takes me off probation."

"Say some of my grandchildren turn out to be Mormon. Could they get baptized for me after I'm dead?"

"Likely so."

He decided not to tell her it might not do her any good even if somebody was baptized in her behalf after her death. From what he understood, people who had a chance to become a Mormon in mortality but didn't take advantage of it, didn't get another chance in the hereafter.

"So remind me which of the three glories will I be in while I wait for my grandkids to get around to being baptized for me?"

"You'll be in the middle one, the Terrestrial Kingdom. That one is for good, decent people who have been blinded by the craftiness of men."

"So I have been blinded by the craftiness of men?"

"Well, yes, more or less, that's the way it is." He paused. "Sorry to have to put it that way. Things are even worse for me, of course—at least right now. If I have the bad luck to get killed before my year of probation is over, I'll end up in the Telestial Kingdom, which is the bottom one. That's where wicked people go. It's like the Baptist hell. People aren't tortured and tormented there. They are just separated from God and Christ for all eternity."

"I think you are already forgiven, Bode," she said. "You just don't know it. I think there's just one degree of glory in heaven and its glory can't be measured. You and me, we'll both be there—and our child, too, no matter whether it turns out to be a Mormon or a Baptist."

They attended the Mormon meeting in Bristol first. They took a seat near the rear entrance so that they could depart quickly at the end of the service. On the platform at the front, a woman played prelude music on an organ. A bishop and two counselors sat to the left of a lectern while a teenaged girl and an elderly couple sat to the right. One of the counselors conducted the meeting. There was an opening hymn, accompanied by the organist and led by a female chorister, and then an invocation. A second hymn followed, during which older teen boys broke bread into bits on trays and blessed the bread.

"Those are priests," Bode whispered. "About seventeen years old, I'd judge. Priest is the office I'm stuck in right now, being a backslider."

Younger teen boys distributed the trays. "Those are deacons—twelve or thirteen years old," Bode whispered.

When a tray filled with small pieces of broken bread reached Iris, she looked at Bode a moment, then took a piece and put it in her mouth. She offered the tray to Bode. He attempted to grasp the handle in order to pass it on without partaking—this from respect for his probation. Frowning, Iris refused to release the tray until Bode, to keep from creating a scene, took a piece. She was, he saw, insistent that they act out the charade of a conventional Mormon couple 100 percent. As he expected, the procedure repeated itself when a tray of water cups, duly blessed, reached them. Bode judged this to be a violation of his probation. He wondered whether another aspect of the charade was also blameworthy—his satisfaction at the possibility of being taken for the husband of the slender, dark-haired young woman at his side.

Following the distribution of the sacrament, the teenaged girl who sat on the stand spoke briefly on a theme drawn from a general conference sermon. She was followed by the elderly couple, who reported on a mission to Montana from which they had just returned. Both emphasized the joys of service in their talks, citing passages from the Bible, the Book of Mormon, and the Doctrine and Covenants. Among several anecdotes, the husband mentioned having recently given a name and a blessing to the new baby of a young woman whose soldier husband was on active duty elsewhere.

This anecdote figured in Bode's and Iris's conversation while they drove on to St. Albans after the sacrament meeting had ended.

"Do Mormon men get to choose a baby's name off the cuff just like that?" Iris said.

"Not off the cuff," Bode replied. "They give the name the parents have chosen. They also give a blessing so the baby will grow up healthy and righteous. It's usually the baby's father that's giving the blessing."

"So could you do that for our baby?"

"Yes. That is, after I have cleaned up my act and have been made an elder. If we were willing to wait for a few months after our baby is born, I could likely do it."

"I would like that," she said.

As they pulled into the parking lot at the Baptist church, Bode brought up another matter. "I expect you'll want me to take part in the communion, as you call it."

"Would you rather not?"

"When the time comes around and our kid is old enough to see how things are, won't it be harder to teach it which church is yours and which is mine if we partake of each other's sacrament—or communion, as you call it?"

"I hadn't thought of that. But yes, I agree, we shouldn't participate in each other's communion."

Again for Bode, that tremor along the spine—he could see they were behaving more and more as if marriage were indeed a cut-and-dried proposition.

The service had already begun when they entered. The pastor—a short, robust man attired in a rumpled double-breasted suit—was leading a hymn a cappella, there being no piano or organ present. The small hall featured a double row of benches, scarcely enough for fifty persons. Close to thirty persons were currently present, mostly men and women accompanied by a few children.

Bode and Iris seated themselves on the last row of benches. At the front was a low stand with a tall lectern, behind which the pastor stood. Two other equally robust men sat in chairs on either side of the pastor. In front of the men, just off the stand, stood a low table covered with a satiny cloth. Trays with handles and shiny stainless-steel plates rested on the table.

At the conclusion of the hymn, the pastor broke directly into a sermon. Stepping off the low stage, he began to pace back and forth like a lion in a cage, his voice assuming a rhythm coordinated with his stride, dropping and rising in force as he strode back and forth. He said he wished to emphasize that it was faith rather than works that took a person to heaven. However, as he went on to make clear, good works inevitably followed a genuine faith in Jesus. They were the necessary product of real faith. Soon he shifted to a new topic. He said Jesus was his best friend. Sweeping an arm toward his listeners, he told them he knew Jesus as well in his inward life as he knew these, the cherished members of this congregation, in his outward life. He said he spoke personally with Jesus many times every day. He said he hoped his listeners had such a relationship.

Despite himself, Bode was transfixed. He listened intently, his mouth slightly agape. The pastor, for all his rumpled, dowdy appearance, could preach. There was no doubting his intense sincerity.

If he misled his followers, it wasn't because of craftiness. He honored Jesus to the core.

Eventually, the pastor declared it time to celebrate the Lord's Last Supper. He said if there was anything amiss in the hearts of his listeners, they should repent of it now. With that, he closed his eyes and called upon Jesus to sanctify the unleavened bread on the plates. He then handed the plates to the two men beside him. Each of them went down an outside aisle, handing a plate to the first person on each bench and waiting until the plate had been handed back before moving on.

When a plate came along the bench on which Bode and Iris sat, he saw it contained small wafers. Iris took a wafer and offered the plate to Bode, who—with unexpected regret—passed it on without taking one. A few minutes later, a tray of tiny cups of grape juice came along their row. Again, Bode abstained.

Shortly, the deacons returned to the front and the pastor said, "That's all for now, folks. Don't forget Bible study tomorrow night at six o'clock. Sister Hoskins will be running a nursery, so bring the little fellows along. God bless you. Drive careful."

Bode and Iris retreated quickly from the church and started for home. Passing through Ephraim, they stopped at a sandwich shop. He ordered a ham sandwich, she a chicken salad. They seated themselves across from each other in a booth by a window looking out onto Main Street and for a period ate in silence, casting fleeting glances into each other's eyes and turning their heads frequently to gaze out the window.

Bode ruminated on the pastor's theme of establishing a personal relationship with Jesus. Bode had never felt that Jesus was close at hand. He wasn't sure he wanted to. Wouldn't that put enormous demands on a fellow? He'd have to take his sandals off, so to speak, like Moses in the presence of the burning bush.

He spoke of the sermon to Iris. "What about you? Have you felt the presence of Jesus?"

"I have. The night I drove to the massacre site to help me make up my mind to have an abortion—the moment I turned off the car lights, I had a panic attack, and I said, 'Sweet Jesus, help me,' and you know, the calmest feeling came over me, and I knew he was close, just as if I was in a room and he was in the hallway just out-side, and I knew I must keep the baby but my sin was forgiven and I could bear whatever disgrace and humiliation came my way." Bode's scalp prickled. For a moment he supposed an uncanny energy sur-rounded Iris. And then it dissipated, and things were ordinary again.

Inertia bound them to the booth. Bode acknowledged the pleasure of simply being there with Iris, gazing out the window at passing automobiles and college students strolling on the sidewalks.

By and by, a boy and a girl passed along the street on a bicycle, the boy pedaling, the girl seated on a rack behind, arms around him and legs spread to keep her feet from interfering with the pedals.

"College students?" Bode queried with a nod toward the scene on the street.

"Probably," Iris said. After a pause, she added, "Do you wish it was us, starting over with enough sense not to get pregnant?"

"Do you?" he said evasively.

"Of course I do. That is, at least a part of me wishes it was us. It would be nice if we were just a Mormon guy and a Baptist girl who knew each other at Snow College once upon a time. As it is—well, our mistake was to hang out in the back seat of a car, wasn't it? But I'm not going to hold our sin against our baby. I'm glad the baby is alive, and I'm glad you are its father."

She picked up the plastic fork with which she had eaten her salad and looked at it abstractly, as if it focused a thought for her.

"I didn't want to fall in love with you, Bode, but I have. Like I said before, I've got used to you. You are considerate, you are kind-hearted. So I'm okay with marrying a Mormon. I'm okay with our child becoming a Mormon, if it chooses to. So I'd be glad to be part of a two-church family. But if you aren't in love with me, I don't think we should do it."

She was still making it easy for him to back out. He considered doing so for only a moment. Under the terms of any parenting plan they were likely to make, he would see Iris only momentarily at the beginning and end of periods of visitation—with a high possibility that some other caretaker than Iris would supervise the exchange of their child. She would essentially disappear from his existence.

Across the table, she watched intently. The irrelevance of her plainness sank in on him with finality. Her overbite, her nose, they were part and parcel of a cherished being. A lifetime with Iris Denning—the prospect filled him with a luminous joy. As for the hereafter with its consequences, it was abstract and remote.

"You've got used to being with me," he said. "Well, I've got used to being with you."

She reached a hand across the table. His hand met hers at the half-way point.

They went on talking for a while, scoping the prospects and problems of a two-church family. Iris accepted that, if Bode blessed and baptized their child, it would be entered upon the records of his church as a member. Bode accepted that Iris would make sure it was also entered on the records of whatever Baptist congregation she attended.

Before they left the sandwich shop, they decided to inform both sets of parents of their intentions that evening. Accordingly, Bode phoned his parents and alerted them that he and Iris would arrive within an hour.

"Will they think I'm a Delilah?" Iris asked while they drove.

"They'll just be glad we've decided to get married," Bode said.

It was after dark when they arrived in Richfield. Bode's parents met them at the front door. They were both in their usual Sunday attire. Taking Iris by both hands, Bode's mother said, "You are welcome in this home." After she had introduced Iris to Alan and Janet, they all took seats in the spacious living room, Bode and Iris on the sofa, the others in chairs. "We've decided to attend one another's church," Bode said.

Alarm showed in his mother's eyes. His father's brow furrowed deeply.

"We've also decided to wait to bless our baby till the bishop has taken me off probation and I've been made an elder, and then I'll bless it in our Mormon ward. Also, later on, when it's eight, I'll baptize it."

Bode saw his parents relax, and he relaxed a little as well. No need to tell them their child would also be on the Baptist records, also no need to bring up the vexing probability that all these arrangements would repeat themselves when they had other children.

Shortly Bode's mother and Iris began a discussion of family connections. Was there a possibility that Iris could be related to a Denning family Esther knew over at Capitol Reef? Not likely, Iris informed her. As far as she knew, her father's family derived from roots in Missouri, where an ancestor had moved immediately after the Civil War.

"Your family is nice," Iris said to Bode as they drove on toward Salina.

"They like you," Bode said, neglecting to add that they would never surrender a hope that Iris would convert. That would remain a given till their dying day.

Bode and Iris found her parents watching television in their living room. "Sorry to interrupt," Iris said, "but we've made up our minds. We want to get married."

Turning off the TV set with a remote control, Merle motioned the young couple toward the sofa. Once they were seated, Merle turned a querying look toward Bode.

"I'll try hard to earn a decent living," Bode said. "I'll do my best."

"We'll have my wages from the café for a while," Iris said. "After that, we'll make do on whatever he earns. We'll live in a shack if we have to."

"We can't have you living in a shack," Merle said. "If you are determined to get married, we'll help."

Woodrow scowled, needing no words to express his disgust with this new turn of events.

"We *will* help," Merle repeated insistently.

The next morning, Merle drove to the Carpenter home and introduced herself to Esther. Over the next two weeks, the two mothers helped their engaged offspring lay out a plausible future. The wedding would take place on the Saturday of the Thanksgiving weekend in a reception room of a new Richfield motel. The officiator would be neither a Mormon bishop nor a Baptist pastor but the Sevier County clerk. Other arrangements included a small one-bedroom apartment for the newlyweds near the truck-stop on the I-70. Bode would continue to work at the AgriCo-op. He planned to enroll in night school when winter semester began at the Richfield branch of Snow College and pursue a major in

natural resources management. As for Iris, she planned on filling her time after she had quit working at the café by pursuing
a degree in elementary education through the online Western
Governors University. Woodrow, having accepted the inevitability
of the marriage, made the couple the gift of a car with a lot of miles
left in it, giving the young couple the mobility of a second serviceable, if aging, automobile.

On the evening before Thanksgiving Day, Avery and Anna
arrived from BYU. They were extraordinarily positive and cheerful,
as if they were determined to ignore the Carpenter family's ship-
wrecked honor. Bode was doubly grateful for their presence, which
distracted their parents from the ignominious necessity of the
pending marriage.

The wedding party gathered as scheduled at 3:00 on the Saturday afternoon following Thanksgiving. Folding chairs were
arranged in rows in a meeting room of the motel. At the front
stood a small table, laden with a bouquet of white, pink, and yellow
flowers. The county clerk, standing in front of the table, called the
gathering to order. Bode and Iris stood before him, Iris wearing a
light blue suit and half-high heels and Bode wearing his dark suit
with a new blue-grey tie—a gift from Iris.

Referring to a few scribbled notes in his hand, the county clerk
spoke briefly on the weighty implications of marriage, urging Bode
and Iris to regard their civil wedding as a solemn contract with
Heaven to love and cherish one another. He then proceeded with
the official ceremony, securing from each the required assent to
taking the other as a life-long spouse. Bode found himself saying
yes with a cracking voice, seized suddenly by the finality of it all.

The wedding party then migrated to a private dining room for
a catered supper. After the meal, the party broke up slowly, the
goodbyes generating brief sallies into new topics of conversation.
At a private moment, Avery asked Bode about the prospects of Iris
becoming a Mormon.

Bode shook his head dolefully. "It'll never happen."

"You are sure of that, are you?"

Bode nodded grimly.

"Well, by golly," Avery said, "at least, you would call her a good person—a *righteous* person—wouldn't you?"

"Absolutely."

"It's certainly not a sin to be married to a righteous non-Mormon," Avery reminded him. "The thing is, don't let her drag you off course. You can still qualify for the Celestial Kingdom. You can still qualify for spending eternity in the presence of Heavenly Father and Jesus. Just be a good Mormon, Bode, and you'll be okay."

Just be a good Mormon—Bode was glad that Avery had backed up the bishop's assurance that a two-church marriage wasn't inherently sinful. Maybe he would see the interior of the Manti temple again after all. He needed to keep his sights locked on the Celestial Kingdom.

The newlyweds spent the night in the Richfield motel, intending to depart in the morning for Bryce National Monument on a brief honeymoon. After they had checked into their room, Iris raised a question. Were they to lounge on the king-size bed for a while and watch wide-screen cable TV, or were they to get down immediately to the business of giving a legitimate consummation to their union?

"I wouldn't mind if we made love first," Bode said, having had the legitimate consummation of their marriage on his mind all day long.

He showered first and put on new pajamas. Iris undressed and put on a robe while he was in the shower. Bode emerged from the shower and sat on the side of the bed. Iris stood before him, fingering the delicate lingerie she intended to wear when she returned from the bathroom. He untied her robe and pulled it open. She was nude beneath the robe—small breasts, trim thighs, a slim waist showing a slight bulge.

"You are beautiful," he said.

He stood and they embraced. Shortly, one thing having led to another, they got onto the bed and made love.

"Well," she said, "we've taken care of that little business."

"I wouldn't mind if we did it again after you've had your shower," Bode said.

She looked at him askance. "If you've got the energy …," she said.

247

As it turned out, he did.

Much later, after they had gone to bed for the night, he failed to fall asleep quickly. He couldn't get his mind off Avery's earnest reminder that, despite being married to Iris for a mortal lifetime, he could still qualify for spending eternity in the presence of Heavenly Father and Jesus in the Celestial Kingdom. He had heard that righteous persons who were not married for time and eternity but who dwelled in the presence of the Father and the Son were considered ministering angels. He had heard that these ministering angels from the Celestial Kingdom could visit the lesser kingdoms. A ministering angel—that was exactly what Bode would be. As such, he would request leave of absence to visit Iris in the Terrestrial Kingdom. He would request that it be an extended leave of absence. He would be there to comfort and sustain Iris and also to comfort and sustain any of their children who had chosen to go the Baptist way. It was a happy thought.

After about half an hour, Bode began to relax, soothed by the soft sounds of Iris's sleep. He slowly slid a hand toward her till it barely touched her arm. He left it there, comforted by her tactile presence.